RED
LETTER
DAY

GW00372827

RED
LETTER
DAY

COLETTE CADDLE

POCKET
BOOKS

London • New York • Sydney • Toronto

First published in Great Britain by Pocket Books, 2004
An imprint of Simon & Schuster UK Ltd
A Viacom Company

1 3 5 7 9 10 8 6 4 2

Simon & Schuster UK Ltd
Africa House
64–78 Kingsway
London WC2B 6AH

www.simonsays.co.uk

Simon & Schuster Australia
Sydney

Author photograph © M. Edwards

A CIP catalogue record for this book is available from the British
Library

ISBN 0-7434-6884-8

Typeset by SX Composing DTP, Rayleigh, Essex
Printed and bound in Great Britain by
Cox & Wyman Ltd, Reading, Berkshire

FOR TONY

RED
LETTER
DAY

Prologue

Celine massaged the wax in and pulled her hair into spikes. Then she put on the vivid purple lipstick that matched her eyeshadow and nail varnish perfectly.

'Celine! Come on, we're going to be late!'

'Coming!' she yelled back as she pulled on her perilously high platforms and clumped down the stairs.

'Hey, you look great!' her husband said, picking her off the bottom step and swinging her around. 'Doesn't she, Frank?'

Celine's father grinned. 'Great.'

'Where's my bag, Dermot?'

Dermot pointed to the spangly purple bag on the floor. 'That thing?'

'Yeah, great. Okay, I think I'm ready.'

'Are you nervous, love?' her father asked as they walked out to his car.

'A bit, Daddy, but I'm excited too. Some of Ireland's top designers are going to be here tonight.'

Dermot grinned as he held open the door for her. 'Sure won't you be there!'

'Idiot!' Celine laughed.

The RTE studios were buzzing when they arrived. Celine was quickly surrounded by her classmates as they all admired each other's outfits and discussed the likely winner. They finally broke up when they were told to take their seats and Celine went in search of her husband. Frank would have to sit with the main audience but thankfully Dermot would be with her in the front row. She clutched his hand tightly as the awards got under way.

'I hope the graduate award isn't last or I'll have no circulation left in that arm,' he murmured.

'What?' Celine's eyes were darting around the room and every so often she'd give a little squeal and point out some big name to Dermot.

It was over an hour before Pat Kenny got to the new designer award. Dermot sat up in his seat and clasped both of Celine's hands in his.

'And the winner of the new designer of the year award goes to . . .'

Celine held her breath.

Pat Kenny's eyes roved across the expectant faces. 'Celine Moore!'

Dermot jumped to his feet and dragged his wife with him. 'You've won, Celine, you've won!'

Celine's expression was bemused. 'What?'

'Go on, love, they're waiting.'

Celine drew herself up, straightened the skirt of the black dress that she'd only finished making that afternoon and started the long walk up the red carpet.

She was only vaguely aware of the congratulatory smiles and handshakes as she walked. She'd won. She was here on the *Late Late Show* surrounded by the big names from the Irish fashion industry – and some from across the pond too – receiving the highest accolade a new designer could get. She nodded and smiled as Pat Kenny shook her hand, only vaguely aware of what he was saying, and moved on to be embraced by Paul Costello – dear God, Paul Costello! If only her mother were here to see this, she'd be so proud. Thinking of her mother reminded her of her dad. She looked out into the audience to see if she could spot him but in the dimly lit studio she couldn't see beyond the first two rows. Clutching the Waterford Crystal trophy and cheque close to her chest, Celine concentrated on putting one foot in front of the other and getting back to her seat without falling flat on her face. Thank God she wasn't expected to make a speech.

'I'm so proud of you,' Dermot said as she sat down.

She hugged him hard. 'Thanks, Dermot, I couldn't have done it without you.'

'You're got what it takes, Celine, and that's why you're here. You've got the X factor.'

'At least I should get a reasonable job now.'

'You're going to be famous in no time and I'm going to retire!'

Celine grinned and put her finger to her lips as the next winner was announced.

*

Frank drove home with a broad smile on his face as his daughter and her husband sang, laughed and relived the moment again.

'I didn't think I'd make it up those steps,' Celine told them again.

'You were brilliant and the best-looking designer in the room!' Dermot said, kissing her soundly. 'What we need now is a curry!'

'Curry, yeah, great!' Celine suddenly felt ravenous.

'Curry?' Frank repeated. 'It's nearly one o'clock in the morning!'

'The best time to eat curry,' Dermot assured him. 'The place at the top of the road should be open, Frank.'

'Okay then.' Frank capitulated and detoured to stop at the takeaway. He'd have travelled to Timbuktu if they'd wanted him to, he was so proud of Celine.

'What will you have, Frank?' Dermot asked as he got out of the car.

'Nothing for me, thanks.'

When they finally pulled up outside the cottage, Frank kissed his daughter. 'I'm proud of you, love, well done.'

'Come in for a drink,' Dermot urged.

'No, lad, I'm for bed.'

'I'll phone you tomorrow, Daddy,' Celine promised.

'Champagne!' Dermot said, making straight for the fridge.

Celine laughed. 'Champagne and curry!'

'You'll be drinking champagne with everything from now on,' Dermot told her as he poured the bubbly into two tumblers.

'I think I need to earn some money first!'

'You'll have your pick of jobs now. They'll all be fighting over you. Celine Moore, Ireland's newest and most exciting designer!'

Celine twirled around, slopping some of her champagne on the floor. 'Today, Dublin, tomorrow, the world!'

Chapter 1

'I'm sorry.' Rose scanned the page in her hand and then looked back at the young woman in front of her. 'But am I missing something? How did someone with your qualifications end up working in a pharmacy?'

Celine shrugged. 'I don't know.'

Rose sighed and put the brief uninformative CV down on the desk. 'Look, Celine, you seem like a lovely girl and between your qualifications and shop experience you're an ideal candidate for the job but, well, I think there's something you're not telling me.'

Celine stared back at her from under a heavy chestnut fringe. 'It's a bit complicated.'

Rose folded her hands in her lap and waited.

Celine sighed. 'Okay, then, let me explain. I'm a widow. My husband died just after I qualified from the College of Art and Design.'

'Oh, I'm sorry!'

Celine carried on, a slight tremor in her voice: 'After he died I lost interest in design.'

'So you took the first job that came along,' Rose surmised.

Celine nodded.

'Why do you want to get back into the rag trade now? Are you going to take up designing again?' Rose watched as the girl's face filled with horror.

'Definitely not!'

'So?'

'Er, well, I wanted to move out of Killmont for personal reasons. I know I could do the job and having a flat over the shop takes care of my accommodation problem.'

Rose bit her lip as she studied the girl. Somehow she felt there was a lot more going on behind those sad eyes but in her gut she felt she could trust Celine Moore. As soon as she'd walked in and Rose felt the cool firm grip of her hand she'd made up her mind. 'How soon can you start?'

Celine laughed, her eyes lighting up. Rose blinked at the transformation.

'Tomorrow?'

Rose smiled. 'No need for that. Why don't you concentrate on moving in over the weekend and you can start Monday. That will give me six weeks to show you the ropes before I go into hospital for a hip replacement.'

'Oh, I'm sorry. Are you in a lot of pain?'

Rose chuckled. 'Yep, but now that I've got you to do all the donkey work I'll be fine.'

'No problem, that's what I'm good at.'

'How are you at making tea?' Rose asked hopefully.

Celine stood up immediately. 'Why don't you be the judge of that?' She filled the kettle and found two mugs.

Rose settled back in her chair and put her foot up on a stool and told Celine of the problems she'd had trying to find a manager for the shop. 'So whatever your reasons for wanting the job, I'm glad you're here.'

Celine set the teapot on the table and went to get the milk and sugar. 'Me too.'

'When we've finished our tea I'll show you the flat. It's a bit basic,' Rose warned.

Celine shrugged. 'I don't need much.'

'It needs airing. The lad that used to live there moved out last month. And I'd better ask Richard to get the immersion checked. It goes on the blink sometimes.'

'Richard?'

Rose nodded. 'My landlord.' She shot a speculative look at Celine. 'A rather handsome and single landlord.'

'Not interested,' Celine said lightly. 'Tell me about the shop.'

Rose obliged, realising that it would be a while before Celine let her guard down. Rose could relate to that. She knew what it was like to have a past and she wasn't the nosey sort. Celine could keep her secrets. As long as she was good at her job, Rose didn't mind. 'We opened Close Second in 1998.'

'We?' asked Celine.

'Me and my son. Oh, he's not actually involved – God forbid!' She chuckled. 'No, I run the shop on my own. I did have a partner for a couple of years but she got bored and asked me to buy her out. Sadie Mitchell, the lady you met on the way in, works part-time.'

Celine frowned. 'Why didn't you give her the job?'

'Oh, Sadie wouldn't want it! She just likes to get out of the house for a couple of hours. Don't ask her to do anything complicated or she'd be a nervous wreck.' Rose chuckled. 'She can't even put on the alarm!'

'Does that mean you have to be here all the time? How on earth do you manage?'

Rose grimaced. 'I get the odd break. My son works for Dominic who owns the newsagent's next door and if I need some time off he opens and closes the shop for Sadie.' She finished her tea and stood up. 'Come on, I'll show you your new home.' Taking a key from the window ledge she led Celine through the shop. 'Sadie, meet Celine Moore. She's going to be our new manager.'

The older woman looked up from her magazine. 'That's nice.'

'I'm just taking her up to see the flat.'

They went outside and Celine watched as Rose opened the front door and began the slow progress up the steep, narrow stairs. 'Why don't you wait down here?'

'I can manage a few stairs,' Rose snapped.

'Sorry.'

Rose reached the top and turned to offer an apologetic smile. 'Don't mind me. Just sometimes it's difficult being treated like a geriatric. Inside I still feel thirty-five!'

Celine smiled. 'You sound like my dad. He retired last year and he's finding it very hard to get used to doing nothing.'

Rose was surprised at this reference to Celine's personal life. 'As soon as you stop working you're ready for the scrapheap.' She bit her tongue as she saw the worried look on Celine's face. 'I bet he keeps himself busy,' she offered.

'He does a lot of gardening and he plays golf.'

Rose beamed at her. 'Ah well, there you are then.' She opened the door and pointed at the small corridor to the right. 'Bedroom and bathroom through there. And this is your kitchen-cum-living room.' She walked on into the main room and turned to face her new employee.

Celine admired the spacious room, with the high ceiling and large sash window that flooded the room with light. 'It's wonderful!'

Rose wrinkled her nose. 'I wouldn't go that far.' She opened a door in the kitchen and peered inside. 'The immersion is in here and yes, as I suspected, the floor is a bit damp. I'll have to get that checked.'

'Great.' Celine retraced her steps and stuck her head into the bathroom and bedroom. They were both small but clean and again had wonderfully large windows.

'It could all do with a coat of paint,' Rose fretted. 'I'm afraid it's been a while since I've been up here.'

'I can decorate it,' Celine offered immediately, her expression brightening.

'There's no need, I'll tell Richard to take care of it.'

'No, really, I'd enjoy it.'

'I bet you could make it really special with your talents.' Rose watched as Celine shrugged and looked uncomfortable. This girl was as prickly as a hedgehog. 'Right, well, you can move in as soon as you want. The central heating switch is over here.' She showed Celine the gas boiler beside the cooker. 'I'll put it on now to air the place.'

'I'll go home and pack.' Celine smiled and held out her hand. 'Thanks, Mrs Lynch, I really appreciate this.'

'Call me Rose, love. Oh, and here's the key.'

Celine pocketed the key and started down the stairs. 'Bye, Rose. I'll bring my stuff over tomorrow.'

'See you then,' Rose called after her, before descending the stairs at a more leisurely pace. When she got back into the shop Fergus was leaning against the counter talking to Sadie. 'Oh, hello, love. That's a pity, you just missed my new manager.'

'So Sadie was saying. That's great, Ma!'

Rose nodded. 'Yes, I think she'll work out very well. 'Now, let's go and eat. I'm starving. I'll only be half an hour, Sadie, and then you can get off.'

'So, what's she like?' Fergus asked when they were

seated in the tiny café across the road eating lunch – an egg sandwich for Rose and a burger and fries for Fergus.

'I have no idea,' Rose replied.

Her son frowned. 'What do you mean?'

'Ah, nothing, love, don't mind me.'

'How's the leg today?'

'Not bad. Are you working in the shop this afternoon?'

'No, Dominic doesn't need me.'

Rose shot him a suspicious look as she poured the tea. 'What do you mean he doesn't need you? What have you done?'

Fergus shook his head. 'Nothing! Things are just quiet, okay?'

'So if you've no work what are you going to do?'

Fergus shrugged. 'I might head into town for a while.'

'Ah don't, son, sure there's nothing much in town.'

Fergus rolled his eyes. 'Ma, stop worrying! Town is a big place, I'll be fine.'

'I just don't want you bumping into any of *that* crowd.'

Fergus rubbed the bridge of his nose. 'Ma, if I wanted drugs I could get them any day of the week. I work in a shelter every night, remember?' He patted her hand awkwardly. 'I'm clean. I've been clean for seven years.'

Rose gripped his hand and nodded. 'Sorry, love, I believe you, honest I do, it's just I can't help worrying.'

He grinned. 'Wait till you're in hospital and I have the house to myself.'

She took a swipe at him that he ducked easily. 'Don't even think about it or I'll get your Aunt Babs to move in and keep an eye on you.'

Fergus groaned. 'No, anything but that! I promise to live like a monk.'

Rose watched him as he wolfed down his burger. 'I wish you wouldn't. It's about time you found yourself a nice girl. You're nearly twenty-four.'

'Yeah, and I'm an ex-drug addict, working part-time in a newsagent's and in a shelter for the homeless; oh yes, I'm a great catch!'

Rose studied her son. He was thin but sinewy with his hair cropped tight against his head and dark chocolate brown eyes, just like his dad's. He was a good-looking lad who bore little resemblance to the skeletal, hollow-eyed automaton of seven years ago. 'You are happy, Fergus, aren't you?'

'Sure, Ma,' he told her through a mouth full of fries.

'Maybe you should look for a better job,' she ventured.

'I'm grand where I am.'

'But Fergus, mixing with all those, those . . .'

'Bums?'

She frowned. 'You know what I mean.'

'Stop worrying, Ma, you'll go grey.' He stood up and tousled her hair. 'Thanks for lunch. Seeya later.'

'Bye.' Rose lifted a hand to smooth her blonde

head. The only way she'd go grey was if she missed an appointment at Annabelle's Hair Studio! Her smile faded as her thoughts drifted back to her son. She'd never wanted him to work in that homeless shelter but his social worker had convinced her that the responsibility would be good for him. He was right of course. As the months went by and Fergus saw first-hand the damage drink and drugs could do, his resolve to stay clean strengthened. But she thought it was time he moved on to a more normal job. He was so young and vulnerable. She didn't want to go into hospital and leave him alone but she had waited a year for this hip replacement and if she pulled out now she knew she'd be waiting as long again. And at least she had Celine Moore to look after things while she was away. Rose knew that if she told Fergus about the girl's background he'd have said she was mad to hire her. But for some reason, she was drawn to Celine Moore and from their short conversation it was clear that the girl understood clothes. Rose paid for lunch and headed back across the road. Dominic was standing outside the newsagent's.

'Hi, Rose.' He smiled at her, rocking on his heels, his hands dug deep in the pockets of his cardigan. 'Beautiful day.'

'Hi, Dominic.'

'How's the leg?'

She made a face. 'Not bad, not bad.'

'Well, you don't have long to go now.' He walked

with her to the door of Close Second, taking off his glasses to polish them on the front of his heavy cotton shirt.

'Have you found someone to run this place for you yet?'

'Yes, thank goodness. She starts on Monday.'

'Wonderful! That must be a load off your mind.'

Rose turned worried eyes on him. 'Yes it is, now if I could only sort my son out. Why didn't you want him to work today, Dominic? Has he been giving you trouble?'

Dominic pushed dark blond hair off his forehead and settled his glasses back on the bridge of his nose. 'Of course not, Rose! There just isn't enough work for us both at the moment.'

Rose frowned. 'That new book shop is really hurting you, isn't it?'

Dominic sighed. 'If only they stuck to selling books, but no, they have to sell stationery and newspapers and magazines.'

'I hate the idea of Fergus having nothing to do all day.'

'I'm sure he'd have no problem finding something else.'

'Yes, but with his background—'

'Forget about his background, Rose. I've left him alone in that shop God knows how many times and he's never touched the till.'

Rose looked shocked. 'I should hope not!'

'If he were still on drugs, Rose, he'd have cleaned

me out long ago and you too. He's a good lad and I'd be happy to give him a reference.'

Rose's face cleared as she recognised the truth of his words. 'Thanks, Dominic.'

Two women approached and turned into the newsagent's. Dominic turned to salute her with a twinkle in his eye 'Don't look now but I believe I have customers! See you later, Rose.'

'Bye, Dominic.' Rose laughed. With all his problems Dominic still held on to his sense of humour. Gosh, what must he think of her? He'd said business was bad and all she'd been worried about was how it would affect her son. She'd bring him in a coffee later and ask him about it, she decided as she went back into her shop. She could imagine how tough it must be and how Dominic's takings must have dropped in the last three months. She'd probably never have that problem. There were only a handful of second-hand shops in Dublin and only one other that dealt exclusively in designer labels. She had a loyal clientele, some of them travelling from the four corners of Ireland. She had the phone numbers of her best customers and she called them if something came in that she knew they'd like. It was this personal service that made it even more difficult to find a suitable manager.

The bell tinkled on the door and she looked up and smiled. 'Mrs Williams! I'm so glad you dropped in. I have a lovely Gina Bacconi dress that I think you'll like.'

*

Fergus stood in HMV debating whether to spend his
last few Euros on CDs or a new game for his
Playstation. The way things were going it looked like
he'd have a lot more time on his hands soon so he
decided to go for the game. After paying for it, he
tucked it into the inside pocket of his jacket and
headed back out onto Henry Street.

'Yo, Gus, how's it goin'?'

Fergus closed his eyes briefly before turning
around. 'Howaya, Mick.'

Mick Garvey leaned closer. 'Haven't seen ye in
ages.'

Fergus stepped back. 'Ah, well, you know yourself,
keeping busy.'

Mick laughed. 'Still working at the shelter, are ye?'

Fergus nodded. 'Yeah, a bit.'

'Ye must meet all sorts down there. Maybe I'll drop
in and see ye some night.'

Fergus smiled but his eyes were cold. 'Sure. And if
I'm not there, Paddy Burns will be. Do you know
Paddy, Mick? He's an ex-cop.'

Mick's eyes narrowed. 'I hope yer not forgetting
who yer friends are, Gus.'

'Oh, I know exactly who my friends are, thanks,
Mick. See you around.' Fergus walked away before
Mick could answer and lost himself in the crowds on
Henry Street. He was breathing heavily and his heart
was racing. Mick was half his size and he could take
him out any time, but as one of Dublin's main dealers,

Mick had a lot of contacts. If Mick Garvey ever wanted to get him, he'd only have to put out the word. So Fergus would continue to do what he'd always done: keep his mouth shut and lie low. He moved quickly in the direction of the bus stop. Maybe coming into town hadn't been such a good idea after all.

Chapter 2

Celine ran a self-conscious hand through her tangled hair as she went to open the door. 'Hi, Marina.'

Marina frowned at her friend's pale, miserable face. 'You look like shit.' She walked through to the kitchen and stopped in the doorway. 'What the hell?'

Most of the shelves were empty, half-filled boxes were on the worktops and table and an assortment of clothes was strewn around the room.

'I'm moving,' Celine explained.

'Excuse me?'

Celine took a pile of clothes off a stool and dumped them on the ground. 'Sit down, it's a long story.'

Marina perched her slender form on the stool and crossed one long leg over the other. 'Do tell.'

'I've been having an affair.' Celine didn't look at her friend, concentrating her attentions on opening the wine that her friend had brought.

Marina stared at her, wide-eyed. 'You're kidding! Who with?'

Celine went in search of glasses. 'Bloody hell, which box did I put them in?'

'Celine!'

She found the glasses and turned to face Marina. 'Kevin Gilligan.'

'Kevin Gilligan? Kevin Gilligan as in the manager of our local building society, pillar of the community, married to that old bag Eileen?'

Celine nodded. 'That's the one.'

'Jesus! How long has this been going on?'

Celine shrugged. 'A few months.'

Marina scowled. 'Why didn't you tell me?'

'Affairs *are* supposed to be secret,' Celine pointed out.

'Not from your best friend they're not,' Marina retorted. 'I'm supposed to be involved, supplying you with alibis and the like.'

'But I don't need alibis. I'm a free agent.'

'Kevin Gilligan isn't. His wife will take you apart when she finds out.'

'She already has.'

'She knows? She didn't come here, did she?'

Celine gave a wry smile. 'Nothing so discreet, she attacked me in the middle of the golf club.'

'Bloody hell.'

'In front of Daddy, Brenda and Alan,' Celine continued.

'Wow, poor you. When did all this happen?'

'Last week. Dad's not impressed.'

'And what about the sainted Brenda?' Marina had never had much time for Celine's sister-in-law.

'Won't even talk to me.'

Marina shrugged. 'Well, that's no bad thing.'

'Brenda's okay.' Celine felt obliged to stick up for Dermot's sister.

'Oh, I know, she's just so, so . . .' Marina fluttered long fingers around as she searched for a word. 'Settled.'

Celine stared out of the window, her eyes sad. 'Settled isn't so bad.'

Marina gave an impatient shrug. 'No, but there's settled and settled. Do you think she and Alan are happy?'

Celine looked surprised. 'I don't know. I suppose so.'

'He's quite good-looking.'

'Alan?' Celine stared at her friend.

'Yes, in a reserved, intelligent sort of way.'

'Don't even think about it. I'm in enough trouble with Brenda without you chatting up her husband.'

'Oh, don't worry, I've had it with married men. It's time poor little Josh had a proper role model in his life.'

Privately Celine thought 'little Josh' was beyond help but she was surprised at the serious look on Marina's face. 'Are you on the look-out for a new husband?'

'Yes, I think it's time,' Marina admitted. 'You should think about it yourself. Don't you miss having someone?'

'I've had Kevin,' Celine reminded her.

'That was just sex – oh, God, you don't love him, do you?'

'Of course not.' Celine laughed. 'I'm not dumb.'

Marina shook her head. 'Dumb enough, my dear. As my old dad used to say, never shit on your own doorstep.'

'Charming.'

'But true,' Marina insisted. 'It would probably be best if you dumped the gorgeous Mr Gilligan. Date married men, by all means, but next time go a little further afield. Have you been blackballed at the golf club yet?'

Celine laughed. 'No, but I'm sure it's only a matter of time. Eileen Gilligan is an important woman.'

'Which is why I'm saying—'

'I know, I know, don't shit on your own doorstep.'

'How on earth did it all start anyway? It's not as if you move in the same circles. It's not as if you move in *any* circles at the moment,' Marina added.

'We met down the gym.'

'The gym!' Marina's eyes lit up. 'I told you it was the perfect place to meet men.'

'Yes, well, I was fed up getting the third degree from the local biddies every time I went swimming, so I started to go down at seven a couple of mornings a week.'

'And Kevin was there perfecting his breast stroke?'

Celine rolled her eyes. 'He's a really nice guy, Marina.'

'He's not exactly hard on the eye either.'

'No,' Celine agreed, a twinkle in her eye.

'So, he chatted you up in the Jacuzzi.'

'No, in the snack bar. We got into the habit of having a coffee after the session. One morning the bar was shut and I invited him back here.'

Marina's eyes widened. 'You little hussy! I didn't know you had it in you!'

'Me neither,' Celine admitted. 'I hadn't intended it to turn into a full-blown affair but, well, Kevin can be very persuasive.'

'I bet he can.'

'It was nice to feel attractive and sexy again.'

Marina leaned forward. 'So is he good?'

'Marina!' Celine cried but she was smiling. 'He's great.'

'So what happens now? I don't suppose he's going to leave Eileen?'

'Of course not, I wouldn't want him to. No, it's over. I feel quite ashamed of myself.'

'Oh, for God's sake, you are only human,' Marina said matter-of-factly.

'It's not just about Kevin, it's my life. I've been so pathetic these past few years. I haven't *done* anything. I didn't even set out to have an affair. It just' – she shrugged – 'happened.'

Marina nodded. 'I've had relationships like that too. I must say, though, I am relieved!' I was beginning to think you were heading for a nunnery. You've been on your own for so long – it's not natural.'

Celine chuckled. 'But now you know different.'

'Yes, thank goodness, you're normal after all.'

'I wouldn't go that far.' Celine gave her a lopsided smile. 'I have to hand it to Eileen, she gave quite a performance. No screaming or shouting – she even apologised for interrupting our meal – and then went on to tell Daddy that I was screwing her husband.'

Marina cringed. 'Ouch.'

'Yeah, I felt like a teenager caught behind the bike shed.'

'So what happened then?'

'Brenda stormed out and Daddy and I drove home in silence. Honestly, I would have preferred it if he'd shouted at me.'

'Hurt silence is much more effective,' Marina agreed, 'but he'll get over it. Give him time to cool off. Moving is a bit drastic though, don't you think?'

'Ah, but you haven't heard the full story. You see, I've also been fired.'

Marina raised her eyebrows. 'Because of the affair?'

Celine nodded. 'Turns out my ex-boss is a distant cousin of Eileen's.'

'God, that woman has more tentacles than an octopus. So what now?'

'I've got myself a new job!'

'Crikey, you don't hang about, do you?'

'Can't afford to, but no, this was sheer luck. I was going through the situations vacant page in the *Times* on Thursday and found it.'

'Not another pharmacy, I hope.'

'Nope. It's a second-hand fashion boutique in Hopefield and as of this morning I'm going to be the manager.'

Marina's eyes widened. 'Not Close Second?'

'Do you know it?'

'Well of course I know it! It's only the best second-hand shop in Dublin. My God, I get most of my clothes there these days!'

'Well, that's great. Now I actually know one of my customers.'

'It's *the* place to go for the perfect little designer number at half the price. You would be amazed at the ladies who shop there.'

'Looks like I'm going to meet them.'

'I hope there will be special discounts for your friends,' Marina purred.

Celine hugged her. 'I'll do my best.'

Marina raised her glass. 'This is great, Celine, congratulations. It's about time you got back into the rag trade. Next thing you'll be telling me you're designing again.'

Celine's smile faded. 'Definitely not.'

Marina tactfully changed the subject. 'But why do you have to move house? You could easily commute.'

'The job comes with a flat over the shop and I think it might be a good idea for me to disappear for a while.'

'Your dad will miss you.'

Celine shook her head, her eyes dark with sadness. 'I think he'll be relieved.'

'Rubbish, you know he's mad about you.'

'And the feeling is mutual, which is why I have to go.' Celine stood up abruptly and brushed her hands on her faded jeans. 'Now are you going to help me pack?'

Marina looked down in alarm at her cream linen trousers. 'Absolutely not!'

Celine laughed. 'Then get out.'

'Charming.' Marina drained her glass and leaned over to kiss Celine's cheek. 'When do you start?'

'Monday, but I'm going to move into the flat tomorrow.'

'Well, the best of luck, darling. I'll drop by during the week and you can sell me something.'

'Ooh yes, that will impress Rose.'

Marina tapped the side of her nose. 'Leave it to me. Before I've left she'll think you're the saleswoman of the year!'

After Marina left, Celine went back to her packing with a lighter heart. It would be exciting to work with clothes again, especially some of the newer designs. When she'd gone for her interview this morning she'd noticed that Rose had a fair representation of Irish designers – one of whom Celine had gone to college with. It would be strange to be selling Emily Park's creations. She had her own shop on Baggot Street now and dressed some of Ireland's most famous women. Celine didn't follow fashion any more but everyone knew about Emily's meteoric rise to fame. She was a media darling and everyone's favourite success story. Celine was happy for her and not remotely jealous. She'd realised when Dermot died that all her creativity had died with him and was resigned to living an uneventful life. She smiled slightly as she cleaned out the fridge. Her life could hardly be called uneventful now that she was the scarlet woman of Killmont! But she would be happy to leave that behind, leave Kevin Gilligan behind and go back to being a shopkeeper. Although working in a clothes shop would be a lot more fun than the local pharmacy and the clientele would be more interesting too. Celine looked forward to blending into the background and watching Dublin's finest up close and personal. It would be a wonderful distraction from her own dreary life and being on the far side of Dublin from Killmont made it all the more attractive.

Chapter 3

Kay Flynn was on her knees picking up pieces of crayon when Marina arrived.

'Mum, what on earth are you doing down there? Where's Josh?'

There was a crash and the sound of breaking glass. Kay closed her eyes briefly. 'At a guess I'd say he's in the kitchen.'

Marina hurried past. 'Josh, darling, are you all right?'

Kay stood up and followed her, groaning inwardly when her worst fears were confirmed. Her beautiful Dublin crystal vase was in pieces on the floor.

Marina sat her son on the kitchen table and began examining him from head to foot. 'Are you hurt, my darling?'

Josh took one look at the frown on his grandmother's face and burst into tears. 'It was an accident, Mummy.'

'Of course it was, Joshie. Mummy and Granny know that, don't we, Granny?'

Kay got back down on her knees and began to pick

up shards of glass. 'Of course we do,' she muttered obediently.

'I think some chocolate buttons will help dry those tears.' Marina smiled lovingly at her son and produced a bag from her pocket.

Josh wiped his face on his sleeve and grabbed the bag.

'What do you say, Josh?'

'Thank you,' he said through a mouthful of chocolate.

Happy that all the glass was off the floor, Kay dumped the daffodils in the bin and mopped up the water.

'He's so brave.' Marina sat down next to him and watched her mother at work. 'Did he eat his dinner, Mum?'

Kay thought of the food that Josh had hurled around the kitchen but decided it was easier to lie. 'He certainly did.' Josh looked up in surprise and she put her finger to her lips.

'You are such a good boy, Joshie, and I think you are Granny's pet.'

Pet Rottweiler, Kay thought, reaching for the kettle. 'Tea, Marina?'

Marina shook her head. 'I don't suppose you have any Evian water?'

Kay nodded towards the tap. 'There's plenty in there.'

'Oh, Mum!' Marina gave a tolerant laugh. 'Well, maybe a cup of weak tea then.'

'How's work?' Kay asked as she fetched two mugs.

'Not great but I'm modelling in the Penney's fashion show tomorrow night.'

Kay tensed. 'Tomorrow's my book club night.'

'Oh, that's okay, Katie is going to baby-sit.'

'Don't like Katie,' Josh piped up.

'Of course you do, darling. Katie's a lovely girl.'

Josh's bottom lip trembled. 'Don't like her.'

Kay rolled her eyes as her daughter gathered him into her arms.

'Don't cry, darling! You don't have to stay with Katie if you don't want to. But if you do, Mummy will bring you back a special present.'

Josh stopped crying. 'What?'

Marina hugged him. 'It will be a surprise. Okay?'

'Okay,' Josh said reluctantly, scrambled down off her lap and went into the other room to watch television.

Kay carried the tea to the table and sat down. 'Penney's fashion show, eh? I didn't think you'd be bothered modelling for them.' While Kay was only too happy to shop in the store, her daughter wouldn't be seen dead wearing chain-store clothes.

'Don't have a lot of choice these days, Mum,' Marina admitted. 'The offers aren't exactly rolling in.'

Kay frowned. 'But you're only thirty-five.'

'Thirty-four,' Marina corrected. After all, it was still two months to her birthday. 'But I'm surrounded by tall, skinny twenty-year-olds.'

'You're tall and skinny—'

'But not twenty. And I'm too young to model for the middle-aged fashion.' She sighed. 'Lord, I never thought I'd look forward to getting older!'

Though Marina was laughing about her situation, Kay could tell her daughter was worried. 'I wish I could afford to help out,' she fretted.

'Don't be silly, Mum, you're poorer than I am.'

Kay's smile was sad. It was true. Donald had never bothered with life assurance or savings, convinced he had plenty of time to make his fortune. Dropping dead at the tender age of fifty-eight had not figured in his plans. His estate agency had been sold to pay off all his bills and Kay had been lucky in the end to hold on to her house. 'Would you not take Josh out of that nursery, darling? I'm sure a childminder would be much cheaper.' She decided not to mention the music lessons, art lessons and now – God help us – the drama class.

Marina was staring at her as if she'd lost her mind. 'Of course not, Mum! That's the best nursery in Dublin and I wouldn't feel happy putting Joshie anywhere else.'

'But he's only four and think of the money you'd save.'

Marina shook her head. 'No, and anyway, since when was I ever able to save? A chip off the old block, that's me.'

Kay winced. It was true, Marina was exactly like her father, which was why she worried so much. Josh was always dressed in the best of clothes and Marina was forever buying him gifts.

'Don't worry, Mum,' Marina continued. 'I'm going to find myself a rich husband.'

'Oh, well get me one too.' Kay patted her hair. 'There's life in the old dog yet!'

Marina laughed. 'How about a father and son? We could double-date.'

Kay chuckled as she sipped her tea. 'Just ask to see their bankbooks first. Knowing our luck we'd end up paying for dinner!'

An hour later, Kay stood at the hall door and waved goodbye as Marina sped away. When she returned to the kitchen she groaned as she looked around. The place always looked like a bomb had hit it after a visit from Josh. She sighed as she thought of her errant grandson. What he needed was an occasional clip round the ear but, of course, Marina wouldn't hear of it. She didn't even see the need of it – Kay couldn't believe how blind her daughter was to Josh's naughtiness. He could do no wrong in her eyes. A pity Donald wasn't here, Kay thought as she fetched the Hoover. For all his faults, her husband had been good with kids and even though he'd adored his only daughter, he'd never spoilt her. And Kay could have forgiven him if he had. From the moment she'd been born, Marina had been as perfect as an angel with her golden curls, blue eyes and creamy skin. Kay didn't know where those amazing looks had come from. She and Donald had looked at each other in awe, wondering how they'd been blessed with such a beautiful child. As Marina got older, it became clear that she had the confidence to match her looks and a taste for the good things in life that led her into the world of modelling. At twenty she was earning more than her father ever had and her life was full of parties and functions. She holidayed three times a year in the best resorts and was seen on the arm of any number of actors and pop stars. Kay and Donald were proud and slightly amazed that they had produced such a successful daughter.

When Marina introduced her fiancé to her parents she was twenty-seven. Kay had thought it was time that her daughter settled down but had disliked Ray Prendergast from the moment she set eyes on him. But Marina was blinded by his model good looks and fell for all the smooth talking that had made her mother so suspicious. It was a stormy marriage from day one, but when Marina discovered she was pregnant, she was more determined than ever to make the marriage work. Through her pregnancy and the first few months of Josh's life, she tolerated Ray's drinking, womanising and allergy to work. As fast as she made money, he spent it, but after he'd lost another modelling job because of unreliability, Marina gave him his marching orders and instead of wasting time feeling sorry for herself, had thrown herself into rearing her beloved son.

*

Kay had been proud of her and was riddled with guilt that as he got older, her grandson irritated her beyond belief. She'd looked after him a lot when he was a baby but since he'd learned to walk and talk, Kay found herself making excuses whenever Marina asked for help. Thankfully, her daughter didn't seem to notice. Kay wondered if it was a maternal defence mechanism that made her daughter oblivious of her son's effect on others.

Kay knew she wasn't the only one who found Josh a handful. Celine had an edge in her voice when she was around the little boy and had turned white the day Josh had knocked Dermot's picture off the desk. Kay cringed at the memory. She'd visited Celine's home a number of times over the years but had never been in Dermot's study. The three women had been chatting over a coffee in the kitchen and hadn't noticed Josh slipping from the room. The crash from Dermot's study had Celine on her feet and heading for the door, Marina and Kay on her heels. Kay would never forget the sight of Celine on her hands and knees, picking up the pieces of the glass frame. As usual, Marina was more concerned with Josh, but Kay realised that her grandson had not only broken a treasured possession but had intruded on a shrine. She hustled her daughter and grandson out of the room to let Celine have a moment's privacy.

'That was very naughty, Josh,' she'd said, her voice sharp.

Marina raised an eyebrow. 'It was an accident, Mum.'

'He shouldn't have been in there,' Kay had hissed. 'Didn't you notice that room?'

Marina shrugged. 'It's positively dreary. I keep telling Celine she should dump the furniture and give it a lick of paint.'

Kay blanched. 'Oh, Marina, really!'

Celine arrived back and flashed a tight smile at them. 'No harm done. I can easily get a new frame.'

'There, Mum, stop fussing.'

Kay bit her lip and glared at her grandson.

'It's fine, Kay, really,' Celine assured her.

And that had been that. But Kay noticed that Celine had kept the door firmly shut on all of their visits since and probably locked if she had any sense.

Kay finished hoovering Josh's crumbs and plumped the cushions on her sofa. She pulled back as her hand came in contact with something cold and sticky and groaned as, on closer inspection, it turned out to be jelly – no wonder Josh had finished his dessert so quickly. 'Little terror,' she muttered and went to fetch water and a cloth. Again.

Chapter 4

Celine stood in line at the checkout in the small supermarket. 'Hi.' She smiled at the woman in front who'd turned to stare.

The woman turned away and Celine saw the look that passed between her and the checkout girl.

She kept the smile plastered on her face until she got outside. 'Silly old cows, nothing better to do with their time,' she muttered as she staggered down the road with her bags. She'd avoided the local shop lately but today she'd had to venture out to get detergent, polish and cloths in order to give the house a good clean before she moved out. She managed to cover the short distance home and get inside the safety of her hall door without meeting any other neighbours. She groaned when she saw the distinctive red envelope lying on the mat – not another one. After unpacking, she went out to the hall and picked it up. She considered throwing it in the bin without opening it but she knew that, before the night was out, she'd go rummaging for it. As usual, it contained one white piece of notepaper with one typewritten line. WHY STAY WHERE YOU'RE NOT WANTED? She tossed it on to the table and slumped into a chair. No matter how much she tried to dismiss these notes that appeared once or twice a week now, they unnerved her. She didn't believe Eileen Gilligan was the culprit. As she had demonstrated that night in the golf club, she was a woman who believed in the direct approach. It could be one of her well-meaning cronies of course – there were plenty of them. Her father would be horrified if he knew about the hate mail but she wouldn't tell him. She'd caused enough trouble already. The phone rang and she decided to let the machine answer. She listened as her voice asked the caller to leave a message after the tone. There was a short pause and then a nervous cough. 'Ms Moore, this is Audrey Thomas from the Willows Golf Club. Just to advise you that the committee have decided that it would be better if you didn't come to the clubhouse for now. If you have any queries or questions, please put them in writing to the captain James Fairchild or myself. Thank you.'

'God almighty, the sooner I get out of this place the better!' Celine laughed but there were tears in her eyes.

She took a can of beer from the fridge and went into what Dermot had laughingly called his study. As she unlocked the door she remembered the day that Josh had broken the picture frame and how she'd cried herself to sleep that night. Thankfully she wasn't quite as emotional these days. Celine sat down in

Dermot's battered leather chair – he'd picked it up at
a car boot sale – and gazed around the room that she'd
never changed. The walls were covered with pictures
of colleagues and patients, some of the latter now also
dead. Dermot hadn't been able to help everyone but it
wasn't for the lack of trying. He had known from an
early age that he wanted to help people. His career
guidance officer at school suggested social work.
Celine had cursed that teacher many times since but
she knew that Dermot wouldn't have been happy
doing anything else. Not that he was ever *really* happy
– he had cared too much. He had been frustrated by
the lack of funds, the helplessness of the police when
it came to domestic disputes, the red tape involved in
rescuing kids from parents that abused them. Every
day was a battle for Dermot. Celine studied the
awards on the wall that lauded his dedication and felt
tears prick her eyes. Poor Dermot. He was way too
young to die. Everyone had told her she should be
very proud of him. They said what a special man he'd
been, that he was a hero. Celine had thanked them,
nodded, smiled, but sometimes, when she felt really
low, she thought that her husband had been a selfish
bloody fool. He shouldn't have died. He shouldn't
have even been there that night. Why did he have to
play the hero? Why hadn't he thought of his own
safety? Why hadn't he thought of her? Why had he
made her a widow at just twenty-one? But it was a
long time ago now and she knew she had to move on.
Maybe Eileen Gilligan had done her a favour.

She picked up the wedding photo that sat on the desk. Dermot was standing behind her and she was leaning back against him. She was smiling into the camera and he was smiling down at her. It was a happy photo; it had been a happy day. Her dad had forked out a small fortune for the reception and everyone had said what a perfect couple they made. 'Perfect,' she murmured, setting the photo back on the desk. She looked at the books and papers that littered the room and mused that she really should clear it all out. One of Dermot's colleagues had taken away any papers relating to his patients but it had barely put a dent in the data that Dermot had surrounded himself with. There were articles, magazines, notes scribbled to himself – these would be the most difficult to discard. When Celine looked at the familiar large untidy scrawl it made her heart beat faster and for a second it was as if he was still here. She stood up and walked out of the room, closing and locking the door behind her. She would clean it out but not today.

As she stood in the hallway, beer in hand, the doorbell buzzed and, realising that she was visible through the frosted glass, she reluctantly went to answer it. Who would it be, she wondered. A personal visit from the lady captain or more harassment from the local kids? She flung open the door, ready for battle. 'Kevin!'

He smiled. 'Hi, honey, I'm home.'

'Are you mad?' she hissed, dragging him inside and closing the door. 'What if someone sees you?'

He pulled her into his arms and kissed her. 'I parked in the next road and walked up the lane. No one saw me.'

Celine groaned as his hands slipped under her shirt and opened her bra with one expert click. 'Marina could have been here, or my dad.'

'No cars outside,' he murmured as he kissed her neck.

'Eileen is probably having you followed,' she protested, but her eyes were closed and she leaned into him, willing him to continue.

'Forget about Eileen.' He moved towards the stairs, dragging her after him. 'We've got some catching up to do.'

And putting Eileen, her dad and Brenda out of her mind, Celine allowed him to lead her upstairs.

Celine stared at the ceiling and listened to Kevin's quiet snores. It was almost midnight and she'd have to waken him soon. She felt more relaxed and at peace than she had in days. Mindless, passionate sex did that for her – at least with Kevin it did. She turned to look at the long dark lashes that fanned his tanned face and marvelled at the slight smile that played around his lips even in sleep. He was an attractive man who always seemed to be in good humour despite his wife's reported nagging. Though nearly thirty-eight, his body was fit and muscular and Celine knew that there were plenty of women who'd happily change places with her. She was ready for someone else to take over as Kevin Gilligan's mistress although she knew she would miss him. She did not love him but when she was in his arms, when he made love to her, she was happy.

Kevin stirred and opened his eyes. 'What are you thinking about?'

Celine raised herself up on her elbow and stared down at him. 'What a nut you are to have come here.'

Kevin leaned over and kissed her breast. 'But a lovable nut.'

'Don't you ever feel guilty?' she marvelled.

'Not any more.'

'What about your wife, your kids?'

Kevin looked away, his face grim. 'My wife is happy once she's got plenty of money to spend and as for my kids, I'm a bloody good father.'

Celine hugged him. 'I know you are.'

He kissed her lips. 'Look, Celine, everything will be fine. We just need to be a bit more careful.'

Celine sat up, shaking her head. 'No, Kevin. Did you know that I've been told to stay away from the golf club *and* someone is writing me nasty letters?'

Kevin's eyes widened. 'God, what a parochial little place Killmont is.'

'What a small-minded, sexist little place, you mean. They want to run me out of town and they turn a blind eye to anything you do.'

'Yeah, great, isn't it?'

Celine poked him in the stomach. 'I've decided to leave.'

Kevin raised an eyebrow. 'Leave?'

'I've got a job running a boutique in Hopefield. I'll be living over the shop.'

'That's great, Celine! Now we'll be able to see each other more often.'

Celine looked away. 'I don't think that's such a good idea.'

'Of course it's a good idea. We're good together, Celine, you know we are.' Kevin pulled her on top of him and buried his face in her hair.

'We don't have time for this,' she protested as his body started to move against hers.

'No,' he agreed and kissed her hungrily.

'You should be going.'

'Yeah.' He rolled her over and moved on top of her. Celine closed her eyes and let her body take over.

Chapter 5

Alan put down his paper with a sigh and looked at his wife. She'd rearranged the flowers in the lounge and the dining room twice already and now she was rubbing at a stain on the carpet that was at least two years old. 'Why don't you call her?' he said gently.

Brenda didn't even look up. 'Never.'

'But, Brenda—'

'Leave it, Alan, please.'

'But I hate to see you so upset.'

'I am not upset, I'm angry and disgusted.' Brenda sat back on her heels and pushed her hair back off her flushed face. 'I never want to talk to the girl again.'

'That's a bit harsh. It's been six years!'

'This is nothing to do with Dermot. My poor brother is not responsible for his wife committing adultery.'

Alan sighed. 'All I'm saying is she must have been lonely.'

Brenda shot him a look of disgust. ''Being lonely is no excuse to sleep with a married man. Trust you to take her side.'

Alan threw down his paper and stood up. 'I'm not taking sides, in fact I'm not going to say another bloody word. I'm going to the golf club.'

Brenda closed her eyes as the front door banged. She really shouldn't be taking it out on Alan but he just didn't understand how betrayed she felt. She went outside and looked impatiently around her tidy kitchen. She needed to keep busy but she'd already cleaned the fridge out, scrubbed the cooker – although as she'd only cleaned it last week there wasn't that much scrubbing to be done – and the floor was polished to the point of being dangerous. 'Scones,' she murmured and went to fetch the ingredients. She turned the oven on to warm, took a large bowl from the cupboard and switched on the radio to Forever FM. They played all Eighties stuff on Saturday mornings which she could at least hum along to. After measuring in the flour and adding the sugar, eggs and milk she started to mix and felt the calm descend on her. Yoga might relax some people but baking did it for Brenda every time. She had some cooking apples so she could make apple crumble too – Alan loved that and it would make up for her snapping at him this morning. And she'd make a ginger cake for Frank. Usually she'd make two – the other one for Celine – but not any more.

She rolled the dough, cut out the scones and slipped the tray into the oven before cleaning her bowl and starting on the cake. Celine would have to buy her own bread and cakes from now on. *And* she'd have to find someone else to make her curtains or advise her on how to get red wine out of wool trousers. Unexpected tears pricked her eyes and pulling out a handkerchief she blew her nose. She shouldn't waste any tears on the girl. How would poor Frank hold his head up in the golf club after this? Celine couldn't have embarrassed him more if she'd done a striptease on the table.

Brenda took the scones out of the oven and put them on to a tray to cool. Celine should have thought about her family before hopping into bed with Kevin Gilligan. She'd behaved disgracefully and hadn't even had the decency to do it with a stranger. She had to carry on her dirty little affair in the middle of Killmont, amongst all their friends. No matter what Alan said, she would never forgive Celine.

Alan teed off and smiled slightly as his ball went high and straight.

'Nice shot.' Frank stuck his tee in the ground.

'How's Celine?'

Frank swung his club and cursed under his breath as the ball swerved off to the left and into the rough. 'I don't know and, to be honest, I'm not sure I even care at the moment. She wants to come round later and talk.'

'Brenda is very upset too,' Alan said as they walked down the course. 'I've tried to calm her down but I always seem to say the wrong thing.'

It wasn't until they'd finished playing the hole that

Frank spoke again. 'I wish I knew why she did it.'

'Maybe she loves him,' Alan suggested.

'Bollocks!' Frank hissed. 'She wouldn't love a sleazy git like him. Oh God, it's an awful mess. You know he has three kids.'

'I know, but from what I've heard the marriage isn't great and Celine wasn't the first.'

'That's no excuse,' Frank retorted. 'I don't know what the hell she thought she was playing at.'

'The only way you're going to find out is if you talk to her,' Alan pointed out.

Frank sighed. 'I suppose you're right.'

'Let's have dinner at the club tonight.'

'Do you think Brenda will want to?' Frank asked.

Alan shrugged. 'We have to do it sometime. The sooner the better, I think.'

Brenda had fallen asleep in the chair when the doorbell rang. She blinked a couple of times and then hurried to answer it, putting a self-conscious hand to her tousled hair. She hesitated when she recognised the silhouette through the glass.

'Brenda? Brenda, please let me in.'

Brenda opened the door. 'What do you want?'

Celine glanced at the curtains twitching in the next house. 'To explain. Let me in, Brenda. You don't want the neighbours to hear, do you?'

Brenda stood back, frowning at her sister-in-law's appearance. She looked about seventeen in her faded jeans, dark hair in pigtails and not a trace of makeup.

Brenda would never dream of leaving the house without makeup, but then she didn't have flawless skin and wide-set grey eyes. 'I'm waiting,' she said.

'It meant nothing. It was a mistake. Kevin was never a replacement for Dermot, you've got to believe that.'

'I do.' Brenda's tone was clipped.

'Then why are you so upset with me?'

'You say it meant nothing, that it was a mistake?'

'Yes.' Celine nodded eagerly.

'Don't you see that that's even worse? You messed around with all of our lives for a bit of fun, a roll in the hay. Eileen, your father, me, you didn't think about what effect it might have on any of us, did you?'

Celine studied her scruffy trainers. 'You weren't meant to find out.'

Brenda's laugh was mirthless. 'Oh, I see. Poor little Celine didn't *mean* to hurt anyone so that makes everything okay.'

'That's not what I'm saying—'

'I don't want to hear it, Celine. Your father might have to put up with you but I don't. Now please leave.'

'But Brenda—' Celine protested but her sister-in-law had already opened the door.

'Just go.'

After her failed attempt to make peace, Celine wandered down to the village and into the coffee shop. Her father wouldn't be back from the golf club until twelve and though she still had a lot of packing to do, she didn't fancy staying in the house all morning. As she queued at the counter, she was aware of whispers nearby. When she looked over, she recognized two women from the golf club. Giving them a broad smile and a cheery wave, she carried her latte to a corner table, sat down and spread out a newspaper in front of her. She was conscious of the women watching her, but she studiously ignored them, sipped her coffee and tried to look absorbed in her paper. It was a wonder she wasn't in it, she thought wryly. She stared blindly at the paper and thought about the mess she was in. She'd burnt her bridges with Brenda, her father was positively frosty – could things possibly get worse? Draining her cup, she took her paper and went back out on to the street. As she marched home she was conscious of stares and whispers but she held her head up high. To hell with them all, she thought, but was relieved to reach the sanctuary of her little cottage. The first thing that she saw when she got inside was a red envelope on the mat. 'Post on a Saturday,' she murmured, reaching down to pick it up. She tore it open and stared at the single white page with one typewritten sentence.

YOU'RE NOT WELCOME AROUND HERE.

Celine put it with the others in a drawer of Dermot's desk. She didn't know why she was keeping them. Tomorrow she'd be gone and the anonymous writer would have to find a new target. Celine threw all her energies into packing up the last of her belongings. Anything personal that she was leaving behind was now stacked in Dermot's study and the estate agent was under strict instructions that his room was off limits to the new tenants.

Two hours later, she stood at her father's hall door. She was determined to work things out with him before she left.

'Oh, it's you,' he said.

'Hi.' Celine smiled nervously and followed him into the lounge. 'Did you have a good game?'

'Not particularly.' He sat down in his chair and closed the novel he'd been reading.

'Oh, Daddy.' Celine perched on the sofa opposite him. 'Don't be like this.'

'Like what?'

'Angry.'

He shook his head. 'I'm not angry any more. Confused, yes, disappointed, yes, but angry, no. I'm just relieved your mother wasn't here to see this.'

'Oh, for God's sake, Daddy! Don't be silly.'

'Silly? I think you're the one who's been silly. You've thrown away the most precious thing you possess, your good name, for an asshole like Gilligan.'

'He hasn't taken advantage of me, if that's what you think, Daddy.'

'Is that supposed to make me feel better? That you went after him? I'm going to make some tea.'

He went out to the kitchen and Celine flopped back in the sofa. She'd always loved this room and even with her father's rather sensible approach to decorating, it was still cosy. Frank had painted the whole place white but the golden glow of the maple floors, the old pine dresser and the faded floral patterns in the curtains and sofas softened the effect. Celine got reluctantly to her feet and followed him out to the kitchen. 'I wasn't saying that I went *after* Kevin, Daddy,' she explained as he handed her a mug. 'Just that he didn't take advantage of me. I went into this with my eyes open.'

Frank looked at her with sad eyes. 'But why? You're a beautiful girl, you could have anyone you want. Why settle for a married man and why hurt his family?'

'I didn't plan to hurt anyone. I wasn't asking Kevin to leave Eileen, Daddy. What we had was just—' She hesitated.

'Sex,' he concluded.

'Yes.' She felt her cheeks grow hot. There was never a right time to discuss such intimate topics with your father.

Frank shook his head. 'And that explains everything?'

'It's what we both wanted. It was uncomplicated.'

'Until Eileen found out. The woman must be devastated.'

'I wouldn't waste too much pity on her,' Celine told him. 'Once Kevin buys her an expensive piece of jewellery she'll forgive him. She always has before.'

'Then it's a bloody strange marriage.'

Celine smiled slightly. 'Well, we agree on that at least.'

'You won't see him again.' It was a statement rather than a question.

Celine shuffled uncomfortably. 'I won't be here.'

'What?' He put down his mug and looked at her.

'I've got a job in Hopefield.'

'But you've got a job here.'

Celine grimaced. 'I was fired.'

Frank sighed. 'So what are you going to do?'

'I've got a job running a boutique and there's a flat over the shop.'

'You don't have to move, surely?' he protested.

'It would be too much hassle commuting without a car, and anyway, I think it would be a good idea if I got out of Killmont for a while.'

'I suppose.'

'It's not far.'

'No, no, I suppose you're right. It's probably for the best.'

Celine noticed his eyes were suspiciously bright and quickly moved to hug him. 'I'm sorry, Daddy. I'm so sorry.'

Frank held her tightly against him 'I know. I don't like what you did, Celine, but you're still my daughter and I love you.'

Celine closed her eyes and breathed in the familiar, comforting scent of his aftershave. 'I love you too, Daddy.'

Chapter 6

When Celine told her father she was planning to move straight away he insisted on helping. 'There doesn't seem to be much,' he remarked later as he put her bags in the car.

'I don't need much. The flat is tiny and I need to buy some clothes.' Celine looked down at her jeans and shirt. 'This isn't exactly suitable attire for running a designer boutique.'

Frank frowned as she locked up. 'But I thought you said it was a second-hand shop.'

'It is, but it only deals in the best designer labels. Marina says it's very popular.'

Frank chuckled. 'Oh, well, she should know! It will be nice to see you in some fancy clothes.'

Celine wrinkled her nose. 'Fancy isn't exactly what I had in mind.'

'Pity.' Frank climbed into the car.

Celine laughed and got in beside him.

'I'll keep an eye on the house for you,' he said as he pulled out onto the main road.

'There's no need, Daddy, the agency will look after it.'

'Still, I'd feel easier in my mind. No harm in wandering past occasionally.'

'Thanks.'

'So will I get to meet your new boss today?'

'Rose Lynch, is her name. Maybe we'll pop in and say a quick hello but Saturday is bound to be her busiest day.'

'And you say she has to go into hospital?'

'Yes, for a hip replacement, so she'll be out of action for a while.'

'Poor woman, it can't be easy trying to run a business when you're in pain.'

Celine shook her head. 'Although she seems like a remarkably capable person and cheerful with it. I think you'll like her.'

Frank shot her a look. 'I hope you're not match-making.'

Celine laughed. 'She's around your age actually, but no, I'll leave that to Brenda.' Celine's smile faded as she thought of their earlier confrontation. 'Daddy, would you talk to her for me?'

'I think that's up to you.'

'I tried to this morning but she wouldn't listen.'

'It will probably take time.'

Celine stared out of the window. 'That's what Marina said but I'm not so sure. Maybe if you had a word with Alan—'

'No, Celine, I'm sorry but I'm not going to get

involved. Alan and Brenda have already had words over this and I don't think it's fair. Leave them both alone.' Frank slowed the car as they neared Hopefield's main street. 'Where to?' he asked, his voice gruff.

'Turn right at the end and it's the first shop on the left.'

After Frank had parked the car he turned to his daughter and forced a smile. 'Come on then – show me your new home.'

They unpacked the car and carried the bags over to the shop. Rose was with a customer and there were a few others in the shop so Celine just waved and said she'd pop down later. She opened the hall door to her new home and led the way upstairs.

'It's very small.' Frank frowned as he wandered around.

Celine smiled. Her father's stature had a habit of making every room look small. 'It's fine.'

'I don't like the look of that immersion,' he continued, poking his head into the airing cupboard. 'There's a damp patch on the floor.'

Celine peered over his shoulder. 'Rose said she'd get the landlord to check that out. I'd better remind her.'

'The place could do with a lick of paint too,' Frank continued.

'I'm going to paint it.'

'But that's not up to you. Get the landlord to do it.'

'But I'd like to do it, Daddy.'

Frank shrugged. 'Do you want to unpack or go shopping first?'

'Shopping, I think,' Celine decided. 'Then at least we'll be able to have a tea break.'

Frank opened the fridge. 'We could have that now. It looks like someone's been expecting you.'

Celine smiled when she saw the milk, butter and bottle of wine. She opened the cupboard above and not only was there a fresh jar of coffee and a box of teabags, but biscuits too. 'Oh, isn't that nice?'

'Very kind.'

'But I still think we should do the shopping first. The later we leave it the worse it will be.'

'You're right.' After a longing look at the chocolate biscuits, Frank followed her to the door.

Celine smiled at him. 'Thanks for this, Daddy, I appreciate the help.'

'Sure if I didn't help you, who would? Oh, I didn't mean—'

'It's okay, Daddy. Let's go.' Before joining her father in the car again, Celine nipped in to say hello to Rose and ask her about the immersion.

'He said it would be taken care of sometime today.'

'Oh, but I'm off to do a bit of shopping.'

'No problem, I'll let him in.'

Celine smiled. 'Thanks, Rose, and thanks for stocking the fridge.'

Rose winked. 'Oh, just the bare essentials, that's all.'

'Maybe you'd like to join me and my dad for a glass of that wine after you've closed up?'

'Well, I'd love to!'

'Great! See you later.'

The rest of the afternoon went by in a flash, as
Celine and Frank followed the supermarket trip with
a visit to the local DIY shop where Celine bought a
mop and bucket, a small table lamp, a pretty set of
mugs and a cheap but cheerful cutlery set.

'Why didn't you bring this stuff from the cottage?'
Frank asked as he lugged the purchases out to the car.

'Because it's being rented fully furnished.'

'They'll probably wreck the place,' Frank warned.

'Don't worry, I've hidden all the good stuff.' Celine
knew her father was thinking about her mother's
china dinner service and silver that he had given her
when she got married. 'It's all safely under lock and
key in Dermot's office.'

'You don't know what kind of people might rent
it.'

Celine scowled as they got into the car. 'Don't say
that, Daddy! I won't be able to sleep worrying about
the place!'

'You don't worry about a thing. I told you I'll be
watching.'

'Thanks.'

'Any chance of a cup of tea now?' he asked as he
drove back to the flat.

'Tea and a sandwich and cakes too,' Celine told
him. 'I stocked up.'

Frank patted his stomach. 'I'm glad to hear it. It
seems a very long time since breakfast.'

Celine checked her watch. 'Oh, goodness, it's nearly five! Sorry, Daddy, I had no idea it was so late.'

'You're just like your mother. Once you start shopping you completely forget about time.'

Celine said nothing. That might have been true once but these days her shopping trips were functional.

Her father pulled into a parking spot right outside the shop. 'Now that was lucky!'

'Yeah, great, only we still have to carry everything upstairs.'

Frank got out and drew himself up to his full six feet one. 'No problem. You go and put the kettle on and I'll take care of all this.'

'Do a few trips, Daddy,' Celine warned. 'I don't want you putting your back out.' Grabbing a couple of the supermarket bags, she opened the front door and went upstairs. 'Oh! Hi!' She stopped in the doorway when she saw two legs in very dirty jeans sticking out of the airing cupboard.

'Out in a minute,' a voice called.

Celine dropped her bags and went to put on the kettle. As she was unpacking the groceries, her father arrived with the first load. 'Here you are – oh, hello there. Come to fix the immersion, have you?'

'That's right.'

Celine's eyes widened as the man crawled out of the cupboard and stood up. His hair was brown and wavy and a little too long for her liking but his eyes were like dark pools of sherry – like a faithful dog, she thought. And the legs were attached to a very attractive, athletic body clad in an old rugby shirt.

'It should be okay now. If you have any problems, tell Rose and I'll drop back.'

'Thanks.' Celine turned around to find her bag. She pulled out a ten Euro note and held it out to him.

'Oh, no, no, that's okay. Seeya.' And he was off down the stairs before Celine could stay another word.

Frank nodded in approval. 'That was nice of him.'

Celine made two ham and cheese sandwiches and a large pot of tea. While her father ate, she finished unpacking the shopping.

'Leave that,' he said between bites. 'You must be hungry too.'

'I am but I just want to tidy up a little. Rose said she'd come up for a drink.' Celine put a second bottle of wine and a six-pack of lager in the fridge. When the groceries were stashed, she put the rest of her purchases in a corner. 'That looks a bit better.' She sat down opposite her dad and bit into a sandwich.

Frank had moved on to the biscuits. 'I suppose it could look quite cosy here.' He looked around at the pale green walls. 'But that colour is too cold for this room.'

Celine nodded. 'I was thinking of yellow.'

'That would be nice but nothing's going to look much around that thing.'

Celine followed his gaze to the tweed-effect brown sofa. 'A few cushions might help,' she said doubtfully.

'Yoo-hoo, only me.'

'Come on up, Rose.' Celine went to the top of the stairs and watched Rose's painful ascent.

'Oh, dear, I think I need that drink now.' The woman stopped to catch her breath when she reached the top.

'Daddy, this is Rose. Rose, this is my father, Frank.'

Frank was on his feet in an instant. 'Lovely to meet you, Rose.'

'And you,' Rose gasped.

Celine pulled out a chair for her and she sank into it, laying her stick down beside her.

'Are you okay?' Frank asked, his face full of concern.

'I'm fine,' Rose assured him. 'And I'll be better when I get a drink inside me.'

Celine had already got the wine and was looking for glasses and a corkscrew. She could only find tumblers and the corkscrew had seen better days.

Rose pulled a face. 'I'm afraid Barry wasn't really into wine.'

'Was that the lad who used to live here?' Frank asked.

Rose nodded. 'I know Richard had intended to restock the place but I'm afraid there wasn't time.'

'Don't worry about it.' Celine handed them their glasses. 'Cheers.'

''Cheers. No, I'll tell Richard that you're going to need a few things. Oh, did he manage to fix the immersion?'

Celine nodded. 'There was a guy here when we came in but I don't think it was the landlord.'

Rose laughed. 'If he was a fine thing, with sexy eyes and wearing scruffy jeans, that was Richard.'

'Lord, and I offered him a tenner.'

Rose guffawed again.

'What?'

'Maybe I should have explained earlier – your landlord is Richard Lawrence.'

Frank stared. 'Richard Lawrence, the property developer?'

'The same,' Rose confirmed, her eyes twinkling.

'He didn't exactly look like a rich tycoon,' Frank consoled his daughter.

Celine frowned. 'No he didn't. He should have introduced himself, after all, I am his new tenant.'

'He should have,' Rose agreed, pulling herself together. 'Still, at least you've got hot water.' Her eyes roved speculatively round the room. 'You need a few things though, and that sofa has to be replaced. You can decide about the bed after you've slept in it.'

Celine flashed her father a delighted look. 'Do you think Richard would agree to replace them?'

Rose waved a hand. 'Oh, yes, he's no skinflint, thank God. '

Frank smiled happily. 'Sounds like you've landed on your feet, Celine.'

'It does, doesn't it?

Rose raised her glass. 'Welcome to Hopefield, Celine, I hope you'll be happy here.'

Chapter 7

Frank whistled softly as he got ready for dinner. He was feeling better tonight than he had in weeks and he was looking forward to an evening in the club. It would be their first dinner there since 'that night' but Alan was right. It was important for Brenda's sake to get back to normal. He hadn't told Celine that they were going out tonight and he'd felt a bit guilty about that, but what was the point? It wouldn't have made her feel any better.

He prayed that Kevin and Eileen weren't going to put in an appearance. Apart from Brenda's embarrassment, he wasn't sure he could be in the same room as Gilligan without slamming a fist into his pretty face. Frank grimaced at his reflection in the mirror as he pulled the knot out of his tie and started again. Why had Celine got involved with that man? Frank was still in shock that his little girl could do something so sordid. But then she hadn't been the same since Dermot died. Oh, she smiled and laughed, but the spark was gone. Celine had always been such a vibrant and confident girl but since Dermot died it was as if her life was on hold, almost as if she were just biding her time until . . . He shuddered. He didn't want to think about it. What mystified him was how she'd got together with Gilligan in the first place. When she wasn't working she was at home. If she was out it was with him or Marina. He checked his watch. Bloody hell, it was late. He ran down the stairs, grabbed his keys and jacket and left the house. It was only a ten-minute walk but he wanted to be there first to ensure that they got a quiet corner table. He would also order a bottle of that white Spanish wine Brenda liked. That might help her to relax.

He was sitting at the table sipping his pint when Alan walked in alone.

'It's okay, she's just in the ladies' room,' Alan assured him when he saw the crestfallen look on Frank's face.

'Oh, good, good.' Frank got to his feet. 'Pint?'

'Yes, please.' Alan glanced quickly around the room.

'He's not here,' Frank muttered.

Alan sat down. 'Thank God for that. How's Celine?'

'Gone. I helped her move today.'

Alan's eyes widened. 'What? Where?'

'To Hopefield. She thought it was for the best.'

'But what about her job?'

'She's got herself a new one.' Frank didn't see the need to tell Alan that Celine had been fired.

'Oh. Well, maybe it's for the best.'

'Maybe what's for the best?' Brenda asked. She kissed Frank's cheek and then slid into the seat between him and her husband.

'Celine's left Killmont.'

'Good.'

Alan grimaced. 'She's moved to Hopefield. Frank says she has a new job there.'

Brenda picked up the menu. 'I'm starving.'

Frank and Alan exchanged glances.

Frank pretended to study the menu, sneaking an occasional glance at Brenda. Though she seemed cool, he could see that her menu was shaking slightly and her eyes were flickering nervously around the room. 'I think I'll have a steak,' he announced.

'And I'll have the fish.' Brenda closed her menu with a snap and took a sip of wine.

'It's your favourite,' Frank told her.

She smiled at him, the first genuine smile of the evening. 'Thanks, Frank, it's lovely.'

He laughed. 'The least I can do for the lady who keeps me supplied with the best bread in Killmont.'

'The best in Dublin,' Alan corrected, and squeezed his wife's hand.

Brenda's lips tightened. 'I know what you're both up to and you're wasting your time.'

Frank looked at her, all innocence. 'Well, I wouldn't mind a ginger cake.'

Brenda scowled at him. 'I'm not an idiot, Frank.'

'No one said you were.' Alan's voice was soothing.

'I'm sorry, Brenda, let's order and enjoy our evening.'

'Thank you, Frank, I'd like that.'

Alan drained his pint and looked around for the waiter. 'Good idea.'

Chapter 8

Dominic was just getting out of the car when he heard a noise and a muttered expletive. He looked around and saw an attractive brunette crouching outside Rose's shop, gathering up groceries from around her. He hurried over to help. 'Afraid your eggs are broke.'

The girl looked up and smiled. 'Oh, well there goes my attempt at healthy eating.'

Dominic put two frozen chicken curries back into her bag. 'It's hard to eat sensibly when you live a busy life. I'm afraid this bag isn't going to last very long. Have you far to go?'

'Just upstairs.'

Dominic's eyes lit up. 'You're Rose's new manager!'

'Er, yes.'

'I'm your next-door neighbour. Dominic Nugent.'

'Celine Moore. I'd shake hands but . . .'

Dominic laughed. "Why don't you put your groceries away and then join me for a coffee?'

She looked less than enthusiastic. 'I'm not sure that I have the time.'

'You don't want to insult me, do you?'

She smiled. 'I couldn't do that to my new neighbour. See you in a minute.'

Dominic went back into the shop, whistling as he went. It would be nice to have a pretty woman about the place and she was certainly pretty. A curvy little figure, a lovely smile and serious wide-set eyes. He was just pouring water into two mugs when the bell on the door jangled. 'Come on through,' he called. Celine appeared in the doorway as he put the mugs on the table. 'It's just instant I'm afraid.'

'Lovely.' Celine sat down and helped herself to sugar and milk.

Dominic opened a packet of biscuits and carried them to the table. 'Well, welcome to Hopefield.' He toasted her with his mug. 'I wish you all the best in your new job.'

'Thanks.' Celine bit into a biscuit.

Dominic wasn't used to such reticent women. In his experience they seemed to see silence as a heinous crime. 'Where are you from?'

'The other side of the city. Have you owned this shop long?'

'Four years.' Dominic allowed her to divert him but his curiosity was piqued. 'I'm originally from Yorkshire. I was in the insurance business over there but I felt it was time to do something on my own.'

'So you swapped selling policies for selling newspapers.'

'And confectionery, stationery, magazines.' He ticked them off on his fingers. 'I assure you this is a professional operation.'

'So it was the right move?'

Dominic frowned. 'It was until that bookshop across the road opened last year.'

'Ah.'

'Indeed. But enough about me. Tell me about Celine Moore.' The girl had seemed quite relaxed but now she moved to the edge of the chair and was fidgeting with her mug.

'Not much to tell. I worked in a pharmacy up until a couple of weeks ago. Now I'm here. That's it.'

Dominic very much doubted it.

She stood up and held out her hand. "I should be going. Thanks for rescuing me and for the coffee.'

Dominic took her hand and grinned like an idiot. 'My pleasure. When do you start work?'

'Tomorrow,' Celine said as they walked to the door.

'If there's anything you need . . .'

'Thanks. Bye.'

'Goodbye.' Dominic watched her leave. Hopefield was going to be a more interesting place with Celine Moore in town.

Celine hurried back to her flat and shut the door with a grateful sigh. It was starting already. How long could she hope to keep her private life private with friendly people like Dominic and Rose around? Still, it made a pleasant change from the way she'd been treated recently in Killmont. Dominic was a darling and it would be nice to have him nearby once Rose went into hospital. She figured he must be in his mid-forties though he wore the clothes of an older man. But the eyes behind those glasses were young, intelligent and very friendly. Celine filled a bucket with warm water and fetched the mop she'd bought yesterday. She'd spent the morning hoovering and dusting and once she'd washed out the kitchen and bathroom floors the flat would be quite respectable. Then in a couple of weeks after she'd settled in she'd think about redecorating. She opened the window as far as it would go as the air in the flat was still stale. She'd taken down the curtains allowing sunshine to flood the room and the difference was amazing. The flat wasn't overlooked so she was in no hurry to replace them. The place looked so much more cheerful this way. If she could only get rid of the drab furniture . . .

A loud buzzing noise made her jump. There was a second buzz and she realised it was coming from the antiquated intercom on the wall by the door. She went over and pressed the button. 'Hello?'

'Hi!' A voice boomed from the box making her jump again. 'It's Richard Lawrence.'

'Oh, hi,' Celine said and then remembered that she had to press the button. 'Hi,' she said again.

'Can I come up?'

'Oh, yes, sure.'

Silence and then: 'You need to buzz me in.'

'Right, sorry.' Celine pressed a second button and moments later she heard his step on the stairs. She opened the door with a guarded smile. 'Hi.'

He grinned. 'Hi. Again.'

Celine blushed and turned away from him, moving in behind the safety of the kitchen bar. 'You should have introduced yourself yesterday. I thought you were the hired help.'

'Sorry. How are you settling in?' he asked, walking past the dreaded sofa and settling himself in an armchair.

'Fine.' Celine noticed he was still wearing a rugby shirt, but his jeans were clean today.

'Good. Rose said that there were a few things needed replacing.'

'If that's okay.'

'Yeah, sure, I'd been planning to do the place up. That's why I never advertised it after Barry left.'

Celine shifted uncomfortably. 'But Rose said the flat came with the job.'

Richard laughed. 'Yes, so I believe.'

'Is that a problem?'

'No, don't worry about it. Look, why don't you make a list?'

'Sorry?'

'Of the things you need?'

'Ah.'

'Except the furniture.'

'Oh.'

'That's already taken care of.'

'Oh!'

Richard laughed again. 'You don't say much, do you?'

Celine offered him a small smile. 'Sorry.'

'Hey, don't apologise. It makes a pleasant change.'

She looked at him in confusion. 'You'll understand when you meet some of the locals. And our Rose never shuts up.'

'I think she's very nice,' Celine protested.

He smiled and stood up. 'Me too. That furniture should arrive tomorrow. I'll drop by the shop sometime for that list. Bye.'

'Bye,' Celine replied and watched as he disappeared back down the stairs. God, I never even offered him a coffee, she thought. As she mopped the floor she wondered what was going on with Rose. It seemed very strange that she should offer the flat as part of the job without even consulting the landlord. If it became a problem, Celine realised, she could always offer to pay rent; money wasn't an issue as the bulk of Dermot's insurance money was still sitting in her bank account. And now that she'd cleaned the place up, she quite liked it here. Especially now that she was going to have new furniture. She paused in her work. Richard hadn't actually said *what* furniture was being delivered. She cast a mournful look at the tweed monstrosity, 'Please, oh, please!' she muttered.

With the floors clean, Celine decided to go for a walk. It was time she got to know her new neighbourhood. After she'd pulled on a clean sweater and brushed her hair, she grabbed her keys and bag and ran downstairs. It was almost noon and the day had warmed a little. Celine turned right past the window of the boutique, pausing briefly to admire Rose's display. Marina was right, the woman only dealt with quality clothes. Celine felt a frisson of excitement at the thought of those rich fabrics, the minute stitching and cuts that could make a size sixteen look like a twelve. It would be a pleasant change from advising on remedies for athlete's foot and indigestion. She wandered up the road past the closed shop fronts of a bookmaker and estate agent and paused briefly to study the offers in the travel agent's window. The last time she had been out of the country was her first year in college when she went to Majorca with three of the other students. She and Dermot had planned to travel. Not to the usual places but to more exotic locations. Though Celine had always joked she would not let him near a Third World country or he would probably never come home! She turned away and headed for the large roundabout that marked the end of the main street. The first turn off it was into an exclusive development of town houses and apartments. Celine noted the expensive cars through the gates and wondered how many of the residents dropped into Close Second. Next was a petrol station and she nipped into the shop to get a Coke. She was picking up a newspaper when she thought of Dominic and put it back on the shelf, resolving to drop into the newsagent's on the way back.

The woman behind the counter was watching her curiously. 'You're the new girl from Close Second, aren't you?'

Celine stared at her. 'That's right. How did you know?'

The woman chuckled. 'It's a small place, love. I'm Mary Boyle. This is my son's garage and I help out when I can. Are you settling in all right?'

'Yes, thanks.'

'Well, you let me know if you need any help. My Gerry is a fine big lad and very good with his hands. He'd be happy to help. He's single too,' she added.

'Thanks. Bye.' Celine grinned and went back outside before Mary Boyle produced her son for inspection. She crossed the road to check out the other side of Hopefield's main street. There was a hardware on the corner that was closed and beside it a large bookshop. Dominic's competition. She went inside, nodded at the man sitting behind the till and wandered around. She could see immediately why business was bad for Dominic. The shop was well laid out and as well as books, it stocked a good range of magazines, newspapers and writing materials. There was no food or drink for sale but, thought Celine, the garage took care of those needs and was open all hours.

'You're Rose's new manager, aren't you?' The man had moved around to stand in front of the counter and was studying her curiously. He was about the same age as her father but his hair was an unnatural reddish-brown, and he wore a garish tie with a wide-striped shirt. Celine took an instant dislike. 'That's right.'

'Welcome to Hopefield. If there's anything you need let me know. Tom Parker is the name.'

Celine reluctantly shook the sweaty hand he was holding out. 'Celine Moore. Thanks. See you around.'

He looked disappointed. 'Oh, okay then. Take care.'

Celine escaped back onto the street, went past the launderette and stepped into the café that was directly across the road from Close Second. She felt her mouth water at the display of cream cakes and pastries.

'Why don't you take a seat right over there?' a buxom, red-haired woman said, smiling at her. 'Thanks.' Celine went over to the small table by the window and sat down. She had only intended to have a coffee but as she studied the menu, she realised she was hungry.

'I can recommend the pasta special and the quiche is very good today.'

Celine nodded. 'The quiche, please, and a black coffee.'

'Sure.'

Celine looked around the large, airy room and admired the paintings on the wall. They all seemed to be by the one artist, and had little cards with prices in the corner. The one on the wall by the front door – a stormy seascape – would look wonderful on the wall of her new living room. She'd check out the price on her way out. It would be nice to add a personal touch to the flat.

'Here you go.' The woman was back with her food. 'You're our new neighbour, aren't you?' The woman nodded across at the flat.

Celine wasn't surprised at the enquiry this time. The woman had probably been watching her move in. 'That's right. Celine Moore.'

The woman stuck out her hand. 'Tracy Cunningham.'

'Is this your café?'

'That's right. Been running it for five years now with Bob – that's my husband. He does all the cooking, bless him.'

Celine sniffed appreciatively at the quiche. 'It smells great.'

Tracy beamed at her. 'Enjoy. Just shout if you need more coffee.'

Celine tucked into her food and was delighted to find that the quiche tasted good too.

'Hello again.'

She looked up to see Dominic standing over her. 'Oh, hi.'

'Settling in okay?'

Celine smiled. 'Getting there. Can I buy you a coffee?'

Dominic pulled out a chair and sat down. 'Why not?'

Tracy was already approaching and Celine asked

her for another coffee. 'Who's looking after the shop?' she asked when they were alone once more.

'Rose's lad. He often helps me out although I can't put much work his way these days.'

'I met your competition, Tom Parker.'

Dominic grunted. 'Oh, yes?'

'I didn't buy anything,' Celine added quickly. 'It is quite a nice shop though.'

'Yes.' Dominic nodded and then smiled his thanks as Tracy brought the coffee. 'I wish I could afford to do a bit of renovation. I put in new shelving when I moved in but the place needs better lighting and display material and the cold cabinets are ancient. Oh, I'm sorry, Celine. We only met this morning and I've done nothing but moan since we met. What must you think of me?'

'I think you're a nice guy who's going through a rough time. It happens to us all.'

He smiled gratefully. 'I'm going to like having you as a neighbour. If you need someone to show you around . . .'

'I've been up and down the main street already,' Celine laughed. 'I think I've seen it all.'

'Don't you believe it,' Dominic told her. 'There's a lot more to Hopefield than is first apparent.'

'Well, there's certainly one hell of a grapevine.' Celine grimaced. 'Everyone seems to know who I am.'

'You *do* live opposite the only café in town,' Dominic pointed out, a twinkle in his eye.

Celine laughed. 'You have a point.'

'So tell me, what do you do for fun? We have a very good sports club – it's at the back of the apartment complex out on the roundabout. They have eight all-weather tennis courts, a great pool, a gym and a couple of squash courts.'

'I'm not really into sport,' Celine lied. The last thing she was going to do was join another sports club. Look where that had got her in Killmont.

'Oh. There's a cinema complex on the outskirts of town.'

'Near the shopping centre?'

'That's the one.'

She nodded. 'I must take Marina there. She's my friend and she's movie-mad.'

'There's also an amateur musical society,' he offered. 'We're putting on "My Fair Lady" this year.'

'We?'

Dominic puffed out his chest. 'I'm the male lead.'

'Henry Higgins? I'm impressed!'

'We could do with some new members, young female members in particular,' he added. 'We have lots of members over fifty – Eliza Doolittle is forty-eight.'

Celine's lips twitched. 'Oh, dear.'

'So if you're interested . . .'

'Me? Oh, God, no! Not my thing at all, I'm afraid. I don't have a note in my head.'

Dominic sighed. 'Shame.'

'I could help out backstage if you like,' Celine offered, feeling sorry for him.

His face broke into a happy smile. 'That would be wonderful. I'll tell Cathy Donlan – she's our producer.'

'Great.' Celine sipped her coffee, already regretting her offer. She was barely in the town twenty-four hours and already she felt more involved with the community than she had been in all her time in Killmont.

'We have a neighbourhood watch scheme too if you're interested in getting involved . . .'

'Er, no, I don't think so.'

Dominic shrugged and smiled. 'I'm sorry, I shouldn't be rushing you into these things, you've hardly moved in.'

Celine glanced nervously at her watch. 'I should be going, I still have so much to do.'

'Of course.' Dominic raised his hand to attract Tracy's attention and patted his pockets in search of his wallet.

'No, I'll get this.' Celine opened her purse and handed Tracy twenty Euro. She put on her jacket and followed Tracy to the counter for her change. 'That was lovely, thanks.'

'Anytime. And if you need anything . . .'

'Thanks,' she said and hurried outside.

Afterwards, when she was back in the sanctuary of her little flat, she realised that in her haste she'd forgotten to check the price on the painting by the door. Oh, well, she could always do it tomorrow.

Chapter 9

'Do you want me to restock the fridges, Dominic?'

Dominic looked up from the stack of bills in front of him. 'Yeah, great. Thanks, Fergus.'

Fergus checked the fridge and then went to the storeroom out the back and loaded a trolley with soft drinks and water. He had just finished and put the trolley away when Dominic came into the shop with a mug of coffee.

'So what do you think of your mum's new manager?'

'Haven't met her yet, but Ma seems happy.'

'Yes, she's a nice girl, good-looking too.'

Fergus grinned. 'Interested, are you?'

Dominic stirred his coffee, a dreamy smile on his face. 'She's a bit young for me but I like her. She's different, very quiet, deep, a bit of a mystery woman. I'd say there's a lot more to Celine Moore than she lets on.'

Fergus frowned. 'She'd better not let Ma down.'

Dominic shook his head. 'I'm sure there's no chance of that. She seems a very good person.

Anyway, you and I will be here to keep an eye on things, Fergus.'

Fergus sighed. 'True. I just don't want anything to worry Ma when she's going in for this operation. She doesn't let on but she's in an awful lot of pain.'

Dominic had also noticed the shadows under Rose's eyes and the slight stoop she'd developed. 'It's a very successful operation, Fergus, don't worry. This time next year she'll be off skiing!'

Fergus chuckled. 'I don't know about that but it would be great if she could go back to her ballroom dancing again, she misses it a lot.'

'Misses all those men fighting over her, you mean.' Dominic drained his cup and stood up. 'Right, I'm off to see my beloved accountant. Can you hold the fort until two?'

'Sure. Will you need me later this afternoon?'

'Er, no, sorry. But if you could open up for me the rest of this week—'

'No problem,' Fergus said immediately.

'Thanks. See you later.'

'Good luck.'

'I'll need it,' Dominic muttered as he picked up his briefcase and headed for the door.

When he'd left, Fergus tidied some of the shelves, brushed out the floor and restocked the cigarettes. In the last hour he'd served three customers and taken the grand sum of six Euro, forty cent. Dominic wouldn't stay in business long if things carried on like this. It looked like he'd have to find another job. The shelter didn't pay enough and though he'd never admit it to his mother, he'd had enough of looking after broken men who were bent on killing themselves with drink or drugs. What he could do instead, he wasn't sure. He'd dropped out of school at sixteen and had only ever worked in this shop and at the shelter. With his background he was probably unemployable. His mother had hinted that he should go back to school but at twenty-four, Fergus couldn't face that. It was a pity his mother didn't own a hardware then she wouldn't need to hire a manager and he wouldn't have to find a job.

Celine Moore. He frowned. That name seemed vaguely familiar but why he wasn't sure. Well, he'd be meeting her as soon as Dominic got back. His mother had insisted that he drop by, not that he had anything else to do. Even sitting in front of the TV and playing games on his PlayStation got boring after a while. And after running into Mick last week, he was going to stay out of town for a while. It would break his Ma's heart but sometimes he thought it would be better if he left Dublin for good. But he'd wait until she was back on her feet and he was sure she could look after herself. She'd stood by him through some very tough times and now it was his turn to look after her. He'd ask down at the shelter about working extra hours. His mother said that Richard Lawrence could probably put some work his way but Fergus didn't like to ask. Richard had done them enough favours over the years.

Fergus's thoughts were interrupted as a large truck pulled up outside. He went to the front door and nodded to the young lad who jumped down on to the pavement.

'Delivery for 12A, Ms Moore?'

'Oh, right, you'll find her in the shop next door.'

'Cheers.' The delivery man went into Close Second and moments later reappeared accompanied by a slim dark-haired girl.

Fergus stepped back into the doorway, his heart hammering in his chest. It had been nearly six years since he'd last seen her but it was definitely her.

Celine watched delightedly as the two deliverymen dragged the dreaded brown suite downstairs. 'Thanks, bye,' she called and then whirled round to pull the plastic from the new suite. She gave a small yelp as she realised it was leather. She flopped down on the sofa and groaned in ecstasy as she sank into the luxuriant cushions. She hopped up again and began to rearrange the furniture, turning the sofa so that it faced the large window and the panoramic views of rooftops with the Dublin Mountains in the background. Nice one, Richard, she thought as she examined the soft, black leather. This had certainly not been cheap but it was a good buy for a flat as it would be hard-wearing and easy to keep clean. As she gathered up the plastic that it had been wrapped in, she noticed another box just inside the door. On inspection, she discovered it was a small microwave.

'Oh, great.' She wasn't the best cook in the world and the oven was old and temperamental. This would make life a lot easier.

There was no doubt she'd landed on her feet with both her employer and her landlord. She'd really enjoyed her morning in the shop and had been very impressed with Rose's stock and monthly turnover. Sadie was the only possible fly in the ointment. Like so many women she'd come across in Killmont, the woman was a gossip and a nosey parker.

'She's harmless,' Rose had said when the older woman had gone for lunch. 'I just switch off and let her talk.'

Celine doubted that but at least they wouldn't have to work together that often. Sadie worked Mondays – which would be Celine's day off – and part-time whenever Celine needed a break. She was there on Saturdays too but from what Rose said, Saturdays were so busy there wouldn't be much time for socialising. Regardless of Rose's assurances, though, Celine was determined to keep Sadie at arm's length.

She closed her eyes, inhaled the wonderful smell of new leather and went back downstairs to the shop.

'Well?' Rose looked at her expectantly.

'My new suite has arrived,' Celine told her. 'Black leather.'

Rose's eyes widened. 'My, Richard's really pushing the boat out.'

'And he bought me a microwave too.'

'Excellent. Have you got your list ready for him? He sometimes drops in around lunchtime.'

Celine took a piece of paper out of her bag under the counter. 'I'm not too sure what to put on it.'

'Give it here.' Rose put her glasses on and looked at the tiny list Celine had put together. 'For goodness sake, love, you need a lot more than this!'

'Well yes, but I thought I should buy them.'

Rose rolled her eyes. 'If you plan to take them with you when you move on, fair enough, but otherwise, Richard should pay for them. He will be more than grateful if you kit the place out properly, believe me.' She looked back at the list. 'You know, I think it would be better if we took care of this ourselves.'

'We?'

Rose looked up and smiled. 'Yes, why not? It's supposed to be my day off and you can't trust a man to go out and buy household goods.'

'He did okay with the suite,' Celine murmured.

'That was luck. Come on, let's go. There are some great shops in the centre outside the village and an Atlantic Homecare further out the road. Between them, we should be able to get everything you need. Sadie?' she called into the backroom. 'Are you finished your lunch yet? Celine and I are going out.'

The little woman came into the shop and eyed them curiously. 'Oh, yes, anywhere nice?'

'Just a bit of shopping.' Rose grabbed her coat and keys and steered Celine towards the door. 'If Richard's looking for us, tell him I'll call him later.'

*

Within a couple of hours, Celine had been through three shops and was now weighed down with bags. For a woman with a dodgy hip, Rose could shop. 'That's plenty,' she said as she saw Rose pause to look speculatively at another shop in the distance.

'Just one more.' Rose led the way down to the opposite end of the shopping centre.

Despite her tiredness, Celine's eyes lit up when she saw the cane and wicker shop that her boss had paused outside.

'They have wonderful linen baskets here.'

Celine needed no further encouragement. Leaving Rose sitting in a comfortable rocking chair surrounded by bags, she wandered around the shop. An hour later, they left having purchased said linen basket, a coffee table, a bedside table and a breadbasket. These would be delivered the following day.

'I can't possibly ask Richard to buy all of this stuff.'

'He can afford it.'

'That's not the point. He only wanted to kit the place out with necessities, not luxuries.'

Rose was in pain now and though she'd only known Celine a couple of days she knew there was no point in arguing with the girl. 'Fine. Let's go home.'

Celine shot her a worried look. 'Are you okay?'

'I'll be fine once I get my shoes off and have a coffee.'

When they pulled up outside the shop, Rose put

her head into Dominic's to ask her son to help Celine take her purchases upstairs.

'Sorry, Rose, he's gone. But if you keep an eye on the shop for a minute, I'll help Celine.'

Rose leaned heavily against the counter. 'Thanks, Dominic, I'd appreciate that.'

Fergus sat in the window of the café and watched Celine Moore and Dominic unload his mother's car. Dominic said something and Celine laughed. Fergus had never heard her laugh. In fact he'd never seen her smile. Over the years, the image that had stayed with him was of a young, pale-faced girl, dressed all in black, with tears coursing silently down her cheeks. He'd never even heard her speak.

Chapter 10

Marina put on her lipstick, pressed her lips with some tissue paper and then added a layer of gloss. 'Josh, are you ready yet?' She pulled on a calf-length suede skirt and black top. After she'd slid on her knee-high black leather boots, she went to her jewellery box and selected some strings of coloured beads to wrap around her long throat and a heavy bronze slave bangle for her wrist. 'Josh?' she called again and began to pick her way through the trail of toys that led to his bedroom. Her son was sitting playing with his train set and there was an ominous dark stain on the Tommy Hilfiger jeans that she'd dressed him in less than an hour ago. 'Have you had a little accident, honey?' She crouched down beside him and fondled his blond head.

Josh didn't bother to reply.

'Come along, darling. Mummy will get you some clean clothes. And remember, when you want to do a tinkle, you must do it in the toilet.'

'Don't want to!'

'Joshie, be a good boy.'

'No!'

'But we have to hurry. We're going to visit Granny.'

'Don't want to. Granny doesn't like me.'

Marina hugged his wriggling body to her chest. 'Oh, silly, of course she does! Granny loves you.'

'Does not.'

Marina sighed. 'Come on, darling. Let's get you out of those wet jeans and if you're a good boy you can have a chocolate biscuit.'

'Two biscuits,' Josh demanded with a belligerent look in his eye.

'Two it is.' Marina beamed at him and led him to the bathroom.

It was thirty minutes before Marina piled Josh into the car and drove the short distance to her mother's house.

Kay led the little boy into the living-room as Marina went back to the car to fetch the bags. Josh would only be here a few hours but Marina always brought enough gear to last the week. There were the medicines – just in case. A complete change of clothes – that Kay usually had to dip into. And enough toys to keep triplets happy.

'Now Mum, no television,' Marina told her mother before she left, 'and make sure Joshie has a little nap.'

Kay nodded as she always did, and manoeuvred her daughter towards the door. 'He'll be fine, Marina, don't worry.'

When Kay came back into the room, Josh had all

her ornaments on the floor and had knocked over a plant. 'Okay, Josh.' She smiled through gritted teeth. 'Why don't I fetch the chocolate biscuits and we can watch Barney.'

Immediately Josh clambered up onto the sofa and beamed at her. 'Yippee.'

Marina's back ached as she held the pose for that 'one more take'.

'That's a wrap, thanks, Marina, you were great.'

Marina kissed the photographer on both cheeks. 'My pleasure, Gerry.' Not bothering to remove the heavy makeup, she went out to the car and headed in the direction of Hopefield. She was an hour late but Celine had said that her boss was relaxed about what time she took her lunch break. And after a much-needed cup of coffee, Marina was looking forward to a rummage through those wonderful clothes.

When Marina walked into the shop she stopped in her tracks and stared at her friend. For the first time in years, Celine was wearing a skirt. The skirt of a very beautiful, well-tailored, toffee-coloured suit, with a thin black vest underneath. And she was wearing makeup. Not much, granted, just some subtle colour around the eyes and a touch of lipstick. But as Marina watched, she realised there was something else. Celine was holding a dress up against a customer, a frown of deep concentration on her face and a light in her eyes that Marina hadn't seen in a very long time.

'Hello there. Can I help you?'

Marina turned to smile at the owner. 'Hi. I'm a friend of Celine. I just came in to wish her luck.'

Rose smiled. 'Well, as you can see, she doesn't need it. I'm Rose Lynch.'

'Marina Flynn.'

'The model?'

Marina beamed at her. 'That's right, and one of your regular customers.'

Rose chuckled. 'I know that, but not everyone likes me to comment on it.'

'Oh, the snobs? Well, ask Celine, I brag about the amount of stuff in my wardrobe that's second hand. Especially evening wear.'

Rose was all business immediately. 'A beautiful cerise cocktail dress came in yesterday – Dior – it would look lovely with your colouring. Would you like to try it on?'

Marina shot a look at Celine. 'It looks like I'm going to have to wait anyway. Why not?'

Celine finally spotted Marina as Rose led her to the changing room. 'Oh, Marina—'

'Don't worry about me, darling, I'm in good hands.'

'Isn't this the most beautiful dress?' Marina and Celine were sitting in Café Napoli and Marina was taking another peek into her shopping bag.

Celine pulled a face. 'I hope you're not going to buy something every time you come to see me or you'll be penniless.'

Marina smiled. 'Ah, but Rose and I have a deal.'

'You do?'

'Yeah. If I only wear it once and bring it back laundered and pressed she'll give me sixty per cent of what I paid for it.'

'Is that good?'

'It's great. In the shop across town they only give me forty-five.'

Celine laughed. 'Where's Josh?'

'With Mum, but I can't stay long.' She checked her watch. 'He has a swimming class at four. Now tell me everything. Are you happy with your new job?'

'Yes, I think it's going to work out very well.' Celine told Marina all about Rose and Dominic and some of the other residents of Hopefield. 'It's a little bit cosier than I would like but I suppose that's the problem with small neighbourhoods.'

'Have you told Rose about Kevin?'

Celine looked nervously around to see if Tracy was within earshot. 'Of course not! She doesn't need to know about him.'

Marina shrugged. 'It's not such a big deal.'

Celine grimaced. 'Tell that to the person who was sending me hate mail.'

Marina stared at her over her coffee mug. 'Celine, why didn't you tell me?'

Celine shrugged. 'It's in the past. Now I'm going to concentrate on making a go of this job and no one in Hopefield is going to know anything about me.'

Marina smirked. 'I wish you luck. This is Dublin, remember. Now, are there any nice men around?'

Celine laughed. 'Well, the guy who owns the filling station down at the roundabout, his mother's trying to fix him up but I haven't seen him yet.'

Marina nodded speculatively. 'There's money in oil.'

'Then there's Dominic Nugent, he owns the newsagent's next door.'

'Oh?'

'Not your type,' Celine assured her. 'Baggy cords and cardigans.'

Marina wrinkled her nose.

'And then there's my landlord. Now he just might be your type.'

Marina brightened. 'Describe him.'

'Well he doesn't dress very well but he's good-looking and loaded.'

'A low-key millionaire, sounds good. What does he do?'

Celine grinned. 'He's a property developer, name of Richard Lawrence. Maybe you've heard of him.'

Marina nearly choked on her coffee. 'The gorgeous Richard Lawrence is your landlord?

'Yep, and a very generous one too.'

Marina looked reluctantly at her watch. 'I wish I could stay and hear all about him but I'm going to be terribly late.'

'Come up and see my flat first.'

'Sorry, that will have to wait till the next time.'

'Oh, okay then.' Celine stood up and went over to the counter to pay. As she stood waiting for her change, she realised that all the paintings were gone. 'Oh!'

'Something wrong?' Tracy asked.

'The paintings, they're gone. Surely you haven't sold them all?'

Tracy laughed. 'No such luck. No, the artist decided he didn't want to sell them after all.'

'What a pity.'

'Celine?'

'Okay, Marina, I'm coming. Thanks, Tracy, bye.'

'Nice lunch?' Rose asked as Celine came back into the shop.

'Yes, thanks.'

'I'll leave you to it for a little while.' Rose suppressed a yawn. 'I could do with putting my feet up.'

'Go ahead, I'll be fine.'

'Just shout if you need me,' Rose told her and went through to the back.

Celine looked around the empty shop and wondered what to do. The shelves were a little untidy so she took down the clothes and started to refold them. She fingered a cashmere cardigan with reverence. The material was a rich shade of royal blue, a colour that had always looked beautiful on her mother. She smiled. Whenever she had designed something or chosen material, her mother had often come to mind. Like Celine, she had loved clothes and had been fairly nifty with a needle. Maybe if she'd been alive when Dermot had died Celine wouldn't have given up her career.

Ann Moore's death at just fifty-three had been a devastating blow to both Frank and Celine. The brain tumour was found after Ann had complained for months of blinding headaches. It had been all downhill from there on.

Celine gave herself a mental shake and turned to re-hang some of the dresses on the rail. She noticed some marks on a black trouser suit and went in search of a clothes brush. After she'd cleaned the suit to her satisfaction she went through all the rails, brush in hand. She was just finishing when two young girls came into the shop. She donned a welcoming smile. 'Hi. If you need anything just ask,' she said and moved quickly back behind the counter. She always hated pushy shop assistants who hung over your shoulder. Thankfully, Rose felt the same way. Her tactics paid off and after trying on several outfits, both girls bought something. Eyes shining, Celine went through to the back to report her success to her boss. Rose was in the armchair with her feet up and eyes closed. Celine backed out immediately.

'Come in, come in, I was just resting my eyes. Is everything okay?'

Celine nodded. 'It certainly is. I just sold the red velvet skirt and the black Rocha dress.'

Rose did a quick calculation. 'One hundred and
forty-five Euro.'

Celine nodded. 'You're good!'

'So are you,' Rose retorted. 'That skirt has been on
the rack for months.'

'I suggested to the girl that she put a fringe or lace
trim on the bottom. She was a student,' she added by
way of explanation.

Rose eyed her speculatively. 'I can see your talents
are going to come in very handy. There are a lot of my
customers who would love advice like that.'

Celine shrugged. 'I'll be happy to help if I can.'

Rose smiled as the bell on the shop door jangled.
'Why don't I go? You put on the kettle. And there's
some shortbread in the cupboard.'

Celine did as she was bid and as she fetched the
biscuits she thought it was just as well she and
Rose would only be working together for a few
weeks or she'd be as big as a house! Rose was
back moments later, a scowl on her face. 'Time-
wasters,' she grumbled. 'I wouldn't mind but they're
always the ones who pull the clothes around and I
can tell from the moment I set eyes on them that
they've no intention of putting their hands in their
pockets!'

'Tea or coffee?' Celine asked.

'Tea, please.' Rose sank back down into the
armchair.

'It's sad though,' Celine remarked as she made the
brew. 'Having nothing better to do but wander

around the shops. They probably can't afford to buy anything.'

'Rubbish. Even a down-and-out could afford something from my bargain basket!'

Celine smiled. 'True. I was wondering . . .'

'Yes?'

'Would it be all right if I bought a couple of things?'

'But of course, and you get the staff twenty-per-cent discount.'

'Oh, there's no need for that.'

'Not at all, there have to be some perks in all jobs.'

Celine giggled. 'I used to get ten per cent off all indigestion remedies at the pharmacy.'

Rose sighed. 'I don't think I can possibly compete with that!' She looked at the wall clock. 'It's nearly five-thirty, let's lock up for the day.'

'Okay.' Celine went through to the shop, turned the sign on the door around and was just turning the key when someone tried the handle. 'We're closed,' she called. There was a knock on the door and she opened it a fraction. 'I'm sorry but we're—'

'Hi, Celine.'

'Fergus?' she gasped, the colour draining from her face.

He grinned nervously. 'Yeah, that's right.'

'But I don't understand. What are you doing here?'

'I've come to collect me ma.'

'Rose?' Celine clutched the door for support.

Rose appeared behind her. 'Oh, hello, love, you're early. Celine, this is my son, Fergus.'

Fergus shot Celine an anxious look. 'Yeah, Ma, we've met.'

Chapter 11

Rose sat in her shop in total darkness, her face wet with tears. She hadn't got much sense out of Fergus but it hadn't taken her long to piece things together. By then, Celine had fled upstairs to her flat and Fergus was pacing the shop, punching his fist into his hand.

'She was Dermot's wife?' she had repeated.

'Yeah, Ma, I told you. I didn't realise until I saw her. Dermot's surname was McKenna. God, did you see the way she looked at me?'

Rose had patted his arm. 'It was just the shock, that's all.'

Fergus shook his head. 'No, she blames me, I know she does.'

'Don't be silly, love.'

He had whirled around, his face almost grey, his eyes haunted. 'Trust me, Ma, she blames me.'

And then he'd left. Rose had followed him out on to the street and called after him but he'd kept walking. She'd tried his mobile several times since but it was switched off. Rose was torn between concern for her son and pity for the girl upstairs who was probably crying her heart out. She decided to go and check on her but when she went out and buzzed the intercom, there was no reply. After a few minutes, Rose gave up. Maybe she'd go by the shelter. It was after seven and Fergus's shift would begin in half an hour. She was just locking up when Richard drove up and beeped the horn. She gave him a small wave and turned quickly away.

'Rose, what's wrong?'

He was already at the door, and Rose felt a wave of affection at the concern in his face. Rose had liked him from the first moment she'd met him and it wasn't long before they'd settled into a comfortable friendship. She'd found herself telling him things that she'd never confided in another living soul and he, in turn, had cried in her arms, the day his beloved uncle died. But it was different this time. This wasn't her secret to tell. 'It's nothing, Richard, I'm fine.'

'Like hell you are. Now we can stay out here and argue the point or you can invite me in.'

'Sorry, Richard, I don't have time. Fergus is expecting me home,' she lied.

'That's strange, I just saw him go into the pub.'

Rose whirled around. 'Which pub?'

'Donnelly's. What is it, Rose. Is it Fergus? Is he okay?'

Rose realised that he wasn't going to give up without some kind of answer. 'Come in and I'll make some tea.'

Richard followed her inside and waited in silence while she boiled a kettle.

'I'm okay now, Richard,' she said when they were sipping their tea. She gave him a shaky smile. 'Fergus and I had a quarrel and I was a bit upset.'

Richard watched her steadily. 'How long have we known each other, Rose?'

Rose could have told him the date, time and place. 'Five years,' she said.

'And would you say we're friends?'

'Of course, Richard, what a question!'

'So tell me what's wrong.'

Rose rubbed her eyes, suddenly feeling all of her sixty years and decided to confide in Richard yet again. 'Before we moved here, Fergus was involved in . . . an incident.'

Richard frowned. 'To do with drugs?'

Rose shook her head. 'No, it was after all of that. You know the shelter where Fergus works?'

'Of course.'

'It was his social worker that got him that job. A man called Dermot McKenna. He stuck with Fergus when he was at his worst, got him a place in a rehab clinic and then, when Fergus was well again, found him the job at the shelter. I was against it at first but Dermot persuaded me that it was important for Fergus to confront his demons. He was right, of course. Fergus has gone from strength to strength since.'

Richard frowned. 'Sounds like a nice guy but what has that got to do with your quarrel tonight?'

Rose sighed. 'There was no quarrel, Richard, just a ghost from the past. Dermot used to drop into the shelter occasionally to check in with Fergus. One night when he arrived, Fergus had just thrown out a drunk who had started trouble and was spoiling for a fight.' She swallowed hard, her hand tightening around her mug. 'They had a cuppa, watched a bit of football on the box and then Fergus walked out to the car with Dermot. The drunk was waiting. He took a swing at Fergus but Dermot stepped in and the two of them went down. When Fergus pulled them apart, there was a knife sticking out of Dermot's chest.'

'Jesus.'

Rose continued, her voice flat, 'He died on the way to hospital.'

'Poor Fergus, he's gone through an awful lot for such a young lad.'

Rose nodded. 'Too much. I often wonder if things would have been different if his father had been around. I don't think I was a very good parent. I couldn't have been or he'd never have turned to drugs.'

'That's rubbish, Rose, and you know it,' Richard retorted. 'These things happen. I can understand why you said nothing before. It's better to forget it, put it behind you and get on with life.'

'And we did. Until today.'

'What happened today?'

'Today, Fergus came face to face with Dermot McKenna's wife. It's Celine, Richard. My new manager, your new lodger. Celine Moore was married to Dermot.'

'I don't understand.'

'I'd never met her, you see – I didn't even know her name. Fergus just knew her as Celine – he didn't know her maiden name. The only time they met was at the funeral. Until today.'

Richard absorbed this in silence for a moment. 'It must have been a shock for her.'

'She never said a word, just ran upstairs. I was trying to get in to talk to her when you drove up but she won't answer.'

'I have a key if you want to—'

Rose shook her head. 'No, I'm sure I'm the last person she wants to see.' She stood up slowly, wincing as pain shot from her hip down into her foot. 'I'd better go and get Fergus before he drinks himself into a stupor.'

'Do you want me to come along?'

'No, thanks. And Richard? Please don't mention this to anyone.'

Richard drew her into his arms and planted a kiss on her hair. 'I won't tell a soul. Keep in touch, Rose. If you need anything, anything at all, just call.'

'Thanks, Richard, you're a good friend.'

Celine sat on her new leather sofa, her knees drawn up under her chin, her arms tight around them. She didn't know how long she'd been sitting like this but it was now dark with the only light coming from the streetlights outside. The phone rang, making her jump. She stared at it. It still sat on the windowsill, had done since she'd moved in as it was disconnected. Obviously not any more. She tried ignoring it but it just went on and on. Probably the operator. She dragged herself out of the chair and went to answer it. 'Hello?'

'Celine?'

'Yes?'

'It's Richard. Glad to see you've been connected.'

'Oh, yeah, thanks, that's great.'

'I'm just down the road, would it be okay if I dropped in?'

Celine froze.

'Celine?'

'It's not really a good time.'

'I won't keep you. It's about the rent. There's a slight problem.'

Celine closed her eyes. 'Okay then.'

'Great! I'll be with you in five minutes.'

Celine hung up and went into the bathroom to wash her face. In the mirror she saw a woman closer to forty than thirty. She washed the mascara off her face, ran a brush through her hair and swapped her crumpled shirt for a black T-shirt. She went back into the living room and switched on a lamp. As she picked up her jacket and bag from the floor, the intercom buzzed. 'Come on up.' She pressed the button and opened the door.

'Hi.' She shifted nervously from one foot to the other.

Richard walked into the room and closed the door. 'Hi.'

'So, the rent—'

'I lied.' He shrugged. 'Sorry, but I didn't think you'd let me in if I didn't make it sound official.'

Celine shook her head. 'Sorry, you've lost me.'

'I was talking to Rose, she told me what happened. I just wanted to make sure that you were okay.'

Celine forced a tight smile. 'So you've seen me and I'm okay.' She walked towards the door but Richard stepped in front of her.

'I'm not sure I'd agree with that.'

'I appreciate the concern but this really has nothing to do with you.'

Richard looked into her eyes. 'I know, but you should talk to someone. Sitting up here on your own isn't going to help. You've got to face Rose sometime. And Fergus.'

Celine turned away from him. 'I don't have to do anything.'

Richard walked over to the sofa and sat down. 'So you're going to run away.'

Celine whirled around to glare at him. 'You don't know what you're talking about.' She looked at him stretched out on the sofa, his hands linked behind his head. Though he was still clad in jeans she could imagine him sitting at the top of a boardroom table. He had presence and oozed confidence. And his calm, measured tone was soothing.

'You're right,' he was saying now. 'So why don't

you come and sit on this very comfortable sofa and tell me.'

Celine saw the kindness in his eyes and couldn't help returning his smile. She crossed the room and sat down. 'I don't really know where to start.'

'Why don't you tell me about your husband.'

Celine smiled slightly. 'Dermot. His name was Dermot. We met at a dance in a rugby club. His friend fancied Marina – my friend – and we were the gooseberries. It's strange, Marina only saw his friend a couple of times.' Celine chuckled. 'He was Dermot's best man and Marina was my bridesmaid.'

'When did you get married?'

'1995. We'd only been seeing each other for a few months, everyone thought we were mad but –' she shrugged – 'we knew it was right. We were so broke! It took ages for us to save a deposit for our house. I was still at college, you see.'

Richard nodded. 'Studying what?'

'Art and Design. I wanted to go into the fashion business.'

'Ah, no wonder Rose loves you.'

A shadow crossed Celine's face at the mention of her boss.

'Didn't you? Go into the fashion business, that is?'

Celine shook her head.

'Sorry, you were telling me about Dermot.'

Celine took a deep breath and gazed out of the window. 'He wanted to change the world. He did for some people. He cared so much. I felt guilty that I wasn't bringing any money in but he said that when I left college we'd be rolling in it.' She laughed. 'He was convinced I was going to become Ireland's top fashion designer.'

'Were you?'

Celine's smile was sad. 'I'd have had a damn good try! After he died it didn't matter though. Success would have been meaningless without him to share it with.'

Richard nodded. 'I can understand that.'

'Dermot talked about his work a lot,' she continued. 'He loved to talk about his success stories. Fergus was one. He was only sixteen when they met. Dermot trailed around Dublin looking for him each night. He brought him food, cigarettes, and eventually Fergus opened up to him. When he finally agreed to get help, Dermot was on such a high. He moved heaven and earth to get him into a rehab centre and then when Fergus got out, he found him a job.'

Richard nodded. 'In the homeless shelter.'

Celine nodded. 'Dermot didn't talk as much about him after that. He'd moved on to another lost soul. He still dropped into the centre from time to time to check on Fergus.' She stopped and stared into space.

'I think I know the rest.' Richard took her hand and held it as tears coursed down her cheeks. They sat like that for some time before Celine excused herself and went into the bedroom. When she returned Richard had opened a bottle of wine. 'I thought you could do with a drink. You can drink it alone if you'd prefer.'

Celine shook her head. 'I'd like you to stay.'

Richard smiled and looked around. 'I like what you've done with the place.'

'The new suite makes all the difference. I was going to paint the whole place a nice golden colour.'

'And you've changed your mind?'

'I won't be here.' Celine took a sip of wine.

'There's no reason for you to go.'

'It would be too awkward.'

'Maybe at first, but Rose is a good woman. I'm sure that she thanks God every day that Dermot came in to Fergus's life.'

Celine's smile was bitter. 'And I wish they'd never met. Rose is great but I'm just not sure I could cope with seeing *him* on a regular basis. It would make me physically sick.'

Richard sipped his drink in silence for a moment. 'Rose will probably have to shut the shop so,' he said finally.

Celine rolled her eyes. 'She can easily find someone else.'

'She'd been looking for months before she found you. There isn't time to find anyone else now.'

Celine put down her drink. 'That's not my problem.'

Richard took both her hands in his. 'I hardly know you, Celine, but I don't believe you're the kind of person to let someone down.'

Celine looked up into his eyes. He was sitting so close she could smell his aftershave. He wasn't as tall as Kevin but he was broader and she thought how nice it would be to be folded in those strong arms. How safe it must feel.

He pushed her hair back off her face and Celine closed her eyes. 'I know this is hard for you,' he murmured, 'but maybe it's an opportunity to put the past behind you.'

Celine's eyes flew open. 'Just like that!'

Richard held her gaze. 'I'm not saying it's easy but I'm sure you're up to the challenge. From what you've told me, Celine, I'd say you've only been living half a life since Dermot died.'

Celine pulled away from him. 'So on the basis of one short conversation not only do you know me, you know what's best for me too!'

Richard smiled. 'Good, aren't I?'

Celine couldn't help smiling. 'You're an interfering do-gooder, that's what you are.'

'I happen to know that you like do-gooders,' he said softly.

Celine turned away. 'I think you should go now.'

'Sure.' He stood up and walked to the door.

'Richard?'

'Yes?' He turned to look at her.

'Do you ever wear anything other than jeans?'

He grinned. 'Only when I have to.'

Chapter 12

Fergus was sitting at the bar when Rose arrived. She nodded at the barman and sat down beside her son. 'Are you okay?'

'Sure.'

'I told Richard what happened, I hope you don't mind.'

Fergus shrugged.

'I don't know what to do, Fergus. How are you going to cope with seeing Celine all of the time?'

'It's not an issue, Ma. Now that she knows I'm your son, you won't see her for dust. She thinks that I'm to blame for Dermot's death. She's right too.'

'Don't talk rubbish,' Rose snapped. 'You didn't stab him.'

'No, but that knife was meant for me.'

'Look, love, it happened and there's nothing you can do about it.'

Fergus drained his pint and nodded to the barman for another. 'You're right there, Ma. There's not a damn thing I can do.'

'Not about Dermot,' Rose said slowly, 'but we can help Celine.'

'I don't follow you.'

'She was training as a fashion designer when Dermot died,' she explained. 'A good one too, from what I gather. This is the first time she's worked with clothes since.'

'So?'

'So maybe we can help her get her life back.'

'No offence, Ma, but you're running a second-hand clothes shop, not a fashion empire.'

Rose scowled and gave him a sharp dig in the ribs. 'I know a lot of important people, I'll have you know. Don't underestimate your mother.'

'Whatever you say, Ma.' He turned to look at her, his eyes sad. 'If there's anything I can do to help, just tell me.'

'For the moment just keep away from the shop, there's a good lad. At least until things settle down.'

Dominic was on the phone when Richard walked into the shop the next morning. He put a hand over the mouthpiece. 'Go on through, I'll be finished in a minute.'

Richard nodded and went into the back room. 'Hey, Fergus, how's it going?'

'Okay,' Fergus muttered as he spooned coffee into two mugs. 'Want one?'

'I'd love one, thanks.' Richard leaned against the counter. 'How are things?'

Fergus glowered at him. 'Oh, fine, never better. Ma told me not to put my nose out of the shop until she gives me the nod, which is great as I'm finished for the day in less than an hour.'

Richard glanced at the clock on the wall. It was just gone eleven. 'That's what I call a half day,' he joked.

'That's what's called going out of business,' Dominic said as he joined them. 'Thanks, Fergus,' he said, taking his mug.

'I'll keep an eye on the shop.' Fergus left them on their own.

'So, business is bad, eh?'

Dominic rubbed his eyes with a weary hand. 'It's going from bad to worse. I think I'd be better off calling it a day.'

Richard's eyes widened. 'That bad?'

Dominic nodded. 'I can't even afford Fergus any more but Rose would be worried sick if I let him go.'

'I might be able to find something for Fergus. I know a guy who's starting up a fitness club across town. I'm sure he'll be looking for help.'

'That would be a load off my mind.'

'I'll have a word,' Richard promised. 'But that doesn't solve all of your problems. Are you really thinking of giving up the newsagent's?'

Dominic shrugged. 'I'm not sure. Maybe I could be a hairdresser!'

Richard laughed. 'Not if you want to make money!' He drained his mug and headed for the door.

'Are you going to buy me a pint later?' Dominic called after him.

'Sure.'

Richard went next door to see Rose. 'How are things?'

She shook her head. 'I don't know. We've been very busy this morning so I haven't had a chance to talk to her.'

'Where is she?'

'In the dressing room with a customer.'

Richard leaned on the counter and looked down at Rose. 'How do you feel about her staying on?'

Rose frowned. 'Fine, I mean, it doesn't change the fact that she's good at the job. Why?'

'I had a chat with her last night,' Richard admitted. 'She was talking about leaving.'

'Oh.'

'I think it's the thought of seeing so much of Fergus. It brings back a lot of bad memories.'

'I do understand that, but what can I do? Fergus will have to drop in occasionally and with him working next door . . .' Rose sighed.

'Leave it with me. Just don't let her go.'

After he was gone, Rose couldn't help wondering why Richard Lawrence was so keen for Celine to stay. Maybe he wasn't the confirmed bachelor she'd thought him to be.

Celine emerged from the fitting room looking slightly flustered. 'Why do most women insist they are a size twelve?'

Rose chuckled. 'They were once. Don't worry. Mrs Warren takes a long time to make up her mind but she usually buys something in the end.'

Celine grabbed two dresses and turned to go back in.

'Celine?'

'Yes?'

'We have to talk. Why don't we go for a drink when we close?'

Celine hesitated for a moment and then nodded. 'Sure.'

Rose closed her eyes briefly and sent up a prayer that she'd be able to persuade Celine to stay. She'd only been here a few days but she'd fitted in immediately. Rose was thrilled at how quickly she learned and how well she handled the customers. It would be such a shame if she left.

At five-thirty sharp, Rose closed up and led Celine down to the pub where she and Fergus had sat the night before. Tonight, she chose a quiet corner.

'What will you have?' she asked Celine as the waitress approached.

Celine shrugged. 'Just a half of lager please.'

'And a white wine for me.' When the girl had left them alone Rose wasted no time in getting to the point. 'Firstly, Celine, I want to apologise.'

Celine looked mildly surprised. 'For what?'

'Blurting everything out to Richard.'

Celine smiled. 'That's okay. I doubt he's the type to gossip.'

'Oh, he isn't!' Rose assured her. 'He tells me you're thinking of leaving.'

'Actually I told him I *was* leaving.'

'Then he must have thought he'd persuaded you to think about it.'

The waiter brought their drinks and Celine waited until he'd walked away before speaking. 'I'm sorry, Rose, I'd like to stay but I honestly don't think I can cope with seeing *him* on a regular basis.'

Rose took a sip of her wine to give herself time to find a reply. It hurt that Celine couldn't even use Fergus's name. 'I'm not going to say I know how you feel, Celine, because I couldn't possibly. It's terrible that you lost your husband at such a young age and it's even worse that he was murdered and died in such a horrific way, but . . .'

Celine's eyes flashed. 'But it wasn't your son's fault, is that what you were going to say?'

Rose held her gaze. 'No, it wasn't. I'm not going to lie to you just to get you to stay, Celine. I realise that Dermot only went there that night to see Fergus but that doesn't mean my son is responsible for his death. All it means is that your husband was a good, kind man who saved my son from drugs and then from a mad drunk.'

Celine stared into her drink. 'Yeah, good old Dermot, he was quite a hero.'

'Yes, he was.' Rose ignored the sarcasm. 'You must miss him.'

Celine stared into the distance. 'You have no idea. He was so vibrant, larger than life. Everyone loved him.'

'Including Fergus.'

Celine drained her glass. 'I've got to go. My dad's dropping over.'

Rose put a hand on her arm. 'Please think about it, Celine. I really want you to stay.'

Celine looked at her, her expression unreadable. 'I'll see you in the morning. Thanks for the drink.'

As Celine walked back to the flat she toyed with the idea of calling her dad and telling him she had to work late but, glancing at her watch, she realised he'd already have left the house. Her thoughts returned to Rose. She really would like to stay but knowing that Fergus could appear in the shop at any time made her shake – physically shake. It reminded her of that terrible year after Dermot died. She had wanted to barricade herself into the house, had been nervous of visitors – even her father – and had been positively terrified on the rare occasion she'd ventured out. She didn't want to end up feeling like that again. This was supposed to be a fresh start, for God's sake. She paused outside her flat and rummaged for the key, her eyes flickering around all the time. When she got inside she quickly closed the door behind her and let out a relieved breath as she climbed the stairs. She went into the bedroom to get changed and then paused as she caught sight of herself in the mirror. Her father would love to see her dressed up and the olive green suit was lovely. It had come into the shop yesterday and Rose had immediately put it under the counter. When she had produced it with a flourish later in the day, Celine's expert eye had recognised an excellent piece of tailoring. It was a designer she hadn't heard of but she would be on the look-out for more of his clothes. Celine had resolved to buy the Irish fashion magazines from now on and make regular visits to Brown Thomas. She was obviously out of touch.

She went into the bathroom, brushed her teeth, combed her hair and touched up her makeup. When she was finished she studied herself closely. No amount of makeup could disguise the pain in her eyes. Would her father notice? He wasn't due to arrive for at least another ten minutes so before she could change her mind, Celine went out to the phone and dialled the number from memory.

'Kevin Gilligan.'

'Kevin, it's me.'

'Hi, good to hear from you. I'm a bit tied up at the moment, can I call you back later?'

With the wife, Celine surmised. 'I'm at the flat, have you got a pen?'

'Yeah, go ahead.'

Celine reeled off her new phone number.

'Great, I'll talk to you then, Harry. Thanks for calling.'

Celine put down the phone, her guilty feelings warring with the need to escape reality. She'd hardly thought of Kevin in the last few days, but now, emotional and frightened, she longed to be in his arms. When he made love to her she could forget about everyone and everything for a while. Her father would be disgusted if he knew but there was no reason for him to find out. She would finish with Kevin, she promised herself, but not just yet. She needed him now more than ever. Celine paced the floor and checked her watch. Where had her dad got to?

Frank took the bunch of daffodils and climbed out of the car. He walked up the path but before he had a chance to ring the bell, Brenda had opened the door.

'Hello, Frank, this is a nice surprise.'

Frank bent to kiss her cheek. 'I just finished working on the garden and I thought you might like these.'

Brenda's cheeks flushed as she took the flowers. 'Oh, Frank, they're lovely!'

'I know daffodils are your favourite.'

Brenda laughed as she led the way into the kitchen. 'I wish you'd give Alan a few lessons. I always have to return his gifts.'

'I'm afraid my talents just apply to flowers,' he admitted. 'Ann loved lilies, Celine's mad about pink roses and you love your daffodils. I do too, I must admit. They make me think of the long summer days to come.'

'And the fact that winter is finally over,' Brenda added. 'How about some tea? I've just taken a batch of scones out of the oven.'

'I don't have much time, Celine is expecting me, but a quick cuppa won't hurt.' Frank rubbed his hands together and pulled up a chair.

They talked companionably for a while and as Brenda seemed more relaxed than she had in weeks, Frank decided to risk mentioning Celine again. 'I'm going over to Hopefield later.'

'You said.'

'Why don't you come with me?'

Brenda lowered her cup and looked at him. 'I don't think so.'

'She's sorry for all the trouble she caused, Brenda. She isn't seeing Kevin, she's started a new life, what more can she do?'

'Probably nothing.'

'Well then, come with me,' he urged.

Brenda stood up and began to clear the table. 'Sorry, Frank, I can't.'

Frank sighed. 'Right, then. I'd better go.'

Brenda moved forward to hug him. 'Thanks for the flowers.'

'You're welcome.'

'You will come and see me again?' she asked, her eyes full of anguish.

'Of course I will, love. Take care of yourself.'

'You too.'

*

Celine answered the buzzer immediately and Frank ran up the stairs. 'Hi, love.'

'You're late, I was worried.'

Frank drew back to look at her. 'I'm here now.'

Celine forced a smile.

'You look lovely. I'd forgotten what your legs looked like.'

Celine laughed. 'My work clothes. I left them on just for your benefit.'

Frank chuckled. 'I'm honoured. So where shall we go?'

Celine walked in behind the kitchen counter. 'I thought maybe we'd phone for a takeaway.'

'No way, not with you dressed up like a dog's dinner. Why don't we go across the road?'

'No!' Celine knew how often Fergus and Rose used the café. She looked at her father's bemused expression. 'I had lunch there today,' she explained. 'How about the Chinese?'

Frank shrugged. 'Fine by me.'

Frank chatted away as they strolled down the street, but Celine was glancing around her all the time. The shop was closed, Rose was gone home and it was highly unlikely that *he* would be around but she couldn't help herself.

'Is everything all right, love?'

'Sorry, Daddy, I was miles away.' She smiled reassuringly and led the way into the warm restaurant.

'I dropped in to see Brenda on the way over,' Frank

said when they were sitting down and their drinks had been ordered.

Celine looked up from her menu.

'Well, I just wanted to make sure she was okay,' he hurried on. 'No harm in that, is there?'

Celine shrugged 'None at all. So is she okay?'

He nodded. 'Yes, well, on the surface anyway.'

Celine gave up the pretence of studying her menu. 'Maybe I'm missing something, Daddy, but exactly what is wrong with her?'

Frank looked away from her cold stare. 'She's upset, love, it's understandable.'

'No it bloody isn't,' Celine hissed. 'I used to be married to her brother. How I live my life now is none of her business.'

Frank patted her hand. 'Of course it isn't, love, but Brenda is very conservative, you know that.'

'Narrow-minded, more like!'

Frank paused as their drinks were put in front of them and shook his head when the waiter asked if they were ready to order. He took a grateful drink of his pint and smiled at his daughter. 'Let's enjoy our evening. Forget about Killmont.'

'Gladly,' Celine snapped and picked up her menu. She couldn't believe it but she was remarkably close to tears. In part she felt hurt that her father was spending so much time consoling Brenda – he wasn't even related to her!

'Beef Chop Suey sounds good,' Frank was saying.

Celine smiled despite herself. 'Have you ever tried anything else, Daddy?'

He closed the menu and smiled at her. 'Why would I when I've found something I like?'

The waiter arrived back and Celine ordered Kung Po Chicken.

'Hah!' her father said. 'The words kettle, pot and black spring to mind!'

Celine laughed. 'Okay, okay, so I'm not feeling adventurous tonight. I need comfort food.'

'And why's that?' Frank asked.

She shrugged. 'Who knows. Tell me about Brenda.'

Frank looked wary. 'I think it would be better if we talk about something else.'

'No, really, it's okay. I promise not to shout or throw your dinner over you.'

Frank smiled. 'Thank God, I'm starving!'

Celine's eyes narrowed. 'Are you trying to tell me you didn't eat in Brenda's?'

Frank's eyes twinkled. 'You know me too well. Just one scone.'

'So, how is she?'

Frank sighed. 'I know you don't want to hear it, love, but she's quite upset. I'm not sure why. Like you say, you're barely related now. Maybe knowing there's another man on the scene means she has to accept Dermot is gone.'

Celine softened. 'I had no idea you were into amateur psychology.'

'Huh!'

'How's Alan coping with all of this?'

Frank frowned. 'Well, that's what worries me. I think he's had enough. He's been very irritable lately, even on the golf course.'

'Really?' Celine was surprised. Alan was the most laid-back, easy-going character she'd ever met. He was a solid, reliable man that you could always depend on.

Their food arrived and Frank waited until they were alone again before answering. 'Yeah, I know, I've never seen him like this.'

Celine piled rice onto his plate. 'Do you think it's serious?'

'I really don't know.'

'I hope they work things out. I can't imagine what Brenda would do without Alan. I'd offer to have a word but I'm the last person she'd want to talk to.'

Frank nodded. 'I asked her to come with me tonight but she wouldn't.'

Celine sighed at the sadness in his eyes. 'Don't worry about it, Dad. You can't make it happen. If she doesn't want to know me, that's her decision. It does bother me, you know. She's Dermot's only sister. We never had much in common but I thought we'd always be friends.'

'I'm sure you will be. Just give her a chance to calm down. Now, tell me about you. How's the job going?'

For all of ten seconds Celine considered telling him about Fergus but decided against it. 'Okay,' she said instead.

'Silly question, I suppose, when you're only a few days in the job.'

'Yeah.' Celine wondered what she would tell him if she decided to leave Close Second and where she would go.

Frank didn't seem to notice her preoccupation and was happily tucking into his food.

'Have you ever met anyone else, Daddy?'

'What do you mean?' Frank looked up at her.

'Another woman?'

'No, of course not!'

'Why "of course not"? You were only fifty-six when Mum died. That's very young to be alone.'

Frank raised his eyebrows. 'That's good coming from you.'

Celine smiled. Her father and Marina had been trying to set her up with a man for years. Kevin Gilligan wasn't quite what they had in mind though. 'Seriously, Daddy.'

He put down his knife and fork. 'Seriously? I got some offers and there were times when I was tempted. Like you say it can be very lonely. But I'm afraid the woman hasn't been born who can take the place of your mother.'

Celine smiled. 'She was pretty special, wasn't she? So many of my memories of her are funny ones.'

'She could always make people laugh,' Frank agreed, 'even at the end.'

'I miss her so much. Even after all this time.'

Frank cleared his throat. 'Time makes it easier but

it doesn't make you forget. And I wouldn't want to.'

'No.' Celine shook her head. 'Me neither.'

'So was Gilligan a replacement for Dermot?' Frank ventured.

'No! God, no!'

Frank grunted. 'You're better off without him, Celine. I wouldn't trust Gilligan as far as I'd throw him.'

Celine kept her head down and said nothing. Her dad had never had much time for smooth operators like Kevin and she knew now that he felt his suspicions were entirely justified.

'You know what they say about every cloud has a silver lining? I think that's true. And I bet that you'll be happy here in Hopefield. Maybe you'll even meet someone special.'

Celine felt sick. She hated lying to her father and the nicer he was to her, the lousier she felt. 'Maybe you're right, Daddy,' she said, forcing a smile. 'Who knows?'

Chapter 13

Fergus finished unpacking the newspapers, opened all the shutters and switched on the lights. Within minutes, the early commuters were arriving, en route to the train station and the bus stop. This was the one time of day when Dominic's customers were loyal – the book store didn't open until nine. It was nearly eight before Fergus got a chance to grab something to eat. He'd just slipped two slices of bread into the toaster when he heard someone in the shop. He went back into the shop to find Richard scanning the headlines on that morning's *Irish Times*.

'Hi, Fergus, how's it going?'

'Okay. Did you want anything else?'

'A bottle of milk please and a quick word if you have a minute.'

'Sure.'

Richard handed over the money. 'It's about a job that's going across town. I wondered if you'd be interested.'

Fergus brightened as he handed Richard his change. 'Go on.'

'A friend of mine, Vincent Bourke, has just opened a new leisure centre and he's looking for people.'

'I'm fairly fit but I'm not trained—'

Richard laughed. 'Oh, sorry, no, he doesn't want you to work as an instructor. He wants you to run the snack bar. Well, obviously he'd want to interview you first.'

Fergus stared at him. 'Are you serious?'

'Yeah. He'd be looking for references but that's not a problem. I'll give you one and I'm sure Dominic will too.'

'Cheers. What kind of hours are we talking about? Do you know how much money he's paying?'

Richard held up a hand. 'Haven't a clue, you need to ask him all that yourself. So you're interested?'

Fergus nodded. 'Absolutely. This is great, Richard, I really appreciate it. Where exactly is this health club?'

'Sandhill.'

Fergus froze.

'Here's his phone number. He's expecting to hear from you today.'

Fergus looked at the card in Richard's hand. 'Yeah, well I'll ring him if I get a chance.'

'What?' Richard shook his head. 'A minute ago you thought it was a great idea!'

Fergus shrugged. 'Maybe I've had enough of standing behind a counter.'

Richard slammed the card down in front of him. 'I don't know what the hell is going on in your head,

Fergus, but you'd better sort yourself out for your mother's sake.'

Fergus frowned. 'What's Ma got to do with it?'

'If you're going to be around on a regular basis, Celine will leave and that means your mother will be without a manager. So do everyone a favour, Fergus, phone Vincent.' Richard left, banging the door after him.

Fergus picked up the card and looked at the address. The sports centre was less than a mile from where he had grown up. His old school was nearby and the park where he'd first bought drugs was just around the corner. Even if he decided to go for the job, he knew his ma would be dead against it. She had sold their place while he was still in rehab and brought him home to the small house on the outskirts of Hopefield. She had told none of their neighbours where she was going, promising to get in touch when they'd settled in. She never had. Rose had left her life and her friends behind in an effort to protect him from the people who had dragged him down. Fergus had pointed out that drugs were available in every town and drug pushers were part of every community but Rose was adamant.

'They don't know you,' she'd said, 'and you don't know them. And that's the way I like it.'

He'd run into Mick and some of the other lads occasionally but so far they'd left him alone. He wasn't sure how it would be if he was working close by, though. His thoughts were interrupted by Dominic's arrival.

'Hi, Fergus. How are things? Have you been busy?'

'Not bad.'

'Right. You go and get some breakfast. I'll keep an eye on things.'

Fergus slid the card into the pocket of his jeans and went into the back.

Richard crossed the road and went into the café. 'Black coffee and a muffin, Tracy.'

'And a very good morning to you too,' Tracy replied as she reached for a large mug.

Richard smiled. 'Sorry. It's one of those days.'

Tracy rolled her eyes. 'What's wrong with everyone this morning?'

Richard followed her gaze to where Rose sat by the window staring across at her shop.

'I'll try and cheer us both up,' he promised and took his breakfast over to Rose's table. 'Can I join you?'

'Of course.'

Rose smiled at him but he noticed the dark circles under her eyes. 'Should I ask what's wrong or will I guess?'

Rose sighed. 'I think you probably know.'

'Well, your manager hasn't buggered off yet, has she?'

'Yet being the operative word,' Rose told him. 'I'm sure it's only a matter of time.'

'Don't be so pessimistic. Celine strikes me as a level-headed sort of girl. Once she's got over the shock I'm sure she'll decide to stay.'

'I'm not so sure but if she does, Richard, keep an eye on her for me, will you?'

'I'll keep an eye on both of them,' he promised. 'Tell me, does Dominic know what's going on?'

'Yes, Fergus told him. I don't think he had much choice. He's been in such a foul mood he had to explain why.'

'Then between us I'm sure we can sort things out and make sure that Celine stays.'

Rose watched him, a speculative gleam in her eye. 'I think you have a soft spot for your new tenant.'

Richard grinned. 'She's very easy on the eye.'

Rose's eyes narrowed. 'You behave yourself. That girl has had enough heartache without you adding her to your list of conquests.'

Richard raised an eyebrow. 'I don't know what you mean.'

'Oh yes you do.'

'It's not my fault that women chase me all the time,' he protested.

'It's a hard life.'

Richard scowled. 'It is. Sometimes I think it would be easier to invent a wife.'

'Or you could actually get married.' Rose suggested.

Richard shivered. 'Let's not get carried away. Anyway, who'd put up with me?'

'You've got a point.'

'Thanks, Rose. You know, I bet Celine Moore could be fun if she ever let herself go.'

'Richard.' Rose shot him a warning look.

He held up his hands in surrender. 'I'll behave myself, I promise!'

Rose got slowly to her feet. 'I'll hold you to that. Now I must get on.'

Richard opened his paper. 'Bye, Rose, and don't worry so much. I'm sure things will work out fine.'

'I wish I had your confidence.'

Richard watched her cross the road and disappear into the shop. An hour ago he had been quite sure everything would be okay but after Fergus's odd change of heart over the job, he wasn't so sure. Richard was convinced that Fergus was as straight as they come and there was no doubt that he adored his mother, so why was he stalling over the job? Richard had seen the expression on his face when he'd first told him about it – he'd been delighted. That rubbish about not wanting to work behind a counter was bullshit. So what was the truth?

Shortly after Rose had opened up, Celine came downstairs. 'Morning,' Rose called before bustling into the back room. Celine took a deep breath and followed her. 'Rose, I'd like to talk—'

'Yes, love, of course, but I'm in a bit of a rush right now.' And before Celine could say another word,

Rose hurried past her out of the shop and into her car.

Celine stood looking after her. Rose was obviously avoiding her but she was just putting off the inevitable, Celine had to leave. She hated letting Rose down. In the few days she'd known her, Celine was impressed with her as a businesswoman and in awe of her courage in the face of such obvious pain. If only she weren't *his* mother. A small woman struggling to push open the door interrupted her thoughts. Celine hurried to help her.

'Thank you, dear. Lovely to see you again.'

Celine frowned. 'Hello.'

The woman laughed. 'Mary Boyle, remember? From the garage.'

'Of course! How are you?'

'Fine, fine. I just dropped by to see how you were getting on.'

'You're very kind.'

'And to bring you this.' Mary shoved a Tupperware box into her arms.

Celine's eyes widened as she peeked inside. 'Shepherd's pie!'

'I know what you single girls are like when you live alone. Live on crackers and coffee, don't you? That's my own recipe, freshly made this morning.'

'I'll have it this evening,' Celine promised and carried it into the back room.

'Ten minutes in a warm oven is all it needs.' Mary was close on her heels.

Celine jumped. 'Great, thanks.' She edged towards the door but Mary was taking off her coat and sitting down.

'It may be spring,' she said, 'but the breeze out there would skin a cat.'

Celine groaned inwardly. 'Would you like a cup of tea?'

'Oh, thank you, dear, that would be lovely!'

Celine put on the kettle and took out cups and saucers – Mary didn't look like the mug sort – occasionally pausing to stick her head into the shop.

'Don't worry, you'll hear the bell if you have any customers,' Mary told her.

Celine smiled through gritted teeth. 'Of course.'

'Are you settling in all right?'

'Yes, thanks. Just a few teething troubles with the immersion.'

'My Gerry could take a look at that for you.'

'That's okay, my landlord, Richard Lawrence, fixed it.'

Mary grunted. 'Did he indeed? Well if there's anything else needs doing you just let me know. My Gerry can turn his hand to anything.'

Celine suppressed a smile. 'Thanks, I'll remember that.'

'You must come to tea,' Mary decided. 'What about Sunday?'

'Eh, well, there's still a lot to do and . . .' Celine stammered as she poured the tea.

'Next week then.' Mary looked with patent

disapproval at the packet of biscuits. 'I have a lovely shortcake recipe. I'll drop it in the next time I'm passing.'

Celine smiled and prayed fervently for a customer to walk through the door.

'Rose was never into baking.'

'She's a very busy woman.' Celine jumped immediately to her boss's defence.

Mary sipped her tea. 'Aren't we all?'

The doorbell chimed before Celine could reply. Saved by the bell, she thought, before muttering her excuses and hurrying into the shop. 'Can I help you?' she asked the attractive thirty-something who was working her way through the rails.

The woman smiled briefly and returned to the job at hand. 'Just looking, thanks.'

Celine sighed. 'Call if you need me,' she said and went back to Mary Boyle.

She was delighted to see the woman was on her feet and hurried to hold her coat.

Mary patted her cheek. 'I must be going. You're very pretty but you really need to put on a few pounds. Make sure and eat that pie.'

'I can't wait.'

Mary looked pleased as she went back through the shop. 'Now drop in and let me know when you can come to tea.'

'Okay then.' Celine opened the door.

'And remember to call Gerry if you need anything.'

'I will,' Celine promised.

'Goodbye then, dear, take care.'

'Bye.' Celine stood in the doorway and waved as Mary Boyle made her way back up the road.

Dominic emerged from next door with Fergus behind him. 'Morning, Celine! How are you getting on?'

Celine stood rooted to the spot.

Fergus muttered something about the loo and retreated inside.

Dominic looked embarrassed. 'I'm sorry about that. Fergus has been doing his damnedest to stay out of your way.'

'So you know?'

'Yes, he filled me in. It's a very small world, isn't it?'

Celine's smile was bitter. 'It certainly is.'

'If there's anything I can do—'

She shook her head. 'There's nothing anyone can do, Dominic. Not now.'

Chapter 14

Marina groaned as she heard the post drop on the floor. 'Joshie, would you get the post for Mummy?'

No reply.

'Joshie?' Marina took off her rubber gloves and walked into the living room. Josh was still in his pyjamas, sprawled on the floor, watching Pokemon. Marina frowned. 'Darling, you know Mummy doesn't like you watching that.'

No reply.

'Joshie, aren't you listening to me?'

Joshie turned to give her a heart-stopping smile. 'Yes, Mummy?'

Marina melted. 'Turn the television off after that programme is finished, okay?'

'Yes, Mummy.'

'Good boy.' She tousled his hair as she went out into the hall. The carpet was strewn with brown envelopes. Marina bent to pick them up, carefully keeping her eyes averted. She brought them into the kitchen and stuffed them into a drawer with the others. Josh came in, rubbing his eyes. 'Can we go somewhere nice, Mummy?'

'Maybe the park.' Marina put the rubber gloves back on and went back to cleaning the worktops.

Josh kicked a chair. 'The park's boring.'

'Of course it isn't, darling.'

'Let's go to the cinma.'

'Cin-e-ma,' Marina corrected. 'No, not today, Joshie. Mummy can't afford it.'

'What's afford mean?'

Marina shook her head and smiled. 'Never you mind.'

'So can we go?'

'No, Josh. I know, why don't we go and see Granny?'

Josh gave the chair another kick. 'I suppose.'

'Come on, you know you always have a good time in Granny's. Maybe she'll have baked some of her wonderful apple tart.'

Josh brightened. 'Okay. Can I bring my Action Man?'

'Sure.'

'And my cars?'

'Of course.'

'And my race track?'

'Yes, Josh, whatever you want.' Marina rubbed at a stubborn stain, then peeled off the gloves. 'Now let's go and get dressed.'

*

An hour later, Josh was running up Kay's driveway while Marina unloaded the boot.

Kay opened the door and forced a bright smile. 'Hello, darling.' She bent to gather a reluctant Josh into her arms. Her heart sank as she watched Marina stagger towards her, her arms full of toys. 'Hi, Mum. Just thought we'd drop by and say hello.'

'Lovely.' Kay took the track from her and set it up in the living-room. She did a quick glance round the room to see if there were any breakables within Josh's reach then went out to the kitchen to put on the kettle. 'How are things?' she asked her daughter.

Marina sighed. 'Quiet.'

Kay turned to look at her. Beautiful and immaculate as ever, Marina had telltale shadows under her eyes and she looked frail. 'No work?'

Marina shook her head. 'No, but then it's a bad time of the year. Give it a week or so and I'll be modelling hats for Easter. It's probably just as well I'm not busy. This is the first afternoon this week that Josh hasn't had some class or other. His life is busier than mine.'

Kay set the table with homemade buns and chocolate bars. Marina bit into a bun and licked her lips. 'These are gorgeous.'

Kay smiled. 'They were always your favourite. Josh, come and have something to eat.'

Josh rushed out to the kitchen, his eyes lighting up when he saw all the goodies. Kay handed him a plate. 'Take what you like, love.'

'Just one of each,' Marina told him as he made a grab for the buns.

'Can I bring them inside?'

Kay thought of her lovely cream carpet. 'I tell you what, you can pretend you're having a picnic.' She took a check tablecloth and spread it on the living-room floor.

Josh carried his plate in and Kay followed with a cup of milk.

'Thanks, Granny.'

He smiled up at her and Kay softened. 'You're welcome, love.'

'You're great with him,' Marina said when Kay returned to the kitchen.

Kay pushed the buns at her daughter. 'Have another, you're very thin. And you look tired. Is everything okay?'

Marina shrugged. 'The bank manager is banging at my door and it's not with a cheque.'

Kay's face filled with concern. 'Oh, Marina!'

'I'm exaggerating, Mum, it will be fine. I'm just a little behind on the mortgage.' And the insurance, and the electricity and the phone, she added silently.

Kay stirred her tea in silence and then with a deep breath she put the spoon in the saucer and looked her daughter in the eye. 'Why don't you move in here?'

Marina lowered her cup. 'Are you serious?'

Kay nodded. 'It makes sense. This house is easily big enough for three. The money from selling your house would pay off all your debts and give you a nest egg. And you'd have a live-in babysitter whenever you needed one.'

'I don't know what to say.' Marina sat staring at her. 'Don't you think we'd hate each other after a week?'

Kay laughed. 'It would take time to adapt but if we gave each other space I think we could cope.'

'What about Josh? I know you love him, Mum, but he's not always easy.'

Kay forced a smile. 'I'm sure I'd lose my temper sometimes and give him the occasional swat on the bum—'

Marina froze.

'And you'd have to let me, Marina, or it would never work. Josh needs to know who's boss.'

Marina nodded reluctantly.

'So what do you think?' Kay held her breath. She had no idea what had made her make such an offer and she knew she'd probably live to regret it but Marina was her daughter and she was in trouble.

'What about men?' Marina asked.

'Yours or mine?' Kay asked and they both laughed. 'I'm sure that I could absent myself from the premises occasionally but I don't want to meet anyone at breakfast.'

Marina looked shocked. 'Of course not!'

'Anything else?'

Marina shook her head. 'I don't think so.'

'Then you'd better call Jack.'

Jack Mullen was an estate agent and an old friend

of Marina's father. Unlike Donald, Jack had grown his business slowly and today was one of the most successful agents in the area.

Marina leaned forward to hug her mother. 'Thank you, Mum, thank you.'

Kay felt the prick of tears in her eyes. 'You're welcome, love.'

After she'd strapped a sleepy Josh into his seat and blown her mother another kiss, Marina drove off in a daze. She wondered if she could cope with living in her mother's house but she didn't have a better solution. Selling her house would clear all of her debts and allow her to put money aside for Josh's education – they might even be able to afford a holiday this year. Her heart sank at the thought of moving back into her old bedroom. And how would Josh react to moving into Kay's tiny boxroom? Marina bit her lip. It probably wouldn't be easy but it wasn't for forever. She would start saving – seriously saving. She would put money aside every month and within a year or so she'd be able to buy another place for her and Josh. Mind you – she pulled up at the lights and smiled at the guy in the Merc beside her – it would be easier to bag a rich man. A rich, old man with a dodgy heart, preferably.

'Mummy, I'm hungry.'

'Don't be silly, darling, you haven't stopped eating since you got to Granny's.'

'I'm hungry,' Josh insisted.

On impulse, she swerved into the shopping mall near her home.

'Where are we going, Mummy?' Josh demanded.

'We're going to McDonald's.'

'Hurrah!' Josh couldn't believe his luck. His mother didn't bring him here very often.

Marina turned her head to smile at her darling boy. 'And then, we're going on a shopping spree!'

Josh sat up, sleep forgotten. 'Can I have a toy, Mummy?'

Marina pulled into a parking spot with a crash of gears. 'My darling, you can have two.'

Chapter 15

Fergus got off the bus and stood looking around him. The neighbourhood hadn't changed much in the seven years he'd been away. The streets were deserted, several houses were boarded up and every wall seemed to be covered with graffiti. Fergus wondered what Vincent Bourke was thinking of opening a fancy sports club in a place like this. And, he wondered as he set out on the ten-minute walk to the premises, how long would it last? But as he got nearer, he noticed a change in his surroundings. There was a lot of building work in progress, apartments and town houses mainly, and the old residential home had been razed, a notice announcing that a large shopping mall was to be built on the site. The other thing Fergus noticed was that in this part of town the cars were a lot newer and bigger. Sandhill must be one of Dublin's new up-and-coming neighbourhoods. He quickened his step, his heart getting lighter as he realised that with the advent of such prosperity, his old 'friends' might have also moved on. When he turned into the entrance of the Sandhill

Sports and Leisure Centre, he was convinced of it. The place oozed class and sophistication and even though it was the middle of the day, the car park was half full with some rather impressive motors. He walked into reception and was greeted by a svelte blonde with beautiful teeth. Fergus was glad he'd opted for black cords rather than jeans and his crisp new Tommy Hilfiger shirt that Rose had bought him. He smiled confidently at the girl and told her he had an appointment to see Mr Bourke.

An hour later, Fergus was following Vincent around the centre and marvelling at the standard of equipment. Finally they came to the small coffee bar that looked out on the pool on one side and boasted a small patio area on the other.

'That's a suntrap,' Vincent told him proudly. 'We made sure of it when we were designing the place.'

'Cool.' Fergus nodded in approval.

'This is Cindy.' Vincent brought him over to meet the girl behind the counter.

Fergus smiled at the girl. 'Howaya?'

'At the moment we only serve tea, coffee and soft drinks but I plan to expand into fruit smoothies, designer coffees and light lunches. So, Fergus, are you interested?'

Fergus stared at him. 'Are you serious?'

'Sure. Your references are great, you have retail experience, you're exactly what I'm looking for. We've talked about the package and I forgot to mention you have free use of the gym and the pool in off-peak hours.'

'It sounds great, Vincent.' Fergus thought of the salary and Celine, and put his worries firmly to the back of his mind. 'I'd love the job.'

'Good. Well, you talk to your boss and see how soon he can let you go. I take it you'll want to continue at the shelter?'

Fergus nodded. 'Yeah, but I'll be able to work my hours there around the centre.'

'Great. Let's go back to my office and do the paperwork.'

Fergus couldn't wait to tell Dominic. As he hurried up the main street of Hopefield, his face buried in the neck of his jacket, he prayed he wouldn't bump into Celine. He practically burst into the newsagent's and shut the door quickly behind him.

Dominic looked up in surprise. 'Hi, Fergus, I wasn't expecting you today.'

'I thought you should know how I got on at my interview.'

'Of course, the interview, I completely forgot! So?'

Fergus grinned. 'I got the job.'

Dominic crossed the room, his hand outstretched. 'Congratulations, Fergus, I'm delighted for you.'

Fergus grinned. 'And relieved?'

Dominic sighed. 'That too. When do you start?'

'That depends on you.'

Dominic shrugged. 'You can finish up here at the

end of the week if you like. Young Grainne will be delighted to do a few extra shifts.' Tracy and Bob's girl had just started college and needed the money but working for her parents did not appeal.

'Then I suppose I start next Monday. It's a great place, Dominic, and I get to use the facilities for nothing.'

'Sounds great. Is Rose pleased?'

'She doesn't know yet.'

'Well, get in there and tell her!'

Fergus studied his feet. 'Not a good idea.'

Dominic nodded. 'Of course, Celine, I was forgetting. Still, I'm sure she'd be glad to hear that piece of news.'

'Ma can tell her. I'm staying well away.'

'I suppose you're right.'

'Right then, I'll be off. Seeya, Dominic, and thanks again for that reference.'

'You're welcome.' Dominic walked to the door and watched him hurry down the road. As he stood there, Richard pulled up in front of the shop and lowered the car window. 'Can I interest you in a pub lunch?'

Dominic shook his head. 'Afraid I'm on my own.'

'Did I see Fergus just leaving?'

Dominic smiled. 'You did and he's one very happy lad.'

Richard raised an eyebrow. 'He got the job?'

'He certainly did.'

'That's going to make two people very happy.' He

got out of the car and stretched. 'I'd better go and have a word with Rose.'

'Well don't say anything about Fergus because he hasn't told her yet.'

'My lips are sealed,' Richard promised.

'Hi, Rose, Celine.'

'Hi.' Celine smiled, thinking that Richard filled the small shop with both his size and his personality.

'Hello, love,' Rose said absently. 'Have you come about the keys?'

Richard frowned. 'Keys?'

Rose shook her head. 'Remember you were getting an extra set cut for the shop? And you were to get the alarm serviced too.'

'All in hand, Rose,' Richard promised. 'There's no hurry, is there?'

Rose glanced sideways at Celine. 'I'd prefer to get it sorted before I go into hospital.'

Richard flashed Celine a sympathetic look.

'Can I take my lunch, Rose?' she asked.

'Sure, off you go.'

'How are things?' Richard asked when she'd left.

'Tense,' Rose told him. 'She's agreed to stay another week but I don't have any hope of finding someone else before then. That's why I need the security sorted.'

'Don't worry about that,' Richard told her. 'Your problems are over.'

Rose rolled her eyes. 'I doubt that.'

'Trust me.'

'Stop talking in riddles, Richard.' Rose was rapidly losing patience with him.

'I think I'll go and talk to Celine, she's much nicer,' he remarked.

'Sorry, but this is my livelihood we're talking about.'

He bent to kiss her cheek. 'I know, Rose, but I really think it will work out fine. See you later.'

Celine was just cutting her cheese sandwich in two when the buzzer went. 'Hello?'

'It's Richard.'

'Come on up,' Celine told him and put a hand up to smooth back her hair as she opened the door.

'I thought you might fancy going out for lunch,' he said as he reached the top of the stairs.

Celine looked over at her uninviting sandwich. 'I've only got forty minutes.'

'Plenty of time. Let's go to the pub.'

Celine grabbed her bag. 'What the hell!'

When they got outside Celine started to look nervous.

'He's not working today,' Richard murmured.

Celine shot him a grateful smile. 'I suppose you think I'm overreacting.'

'Not at all.'

'Does that mean you're not going to try to persuade me to stay any more?' Celine couldn't help feeling disappointed.

Richard pushed open the door of the pub and stood back to let Celine go first. 'I don't think I have to.' He broke off to say hello to the pretty waitress who had hurried over to their table. 'Hi, Lucy.'

'Hi, Richard, good to see you,' she purred before giving Celine a malevolent look.

After they'd ordered and she'd left, Celine burst out laughing.

'What?' Richard asked, bemused.

'Is she one of your girlfriends?'

'One of?' he said reproachfully.

'Rose warned me about you.'

'It's all lies.'

'Can I ask you a personal question?'

Richard moved closer. 'Please do.'

'Do you really live in a penthouse?'

Richard threw back his head and laughed. 'I really do. Would you like to see it?'

Celine shrugged. 'I'd like to see the view.'

'But do you think it's safe given my reputation?'

Celine held his gaze. 'Probably not.'

Richard jumped as Lucy banged down their drinks and flounced off. 'Service with a smile, eh?'

Celine frowned. She was already labelled 'the other woman'. She didn't need to complicate her life further.

'So when are you coming to see the view?' Richard asked.

Celine moved away. 'Maybe it's not such a good idea.'

'What, because of Lucy? Celine, I assure you, I've never even gone out with the girl. Ask Dominic.'

'Dominic?'

'He's the one I usually drink with,' Richard explained. 'And he'll tell you what it's like around here. Being a single, wealthy man in a small town full of single women isn't easy.'

Celine laughed at his woebegone expression. 'Poor you.'

'That's what everyone says,' he complained, 'but it's not all it's cracked up to be.'

'What isn't?'

'Being an eligible bachelor. Women seem to see me as a challenge.'

Celine grimaced. 'Well, you don't have to worry about this woman. I've no intention of chasing you.'

'Exactly! That's what I like about you.'

Celine looked at him. 'Look, Richard, I was flirting with you, having a bit of fun, that's all.'

He grinned. 'I liked it.'

'Don't get used to it, I'll be gone in a couple of weeks.'

He shook his head. 'No you won't.'

'There you are.' Lucy banged down their lunch, making the drinks slop over.

Richard scowled at her. 'She won't be getting a tip today,' he muttered as she tottered away. 'Now, as I was saying before that rude interruption, you don't have to go.'

Celine sighed. 'I know you mean well, Richard,

and I appreciate that, but you don't understand.'

'No, *you* don't understand. You want to leave because you can't handle seeing Fergus about the place, right?'

Celine nodded.

'Then you'll be happy to hear that he's starting a new job on Monday on the other side of town.'

'Really?'

'Really.' Richard turned his attention to his toasted sandwich.

'I can't believe it. Is he leaving because of me?'

Richard shook his head. 'No, Dominic can't afford to keep him on, it was only a matter of time. You may have accelerated it but that's all.'

'Did you have something to do with it?'

'Now what makes you say that? Eat your lunch, it's getting cold.'

Celine shot him a suspicious look. She didn't really care why Fergus was going, she was just relieved he was. Now she could stay. Now Rose could go into hospital and not have to worry about the shop. Now Celine could relax again and throw herself into the job. Maybe things would work out after all. Tears welled in her eyes.

'Hey, are you okay?' Richard was looking at her.

Celine jumped to her feet. 'There's just something in my eye.'

'Let me look.'

'No, it's okay. I'll be back in a minute.' She hurried out to the toilets, splashed water on her face and smiled at her reflection in the mirror. 'It's going to be okay,' she murmured. 'Everything's going to be okay.'

Chapter 16

Brenda pushed a trolley around the supermarket, throwing things into it without much thought or interest. They'd had another row that morning. As usual it had started over something silly. This time, Brenda was annoyed because she'd asked Alan to put out the bin and he hadn't.

'I will put the bin out, I always put the bin out,' he'd told her. 'What is your problem?'

And Brenda couldn't answer that. She didn't know why she felt angry all of the time. She didn't even know what she was angry about. And she couldn't explain to Alan why he was the focus of all this anger. At the bakery, she tossed random packets of bread and cakes into the trolley – she didn't feel much like baking lately. Frank had noticed. Dear old Frank, he was so kind. He was dropping around more than ever, bringing her flowers and sometimes vegetables from his garden. The vegetables usually ended up in the bin. Brenda would plan to cook something nice for dinner but as the day progressed she would find herself curled up in a ball in front of the television.

When Alan arrived home from work she would stick a ready meal from the freezer into the microwave and leave him to eat alone.

After this behaviour had continued for a couple of weeks, Alan had begged her to go to the doctor. Brenda had screamed at him that all he was interested in was his dinner and he didn't give a damn about her. She could still see the look of hurt and confusion in his eyes.

'Excuse me? That's my trolley.'

Brenda looked from the woman down to the trolley full of nappies and baby formula and stammered an apology. Abandoning her shopping, she ran out to the car and cried her eyes out. When she'd calmed down a bit, she drove very carefully to the medical centre in the village. It took all of her willpower to go into reception and ask for an appointment without breaking down.

Jim Gallagher was walking another patient to the door when he spotted her. Alan had called him a number of times over the last couple of weeks but Jim had told him that unless Brenda was willing to come in and see him, there was nothing he could do. He went back into his room and buzzed reception.

'Maria? I'll see Brenda Foley after the next patient, don't let her go.'

The receptionist put down the phone, consulted the appointments book and smiled at Brenda. 'You're in luck, there's a cancellation.'

Brenda sat down in the waiting room and leafed

through a magazine without seeing it. She felt a sudden urge to run away but she knew that if she did she might never come back.

'Brenda?' She looked up to see Dr Gallagher smiling down at her. 'Come on in.'

She didn't remember much of the consultation afterwards except that she'd cried through most of it. Dr Gallagher had diagnosed depression.

'I'm not an expert, Brenda, and I want you to see someone who is. For the moment, I'm putting you on an antidepressant. I'll call you when I have an appointment for you to see someone.'

Brenda had dabbed at her tears with a sodden tissue. 'Do you mean a psychiatrist? Are you saying I'm mad?'

Jim chuckled. 'You are far from mad, Brenda, but you are sick. If you had angina I'd send you to a heart specialist, if you had cancer I'd send you to an oncologist. Depression is a disease too and it needs to be treated by an expert.'

Brenda was still frightened. 'Will he want to lock me up?'

Jim shook his head. 'Of course not! All he will do is talk to you and monitor your medication.'

So Brenda had gone to the pharmacy and then gone home. She couldn't wait to tell Alan the news. He would be so happy that she had gone to the doctor and relieved that there was apparently a reason for her strange behaviour.

*

She took her first tablet and then went upstairs to lie down. For some reason she felt completely exhausted. It took her a few moments to realise that all was not quite right in the bedroom. There were hangers on the bed, the wardrobe was open and the shelf where Alan kept his ties was almost bare. When Brenda investigated further, she realised some of his clothes were missing and the suitcase that usually sat on the top of the wardrobe was gone. She went back downstairs in search of a note but there was nothing. She went to the phone and saw that the light on the answering machine was flashing. She pushed the button with trembling fingers.

'Brenda, it's me. I'm going to London on business for a few weeks. Given the way things are between us I think it's for the best. I'll be in touch. Take care of yourself. Bye.'

Brenda listened to the message three times. She remembered Alan had mentioned that head office wanted him to come over for some training but he'd kept putting it off, saying he was much too busy to go. She tried to call him on his mobile but it was switched off. She was sitting on the bottom stair staring into space when the doorbell rang.

Frank stood on the step, his face full of compassion. 'Are you okay, love?'

Brenda stood back to let him in. 'Alan's left me.'

'No, love, he's just taking a break.'

Brenda looked at him. 'You knew?'

'He called me from the airport and asked me to

keep an eye on you.' Brenda stared at him, her eyes bright with tears, and Frank took her in his arms. 'Don't worry, Brenda, he's only gone for a few weeks. He'll be back before you know it.'

'I've been so awful to him, Frank, but Dr Gallagher says it wasn't my fault. He says I'm suffering from depression.'

'You went to the doctor?' Frank led her into the living room and sat her down. Brenda smiled through her tears.

'Ironic, isn't it? Alan's been at me for weeks to go and I do it the day he leaves me.' She broke into a fresh flood of tears.

'Oh, love, I'm telling you he hasn't left you. And when you tell him about the depression I'm sure he'll be on the first plane back.

Brenda shook her head. 'No, that's not what I want.'

'Now, Brenda—'

'No, Frank, he was right to go. As long as I know that he's coming back I'll be fine.'

Frank squeezed her hand. 'You're an amazing girl, do you know that?'

Brenda laughed. 'I can think of lots of words but amazing isn't one of them.' And she burst into tears again.

'I'll make you some tea,' Frank said.

'Why do people always make tea in a crisis?' Brenda hiccupped.

Frank sighed. 'Because they've no idea what else to do.'

*

After the tea, Brenda decided to go back upstairs and have the nap she'd planned earlier.

'Are you sure you'll be okay?' Frank asked. 'I could stay if you want.'

Brenda kissed his cheek. 'That's okay, Frank. Strange as it may seem I feel better now that I know what's wrong and I'm doing something about it.'

It was six when Frank left her and he thought about going over to see Celine. He'd love to talk to her about Brenda but under the circumstances, that probably wasn't a good idea. Despite his and Alan's best efforts, Brenda had refused to talk about Celine, never mind see her. Maybe now she was on the medication all of that would change. Frank was glad the girl was finally getting help. He and Alan had been watching her fall apart for weeks now. Alan had been at his wits' end and Frank knew he must have been desperate to go to London without saying goodbye properly. 'Maybe it will shock her into sorting herself out,' he'd told Frank when he'd called from the airport, his voice weary.

Frank had promised to look after Brenda but he couldn't help feeling that a woman would do a better job. And his thoughts returned to Celine. He decided to drive around by her cottage and check that everything was okay. A young couple had rented it and Frank was relieved to see that they seemed to lead a quiet life. As he drove past the girl was just coming in from work and the lad came out to meet her. As they kissed, Frank thought with a pang of all the times Celine and Dermot had stood in that driveway arm in arm. It was criminal that his poor daughter was alone at such an early age. Thoroughly fed up now himself, Frank decided to go to the golf club for a pint.

When he walked into the bar, Kevin Gilligan was in a corner with some friends. He waved but Frank turned his back on him and went to the other end of the bar. 'Give us a pint, Robbie,' he said to the barman.

'We don't usually see you on a Thursday evening, Frank.'

Frank shrugged. 'Yeah, well, I've had a bad day.'

'Don't look now,' Robbie murmured, 'but I think you've got company.'

Frank looked up to see Kevin approaching.

'Frank, how's it going? Let me get you a pint.'

'I've got one.'

'Put that on my account, Robbie, would you?' Kevin slid onto the barstool next to Frank.

'No, thanks,' Frank said through gritted teeth.

'Oh, come on, Frank,' Kevin murmured. 'Don't you think it's time to put the past behind us? Everyone else has.'

'Thanks to you, my daughter had to move to the other side of town,' Frank retorted.

'And from what I hear, she's doing very well.'

Frank shot him a suspicious look.

Kevin smiled. 'Dublin's a small town, Frank. I'm

happy for Celine. She's an intelligent woman and she was wasting away in that pharmacy.'

Frank grunted.

Kevin stood up and clapped him on the back. 'Every cloud has a silver lining, Frank. Ask Celine.'

Frank fumed inwardly as Kevin went back to join his friends. He'd never really liked the man but he positively hated him now. It disgusted Frank that while Celine's life had been devastated when their affair became public Kevin's had gone on as before. Frank would never understand what Celine saw in him. He was nothing like Dermot.

Chapter 17

Celine had really tried to break up with Kevin but after discovering Fergus was Rose's son she felt in need of comfort. On his first visit to her flat, she had practically fallen into his arms.

'So it's true that absence makes the heart grow fonder,' Kevin had said when they came up for air.

Celine hadn't bothered answering but led him into the bedroom. Their lovemaking had been frenzied and rough. Kevin couldn't take his eyes off her and she was only just getting her breathing under control when he was on top of her again. 'God, you are gorgeous,' he'd muttered into her neck. 'Always so cool and calm on the outside and like a complete tart in the bedroom.'

Celine had pressed a hand over his mouth. She hated it when he talked like this. She pulled his face to hers and kissed him long and hard, the sure way to shut him up. When she was finally sated she went into the kitchen and returned with a bottle of whiskey and two tumblers.

'That was great.' Kevin had dipped a finger in his drink and trailed it across her stomach.

'You should probably go, it's late.'

'That's okay, Eileen's away. I can stay the night if you like.'

Celine had closed her eyes briefly. 'If you did that, I wouldn't get any sleep and I have an early start in the morning.'

'Turning into quite the little businesswoman, aren't you?'

Celine had bristled at his amused tone and prayed that he'd leave soon. It was weird that a body that had aroused her only minutes before could so quickly lose its appeal. After pouring another whiskey into him and flattering his ego for half an hour, Celine finally got Kevin to the door.

'I'll be in touch,' he'd told her after another long, languorous kiss.

'Great.' Celine had waved him off and promised herself that she wouldn't call him any more.

And now here she was again agreeing to see him. She put down the phone and went to make the bed. When she'd finished tidying her room, she went into the kitchen and poured herself a large drink. She took it over to the window, curled up on the ledge and stared out at the skyline.

She didn't feel as turned on as she usually did when Kevin was on his way. How much that had to do with Richard Lawrence she wasn't sure. She felt very attracted to him but a relationship with him would be messy. She didn't have to worry about commitment – he was clearly not interested in that. But he was her landlord and would be in her life as long as she was running the shop and that could prove awkward. Being attracted to the wrong men seemed to be her forte. How had she managed to end up with Dermot? She smiled as she remembered that she wouldn't have if it hadn't been for his perseverance – he just wouldn't take no for an answer. He hadn't been her type, Celine had thought, and dismissed him, but Dermot wouldn't leave her alone. There were flowers, cards and phone calls until she'd eventually agreed to go out on a date with him.

That evening had been a revelation. Within minutes, they were talking as if they'd known each other for years. Celine had never felt so comfortable with a man before. A week later, Dermot had told her he loved her and asked her to marry him. She'd refused, told him he was silly, that he didn't know what love was. The following week she had capitulated and six months later they were married.

They had laughed at couples that said you had to work at the first year of marriage. They settled into life together as if they'd never known any other way. They finished each other's sentences, read each other's thoughts and agreed on all the important issues. Celine's eyes filled at the memory of her perfect marriage. That, she realised, must be why she was attracted to such unreliable men these days. She knew that it would be impossible to replace Dermot.

The noise of the buzzer made her jump. Kevin was early. She would dearly love to turn him away because thinking of Dermot had killed any sexual urges. She went to the door and pressed the button. As she opened the door she was surprised to see Richard.

'It's not a good idea to open the door without knowing who's there, Celine.'

'I was expecting someone.'

'Oh.' He looked disappointed. 'I was going to ask you to come for a drink.'

'I'm sorry but—'

'Yeah, you're expecting someone.'

Celine smiled and found herself wishing again that Kevin wasn't coming over. 'You could join me for a quick drink here, if you like.'

'Yeah, why not?' Richard sat down on the sofa while Celine went into the kitchen.

'Wine, beer or something stronger?'

'A beer please.'

Celine brought him a beer and then poured herself some more wine.

'How are you and Rose getting on lately?'

'We're doing okay.'

'I'm glad.'

'You're a very involved landlord, aren't you?'

'Just nosey.' He winked at her. 'No, Rose has been a friend as much as a tenant. She really needs this operation but I know she'd cancel it in a heartbeat if she was needed. So are you looking forward to running the shop on your own?'

Celine nodded. 'I am actually. It should be fun.'

'Well, you've got me and Dominic to call on if you need anything.'

'And Mary Boyle and Gerry,' Celine added.

'Oh, is Mary trying to fix you up already? She doesn't waste time. Next she'll be inviting you to tea.'

Celine chuckled. 'She already has. I can't wait to meet Gerry.'

'I'd love to be a fly on the wall.'

'How old is he? Thirty-five, forty?'

Richard nearly choked on his beer. 'Closer to fifty.'

'You're kidding!'

'Nope.'

'And he's still at home with his mother?'

'Yep.'

Celine shook her head. 'I can't believe that she'd think someone of my age would be interested.'

'She's getting desperate,' Richard explained.

'So you're chased by desperate women and I'm going to be chased by desperate mothers?'

Richard moved a little closer. 'Who would you rather be chased by?'

Celine's pulse quickened as she felt his breath on her cheek. 'Maybe I don't want to be chased at all.'

'That would be a shame.'

He traced a finger across her lips and Celine shivered in anticipation. When he bent his head to kiss her she closed her eyes but before his lips touched hers the buzzer went.

'Ignore it,' Richard murmured.

Celine was tempted to but when the buzzer went again she pulled away from him, stood up and straightened her clothes. 'I can't.' She crossed the room and spoke into the intercom. 'Hello?'

'Hi, baby.'

Richard stood up, a slight smile on his lips. 'Ah.'

'I'm sorry—'

He held up a hand. 'Don't apologise. I was being very presumptuous.'

'It's not like that,' Celine started to explain as she opened the door.

On cue, Kevin reached the top stair, pinned her against the door and kissed her. When he finally stepped back he noticed Richard. 'Hello, there.'

Celine looked at the floor. 'Richard, this is Kevin. Kevin, this is Richard, my landlord.'

Kevin immediately stretched out his hand. 'Pleased to meet you.'

'You too. Right then, I've got my rent so I'll be off. Good night.'

Celine watched him until he got to the bottom of the stairs. 'Good night.'

Kevin pushed the door closed and dragged her into his arms. 'You look good enough to eat and I'm feeling very hungry.'

Celine slipped out of his arms. 'Let me get you a drink.'

Kevin pulled off his tie and stretched out on the sofa. 'I thought this place was rent-free?'

Celine returned with a large whiskey. 'It is. He just has a strange sense of humour.'

'So what did he want?'

Celine smiled slightly. 'He wanted to take me for a drink. Why, are you jealous?'

Kevin laughed. 'I'm not the jealous type, Celine, you know that. Let's go to bed.'

'No, I'm not in the mood.'

Kevin raised an eyebrow. 'Really?'

'Sorry, Kevin, but I've got a lot on my mind at the moment.'

He moved closer. 'I could help you forget.'

Celine looked at him and thought that Richard had sat where he was sitting less than ten minutes ago. 'I told you, I'm not in the mood.'

Kevin's smile disappeared as he picked up his tie and walked to the door. 'I tell you what, Celine. Why don't you give me a call when you are in the mood?'

She looked at him, her face grave. 'I don't think so.'

Five miles away, Rose was lowering herself into a herbal bath that would hopefully help her sleep. She winced as she tried to find a comfortable position and then rested her head against the inflatable cushion. Usually she tried to practise relaxation techniques in the bath but tonight all she could think of was Fergus and that damn job of his. She had been thrilled when he'd told her about it, it sounded wonderful and the pay was good too, but she knew her son well enough to know that he was holding something back. She'd let him talk for several minutes – the fact that he was babbling so much was a sure sign that he was nervous – and then she'd looked him in the eye. 'So what's the problem?'

Fergus had looked away. 'There's no problem, Ma.'

'Don't give me that, Fergus Lynch, I know you too well.'

Fergus had been silent for a moment and then he'd nodded slightly. 'The club is in Sandhill.'

Rose had felt her whole body tense. 'You can't take it.'

'Come on, Ma, it's a great opportunity.'

'It's a great opportunity to get yourself killed.'

'The place has changed, you wouldn't recognise it. They've built all these fancy apartments and there's a new shopping centre being built too.'

'It's too risky.'

'So what if I run into some of the gang? I'm not a kid any more, I can take care of myself.'

Rose had seen the look of determination on his face and given in. She had learned over the years that Fergus could only be pushed so far and the last thing she wanted was to drive him away. 'Are you sure, love?'

Fergus had beamed at her. 'I'm sure, Ma. It will be great, you'll see.'

But now as Rose lay in the bath, willing the water to take away her pain, her doubts resurfaced. Fergus had been involved with some very nasty characters and they had done their damnedest to get him back into drugs in the early days. He had resisted but only because he wasn't running into them on a daily basis. They had come to the shelter occasionally but Fergus was stronger and more secure there because he was never alone. Rose dreaded the thought of him coming face to face with any of that crowd on a regular basis. God only knew what they were into these days. But, she tried to console herself, he was older and wiser now. Rose closed her eyes and tried to persuade herself that everything would work out fine, but it was hard to ignore the sick feeling in her stomach.

Chapter 18

'Thanks so much, Jack,' Marina blew the estate agent a kiss as she closed the door and walked the short distance to Close Second. When she went in, Celine was talking to a rather attractive man.

'Well, hello.' She moved forward to kiss her friend's cheek but her eyes were on him.

'Hi, Marina. This is Dominic Nugent, he owns the newsagent's next door. Dominic, this is my best friend, Marina Flynn.'

Dominic held out a hand. 'Pleased to meet you.'

'And you,' Marina murmured.

Celine raised her eyebrows at her friend's sexy tone. She was used to Marina chatting up men but not average guys like Dominic. 'It's a bit early for lunch, Marina, and I'm on my own so I can't take a break.'

Marina dragged her eyes away from Dominic. 'Oh, that's okay. I just dropped in to say hello. I had an appointment with Jack Mullen, the estate agent.'

'Are you looking for a new house?' Celine asked in surprise.

'No, I'm selling up.' She took a deep breath. 'And moving in with Mum.'

'Oh.' Celine stared at her.

'I'll leave you two to chat,' Dominic moved towards the door. Marina didn't move a muscle so he had to squeeze past her. 'Excuse me. Nice to meet you.'

'The pleasure was mine,' Marina purred.

'Bye, Dominic,' Celine called as Dominic went out the door like a scalded cat. 'Honestly, Marina, you scared the poor man to death.'

'He's lovely, isn't he?'

Celine blinked. 'I can't say I noticed.'

'Oh, great eyes – I do love men in glasses – and he's got a gorgeous bum.'

'Dominic? He's not really your type, Marina. I mean, what about those cords?''

Marina shook her head. 'Don't be silly, Celine, clothes are easily sorted. He's not married, is he?'

'I don't think so.'

'Excellent.' Marina rubbed her hands together.

'Look, forget about Dominic for a minute, will you? Are you really moving in with your mum?'

Marina sighed. ''Fraid so. She has room, I'm broke . . .'

Celine frowned. 'I've told you before that I can lend you money—' She would be only too happy to hand over some of Dermot's insurance money to her friend.

Marina held up a hand. 'And I've told you thank you, but no thank you.'

'You are a very stubborn woman.'

'And you love me dearly.' Marina turned to examine the clothes rails. 'So how's the job going?'

Celine smiled. 'Good.'

'When does your boss go into hospital?'

'Next Sunday. The operation is on Monday.'

'So does that mean you won't be able to meet me for lunch any more?'

'Sure. Mondays I'm off and then Sadie works part-time when I need a break.'

'Excellent! Can't have you stagnating here all alone,' Marina said as she inspected a hound's-tooth trouser suit.

'No chance of that, someone always seems to be dropping by.'

'I'm glad.' Marina put the suit back and looked at her watch. 'I'd better go and collect Josh.'

'How does he feel about moving in with Granny?'

Marina made a face. 'I haven't told him yet.'

'I'm sure it will all work out fine. Kay is wonderful with him.'

Marina beamed at her. 'She is.' She hugged Celine and went to the door. 'We must go out for a drink soon, it's been ages.'

'I'd like that.'

'Great. I'll call you.'

Celine watched her leave. She hadn't told Marina about Fergus yet. Now that the worst of the crisis was over, though, she'd fill her in when they went for that drink. It would be nice to talk to someone who had been around when Dermot died and would understand why meeting Fergus after all this time was so hard for her. She moved around the shop, tidying shelves, re-hanging clothes and humming as she went. Now that Fergus was out of the picture it was as if a great weight had been lifted. He would not be visiting the shop at all in Rose's absence. If there was a problem, Richard would liaise between them. Celine smiled at the thought. That was another plus. She had seen him a couple of times since the night Kevin had walked in on them but he hadn't mentioned the episode. She stopped humming as she realised he hadn't asked her out again either. She had to make it clear that Kevin was out of her life, but how could she do that without looking too eager? Marina would chastise her for being so old-fashioned. If she fancied a man, she didn't think twice about letting him know. But that wasn't Celine's style. She'd just have to try and drop Richard a hint.

Dominic's smile froze when he turned to greet the customer, only to find it was Celine's friend.

'Oh, hello again.'

Marina leaned against the counter and smiled. 'Hi there. I hope you won't be shocked, Dominic – may I call you Dominic?'

'Of, of, course,' Dominic stammered.

'But life's too short for pussyfooting around, don't you think?'

'Well, I suppose—'

'So I'll just come right out and say it. Would you like to have a drink with me?'

'Er, well, I—'

Marina turned on her heel and went to the door. 'Please don't feel pressurised.'

'No! No, I don't!' Dominic stared at her. 'I'd love to have a drink with you.'

Marina beamed at him. 'Wonderful. How about the bar in the Four Seasons tomorrow night?'

'Er, that's fine. Shall I pick you up?'

'I just knew you were a gentleman! But no, thank you for asking, I'll be in town working tomorrow. Shall we say seven?'

Dominic nodded. 'Seven is fine.'

'Lovely, see you then.'

'See you then,' Dominic replied, but she'd already gone. He sniffed the air, breathing in the perfume she'd left behind. What an incredible, scary, beautiful woman. What on earth did she see in him? He moved into the back room and stood in front of the small mirror on the wall. He was in pretty good shape for a man of forty-three – playing squash with Richard helped. His hair was still thick and the grey bits blended into the sandy colour rather well. He grinned at himself as he adjusted his tie and straightened his glasses. As he went back into the shop, the door opened and two gum-chewing schoolboys came in. 'Hello, lads, what can I get you this lovely day?'

*

Marina hummed as she waited at the school gate for Josh. Who'd have thought that she'd meet such a lovely man at Close Second? She'd have to take things slowly though, because Dominic seemed the sort to scare easily. But she could be patient when she needed to be.

'Mummy!'

She crouched down and held her arms out as Josh ran towards her. 'Hello, darling, did you have a nice time?'

'Yes. Can we go to the playground, Mummy?'

'There's no time, darling, your music lesson starts in ten minutes.'

Josh scowled. 'I don't like music, I want to go to the playground.'

Marina thought of the money she'd already handed over for the lessons, but it was a lovely day and the fresh air would do Josh good. 'Okay, then, we'll go to the playground.'

'Hoorah! Thanks, Mummy.'

Marina tousled his hair and then pulled out her mobile to phone the music teacher. It was only money, after all. Later as she pushed her son on the swing, her thoughts returned to Dominic. She couldn't explain why this quiet man in his drab clothes had made her heart beat faster. Maybe it was because he was so different from the men she usually met and very different from her ex-husband. As a model, Ray had been very proud of his looks and, she suspected, had always loved himself more than his

wife or son. He did still see Josh occasionally on his
infrequent trips back from Birmingham but he was
more like an affectionate uncle than a loving father.
Marina knew her mother thought Josh was spoiled
and could do with a strong father figure in his life.
Maybe Dominic could be the one. Kay would like
him, that Marina was sure of. She had never approved
of Ray and though she didn't agree with divorce, she
hadn't been too upset when they split up. 'You were
too good for him,' she'd told her daughter.

'Mummy, can we go for an ice cream?' Josh asked.
Marina helped him off the swing. 'Why not?'

Chapter 19

Rose put another nightie in her bag and then sat down on the bed, exhausted. Tomorrow she would have her hip operation and now that it was so near, she felt nervous. What if something went wrong? What if it was unsuccessful? What if she ended up even more disabled? She heard Fergus coming up the stairs and forced a smile.

'You ready, Ma?'

'Ready.'

'The taxi should be here in a minute.' He took her bag and held out a hand to help her up.

'Now remember, I've left the freezer well stocked with food, there's emergency cash in my jewellery box and just talk to Richard if you have any problems.'

Fergus scowled. 'Ma, I'm twenty-four, I don't need babysitting.'

Rose patted his hand. 'I know love, but just in case.'

'Richard can take care of the shop but he's not taking care of me,' Fergus told her.

'Fine.' The last thing Rose wanted now was a row.

At the bottom of the stairs Fergus gave her a quick hug. 'Sorry, Ma.'

'That's okay, love, I know I'm fussing. Just put it down to nerves.'

'You'll be fine.'

'Of course I will.'

'Are you sure you've got everything?' he asked.

Rose chuckled. 'Now who's fussing?' A horn blasted outside. 'Right, let's go.'

Celine was having a late breakfast and reading the newspapers when the buzzer went. She went to answer it, wondering who could be calling on a Sunday morning. 'Hello?'

'Hi, Celine, it's Richard.'

Celine looked down in dismay at her grey jogging pants and old T-shirt. 'Come on up,' she said, opened the door and went back into the kitchen. 'Coffee?' she offered when he appeared in the doorway.

'I'd love one, thanks.'

Celine poured the coffee and put it in front of him. 'Have you been jogging?' she asked, noting the tracksuit and damp hair.

He shook his head. 'Just thrashed Dominic on the squash court.' He pulled down the zip of his top and Celine felt her eyes drawn to the dark curly hair on his chest.

'Are you bringing Rose into hospital today?'

'No, she was taking a taxi. Are you ready to take over the reins?'

Celine sliced a few more chunks off the French stick on the table. 'Yeah, no problem. Marmalade, cheese?' she offered.

'Cheese, please.' Richard spread butter on two pieces of bread. 'Well, if you need anything, let me know.'

Celine produced the cheese and watched as he cut two generous slices. 'Just keep Fergus out of my way.'

'No problem. He's got his hands full as it is with this new job.'

Celine didn't want to know. 'So have you any plans for the day?' she asked instead.

Richard nodded. 'I've a few things to do.'

'Oh.'

'But the reason I dropped by—'

'You wanted some breakfast?'

'That too.' He grinned. 'But the other reason was to ask you if you'd like to come over for dinner this evening. Unless of course you're seeing Kevin.'

Celine looked him in the eye. 'I'm not seeing Kevin any more.'

Richard raised an eyebrow. 'I see. Does that mean you're free?'

'I'm free,' Celine murmured and hid a smile behind her coffee cup.

Richard drained his cup and headed for the door. 'Good. Seven o'clock, don't be late.'

'Hang on, I don't even know where I'm going.'

Richard paused in the doorway and grinned. 'First

apartment block after the garage, in the front door and take the lift all the way to the top. See you later.'

Celine mentally went through her wardrobe as she finished her breakfast. Something sophisticated but not too dressy – it wouldn't do to look too eager. God, she felt like a teenager again! She wondered if Richard would ask her to stay the night. She wouldn't, of course she wouldn't, that would send the wrong message. Although she wasn't entirely sure what message she did want to send. She stood up and cleared away the breakfast things. She wasn't going to spend the day wondering about tonight. Perhaps she'd go for a walk or head into town, maybe visit the art gallery – it had been ages since she'd done that.

On impulse she phoned her dad to see if he could meet her. 'I was afraid you might be on the golf course,' she said when he answered.

'No, I thought I'd do a bit of gardening.'

'I was going to suggest we meet up in Dwyer's for a bit of lunch.'

'Sorry, love, but I'll never be finished by then. You could come over here though.'

'I don't think so.'

'Oh, come on, love, you can't stay away from Killmont for ever.'

Celine thought about it for a moment. Sundays were quiet and her father's house was on the outskirts of the town. It was unlikely she would meet anyone she knew. 'Okay, Dad, I'll see you about two and I'll bring lunch.'

'Great, see you then.'

Celine combed her hair, pulled on a denim jacket and grabbed her bag and sunglasses. As she stepped out on to the street she saw a bus coming around the corner.

'Celine!'

She turned to see Dominic. 'Hi, Dominic, sorry, got to run.'

'No problem, I just wondered if it would be okay if I gave Cathy Donlan your phone number.'

'Who?'

'The producer of "My Fair Lady"?'

'Oh, right, yeah, that's fine.'

'Great. See you later.'

Celine got to the stop just as the bus pulled up. When she'd bought her ticket, she went upstairs and sat at the front. This had always been her favourite place to sit as a child. She felt unusually optimistic and positive today as she looked out on a Dublin bathed in spring sunshine. The prospect of running the shop alone excited her. She also felt more relaxed now that she didn't have to creep around for fear of bumping into Fergus. And the thought of the evening ahead alone with Richard made her shiver with anticipation. Even going back to Killmont didn't seem so hard now that she was finished with Kevin and had a clear conscience.

As it was such a nice day, Celine opted to wander around Merrion Square instead of going into the gallery. As usual, the railings were chock-a-block with paintings and the artists sat in deck chairs talking among themselves and watching the world go by. Celine liked to come here just to browse but today she was on the lookout for something for her living room. She saw a few paintings she liked but nothing compared with the one she'd seen in Café Napoli. As she left the square, she promised herself she'd ask Tracy again about the artist. She could always call him or her and make an offer. Making her way to the supermarket at the top of Baggot Street, she bought ham, turkey, a mixed salad and fresh bread rolls. At two on the dot, she stepped off the bus in Killmont and started the short walk to her family home. As she'd hoped, there was no one about and she breathed a sigh of relief as she turned into the driveway without incident.

'Oh good, you're here, I could eat a horse.' Her father kissed her cheek. 'Just let me wash my hands.'

'Shall I put on the kettle or would you prefer a beer?'

'Definitely beer,' he called.

Celine chuckled as she set the food out on the table and rooted in the fridge for the beer.

Frank reappeared, drying his hands in a towel. 'We can have it in the garden if you like, it's quite warm now.'

'Lovely. Shall I make you up a roll or would you prefer it on a plate?'

'A roll would be lovely.' Frank twisted the top off

his beer and downed half of it. 'Thirsty work. So what did you do this morning?'

'Went into Merrion Square.'

'Nice day for it.'

Celine sighed. 'Yes, but I couldn't find what I wanted.'

'Oh, you want to buy?'

'Yes, something for the living room. Ham or turkey?'

Frank grinned. 'Both.'

Celine crammed the meat into a buttered roll and added some salad and mayonnaise. 'There you go.'

'Thanks, love.'

When Celine had made herself a small salad they took their lunch outside and sat on the deck at the back of the garden. 'You did a good job,' she said, looking around at the manicured lawn and colourful flowerbeds.

'I need to plant some more shrubs but I'll wait for a couple of weeks. There's still a bit of frost at this time of the year.'

Celine sighed and stretched out her legs. 'I can't believe it's almost May.'

'You'll miss your garden,' Frank remarked.

'Yes, but there's a tiny little courtyard at the back of the shop and apparently it's a real sun trap. I can nip down the fire escape any time I want.'

'That's nice.' Frank finished his roll and sat back to enjoy his beer.

'How's Brenda?'

He shot her a wary look. 'Why do you ask?'

Celine shrugged. 'Just wondering if she's forgiven me yet.'

'She has other things on her mind at the moment,' Frank murmured.

Celine pushed her food away and leaned forward on the table. 'What do you mean, Daddy, what's wrong?'

Frank sighed. 'I shouldn't really be telling you but to tell the truth I'm worried.'

'For God's sake, Daddy, what? Is Brenda sick?'

'No. Well, yes, I suppose she is. She's suffering from depression. The doctor has put her on anti-depressants and she's going to see some kind of specialist next week.'

'A psychiatrist?'

'Yes, that's it. Oh, Celine, she's not the same woman at all.'

'In what way?'

'She cries all the time and she won't go out. The house is a mess and I don't think she's cooked in weeks.'

Celine's eyes widened. Brenda had always been the perfect housewife, her house always smelling of either polish or freshly baked bread. 'What does Alan think?'

'He's in England on some course or other.'

'He must come home. She shouldn't be in the house on her own.'

'I agree but Brenda won't tell him she's sick and she's sworn me to secrecy.'

Celine banged her beer down on the table. 'But how could he go away and leave her when she's like this? What was he thinking of?'

'To be fair, he left before she had her breakdown.'

'Breakdown? Jesus, Daddy, why didn't you tell me?'

'The way things were between you I don't think she'd have appreciated it.'

'But she needs someone to look after her, Daddy. We can't just stand by and do nothing.'

'I call in every day,' Frank protested. 'I bring her a few groceries, though, from the look of her, I'd say she doesn't eat any of it. And I stay to chat for a while.'

'Does she chat?' Celine asked.

He shook his head. 'No, I waffle on for half an hour and then she tells me she's tired and wants to have a nap.'

'I'm going over there,' Celine announced.

'I don't think—'

'Daddy, I'm going over there right now and it would make it easier if you came with me.'

Frank stood up slowly. 'Yes, okay then. Let me get changed.'

Twenty minutes later, Frank drove them the short distance to Alan and Brenda's house. The first thing Celine noticed was litter in the garden and junk mail hanging out of the letterbox. She watched as her father went to pick up the offending rubbish and then rang the doorbell.

'She doesn't always answer,' he warned, and rang the bell again.

The door opened slowly and Brenda peeked out. She opened the door properly when she saw Frank but stopped when she caught sight of Celine.

'Hello, Brenda.'

Brenda shot Frank a venomous look.

'I'm sorry, love, but I was worried about you. Celine wants to help.'

Brenda turned her back on them and went into the living room. Celine and Frank exchanged glances and followed.

'How are you, Brenda?' Celine asked. She was shocked by her sister-in-law's appearance. Normally neat and tidy, Brenda was wrapped in a stained housecoat and her hair was dirty. But it was her gaunt, pale face and haunted eyes that really frightened Celine.

'Fine.' Brenda sat down, her expression blank.

Celine dropped to her knees and took Brenda's hand. 'Oh, Bren, what is it, what's wrong?'

Her sister-in-law refused to look at her. 'Go away.'

Celine shook her head. 'No chance. It doesn't matter what you do or say, Brenda, I'm not leaving. So you may as well talk to me.'

Brenda looked at her for the first time, her expression bleak. 'Oh, Celine.'

'I'm here, Brenda. I'll take care of you.'

Brenda fell into her arms and started to cry like a child. 'He's gone, Celine, he's gone.'

'Alan will be back, love,' Frank patted her shoulder. 'He'll be back as soon as the course is over.'

'Not Alan,' Brenda sobbed.

Celine sat back on her heels and looked into Brenda's eyes. 'Dermot?' she asked softly.

Brenda nodded. 'I miss him so much.'

Celine felt tears prick the back of her eyes. 'I do too.'

Chapter 20

By the time Celine got back to the flat it was almost
seven. There was no time for a shower so she splashed
some water on her tear-stained face and pulled on
black jeans and a pink silk top. Having let her hair dry
naturally this morning it was now like a wild bush
around her face so she slicked it back with gel. A
quick slash of pink lipstick and a spray of perfume
and she decided she'd have to do. She put on earrings
and a bracelet as she went in search of her boots and
then, grabbing a bottle of wine and her jacket, she ran
out the door and down the stairs. As she hurried up
the road she thought about the emotional afternoon
she'd spent with her sister-in-law. When they'd both
started to cry, Frank had withdrawn and left them to
it. In the time-honoured tradition, he had made a
large pot of tea, found himself an ancient newspaper
and retreated to the garden.

Celine kept her head down now as she hurried past
the garage – she couldn't cope with Mary Boyle
tonight – and turned into the gravelled driveway of
the modern apartment block. When she pressed the

buzzer for the top floor she heard Richard telling her to come up. Inside the silent, luxurious reception area, she crossed the deep pile carpet to the lift and stepped inside. When the door opened on the top floor she found herself in a cosy little hallway with just one door.

Richard opened it immediately. 'You're late.'

'Sorry,' Celine said, breathless after all the rushing. 'I got delayed.' She was glad she hadn't had time to dither over her wardrobe as he was wearing his customary faded blue jeans and a black shirt.

Richard steered her across the living room to a comfortable sofa. 'Relax, I'll get you a drink. Is champagne okay?'

Celine raised an eyebrow. 'Are we celebrating something?'

He grinned. 'Of course.' As he disappeared around the corner into what Celine presumed was the kitchen, she looked around her. The large room was decorated in pale, neutral colours and a number of lamps of various shapes and sizes were dotted around, but it was the view that Celine couldn't believe. Hopefield was spread out below and in the distance the sun was disappearing fast behind the Dublin Mountains.

'It's amazing,' she murmured as Richard reappeared at her side with two glasses.

'Now you see why I told you not to be late. Five more minutes and you'd have missed it.' They watched until the last sliver of light was gone and then Richard took a remote control and turned up the lights.

'Very nice,' Celine murmured and moved around the room to study the numerous paintings on the wall.

'Are you an art lover?' Richard asked.

'Oh, yes. I was in Merrion Square today looking for something for my sitting room.'

'Any luck?'

She shook her head. 'No, but then I'd already seen something that was perfect. Did you see the paintings that Tracy had up in the café?'

'Er, yes.'

'I don't suppose you know who the artist is.'

'I do actually.'

'Fantastic! There was one just beside the door—'

Richard took her hand and led her down a corridor.

'Where are we going?' she asked. Surely it was manners to feed her before trying to get her into bed?

Richard paused in front of a door and nodded for her to go in.

Celine opened it and Richard flicked a switch, flooding the large room with brilliant light. The room was lined with built-in cupboards that were littered with paints and brushes, an easel stood near the window and canvases were stacked in one corner. As well as a floor to ceiling window that took up most of one wall, there were two skylights in the wood-panelled ceiling. 'I had no idea,' Celine breathed. And then she gasped when she turned around and saw the painting that she'd coveted in the café. 'Did you do this?'

Richard looked almost shy. 'Yeah.'

'It's fantastic. I didn't know you were an artist.'

He shrugged. 'It's just a hobby.'

Celine shook her head as she moved over to the stack of canvases. 'May I?'

'Sure.'

Celine flicked through the paintings, pausing now and then to have a closer look. Most of them were landscapes or seascapes and there were a couple of portraits. 'That's Rose!' She pulled out the small canvas and smiled. 'It's excellent. Did she pose for you?'

Richard grinned. 'Not consciously.'

Celine put it down. 'When you dragged me in here I really didn't expect you to show me your etchings!'

Richard laughed. 'I never bring anyone in here.'

Celine smiled. 'Then I'm honoured.'

The buzzer sounded and Richard excused himself.

Celine froze. God, had she got it wrong? Maybe this wasn't going to be a cosy dinner for two after all.

'Celine, dinner!'

'Coming,' she called and went back out to the living room.

'We're eating in the kitchen, I hope you don't mind.'

Celine followed his voice and smiled when she saw the table by the window set for two. 'Mind? With a view like that?' Looking out on the small town bathed in twilight, Celine thought that just living here would be an inspiration to paint.

'Then I'll just apologise for the food,' Richard said as he carried several containers to the table. 'I lost track of time today and didn't get to cook,' he explained. 'But our local Indian restaurant delivers.'

Celine laughed. 'Smells wonderful.'

'It does, doesn't it? Now, more champagne or would you prefer something else?'

Celine shook her head. 'Champagne and Indian food, sounds like the perfect combination.'

'And you are the perfect guest,' he told her as he removed the lids. 'I didn't know what you liked so I just got a bit of everything.'

Celine laughed. 'It's just as well I never got to finish lunch.'

'Why was that?'

Celine sobered at the question. 'Oh, nothing, just a family crisis.'

'Are there many in your family?'

'Just me and my dad,' Celine explained. 'But I have a sister-in-law, Brenda.'

'Are you close?'

Celine thought about the way she and Brenda had clung to one another that afternoon. 'We weren't but I think that's changed. Have you any family?'

Richard shook his head. 'My parents were killed in a car crash when I was five. My father's brother raised me. He died last year.'

Celine nodded. 'Ronan Lawrence? Yes, I remember reading about it. Were you close?'

He smiled. 'Very. From the moment he took me in, I went everywhere with him. He even got a hard hat specially made for me so that I could visit all of the building sites.'

'He wanted you to follow him into the business then?'

Richard shrugged. 'It was taken for granted. It was the family business.'

'What about your painting? Surely you must have wanted to pursue a career in art?'

Richard's smile was sad. 'I thought about it,' he admitted, 'but Ronan had a stroke when I was eighteen and I had to join the business a lot earlier than we'd expected.'

'That must have been hard.'

'Not really. Ronan was alive and that's all that mattered.'

'Did he know you were interested in painting?'

'Oh, yes, he encouraged it. He thought I should study architecture at college and put my talent to good use. It would never have occurred to him that I might just study art.'

'Do you resent that?'

He looked shocked. 'Of course not! If I'd explained the situation to him he would have supported me one hundred per cent, he was that kind of guy.'

Celine considered this and thought that Richard must be a very special man to act so unselfishly. 'So, if it's just a hobby, how come your paintings were hanging in Café Napoli?'

'That was Bob's idea and it was a one-off.'

'But that's such a shame,' she protested. 'There were plenty of paintings in Merrion Square today that weren't nearly as good.'

'Well, thanks for the compliment but I'm not interested.'

'But it's such a waste,' she persisted.

'That's good coming from you,' he retorted. 'Weren't you once the most promising young designer in Ireland?'

Celine put down her fork. 'Who told you that?'

'Rose, of course. She couldn't believe her luck when you walked into her shop.'

Celine picked up her fork again and pushed the food around on her plate. 'She exaggerated. Anyway, it was a long time ago.'

Richard smirked. 'Ah, of course.'

'Look, I don't design any more but you paint. Why hide it?'

'Like I said, I do it for my own enjoyment.'

Celine looked around her. 'Well, I realise you don't need the money, but if you sold your work you would be giving enjoyment to others too.'

It was Richard's turn to put down his fork. 'Let's make a deal. If I promise not to nag you about designing will you stop hassling me about painting?'

Celine smiled. 'I'm sorry, I didn't mean to hassle you, it's just that you're so good—'

Richard raised a finger to his lips. 'Ah-ah.'

'Sorry,' she muttered and concentrated on her food.

Richard smiled. 'Let's talk about something more interesting. Tell me about Kevin.'

Celine choked on a piece of chicken and reached for her wine. 'I don't think I want to talk about him either,' she said when she'd recovered.

'Did he break your heart?'

Celine burst out laughing. 'Certainly not!'

Richard smiled. 'Glad to hear it.' He leaned across and touched the side of her mouth. 'Sauce,' he explained and licked his finger.

Celine gulped and dabbed at her mouth with a napkin. 'Gone?'

'I'm not sure, come closer,' he murmured.

Celine's eyes flickered between his eyes and mouth as she moved closer.

'There's just a little bit here.' He pressed his mouth to the side of hers and she felt his tongue on her skin. She shivered and closed her eyes. 'And here.' He moved to the other side of her mouth and she barely suppressed a moan. 'And here.' This time his lips touched hers in a very light kiss. When he stopped, she opened her eyes to find that his face was barely an inch from hers. Without stopping to think about it, Celine snaked a hand around his neck and pulled his mouth to hers. Without taking his lips from hers, Richard lifted her to her feet, pulled her around the table and dragged her onto his lap. Celine rubbed her body against his and dragged her hands through his thick, wavy hair. Richard slipped his hands under her silk shirt and ran them up and down her back. 'Would you like to move somewhere more comfortable?' he murmured against her lips.

'Okay.' Celine looked at him through half-closed eyes.

Richard stood up, kissed her again and then led her into the living room. He reached for the remote with one hand, dimmed the lights and pushed her down on the sofa. Celine wound her legs and arms around him. 'Now you can't go anywhere,' she whispered and kissed his ear.

'Trust me, I don't want to,' he said and pulled her mouth to his. Celine knew that things were moving much too fast but she couldn't stop it and she didn't want to. Richard dragged her top over her head and when her bra followed, she went to work on his shirt and soon it was skin against skin. Richard pulled her to her feet again. 'Come to bed with me.'

Celine pressed her lips against his chest and then looked up into his eyes. 'I thought you'd never ask.'

Chapter 21

Fergus loved his new job but he was finding it hard to concentrate this morning. His eyes kept flicking to the clock but the time seemed to be dragging. The nurse had told him the operation wouldn't be over until after eleven and then Rose would be in recovery for about an hour. All in all, there was no point in him visiting before the afternoon. The club was quiet and after cleaning down the tables, he went for a wander around the gym and pool area. There weren't many customers on a Monday morning so the trainers were hanging around too. They were a nice enough gang, most of them younger than he was, and John, the supervisor, had offered to give him a few tips. 'You could do with some weight training,' he'd said, running a practised eye over Fergus's wiry frame. 'Are you fit?'

Fergus had shrugged. 'Probably not. I used to play football in school but now the only exercise I get is running for the bus.'

'I could give you a programme to follow if you're interested,' John offered.

'That would be great.' Fergus thought it might be a good idea to be fit now that he was back in Sandhill. So far, he had seen none of the old gang and he was hoping that it would stay that way. He wandered over to the window that looked out onto the pool. There was a man doing relentless laps in the lane, two young girls messing about in the shallow end and a mother teaching her toddler to float.

'It's very quiet today, isn't it?'

Fergus looked around and smiled at the tiny blonde. 'Hi, Sarah, how's it going?'

'Oh, I'm bored. One of my ladies was supposed to come in for a workout at ten but she phoned to cancel. Honestly, the number of people who pay a fortune to join this place and then throw in the towel after a couple of weeks.'

Fergus grinned. 'Vincent must love customers like that.'

Sarah sighed. 'Maybe but I find it very demoralising. I'm working my butt off to get these people fit and they give up so easily.'

Fergus took her hand and led her back into the snack bar. 'What you need is one of my special fruit smoothies.'

Sarah groaned. 'You're just looking for a guinea pig.'

'Rubbish, my smoothies are legendary.'

'That's what worries me!' Sarah laughed and climbed onto a stool. 'Go on then, but give me something with strawberries, I love strawberries.'

Fergus looked up his notes. 'I've got just the thing, you're going to love this.'

Sarah watched as he chopped fruit and dropped it into the juicer. Within minutes, he presented her with a pink concoction in a tall glass. 'It looks pretty,' she admitted and then took a tentative sip. 'Oh, it's lovely, Fergus.'

He grinned. 'You see, I told you I was good.'

Sarah fluttered her eyelashes over the rim of her glass. 'Have you any other talents?'

Fergus felt his face redden and he busied himself tidying up behind the counter.

'A few of us are going out for a drink on Wednesday, would you like to come?'

Fergus stopped. 'Er, well, I'm not sure—'

She shrugged. 'No big deal.'

Fergus nodded. 'Yeah, why not, that would be fun.'

Sarah smiled. 'Great.'

An hour later, he was on his way to the hospital to visit his mother. She probably wouldn't be back in her ward yet but when Vincent had come in search of a coffee and seen him drumming his fingers nervously on the counter he'd told him to go.

'You'll make the customers nervous,' he'd said with a sympathetic grin. 'Go and check on your mother and we'll see you later.'

Fergus smiled as he looked out the window of the bus. This job was turning out to be great. An understanding boss, free workouts and a gorgeous girl like Sarah chatting him up. The bus pulled up outside the hospital and he jumped off. When he arrived in St Bridget's ward on the second floor, the nurse recognised him immediately. 'You're Rose's son, aren't you?'

He nodded. 'How is she?'

'Why don't you see for yourself?'

Fergus hurried in and was amazed to see his mother awake.

'Hello, love,' she croaked.

The nurse followed him in. 'How are you feeling, Rose?'

'A bit groggy and my throat hurts. Can I have a drink?'

'Not yet, love. I'll get you some water and swabs and you can wet your lips.'

When she'd left, Fergus sat down beside his mother. 'Are you really okay, Ma?'

'Fine, love, but I could murder a cup of tea.'

'Did they tell you if everything went all right?' He looked nervously at the cage that covered her leg.

'The surgeon said it all went fine but he's going to come and talk to me tomorrow.'

The nurse returned with a glass of water and swabs and handed them to Fergus. 'Just wet her lips for the moment. She can have a proper drink in a few hours. Now, Rose, as soon as you feel any pain, let me know and I'll get you something.'

Fergus held a wet swab to Rose's mouth and she sucked on it. 'I don't think you're supposed to do that, Ma.'

'Are you going to tell on me?' Rose asked, her eyes twinkling. 'How's work going?'

'Fine. Really good.'

'You haven't met any of *them*, have you?'

Fergus sighed. 'No, Ma, I haven't. Now stop worrying about me and concentrate on getting well.'

She nodded and then froze, a grimace on her face.

'Pain?' Fergus asked.

'Yes.'

'I'll get the nurse.' He stood up and went out to the desk. 'My mother's in a bit of pain.'

'I'll be right in.'

Fergus went back to his mother. She had her eyes closed and Fergus thought she looked very vulnerable – not at all like his ma.

The nurse appeared at his side. 'Now, Rose, I'm going to give you an injection and then I think you should get some sleep.'

'Right, I'll go, Ma. I'll be back in this evening.'

Rose opened her eyes. 'Leave it until tomorrow, love.'

'Are you sure?' He looked at the nurse.

'Sleep is the best thing for your mother now,' she assured him. 'She'll be off the drip and ready for visitors tomorrow.'

'Okay then. Do you want me to bring in anything, Ma?'

Rose shook her head. 'Just you.'

He bent to kiss her forehead. 'See you tomorrow.'

As he left the hospital, Fergus took out his mobile and sent Richard a text message. SURGERY SUCCESSFUL. NO VISITORS TIL 2MORO.

Celine was on her knees taking up the hem on some trousers when Richard came in. She removed pins from her mouth. 'Do you want to go through and I'll be with you in a minute?'

Richard disappeared and Celine smiled up at the girl balancing on the chair. 'Nearly finished.'

'I'd hurry too for a guy like that,' the girl said.

Celine's smile got broader. 'There! Now, have a look in the mirror.'

The girl stepped down and studied the shortened trousers. 'Oh, that's great! They hang so much better now. So how much for these and the jacket?'

Celine picked up the jacket. 'The collar is a little worn so let's say fifty-five for the lot.'

'Great, thanks.'

Celine nipped out the back while the girl went into the dressing room to change. 'Hi, there.'

Richard pulled her into his arms and kissed her. 'I just dropped by to tell you Rose is fine.'

Celine grinned. 'You could have phoned.'

He shook his head. 'Then I wouldn't have been able to do this.' And he kissed her again.

Celine broke away. 'So tell me about Rose.'

'All I know is she's fine and she's not allowed visitors until tomorrow.' He bent his head to kiss her again.

'I've got to get back to my customer,' Celine whispered, her cheeks flushed. 'Don't go away.'

Celine quickly wrapped the clothes in tissue paper, put them in a bag and waited until the door had closed before she hurried back to Richard. 'Sadie will be back from lunch soon and then I'm free for the afternoon,' Celine told him after another long lingering kiss.

Richard slipped a hand under her jacket. 'Oh?'

'If you've nothing better to do, you could go on up to the flat and make yourself a drink while you're waiting.'

Richard's hand hovered around the catch on her bra. 'I don't like waiting.'

'I'll make it worth your while,' Celine assured him.

'Okay, then, but don't be long.'

'Fifteen minutes at the most,' she promised, leading him back into the shop.

When Sadie returned, Celine grabbed her bag and jacket.

'Is there any news on Rose?' the older woman asked.

'Yes, she's fine.'

'Thank God.'

'Yes, I'll see you later then, Sadie.'

'You will be back, won't you? Only I can never manage that bugger of an alarm.'

'I'll be back,' Celine promised, halfway out the door.

'Is there enough change in the till?'

Celine took a deep breath. 'Yes, there is.'

Sadie nodded. 'Okay, then, see you later.'

Richard had left the front door open and Celine went in, shut it firmly behind her and hurried upstairs. The kitchen and living room were empty so Celine went into the bedroom. 'Presumptuous, aren't you?' she said when she saw him stretched out on the bed, his arms behind his head.

'Optimistic,' he countered. 'Come here.'

Chapter 22

After Celine had closed the shop, she decided to go and see Brenda but on the two bus rides to Killmont, it was thoughts of Richard that filled her head. She had been sexually attracted to him from the beginning, but she hadn't been prepared for his tenderness and consideration. Lying in bed with him this afternoon, talking and laughing, had reminded her of how good it was to be part of a couple. She hadn't thought she'd ever want to be with any man like that again but Richard was changing her mind. His paintings were a part of it. He had to be a sensitive soul to create such beauty. It was such a pity that he wouldn't let anyone see them. She smiled slightly. That he'd shown them to her, that must mean something.

The bus pulled up at the end of Brenda's road and she hopped off. She walked quickly, her head held high. Somehow she didn't feel like apologising for being alive today. As she turned into the drive of the modern, detached bungalow, Celine hoped that Brenda wasn't regretting talking to her yesterday, so she was relieved when her sister-in-law opened the door, smiling.

'Celine, what are you doing here?'

Celine hugged her. 'I just wanted to make sure that you're okay.'

Brenda nodded. 'Getting there. Come on in, I'll open some wine.'

'Wine?' Celine followed her inside. Brenda never drank during the week and she rarely offered alcohol to anyone else either.

Brenda noticed the look on Celine's face as she fetched a corkscrew. 'It must be the tablets.'

Celine chuckled. 'It's good to see you smile.'

Brenda poured the wine and handed her a glass. 'Don't get your hopes up, I'll probably be crying again in a minute. But I felt better after our talk yesterday.'

Celine shook her head. 'I had no idea that Dermot's death was still such a problem for you.'

Brenda sighed. 'Neither did I. My GP says it's quite normal for people to lapse into depression years after an event. He says talking to the psychiatrist will help.'

'How do you feel about that?' Celine knew Brenda would not find it easy opening up to a stranger.

'I don't have much choice. If I don't pull myself together soon I'll lose Alan.'

Celine's instincts were to assure her that Alan would never leave but she didn't know that so she kept her mouth shut.

'I called him last night,' Brenda continued. 'I knew he'd be happy that you and I had talked.'

'When will he be home?'

'The week after next. He did offer to come home straight away,' Brenda assured her, 'but I thought it might be a good idea if I had some time to myself.'

Celine nodded. 'Can I ask a question?'

'Sure.'

'Why were you so upset about me and Kevin?'

Brenda studied her hands. 'Alan had an affair last year.'

Celine instinctively reached out a hand. 'Oh, Brenda!'

'It wasn't really an affair. It didn't last more than a couple of weeks.'

'How did you find out?' Celine stared at her, wide-eyed.

Brenda gave a mirthless laugh. 'A well-meaning friend told me she saw them together. I wish she hadn't. I would have been better off in ignorance.'

'Did you confront Alan?'

'Yes. He admitted it straight away. It was already over by then. He said he was sorry, I forgave him . . .'

'But you didn't forget?'

'I tried but I knew things would never be the same again.'

'And finding out about me and Kevin didn't help. I'm so sorry.'

'To be honest, when he hightailed it to London I was afraid he'd found someone else.'

'He hasn't, has he?'

'No. it's strictly business, thank God. I asked him

last night. We talked for ages, Celine, it was wonderful. He may be miles away but I feel closer to him today than I have in years.'

'I'm so glad.'

'Don't get me wrong, I know I'm not out of the woods yet. The doctor said there would be plenty of ups and downs.' Brenda shook her head. 'I'm glad I finally cracked, to be honest. It was going to happen sooner or later.'

'I know it's not going to be an easy time but I'll be with you all the way. You know, I don't think I'd have got through those first few months after Dermot died if it wasn't for you.'

'It was such a horrible time,' Brenda murmured. 'Poor Dermot.'

Celine was wistful. 'I used to hate it when people said that. Part of me was furious with him for getting himself killed.'

Brenda looked surprised. 'I didn't know that.'

'Nobody did,' Celine admitted. 'Why do we keep these things locked inside? Do you think it's just women that do it?'

'I doubt it. And we don't do it consciously, isn't that half of the problem?'

'I suppose.'

'Did you get counselling at the time, Celine? I can't remember.'

'I was supposed to but I couldn't face it.'

Brenda frowned. 'I think you should seriously consider it.'

'Now?' Celine looked at her in surprise. 'But I'm fine now.'

Brenda raised her eyebrows. 'Is that why you had an affair with Kevin Gilligan?'

Celine sighed. 'I told you, Kevin has nothing to do with Dermot.'

'I'm not so sure.'

Celine laughed. 'You're supposed to be getting counselling, not giving it!'

'But I've been thinking about it a lot. We all handle grief differently. I transferred my attention to you and you' – she shrugged – 'had an affair with a man who was unavailable.'

Celine's fingers tightened around the stem of her glass.

'I'm sorry, Celine, I should learn to keep my mouth shut.'

'It's okay, Brenda.'

'Alan's right, I just don't know when to mind my own business.'

'You care,' Celine told her and knew it to be true. 'And I do appreciate that.'

Brenda shot her a tremulous smile. 'You're more understanding than I am.'

'Ha! Don't you believe it! Are you okay?' she asked when she saw the smile fade from Brenda's eyes.

'Yes, I just get so afraid sometimes. I don't think I could cope if I lost Alan.'

Celine reached across and squeezed her hand. 'Alan's a good man and he loves you. He made a mistake but it's in the past now. You're the one he wants to spend his life with.'

Brenda took a gulp of her wine. 'I hope you're right, because I'm not as strong as you. I don't think I could go on alone.'

Celine's eyes narrowed. 'Don't talk like that, Brenda. You're not alone. You've got me and Daddy too.'

'I know.'

Celine stood up. 'I think you should have a nice bath and an early night. Do you have anything to help you sleep?'

Brenda nodded. 'The doctor gave me tablets that knock me out for the count.'

'Good. Look, I'll phone you tomorrow. Will you be all right?'

Brenda went with her to the door. 'Sure. Thanks for coming over.'

Celine hugged her. 'No problem. And call me any time, morning or night, if you need to talk.'

She was lost in thought as she walked down the road and never noticed the woman walking towards her.

'Well, really! I didn't think you'd have the nerve to show your face around here again.'

Celine smiled thinly at the lady captain of Killmont golf club. 'Hello, Audrey, nice to see you too.'

Audrey almost snorted. 'Some people have no idea how to behave!'

'I agree,' Celine said through gritted teeth. 'You should do something about that.'

Audrey stood staring, her mouth opening and shutting like a goldfish, as Celine marched off.

Celine prayed that a bus would come soon. She was sure that once Audrey got her breath back, she'd be back for round two. She sneaked a look over her shoulder but Audrey hadn't moved. Out of the corner of her eye, Celine saw the bus rounding the corner. With a cheery wave, she climbed on and went to the back of the bus so that she could continue waving until Audrey was out of sight. 'Totally childish,' she murmured, turning around in her seat, but the old bitch deserved it. Maybe she was the one behind the red letters. She was self-righteous enough to do something like that. Celine let out a long sigh as the bus headed for the city and left Killmont behind. Leaving home had definitely been the right thing to do for a number of reasons. And though it had only been a couple of months, Celine felt as though she belonged in Hopefield.

It was just gone nine when she got home and there was a note on the floor. Fleetingly, Celine wondered if her tormentor had discovered her new address, but the paper was an innocuous white. She picked it up and smiled as she read.

Fancy supper in my place? Home-cooked this time, I promise! Richard.

Celine picked up the phone and called his

apartment. 'I only just got in. Am I too late for supper?'

There was a short silence. 'I thought you might have got a better offer,' he said finally.

'I was visiting my sister-in-law,' Celine told him.

'Oh.'

'So, does the invitation still stand?'

'Yes, of course, I'm sorry.'

Celine smiled. 'That's okay. See you in five minutes.'

When she stepped out of the lift, Richard was waiting for her. He took her in his arms and kissed her. 'I'm sorry for behaving like a jealous schoolboy.' He looked down at her, his eyes suddenly serious. 'I've never felt like this before.'

Celine laughed. 'Then you're very lucky.'

He continued to study her. 'No, I just never cared before.'

Celine sidestepped him and went into the apartment. 'Where is this supper? I'm famished.'

Richard smiled. 'I'll allow your pathetic attempt to change the conversation but we will return to it later.'

Celine shot him a flirtatious look. 'I'd hoped you'd have other plans for me later.'

'Cheeky!' Richard said, leading her to the kitchen. 'I hope you like Italian.'

'Let me guess, spaghetti bolognese?'

'How did you know?'

Celine chuckled. 'Because that's all most men can cook.'

'I can cook more than that,' he protested.

'Oh, yes?'

'Yeah, I can do a mean mixed grill and my beans on toast are amazing.'

'A regular Jamie Oliver,' Celine teased.

'Pukka!' Richard grinned back as he gave the pasta a stir. 'So you and your sister-in-law must be very close, seeing each other two days running.'

'Not really, but she's going through a difficult time and I wanted to make sure she was okay. Can I do anything to help?'

'Just pour the wine.'

Celine filled two goblets with the Barolo that was open on the counter. 'I'm only going to have one. I've already had a couple with Brenda and I don't want to be hung over in the morning. Did you get any more news on Rose?'

'No. I'll go in and see her tomorrow, do you want to come?'

'I don't think we should go together. Why don't you go in the afternoon and I'll drop by in the evening?'

Richard raised an eyebrow. 'Are you ashamed of me?'

'No, I just like to keep my private life private. Anyway, she shouldn't have too many visitors so soon after surgery.'

Richard ladled the food onto two plates and carried them to the table. 'Yes, you're probably right.'

'Looks good,' Celine admitted.

He grinned. 'You must be hungry!'

'Ravenous.'

'Well, eat up, you're going to need the energy.'

Celine frowned. 'Actually, I have a bit of a headache.'

'You're kidding.'

She smiled. 'Yes, I am.'

Chapter 23

Marina applied a second coat of red lipstick and pouted at her reflection. She was getting ready for her third date with Dominic Nugent and she felt uncharacteristically nervous. The first night they'd met for drinks, the second, they went to dinner, but tonight she was going to Dominic's house. So far, he had kissed her hand or her cheek. Tonight, Marina had other plans. She was convinced that under that quiet demeanour lurked a passionate man just waiting for the right woman to discover him. And she, Marina decided, was the right woman. She'd chosen to wear a demure black dress that fell to the knee but which showed off her beautiful figure. And her underwear – as Dominic would find out – was far from demure. She smiled at her reflection and turned her attention to her jewellery box. She ignored her more dramatic pieces and instead chose some simple gold earrings and a heavy bangle. Slipping her stockinged feet into low black pumps, she ran downstairs.

'You look lovely, dear,' Kay said, looking up from her newspaper.

'Thanks, Mum. What do you think, Josh?'

Her son scowled. 'You look yuck.'

'That's very rude,' Kay snapped.

'It's okay, Mum, I think he's a little bit upset at me going out again.'

'That's no excuse.'

Marina sighed and wondered if she should take her mother aside and have a chat. If they were going to live together there would have to be some rules about disciplining Josh. Marina had no objection to Kay taking control when she was at work but when Marina was there, Kay would have to learn to keep quiet. She was about to say something when Josh ran to her mother.

'Granny, will you help me make my jigsaw?'

'Of course, love.' Kay put aside her paper and got down on the ground beside him.

Marina smiled. Maybe it would be better to say nothing for the moment. Her mother might be a tough disciplinarian but there was no doubt she was great with Josh. 'I'll leave you to it,' she said, slipping her wrap around her shoulders.

'Josh, give Mummy a kiss,' Kay ordered.

Josh obediently ran to Marina.

'I love you, darling,' Marina murmured into his hair. 'I won't be late. Be good for Granny.'

'We'll be fine, love, you go and have a good time.'

Marina blew her a kiss. 'I will, Mum, thanks.'

*

It was about twenty minutes' drive to Dominic's house. His directions were excellent and Marina found the tiny cottage quite easily. She eased the car into the driveway and parked beside his ancient, grey Volvo estate. She smiled as she saw that Dominic was standing in the porch waiting for her. So much for her plans of finding herself a rich husband!

She joined him and lifted her cheek for his kiss. 'What a beautiful house.'

'Would you like a tour?' he offered as he drew her inside.

'Maybe later.'

'Then come through and I'll get you a drink.'

As Marina followed him, she admired the understated décor that allowed the beauty of the house to shine through.

'Gin and tonic?' Dominic asked as she settled on a small but comfortable sofa.

'Just a small one.'

'Did you find the house okay?'

'No problem.' She offered him a brilliant smile as he handed her the drink and went to make himself one. Marina noticed with satisfaction that his was rather larger and that his hand trembled slightly as he poured. She tapped her foot gently to the music playing in the background. 'I do love Bizet.' She noticed with amusement the surprise on Dominic's face. 'Just because I'm a model doesn't mean I'm completely uneducated,' she chided.

'I never thought that for an instant,' Dominic protested.

'I'm just teasing.'

Dominic took a seat opposite her. 'Sorry. Do you like opera?'

Marina nodded. 'Yes, but only the cheerful ones.'

Dominic threw back his head and laughed. 'I know what you mean. All that dying in garrets can be a bit wearing.'

'And it always takes so long for them to actually die,' Marina complained.

'You must come to see my Henry Higgins.'

'Pardon?'

'Didn't Celine tell you? Hopefield Musical Society are putting on "My Fair Lady".'

Marina's eyes widened. 'And you're the lead? Well, I didn't know you were a celebrity.'

'Hardly.'

Marina noticed with amusement the pleased look on his face. 'You must have a very good voice.'

He shrugged. 'It's not bad but to be honest, I think I got the part because of my age. Most of the male members are pensioners.'

'I'm sure you're just being modest. I'll look forward to your performance.'

Dominic paused, his drink halfway to his mouth. 'You'll come?'

'Well, of course I'll come.'

Dominic smiled. 'That would be nice. Now, I must go and check on dinner.'

'It smells lovely.'

'It's nice to have someone to entertain. I love experimenting.'

Marina made a face. 'I'm a lousy cook. I think it's the main reason Josh didn't object to moving in with Mum. He knew Granny would feed him well!'

Dominic chuckled and excused himself and Marina took the opportunity to have a closer look at his bookcase. Intertwined with some classics were biographies, murder mysteries and thrillers. Taking up a large spot on the bottom shelf was a copy of *Ulysses*.

'Have you actually read this?' She held it up for Dominic's inspection when he returned.

'Of course not,' he laughed, 'but it looks good, doesn't it?'

'It would if it weren't for all these thrillers next to it.'

'I'm a sucker for blood and guts,' he admitted.

Marina shook her head. 'You surprise me. You're such a gentle man.'

Dominic's eyes twinkled. 'Ah, never judge a book by its cover.'

Marina looked at him from under heavy lashes. 'I look forward to delving between the covers,' she murmured in a sexy drawl.

Dominic visibly gulped. 'Er, right, well, I'd say the food is ready.'

Marina stood up and crossed the room to stand just inches away from him. 'Good, because I'm really hungry.'

Dominic ducked out the door. 'This way then. I'm afraid I've no dining room so we're eating in the kitchen.'

'Much cosier,' Marina assured him and smiled when she saw the table was set with candles, flowers and linen napkins. 'You've gone to so much trouble.'

Dominic shrugged. 'Now, for starters, we have salmon pâté. Oh, God, you do like fish, don't you?'

'Love it.'

'Thank God for that, because you're getting more of it for the main course.'

Marina put her napkin in her lap and looked at the plate he put in front of her. At least five hundred calories, she figured. She'd have to starve tomorrow.

Dominic pulled a bottle of Chablis from an ice bucket on the window ledge and poured it into crystal glasses. 'Cheers.'

'Cheers.' Marina smiled at him. 'Thank you so much for inviting me.'

Dominic beamed happily as he took his seat opposite her. 'It's my pleasure.'

'So apart from music and books have you any other hobbies?'

'I play squash.'

Marina nodded in approval and her eyes slid to the outline of his torso under the heavy cotton shirt. 'I like a man who keeps in shape.'

Dominic reddened. 'Not as much as I should. Richard drags me out for a game when he's about.'

'Richard Lawrence?'

'Yes, have you met him?'

'No, I haven't had the pleasure yet.'

'He's a nice guy, you'll like him.'

'How are he and Celine getting along?'

'Okay, I suppose. He's a very decent chap and I believe he bought a lot of new stuff for the flat.'

Marina rolled her eyes. 'That's not quite what I meant.'

'Oh? Oh!' Dominic nodded as the penny dropped. 'Well, I don't know if there's anything else going on. Celine is obviously a terrific girl. But Richard . . .'

'Yes?' Marina prompted.

Dominic sighed. 'Well, he's not really the settling-down type.'

Marina shrugged her slim shoulders. 'Neither is Celine.'

'She's a widow, I believe.'

Marina nodded. 'She was only twenty-one when Dermot died.'

'She must have been distraught.'

Marina put her head on one side. 'She was quite strong, actually. I'd have preferred it if she'd cried her eyes out.'

'More therapeutic,' Dominic agreed, 'but sometimes it takes a long time for people to deal with their feelings.'

Marina reached across and touched his hand. 'You seem to be speaking from experience.'

'Not really, I wasn't bereaved, although it felt like it at the time. I went out with a girl for nearly five years – we were engaged for three of them. But she found someone else.' He gave a short laugh. 'Unfortunately, she neglected to mention her new love to me. She left her father to do it at the church.'

'Oh, Dominic! How terrible!'

'I was pretty devastated,' he admitted.

'Is that when you decided to move to Ireland?'

He nodded. 'You see, they didn't have the decency to run away together. They set up home just around the corner. I couldn't take that, it was the final humiliation. So, I ran away.'

'Anyone would have in such an impossible situation,' Marina assured him.

'Maybe. Have you finished?' he asked.

Marina nodded and he took their plates over to the counter. She stared out of the window at the small garden and wondered why nice people always seemed to draw the short straw.

When Dominic had served their main course – monkfish stuffed with prawns – and topped up their wine glasses, Marina waved a hand around at their surroundings. 'I just love your house. Did you do all the decorating yourself?'

'I had to. I didn't have the money to pay anyone else to do it! But it was a labour of love. It was almost uninhabitable when I bought it but I just knew it was exactly what I wanted. It helped that it was cheap, of course!'

Marina stared at him in admiration. 'You turned a dilapidated shell into this, alone?'

'Not quite. I let the experts take care of the electrics and the plumbing. Knowing a property developer helped enormously.'

'Richard helped you?'

Dominic nodded. 'He took a look at the place and told me what needed doing. He also got me all the materials I needed at cut price.'

'A nice friend to have,' Marina remarked.

'He is.'

'And you live here alone?'

Dominic smiled. 'Yes, all alone. Once bitten, etcetera.'

Marina frowned. 'Maybe I should leave right now!'

'No! Please, I haven't enjoyed myself so much in a very long time.'

'I haven't either.' Marina put down her knife and fork and dabbed her mouth with a napkin. 'And now I'm going to be very forward.'

'Oh?'

'Yes, I'd like that tour of your house now. And I'd like to start in the bedroom.'

Chapter 24

Fergus pushed open the door to the fitness club, nodded at the receptionist and wandered down the corridor whistling. He'd just come from the hospital and Rose was doing very well. She was able to get about now with the aid of a walker and her confidence was building. In a couple of days she'd be discharged and would go to stay with her sister, Babs, for a few weeks in Arklow. He had offered to take time off to look after her but, given that Rose would need help in and out of the bath, she'd decided that she preferred the help of a woman. Besides, she said, Fergus was still so new in the job it would be a bad idea to take time off so soon.

Fergus didn't argue. He was a bit nervous of caring for his mother and he knew she'd be fine with Aunty Babs. The woman never stopped talking but she had a heart of gold and would treat Rose like a queen. In the snack bar, Fergus went behind the counter and slipped into his white jacket. 'How's it going?' he asked Cindy.

'It's been very busy and there's a class just finishing so prepare for a rush.'

'No problem.' He smiled at her. 'You go ahead and have your break.'

Cindy slipped out of her jacket and adjusted her tiny blue top. 'See you later then.'

'She fancies you.'

Fergus whirled round and grinned as he saw Sarah approach. He pulled her to him and kissed her. 'There's no competition.'

'Don't do that here or you'll get us both fired.' Sarah pushed him away but she looked pleased. 'How's your mum?'

'Very well.'

Sarah sighed. 'She'll be home soon, then?'

Fergus grinned. 'Didn't I mention? She's going to stay with her sister for a few weeks.'

Sarah punched him in the stomach. 'You sod! You know you didn't tell me!'

'I thought it would be a nice surprise,' he murmured, pulling her close. 'We'll have the place all to ourselves for a while yet.'

Sarah squirmed in his arms. 'You're just looking for an unpaid housekeeper.'

'Oh, isn't this touching. Not bad, Gus. I didn't think ye'd ever get a woman, never mind one as cute as this.'

Fergus froze as he looked over Sarah's head into the cold eyes of Mick Garvey. 'What are you doing here?' He moved so that he stood between Sarah and Mick.

'I'm a member, of course. It's important to stay in shape, Gus, isn't it?'

Fergus turned to Sarah. 'I'll see you later.'

She looked worriedly from Fergus to the thin man with the hard features and the scar above his left eye. 'Are you sure?'

'Sure.' He waited until she'd left before turning back to Mick. 'What do you want?'

Mick looked up at the menu. 'Coffee, I think.'

Fergus thought about throwing him out but the snack bar was filling up with women from the aerobics class and Fergus knew that Vincent wouldn't be impressed if he caused a scene. He poured a coffee and handed it to Mick.

'Thanks, mate. Oh. Sorry, I don't think I have any cash on me.'

'It's on the house,' Fergus said through gritted teeth.

'Very decent of ye. Nice to know ye remember yer mates.'

'I've got to get on,' Fergus said as a queue started to grow behind Mick.

'Course ye do. We'll catch up some other time.' Mick winked. 'When it's quieter.'

Fergus felt physically sick as he served, all the time keeping one eye on Mick who sat in the corner watching his every move. Fergus thought he should talk to his boss about banning Mick from the club but then Vincent would want to know why. Maybe he should just keep quiet. He was cleaning down the counter when Mick rose to leave, giving him a small salute before disappearing down the corridor. Fergus stared after him and decided that he'd have to deal with this himself, sooner rather than later. After all, he wasn't a kid any more and he wasn't on drugs. Mick Garvey had no hold over him. Not any more.

Rose opened her eyes and smiled when she saw Richard sitting by her bed. 'Have you been here long?'

'Just a few minutes. I didn't want to disturb you. How are you feeling?'

'Not bad at all.' Rose pushed herself up on the pillow.

'The nurse says you're making a good recovery.'

Rose made a face. 'The food in here is a great incentive. I can't wait to sit down to a decent steak and chips. Have you heard how Fergus is getting on?'

'Vincent seems very pleased with him and I think Fergus is happy.'

'I hope so.'

Richard shook his head. 'Stop looking for something to worry about, Rose, everything is fine.'

'I know, but it's not easy given that he's back in Sandhill.'

Richard looked at her. 'What do you mean?'

Rose sighed. 'That's where he grew up, Richard. That's where it all started.'

Richard blanched. 'Jesus, Rose, I'm so sorry. I had no idea!'

'Why would you? Oh, Richard, I'm so afraid of him

meeting up with the lowlifes who dragged him down.'

'I'm sure you don't have to worry about Fergus, he's a different person now.'

'I know that but some of those lads were downright thugs. Who knows what they're capable of?'

'They're probably all married with kids now and working for the civil service.'

Rose smiled slightly but she wasn't convinced. 'I wish Fergus would settle down. He's too much of a loner.'

'He's only twenty-four,' Richard protested. 'Worry when he's as old as me.'

'So what about you?' Rose smirked. 'Any action?'

'Rose Lynch, what a question!'

'How's Celine?'

He chuckled. 'Is there a connection between those two questions?'

'You tell me.'

'She'll be in to see you later,' he said standing up. 'Ask her.'

Rose smiled as he bent to kiss her. 'I wouldn't dare! Thanks for coming, Richard. Keep an eye on Fergus, will you?'

'Sure, but there's no need.'

'I'd feel happier.'

Richard sighed. 'You're a meddling old woman, do you know that?'

'Less of the old please!'

*

Before he started the car, Richard sent a text message to Celine. ROSE FINE. EXPECT QUESTIONS! Then he sent a message to Fergus. MEET ME 4 A PINT?

He was climbing into his car when Celine's reply came through. He looked at it and laughed.

WHAT HAVE U SAID?!

He keyed in his reply. NOTHING. HONEST.

As he started the engine, a reply came back from Fergus.

8.30, DONNELLYS?

Richard sent back a reply immediately. FINE. He reversed out of the parking spot and headed north, smiling as he imagined what Celine must be thinking. For days he had been threatening to tell Rose about their relationship and she'd made it clear what she'd do to him if he did. He understood her need for privacy but he was so happy lately that he wanted to tell the world. Failing that, he'd love to tell Rose. She knew how to keep a secret. He was disappointed he wouldn't see Celine tonight but he wanted to talk to Fergus as soon as possible. Now that he knew Fergus and Rose used to live in Sandhill, he understood the lad's reluctance to take the job at the leisure centre. He cringed as he remembered the tough time he'd given Fergus over it. Tonight he would apologise and try to find out if Fergus was having any problems in his old neighbourhood. Maybe if they finished up early he'd still get to tuck Celine in.

The object of his affection was at that moment trying

to politely tell a customer that she could not return a
soiled jacket. 'This has obviously been worn,' she
said, looking the woman straight in the eye.

'Not by me. That stain must have been there when
I bought it.'

Celine stared at her in disbelief. 'We don't have any
stock in that condition. I'm sorry but I will not
exchange this jacket.'

'Well, really. Wait until the owner gets back and
you'll be looking for a new job!'

'Have a nice day,' Celine muttered as the woman
marched out of the shop, banging the door after her.
Celine's thoughts were interrupted by the phone.
'Close Second, can I help you?'

'Is that Celine Moore?'

'Yes, that's right. Who is this?'

'Cathy Donlon, Hopefield Musical Society?'

'Oh, yes, hello.'

'I'm sorry for calling you at work. Dominic did
give me your home number but I lost it. Not very
organised, I'm afraid.'

'That's okay, I'm on my own at the moment.'

'Excellent. Dominic said you were interested in
getting involved backstage. It's very kind of you.'

'No problem, I'd be happy to help.'

'Wonderful! Do you think you could come along to
rehearsals the Thursday after next at eight?'

'Er, yes, that should be fine. You meet in the
community centre, don't you?'

'That's right. Now, as you're in the rag trade we

were going to ask you to help out with wardrobe, if that's okay.'

Celine smiled. 'Fine.'

'It won't take too much of your time. We hire in the costumes and they just need to be taken in or let out – usually the latter, ha, ha – nothing too onerous.'

'It sounds like fun.'

'Don't you believe it,' Cathy told her. 'Amateur musicals are serious business.'

Celine laughed. 'I'll take your word for it.'

'Okay then, see you on Thursday. And thanks again. Bye-bye.'

'Goodbye.' Celine was still smiling when she hung up. She checked her watch. It would be another hour before she could close up and then she was going straight in to see Rose. It was wonderful to see her getting stronger, but with the return of health, Rose's antennae were back in full working order. And Celine knew that Richard was dying to tell her that they were an item. But she wanted to keep it secret for as long as possible because that way, no one could spoil it. Marina, on the other hand, was doing the complete opposite. She and Dominic were always together and their lovey-dovey behaviour was enough to make Celine hurl. It was amazing, she would never have dreamed that they were compatible, but there was no doubt they were good together.

As Celine labelled up some new stock, her thoughts returned to Richard. She couldn't believe how close she felt to him already and how relaxed and comfortable their relationship was. She hadn't expected to feel that way with anyone ever again. She just hoped that he felt the same. It would be devastating if she was just one of Richard's flings.

Chapter 25

Fergus pushed his way into Donnellys and went up to the bar. The pub was full and noisy. Not ideal for a quiet chat, he thought with a grin as he ordered a pint of orange. He knew that Richard was on a mission from his mother to find out how things were going in Sandhill. It didn't really bother him. He'd given her enough cause for concern in the past. But she didn't need to know about Mick. Fergus ran a hand through his cropped black hair and sank on to a barstool. He had just had a rigorous workout at the club and ached all over but he loved the feeling. He wanted to get fit and build up his strength. Now that Mick Garvey was back in the picture he would feel better if he was able to defend himself.

'How's it going?' Richard appeared at his side. 'Ready for another one?'

'Yeah, thanks. A pint of lager.' Fergus drained his glass in one gulp.

Despite the crowd, a barmaid was already moving towards Richard. 'What can I get you?'

Richard gave the order and then turned back to Fergus, who was shaking his head. 'What?'

'The bar is packed and you get served straight away. How do you do that?'

Richard grinned. 'I'm irresistible.' As the girl returned with their drinks, he winked at her and gave her a hefty tip. 'Let's find a table.'

Fergus stood up and followed him to a slightly quieter corner of the pub. 'Were you in with me Ma today?' he asked as they sat down.

'I was. She's doing very well.'

'She is, isn't she?'

'Worrying about you, of course.'

'No change there then.'

'She told me about Sandhill.'

'Ah.'

'I'm sorry I gave you a rough time, Fergus, I had no idea.'

'Why would you? We didn't talk about it.'

'So how does it feel being back there?'

For a moment, Fergus was tempted to tell him about Mick but decided against it. 'No problem. I like the job and there's a great crew working there.'

'I'm glad.'

'So you can report back that I'm fine.'

Richard feigned innocence. 'I don't know what you mean.'

'Yeah, right. How's Celine doing?'

Richard nodded. 'Great.'

'Does she talk to you at all?' Fergus asked. 'About me, I mean.'

Richard shook his head. 'She talks about everything except you. Sorry.'

'I can't say I blame her. At least she doesn't have to worry about bumping into me any more.'

'I think it's worked out well all round, most importantly for Rose. Knowing the shop is in safe hands must be a relief.'

Fergus nodded. 'Yeah, it's just a bit weird that the perfect candidate for the job turned out to be Dermot's wife.'

'Tell me about Dermot.'

Fergus sighed. 'I hated him to begin with. Wherever I went, he seemed to find me.'

'Did he try to persuade you to give up the drugs?'

Fergus shook his head. 'Nope. He just talked, gave me smokes, and when I ended up on the streets, he brought me food.'

'I never realised you left home.'

Fergus chuckled. 'I didn't, Ma threw me out. It was probably the best thing she ever did, though I know it was very hard for her.' His eyes glazed over. 'I was a little bastard, Richard. I took money out of her purse, I nicked jewellery. One time I was so desperate for cash, I flogged our toaster! Sometimes, I wouldn't come home at night and she'd be worried sick. But I just didn't care. The only thing that was important was the next fix. Anyway, once I was on the streets,

Dermot would come looking for me. If he found me, he'd drag me off to the nearest shelter.'

'So when or how did you give up?'

Fergus closed his eyes briefly.

'Hey, if you don't want to talk—'

'No, it's okay. When I got really desperate, I agreed to do a bit of pushing. I had no way of paying for the stuff, you see. One of my customers – God, she was only a kid – had a bad reaction. I should have known that Mick would be involved in dodgy gear.'

'Mick was your dealer?'

Fergus gave a reluctant nod.

'Did the kid die?'

'No, she had some kind of a seizure. I called for an ambulance and they were able to help but Jesus, I got such a fright. That night, when Dermot came looking for me, I agreed to go into rehab.'

'And then he got you a job?'

Fergus nodded. 'I wasn't sure it was a good idea and Ma was dead against it but Dermot knew what he was doing. When I saw kids even younger than me coming in totally wasted I knew I could never use again.'

'It can't have been easy.'

Fergus shrugged. 'It wasn't, but I didn't have a lot of choice.'

'What did you use?'

'Crack and speed, mainly. I kidded myself that as long as I stayed away from heroin I'd be fine.'

'How did it start?'

Fergus's face twisted into a bitter smile. 'I wanted to be one of the gang. I was fourteen, a very average student and too shy to be popular. One of the older kids offered me an E. I had it for nearly a week before I worked up the courage to take it. I couldn't believe how happy I felt. Suddenly, for the first time, I was one of the gang. I was sensible enough to begin with, I was almost seventeen before it got out of hand. I was supposed to be studying for my Leaving Certificate but I rarely picked up a book. That's when Ma started to get suspicious. She went through my room one night and found some pills. We had the mother of all arguments and she told me to give up or get out. I promised to toe the line and I really did try.' Fergus swallowed hard. 'It was harder and harder to find money for the drugs and I was getting desperate. One night I took her chequebook out of her bag. She walked in on me when I was practising her signature. That's when she threw me out.'

Richard put a hand on his shoulder. 'Sorry, I shouldn't have asked. It's not a good idea to look back.'

Fergus pulled out a handkerchief and blew his nose. 'It's okay. Looking back reminds me of how lucky I am. If Ma hadn't thrown me out, if Dermot hadn't believed in me, I wouldn't be here now. Dermot was based in the city centre,' he continued. 'He didn't have any reason to come to the shelter that night. But he often dropped in to see how I was doing. We talked a lot. He used to tell me about Celine and

what a success she was going to be. He was very
proud of her. I'll never forget how she looked the
morning of the funeral.'

'She's okay now,' Richard pointed out.

'Is she?' Fergus looked miserably into his pint.
'She's not the big-shot designer that Dermot said she
was going to be. She's working in a shop, what does
that say?'

'You can't take the blame for that, Fergus. It wasn't
your fault.'

'You know, I might have believed that before I met
her again but now I'm not so sure.'

'Take it from me, Fergus, she's fine. Yes of course
she had a rough time,' he added when Fergus looked
at him in disbelief, 'but she's still young. There's
plenty of time for her to get her life together.'

'God, I hope you're right.'

'I am. Now you must concentrate on your life.
Have a good time and date some women.' He stopped
when he saw the slow smile on Fergus's face. 'Ah,
you've met someone.'

Fergus nodded. 'Her name's Sarah, she works at
the club.'

'I'm happy for you, mate. It's time you had a bit of
fun.'

Again, Fergus was tempted to tell Richard about
Mick but he was already standing up and reaching for
his jacket.

'I've got to go. Keep in touch, Fergus, and I'll
give you a call if there's anything relating to the shop

that you need to know about. Now, can I drop you home?'

Fergus checked his watch. 'No, that's okay. Sarah will be finished work in an hour so maybe I'll go and meet her.'

'You do that, but don't go walking down any dark alleys.'

Fergus grinned. 'Yes, Dad.'

'Cheeky bugger!' Richard punched his arm and started to push his way out of the pub.

Fergus followed and, after saying goodbye, sprinted to the bus stop. He was surprised that he had told Richard about Sarah, he certainly hadn't planned to. But he was so happy it was hard to hide it, especially as he went around with a smile on his face most of the time. It made a pleasant change. He hadn't done a lot of smiling since Celine had moved to Hopefield. He sobered as he thought of the rest of the stuff he'd told Richard. It had been a long time since he'd talked about Dermot's death. But between Celine's sudden arrival and Mick's reappearance, those sad, bad days were on his mind. Just over an hour later, he walked into the Centre.

The receptionist looked up. 'Hi, Fergus. If you're looking for Sarah she's gone to the pub.'

'Thanks.' He smiled at the girl and headed towards the pub on the corner. He was halfway across the busy, smoky room when he heard someone call his name. He turned to see Mick Garvey waving at him, a broad smile on his face.

'Hey, Gus, over here. We were just talking about you, weren't we, Sarah?'

Fergus's heart sank as Mick moved to one side to reveal Sarah sitting on a barstool beside him. She smiled and waved. As he approached, Fergus shivered at the cold calculating look in Mick's eye.

Sarah stood up to kiss him. She was more than a bit tipsy and he slipped an arm around her waist to steady her.

'Fergus, what a lovely surprise.'

'I thought I'd come by to take you home.' Fergus kept his eyes on Sarah as he spoke.

'Did you hear that?' She turned to Mick. 'Isn't he lovely?'

'Oh, yeah, he's just great.'

'Let's go, Sarah.'

She waved him away and sat down. 'I'm not finished my drink. Pull up a chair, Fergus, and have a drink. Mick's being telling me all about the old days. You never told me you used to live around here.'

'It was a lifetime ago.'

Mick chuckled. 'Not that long, Gus!'

'Oh, cheer up, Fergus,' Sarah pouted his grim expression. 'Aren't you happy to meet an old friend?'

'Thrilled. Now come on, Sarah, time we went home.'

'Pity we don't have more time to catch up, Gus,' Mick murmured, an amused smile playing around his lips.

'Yeah, sorry about that.'

'Oh, don't worry about it. I work out on a regular basis so you'll be seeing plenty of me. I think it's important to look after yer health, don't you, Gus?'

Fergus looked at his yellow teeth and pimply skin. 'Whatever you say, Mick.'

'Seeya, Mick.' Sarah struggled to focus on him. 'And if you need any help with your exercise programme you just let me know.'

Mick winked at her. 'I'll do that, thanks, Sarah.'

Fergus gripped her arm and steered towards the door.

Chapter 26

Celine plumped the cushions on the sofa, opened the window and leaned out to sniff the air that smelled of cut grass and lavender. It was a perfect May evening and Marina would be here any minute. As it was so nice, Celine was planning to bring her down to the courtyard at the back of the shop. She had already been down to dust off the chairs and set out wine, glasses and some nibbles. This was the first time that she and Marina had got together since Celine had discovered Fergus was Rose's son and since she'd started dating Richard. They had a lot to talk about. The phone rang and she jumped on it, thinking it would be Richard.

'Hello, Celine.'

Celine groaned inwardly. 'Kevin!'

'I've missed you.'

'Oh, Kevin, please don't say that.'

'But it's true. When can I see you?'

Celine took a deep breath. 'I'm sorry, Kevin, but you can't. It's over between us.'

'You don't mean that. If this is because of Eileen—'

'It's not Eileen. I'm . . . seeing someone else.'

'It's that landlord of yours, isn't it?'

'It doesn't matter who it is, Kevin, there was no future for us anyway.'

'You've said that before, Celine, but you've always come back.'

'Not this time.'

'We'll see.'

When she heard the dial tone, Celine put down the phone with a shaking hand. Kevin was charm itself when he was happy, but upset him and he could get very nasty. Perhaps she should invite him over some evening and try to finish it in a more amicable manner. The buzzer interrupted her thoughts and she hurried to let Marina in.

'Hello, darling,' Marina called as she climbed the stairs. 'Sorry I'm late. Just had to nip next door for some mints.'

Celine's lips twitched. 'Mints, eh?'

Marina's eyes widened. 'What else?'

'So I take it the romance is going well.'

'Wonderful,' Marina purred. 'Dominic is a darling and he's great with Joshie.'

'Wow, you've finally introduced them?'

'We've been to the park twice and the cinema once,' Marina reported. 'Do you know that Dominic's the first man that ever showed an interest in my son?'

'And what does Josh think of Dominic?

Marina's smile faded. 'He's been very quiet but it's early days. Dominic is being wonderfuly patient.'

'He's definitely an angel,' Celine agreed. 'Even if he did get me involved with his damn musical society.'

'I'm still in shock about that. It's so unlike you to be sociable.'

'Thanks.' Celine picked up her sunglasses. 'Let's continue this conversation in the courtyard.'

Marina frowned. 'I didn't know you had a courtyard.'

'Well, I don't, but there's a pretty little yard behind the shop and Rose says I can use it whenever I want.' She went over to the window and stepped out onto the fire escape.

Marina leaned out of the window and looked down. 'Are you sure that thing is safe? It looks ancient.'

'It's fine,' Celine assured her. 'Come on.'

Marina pulled on her baseball cap. 'Okay, lead the way.'

Celine was pouring the wine by the time Marina joined her. 'Oh, it is nice down here!' She looked around in appreciation at the tiny courtyard with its potted plants and climbing roses. She pulled a chair under the protection of the large multi-coloured parasol and Celine handed her a glass of chilled white wine.

Celine placed her chair directly in the sun and stretched out, raising her face to the warm rays. 'Isn't it heaven?'

'I hope you're wearing sunscreen,' Marina remarked.

Celine waved a lazy hand at her. 'It's nearly seven o'clock, Marina. Anyway, I'm not a model, I don't have to worry about my skin.'

Marina studied her pretty friend. 'You could be if you weren't so short.'

Celine opened one eye. 'I am not short!'

Marina grinned. 'Course not, shorty. Anyway, tell me all your news. How's Rose doing?'

'Really well. She called this morning and she was telling me that she can get about the house without her frame now. She hates doing the physio though.'

'When will she come back to Dublin?'

'Probably next month, but she won't be able to work for a while yet.'

'And when she is, what will you do?'

Celine shrugged. 'I'll worry about that when the time comes. I almost left a few weeks ago.'

Marina stared at her. 'But why?'

And after taking another sip of her wine, Celine told her friend about Fergus.

'That's incredible!' Maria gasped when she'd finished. 'I know Dublin is a small town but that he should turn out to be Rose's son! Oh, Celine, why didn't you tell me? This must have been a very hard time for you. What did your dad say?'

'I haven't told him.'

'So you've gone through this all alone.' Marina shook her head in disbelief.

'Not quite,' Celine told her with a smile.

Marina rolled her eyes. 'You're still seeing Kevin then?'

'No! It's . . . someone else.'

'Celine! Who? For God's sake, tell me!'

'It's Richard.'

'Richard Lawrence? You've been dating the most eligible bachelor in the country?'

'Don't call him that,' Celine complained. 'He's actually a very ordinary kind of guy.'

'I'll have to take your word for that. So is it serious?'

'Oh, come on, Marina, we've only gone out a few times! What about you? Has Dominic popped the question yet?'

Marina gave her a small, satisfied smile. 'Shouldn't be long now.'

'You only met a few weeks ago!'

'Let's face it, Celine, when you know, you know.'

'I thought you were holding out for a rich man. Dominic is almost on the breadline!'

Marina made a face. 'That's a slight exaggeration but it's true, he's not exactly what I was looking for.' She sighed happily. 'But when you're in love, who cares about money?'

Celine put a hand to her friend's forehead. 'Are you feeling okay?'

Marina laughed. 'Never better.'

'I'm so happy for you,' Celine said, genuinely delighted. 'You couldn't find a better man than Dominic.'

'What about Richard?' Marina asked with a sly look.

Celine laughed. 'Yeah, you're right. He's perfect too!'

'I want to meet this man for myself. We shall set up a foursome.'

'We'll see.'

'Don't give me that! What could be more natural? He and Dominic are friends. You and I are friends. We must go to dinner. I'll tell Dominic to arrange it.'

Celine bit her lip as she saw the determined look on Marina's face. 'Promise me you won't grill him about his intentions?'

'But of course not, darling, I'll be on my best behaviour. Tell me something. Does Dominic know all about you and Fergus?'

Colin nodded. 'But don't be cross with him, Marina, it was a very delicate situation.'

'I'm not cross, darling. I'm impressed. How wonderfully discreet of him. Is there no end to his good points?'

A week later Celine arrived at the church hall just as the cast of 'My Fair Lady' finished a rousing rendition of 'With A Little Bit of Luck'. She applauded delightedly as she pulled up a seat next to Cathy. 'Gosh, they're really good, aren't they?'

'Not good enough,' the producer replied out of the side of her mouth, 'but they will be.'

'So what do you want me to do?' Celine asked.

'The costumes for the ballroom scene have arrived, so maybe you could work with the ladies on those?'

'Sure.'

Cathy clapped her hands. 'Okay, everybody, this is Celine Moore and she's very kindly offered to look after the wardrobe for us.'

There was a polite round of applause and Celine smiled. She was amazed at the number of faces she recognised.

'So,' Cathy continued, 'any of the ladies not involved in the Ascot scene, please go into the next room with Celine and she will organise your ballgowns.'

The women chattered excitedly as they moved down to the door at the other end of the room.

Dominic appeared at her side. 'Hi, Celine, all set for Saturday night?'

'Yeah, looking forward to it. I just hope Marina doesn't give Richard the third degree!'

'She'll behave herself, I'll make sure of it,' he promised.

Celine shot him an amazed look. She didn't think any man was capable of keeping Marina in check, least of all a softly spoken gentleman like Dominic. 'See you later,' she said and went to join the ladies of the cast. When she saw the rails of clothes she almost groaned aloud. She should have spent some time going through the stuff before dragging everybody in here. She clapped her hands together and smiled nervously. 'Hi, everybody, why don't you all have a rummage and see if you can find something to suit you?' She went to the nearest rack and flicked through some of the dresses. 'Yes, the sizes are all clearly marked so it should be straightforward enough. When you've found something you like, try it on and come to me if it needs some adjusting.'

She watched as the women started to rummage through the racks. With a couple of exceptions, they were all middle-aged and Celine thought that most of the adjustments would be to the rather revealing bodices.

'Hello, dear, how nice to see you.'

She turned around to see Mary Boyle bearing down on her. 'Oh, hello, Mrs Boyle, I didn't know you were a member.'

'Thirteen years.' Mary stuck her chest out and cast a scathing eye over the other women. 'I planned to retire this year but Cathy begged me to stay on. There aren't many strong sopranos,' she confided.

'Oh, I see.' Celine nodded gravely.

'You still haven't come for tea.'

'Yes, sorry about that,' Celine murmured. 'But now that I'm running the shop alone, it's been quite hectic. And then I normally spend Sundays with my dad.'

Mary was slightly mollified. 'Well, family is important.'

'Isn't it?' Celine grabbed a flamboyant pink creation off the rail and shoved it into the woman's hand. 'Why don't you try that on, Mrs Boyle? I think that colour would be very good on you.'

Mary preened. 'Really?'

'With your wonderful skin I'm sure of it,' Celine said, backing away. 'Excuse me a moment, I think I'm needed.' She hurried across the room to where a large, red-haired woman was trying to squeeze into an orange dress with layers of netting. Celine ran her eye along the nearest rail and seized a more regal gown in royal blue. 'I think this would suit you much better,' she suggested with a tentative smile.

And so the evening continued, with Celine feeling more like a peace commissioner for the UN than a costume mistress.

'You survived then,' Dominic remarked as he walked her back to the flat.

Celine grinned. 'Only just. No, I had fun. You make a wonderful Henry Higgins, by the way.'

Dominic looked surprised and pleased. 'I didn't think you'd seen any of the rehearsals.'

'I just caught a few minutes of you singing "I've grown accustomed to her face". It was lovely.'

'I think you're being kind.' They stopped outside her flat.

'Would you like a coffee?' Celine asked.

Dominic sighed. 'I'd love one but I promised myself I'd go over the books this evening. Not my favourite occupation.' He handed her the clothes he had been carrying for her. 'Mind you, looking at that little lot, it looks like you're going to be busy too.'

Celine laughed. 'It's just some minor alterations, it

won't take long.' As she turned to open the door, a car pulled up alongside them and Kevin got out.

'Hello, Celine.'

'Kevin!' She quickly turned back to Dominic. 'See you tomorrow.'

Dominic hesitated for a moment and then nodded. 'Right, bye.'

'Pleased to see me?' Kevin asked when they were alone.

'I am, actually. We need to talk. Let's go upstairs.'

Chapter 27

The following morning, Celine was in the shop bright and early and singing along to the radio as she dusted the shelves and hoovered.

'Someone sounds happy.'

She turned to see Richard standing in the doorway and switched off the Hoover with her foot. 'Hello, there.'

After a long kiss Richard drew back to look at her. 'You're gorgeous.'

Celine laughed. 'Rubbish.' She'd pulled on jogging pants and a T-shirt and her hair was pinned on top of her head and she just knew her face would be shiny from all the exertion. 'Come back in an hour and I'll be scrubbed up.'

'You're gorgeous,' Richard repeated and ran a finger down her cheek and across her lips.

Celine pushed him away. 'Don't start, mate, I've got a shop to run.'

'I'm going. I just wanted to check what time I should pick you up tomorrow night.'

'Marina's booked a table in the Thai restaurant for

eight-thirty but we're meeting for drinks first in the Shelbourne.'

'Fine, I'll pick you up around seven.'

Celine put the Hoover away, let herself out of the shop and went back up to her flat. As she undressed, her thoughts returned to the reason for her good mood and she smiled. Finally she'd got through to Kevin that they were finished and they'd parted last night on reasonably good terms. She just hoped that Dominic wouldn't mention his visit – it was unlikely that Richard would understand. He was a laid-back man but Celine suspected he was the jealous type.

After a quick shower, Celine dried her hair, applied some eye makeup and lipstick and then lowered a simple cream linen dress over her head. After zipping it up, slipping on her shoes and running a comb through her hair, she was ready. As she lowered the comb she stared at her reflection in the mirror. She hardly recognised the confident, happy woman staring back at her. She wasn't sure if it was because Richard was in her life, Kevin was out of it or the fact that she was doing a job she enjoyed, but whatever it was, she looked happy. Taking her bag and her keys, she ran downstairs and let herself back into the shop. After she'd put on the kettle, she switched on the lights, flicked the open sign and opened the door to allow a soft breeze into the shop.

Before she got a chance to make any coffee though, her first customer had arrived. After that, there was a constant stream of women and it was almost twelve before Celine got to make a cuppa. Realising that it would probably be her only chance to eat, she hurriedly made herself a sandwich. Fridays were always busy and though she'd be exhausted by five-thirty, Celine preferred it like this. She groaned as she heard the bell and looking longingly at her sandwich and cooling coffee she went back out front where Mary Boyle was poking in the bargain bin. In all the time she'd been here, Celine had never seen Mary buy as much as a scarf. If she was here it would be purely to gossip. She forced a smile to her lips. 'Good morning, Mrs Boyle. Beautiful morning, isn't it?'

'There's still a chill in the air.' Mary cast a critical eye over Celine's light dress. 'My mother always said, "Never cast a clout till May is out".'

'Really?' Celine nodded and nipped back outside to take a quick sip of her coffee. When she returned, Mary had moved on to the hats.

'This doesn't look very clean,' she remarked, holding up a cream beret.

'It's the light.'

Mary threw it back on the shelf and moved on to root through a rail of cardigans. Celine was about to go back to her coffee when the door opened again. 'Good morning, may I help – oh!'

Eileen Gilligan stood in the doorway glaring at her. 'Help me? Well, I don't know, you tell me, Celine. I told you once before what I wanted.'

Celine glanced over at Mary who was standing

still, her ears pricked. 'Why don't you come through—'

'I told you to leave my husband alone,' Eileen said, not moving an inch. 'But it seems you didn't listen.'

Celine took a deep breath and then crossed the room to Mary, took her by the arm and escorted her to the door. 'I'm afraid I must ask you to leave, Mrs Boyle.'

'But you can't do that,' Mary spluttered.

'I'm sorry.' Celine shut the door on the indignant woman and flicked the sign to closed.

'What was Kevin doing here last night?' Eileen demanded. 'And don't try to deny it, because I followed him.'

'Okay, Eileen, I'll be honest with you. I told Kevin it was finished, he had other ideas, but now he's got the message. I'm in another relationship and I've no intention of seeing your husband again.'

Eileen slumped against the counter. 'Do you mean it? Really? Because I'm not sure I can stand much more of this.'

Celine looked at her in amazement. 'I didn't think it bothered you. Kevin told me . . . well . . . I wasn't the first.'

Eileen flinched. 'No, you weren't, but he's never stayed with anyone as long as you.' Her eyes searched Celine's face. 'I was afraid he'd fallen in love.'

Celine reached out a hand to her. 'No! No, I promise you it's over. I'm so sorry, he told me you didn't really care what he did.'

'I was afraid I'd lose him,' Eileen said, tears running unchecked down her face. 'So I ignored what was going on.'

'I'm the last person to give you advice,' Celine murmured, 'but maybe that wasn't such a great strategy.'

'Apparently not.' Eileen pulled out a handkerchief and dabbed at her face.

'Right now, he's not seeing anyone and I promise, hand on heart, I have finished with him for good. I am really sorry for all the hurt I've caused you.'

Eileen gave a brief nod and went to the door. 'Thank you for your honesty,' she said and was gone.

Celine closed her eyes. 'Oh, Kevin, how did you get it so wrong?' After taking a few deep breaths, she turned the sign around again and opened the door. She peered out to see if Mary Boyle was still hanging about but thankfully she was nowhere in sight. Celine could imagine the gossip at next week's dress rehearsal.

'Shit, Dominic!' She sank back against the counter and dropped her head in her hands. He was bound to hear about this and then he'd remember meeting Kevin last night. Lord, even if she'd introduced them it wouldn't have looked so suspicious. He was bound to put two and two together and come up with five. And what would he do then, tell Richard? Damn it, she'd have to tell him first except she wasn't going to see him until tomorrow night. Still, it was unlikely that Mary would have got to Dominic before then. She went out back, threw her cold coffee down the drain and dropped her sandwich into the bin. Suddenly she didn't feel hungry any more. She sighed as the bell went again. Going back into the shop, she prayed that it wouldn't be Mary.

Her face cleared and she smiled in relief when the customer turned out to be her father. 'Hi, Daddy.' She reached up to give him a hug and a kiss.

He touched his cheek. 'What was that for?'

'Oh, it's just nice to see a friendly face.'

'One of those days, eh?'

'Yep. But never mind that, tell me all your news.'

'No news. Can't stay long, I'm on my way to leave the car in for a service. I just wanted to ask you to lunch on Sunday.'

Celine raised an eyebrow. 'You're cooking?'

Frank chuckled. 'God no, I don't want to kill you. I thought we could go out.'

Celine thought of the conversation she'd planned to have with Richard. 'I don't know, Daddy—'

'Oh, please, love, Brenda's coming too. It will be the first time she's been out since all of this happened.'

'Okay, Daddy, as long as we don't go to the golf club.'

'That's a promise,' Frank said, already halfway out the door. 'Come over about one. Bye.'

'Bye.' Celine stood waving in the doorway as he drove away. It looked like her chat with Richard would have to wait. As she turned to go back inside, one of Rose's regular customers arrived and

Celine put her personal problems to the back of her mind.

The rest of the day was uneventful and after Celine had lodged the takings in the bank she walked back to her flat, weary and glad that she was having a quiet night in. She wanted to go through the accounts and check the week's takings but she could at least do it outside and enjoy the last of the sunshine. Pouring a glass of wine she took it and her file down to the yard. She sank back in a chair and closed her eyes, enjoying the warm sun on her face. Just five minutes and then she'd start work. It was another thirty minutes before a dog barking woke her. 'Oh, damn.' She stretched, took a sip of wine and opened the file. As she worked through the sales for the last week she started to smile. After checking it three times she threw the file on the table and sat back with a triumphant 'Yes!' The sales figures were the best since she'd come to Close Second and that included the period when Rose was still there. She was glad she was going to Arklow on Monday. It would be nice to be the bearer of good news.

She was looking forward to seeing her boss especially as business was so good. Celine could never imagine herself returning to the world of design but she could still do something in fashion. She'd have to put some thought into that. In a month or so, Rose would return part-time. Celine didn't relish the thought of leaving the shop and leaving her flat. But, she thought, a smile playing around her lips, she'd a feeling she'd be staying in Hopefield. Richard had hinted a couple of times that he'd like her to move in. Perhaps it was time that she became part of a couple again.

Chapter 28

Kay rummaged among the bottles and tubes on the bathroom shelf in search of anti-inflammatory cream. 'Bloody hell, what does she use all of this stuff for?' she muttered. Josh appeared at her side.

'What are you doing, Granny?'

'Looking for something.'

'What?'

'Never you mind. Have you brushed your teeth?'

'I don't like brushing my teeth.'

'Well, you have to, or they'll all fall out.'

'Mum, you'll scare him.' Marina stood in the doorway bristling with disapproval. 'What are you looking for?'

'The cream for my shoulder.'

Marina scanned the shelf and then looked in the cabinet on the wall. 'It's not in here. It must be in your bedroom.'

'It is not in my bedroom,' Kay snapped.

'I don't like your cream, Granny, it smells yuck.'

'Joshie!' Marina shot her son a warning glance.

'Well, it does,' he insisted. 'It made my Action Man smell yuck too.'

Kay froze. 'Did you take my cream, Josh?'

Josh twisted his toes into the bathroom mat and said nothing.

'Josh, answer Granny,' Marina told him and left to search his bedroom.

'My Action Man had a sore leg,' Josh muttered. 'He fell.'

Kay pushed past him and went after her daughter. Marina was sitting on the bed, holding a white Action Man in one hand and a scrunched-up tube in the other. 'Sorry, Mum. I'll go to the chemist and get some more.'

Kay took a deep breath before replying. 'Throw open the windows, the place stinks.'

'Sure, Mum.'

'And do me a favour? When you go to the shops, take your son with you.'

Marina went into the bathroom. 'Josh, go to the loo, brush your teeth and then come into my bedroom. We're going out.'

'Oh, goody, where are we going?'

'It's a surprise,' Marina told him, knowing that it would be counterproductive to tell him the truth. And from the look on her mother's face, the sooner she got him out of the house the better. They had been getting on much better than Marina could have hoped but there had been a couple of small hiccups, usually relating to Josh. Her mother took rather too hands-on an approach for Marina's liking but that was only natural, she told herself. She must be patient with her mother after all, it was her house.

Kay was sitting in her bedroom with the door firmly closed when she heard Marina and Josh leave. With a sigh of relief, she went down to her kitchen to make a much-needed cup of coffee. As she sat at the table cradling a mug in her hands, Kay wondered what she had been thinking of when she invited her daughter to stay. It would never work out, not in a million years. Marina floated in and out looking beautiful but did nothing to help out around the house. And cleaning it took longer than ever now that Josh lived here. The child was completely out of control and Marina didn't seem to even notice. Kay had tried several times to give him some chores to do but Marina had been horrified.

'He's only a little boy, Mum, you can't expect him to help out yet.'

'He could at least tidy up his toys before bedtime,' Kay had retorted. It was only since they'd moved in that her back had started acting up again. Not surprising, as she seemed to spend all day every day picking up after the child. And now she had to baby-sit tonight; she put her head in her hands at the thought. Most four-year-olds she knew were in bed asleep by eight-thirty but not Josh. Bedtime was a nightmare and even after several stories, he'd appear back downstairs and eventually fall asleep on the sofa. And of course, they couldn't have the TV on while he was there because it would give him nightmares. So instead of settling down in front of Corrie or The Bill, Kay would have to sit through a Walt Disney film. She was determined to buy a television for her bedroom. Then at least occasionally she could get some peace and quiet. She shook her head sadly as she considered her dilemma. Marina seemed to be happy with the arrangement so she was unlikely to move out and Kay would never ask her to leave. Maybe when Josh started school in September he'd be less of a handful but Lord, that was almost three months away. She heaved herself to her feet. Sitting here feeling sorry for herself wouldn't help anyone. Time to go and clean up the Action Man mess in Josh's bedroom. She knew that Marina wouldn't have done it.

'Now, Josh, you need to be nicer to your Granny, she's getting old.'

'Is she going to die?' he asked, his eyes alight with curiosity.

Marina looked over her shoulder at her son in the back seat. 'Of course not. But you must be a good boy for her.' She turned back to concentrate on her driving.

Josh groaned. 'I want to go home to our house.'

'We don't have a house,' Marina told him, her face grim. 'We live with Granny now.'

'But I don't want to.'

'Now, darling, don't be silly, you know how much Granny loves you. She was just cross this morning because you took her cream.'

'But my action man was sick,' he protested.

'I understand that, Joshie, but remember, you should always ask before taking something that isn't yours.'

Josh said nothing but started kicking the back of the front seat. Marina sighed. She probably shouldn't go out tonight but she was so looking forward to meeting Richard. 'Josh, if you're a very good boy today and tell Granny you're sorry I'll bring you to the cinema tomorrow.'

'Hoorah!' Josh broke into a broad smile. 'I love you, mummy, you're the best Mummy in the world.'

Marina gulped. 'I love you too, darling. Do you promise you'll be good?'

'I promise, Mummy.'

'Excellent.' Marina cut off a Punto and swung into a parking spot outside the chemist. She hopped out of the car, flashed the irate driver of the other car a huge smile and went round to open the door for Josh. 'Come on, darling, if we hurry we'll have time for an ice cream.'

Marina clasped his hand in hers. How did she get to be this lucky? As much as she detested Ray at least he'd given her Josh. She knew that he was a little bit spoiled but she'd always felt that she had to make it up to him for throwing out his dad. Of course Josh was only two when Ray had left so he didn't miss him. Marina looked down at his blond head and thought that she hadn't done too bad a job. After they'd got Kay her cream, Marina bought Josh the promised ice cream and then picked up a packet of the chocolate muffins that her mother loved. She was about to head back to the car when she had an even better idea. Stopping off at the off-licence she picked up a bottle of wine and then rented a movie from the video shop. 'Now, Granny is all set for a nice night on her own,' Marina told Josh. 'I hope you remember your promise, Joshie.'

He smiled up at her, his blue eyes full of sweet sincerity. 'I'll be good, Mummy, promise. Can I have popcorn when we go to the cinema tomorrow?'

Chapter 29

Celine wandered around her flat, occasionally taking an anxious peek at her watch. She wasn't sure why she was so nervous about Richard meeting Marina. It should be a relaxed evening given that Dominic would also be there. Celine had only seen Dominic once since Thursday and then it had been just for a quick hello outside the shop. He had been with two sober-looking men with briefcases and the three had disappeared into the newsagent's. Celine had hoped that Dominic was as preoccupied as he looked and didn't have time to listen to gossip.

She went into the bedroom and paused in front of the mirror. She was wearing a black, almost transparent skirt but the different layers and clever cut ensured that it was sexy without being too revealing. She had teamed it with a sleeveless crocheted top of silver grey that complimented her large grey eyes. She wore no jewellery. The outfit was finished off with high sandals that were so delicate she'd be lucky to get a second wear out of them. She smiled as she imagined Marina's reaction when she saw her. Her friend took Celine's usual wardrobe as a personal insult.

'She still has legs,' she'd remarked the first time she'd seen her in the shop. Celine smiled at the memory. She knew how frustrated Marina had felt at her total withdrawal from the world after Dermot died but she had stood by her, sometimes annoying, sometimes loving, but always there. Celine was looking forward to seeing her face tonight when she saw her looking well and happy. And, despite everything, she was happier than she'd been in years.

When Richard arrived to collect her, he stopped in the doorway and stared.

Celine twirled around with a self-conscious laugh. 'Will I do?'

Richard moved forward and took her hands in his. 'You look beautiful.'

'You're not so bad yourself,' she said, admiring the beautifully tailored dark suit.

Richard tugged at his tie and grimaced. 'I still prefer jeans!'

Celine closed her eyes as he bent to kiss her. 'I've missed you,' she whispered against his lips.

'I've missed you too.' He smiled down at her. 'It's a pity we have to go out.'

Celine pulled away. 'Well, we do and we should get going.'

'Do you think Marina will approve of me?' Richard asked as they went out to the taxi.

'You're single, rich and not too hard on the eye so yes, I think she'll be quite happy.'

When they arrived, Dominic and Marina were sitting at the bar. Dominic stood up to kiss Celine and gave her his stool. 'You look lovely,' he told her before turning to shake hands with Richard. 'Richard, I'd like you to meet Marina Flynn.'

Marina tossed back her hair and appraised him with twinkling, blue eyes. 'Richard, nice to meet you at last.'

'The pleasure is mine.' Richard bent his head to kiss her outstretched hand.

'Enough of that,' Dominic told him with mock severity. 'What would you like to drink, Celine?'

'White wine, please.'

'And a pint for you, Richard?'

'Please.'

'So, Richard, you're in the property business?' Marina said, ignoring the glare that Celine was directing at her.

'And you're in the modelling business. I can see why. Dominic told me you were beautiful and he didn't exaggerate.'

Marina flashed him a dazzling smile. 'Quite the charmer, Celine, isn't he?'

'Isn't he just!' Celine smiled at Richard and then turned to take her drink from Dominic. 'Thank you.'

'How are the alterations going?' Dominic asked.

Celine laughed. 'Okay. I should be ready by Thursday.'

'What's this?' Richard asked.

'Celine is Hopefield Musical Society's new wardrobe mistress,' Dominic told him.

Marina touched Dominic's face. 'I still don't know how you talked her into it.'

Richard's eyes rested on Celine. 'Are you enjoying it?'

'It's fun,' Celine said with a casual shrug. 'And I get to watch the star of the show in action.'

Marina smiled delightedly. 'Is he wonderful? I've heard him practising in the shower.'

'He's excellent,' Celine confirmed, 'both at the singing and the acting.'

Dominic gave a slight bow. 'You're too kind.'

'When does the show open?' Richard asked. 'We must book front-row seats.'

'Four weeks' time so I don't think you need to book your tickets just yet.'

'I wouldn't bet on it, Dominic. Some of the women were telling me that their whole families are coming, right down to the great-grandchildren,' Celine told him.

'Good. The screaming kids will drown out my singing. We're sure to get rave reviews.'

'I'm sure my mum would like to come, she loves musicals,' Marina said.

'Daddy loves that kind of thing too,' Celine

remarked. 'And Brenda would probably enjoy a night out.'

Richard glanced at his watch. 'Shouldn't we be heading over to the restaurant?'

Dominic nodded. 'Yes, the reservation is for eight-thirty.'

'Just let me slip out to the loo,' Celine said, standing up.

'I'll come with you. I like him,' Marina said when they were out of earshot. 'He's even better-looking in the flesh.'

Celine laughed. 'Glad you approve.'

Chapter 30

'Is that all you're eating?' Frank looked in disgust at Celine's chicken salad.

She gazed at her plate and wondered if eating at all was such a good idea. 'I was out last night, Daddy,' she admitted.

'Ah, feeling a bit rough, eh? We'd better not talk too loud then.' Frank laughed and winked at Brenda.

Celine touched her temple and winced. 'That would be appreciated.'

'Do you know, I don't think I've ever had a hangover,' Brenda remarked.

'We'll have to take care of that,' Frank replied. 'We must have a night out when Alan gets back next week. What do you think, Celine?'

Celine managed a faint smile. 'Good idea.'

'How's life in Hopefield, Celine?' Brenda asked.

'Great. The shop has been really busy and this week the takings were higher than they've been since I started.'

'Good girl.' Frank beamed at her. 'I'm sure Rose will be pleased to hear that. How is she?'

'She's fine, Daddy. You ask about her a lot. If I didn't know any better I'd say you fancied her.'

Frank almost choked and reached for his pint. 'Well, really,' he gasped when he'd got his breath back. 'It's a sad day when I can't ask after a woman's health without being accused of all sorts.'

'Calm down, Daddy, it was a joke.' Celine glanced at Brenda and rolled her eyes. 'It wouldn't be a crime if you liked the woman.'

Frank glared at her. 'I do like her and that's all. Now, can we please talk about something else?'

'We seem to be running out of things,' Celine murmured.

Brenda started to giggle. 'I'm sorry,' she said when Frank shot her a dirty look. 'It's just this is so nice, sitting here, quarrelling, it's like old times.'

Celine laughed and even Frank managed a reluctant smile.

'If all you needed was a row to make you feel better you should have said!' Celine told her.

'Indeed, we're experts at that,' Frank agreed. 'It's nice to hear you laugh, love,' he added, smiling at Brenda.

'Those antidepressants are wonder drugs, aren't they?' Celine marvelled.

'The tablets help but talking to the psychiatrist is what's really making the difference.'

'I'm glad, love, I've been so worried about you. You know you're like another daughter to me.'

'Don't, Daddy, or she'll start blubbering,' Celine warned.

'She's right.' Brenda blew her nose.

'Blubber away,' Celine told her, 'and if it will make you feel better, we'll argue while you blubber.'

'Don't mind her, Brenda, she always acts the eejit when she's hung over.'

'You know? I'm beginning to feel better,' Celine replied. 'I wonder what's for dessert.'

Later that evening, Celine walked into the pub and frowned at the sight of Richard talking to the waitress.

'Hi,' she said, climbing onto the barstool beside him.

'Hi, Celine, what would you like to drink?'

'A glass of white wine, please.'

'Lucy, can I have a white wine and another pint for me, please?'

After glowering at Celine, the waitress did as she was bid.

'I hope I didn't interrupt anything.'

Richard grinned. 'Just the usual. So, what is it you want to talk to me about?'

Celine stared at him. 'Sorry?'

'Last night on the way home in the taxi you were going on and on about something you had to tell me.'

'Was I? Gosh, I must have been a bit more tipsy that I realised.'

'We all were. It was a good night.'

'What did you think of Marina?' Now that the time had come, Celine was feeling a bit nervous about telling Richard about Kevin Gilligan. Lucy appeared with their drinks and she grabbed her glass.

'She's good fun,' Richard was saying. 'Dominic is nuts about her, isn't he?'

'I think they're nuts about each other.'

'I hope so. I'm not sure Dominic could handle being dumped again.'

'He was dumped?' Celine was momentarily diverted.

'Yeah, at the altar, poor bastard. He hasn't gone out with a woman since.'

'How long ago was this?'

Richard shrugged. 'I'm not sure, but it must be at least ten years.'

'Crikey!'

'So I hope Marina is serious about him.'

'She is.' Celine took a drink from her glass and winced. 'God, this is awful stuff.'

'Let's go back to my place,' Richard suggested. 'I happen to know there are a couple of bottles in the fridge and the waiter is very friendly.'

Celine laughed. 'How can I say no to such a tempting offer?'

They ended up taking the wine into the bedroom and somehow Celine never got around to telling him about Eileen's visit. Later as he slept in her arms she convinced herself that he really didn't need to know at all. If Dominic did hear about it she would easily convince him that it was nothing but gossip. And Dominic was not the sort to spread gossip.

Chapter 31

Fergus felt bile rise up in his throat as he watched them. Sarah was laughing and talking, obviously enjoying herself. And that bastard—

'Excuse me? I asked for a latte not a cappuccino.'

'Sorry.' Fergus dragged his attention back to the queue of impatient customers. By the time things had quietened down, Sarah had gone and Mick Garvey was sitting alone. He looked up, caught Fergus's eye and winked. Fergus walked over to him.

'Leave Sarah alone.'

Mick looked offended. 'Don't be like that, Gus, we were only talking. Ye don't have to worry about her, she's crazy about ye, can't stop talking about ye.'

Fergus shrugged and turned away.

'Yeah, talks about you and yer ma – sorry to hear she's not too well.'

'Thanks,' Fergus muttered.

'She must miss the shop.'

Fergus froze.

'A boutique, isn't it? And in Hopefield, nice spot

that. That's where you and yer ma live now, Sarah was saying.'

Fergus turned back to him. 'Leave us alone.'

Mick's hand shot out and grabbed Fergus's wrist. For a little guy he was surprisingly strong. 'Don't be like that, Gus, it's no way to talk to an old friend.'

Fergus looked around the small bar but no one seemed to have noticed what was going on. 'What do you want?'

Mick released his hand and patted the chair beside him. When Fergus sat down, Mick leaned so close that Fergus could feel his breath on his cheek. 'I think ye know what I want, Gus.'

'I'm clean, Mick, and I'm going to stay that way.'

'Good, that's good, it's better for business to have a clear head.'

'This is my business now.' Fergus waved a hand around the small snack bar.

'Oh, come on, Gus, how much do ye make here, a few hundred a week? Work for me and ye could be making that much a day.'

'Thanks, but no thanks.' Fergus went to leave but Mick grabbed his wrist again, the skinny fingers pinching his skin.

'I'd feel a lot more comfortable if we were working together again,' Mick hissed. 'That way I'd be sure that ye wouldn't go running to the law.'

'I'm not going near the law, Mick, as long as you leave me and Sarah alone.'

Mick's eyes were cold. 'Hey, I'm a member here,

Gus. Ye'd better be nice to me or I'll have to have a word with the boss.'

Fergus pulled his hand away and stood up. 'Just leave me alone to get on with my life, Mick, and I'll do the same.'

Mick gave him a twisted smile. 'Yer making a mistake, Gus. We could be a really good team.'

'I'm doing fine as I am.' Fergus escaped back behind his counter and started to chop fruit to make another batch of smoothies. His hand trembled slightly and he forced himself to take deep breaths and keep his eyes on his work. He felt rather than saw Mick leave and it was only then that he put the knife down and slumped against the counter. He felt cold but he was sweating and his stomach felt sick. The fact that Mick knew he lived in Hopefield, knew about the shop, scared him. Thank God his ma was staying with Babs – at least he didn't have to worry about her for the moment.

'You're overreacting,' he muttered to himself. Mick was probably just making sure that he kept his mouth shut. And he had no worries on that score. All Fergus wanted was a quiet life.

Marina and Dominic sat in Café Napoli, drinking coffee and chatting. Marina was conscious that Dominic was a bit preoccupied but then he'd had another meeting with his accountant and those sessions usually took it out of him. 'How's business, or shouldn't I ask?'

Dominic took off his glasses and started to clean them, a sure sign there was something on his mind. 'Not good but I've had an idea.'

'Oh?'

'Yes, I think it's time to close the newsagent's.'

Marina's eyes widened. 'You're going to sell the shop?'

He held up a finger. 'That's not what I said. No, I think I just need to change what I sell.'

'How exciting! What have you got in mind?'

'I wanted to come up with something to appeal to the residents at Richard's apartments.'

Marina grinned. 'You mean rich people.'

'Rich people with busy lives who don't have time to cook.'

Marina chuckled. 'Or who, like me, don't particularly want to.'

'Exactly. And the only choice is to eat out or order in. Then the choice is pizza, Indian, Chinese.'

'Yes?' Marina prompted, getting impatient.

But Dominic wasn't to be rushed. 'But at the same time we're much more health-conscious. So—'

'So?'

'I was thinking of opening a delicatessen with a difference.'

'A deli! That's a good idea. There's none for miles around here.'

'Exactly. But it would be more than just a normal deli. We could provide a limited catering service as well.'

Marina frowned. 'You're a great cook, Dominic, but I'm not sure you're up to that.'

He laughed. 'I wouldn't be doing the cooking. I'd hire someone to take care of that end.'

'It sounds like a great idea. You could have special low-cal menus.'

'Low cholesterol, low fat, the possibilities are endless.'

'It's a great idea, Dominic, really great.'

Dominic glanced up as Tracy walked by. 'You don't think they'll mind, do you?'

'Of course not,' Marina assured him. 'You won't be in direct competition with them.'

Dominic nodded. 'Some of their customers get coffee and cakes to take away but we won't be doing that sort of thing.'

'How would you handle the catering side?' Marina asked.

'I thought we could have a set menu each day so that people could just come in and order a meal for one or two at the last moment. For larger orders they'd have to give us twenty-four hours' notice and then we could do special menus for larger parties. If it took off, I'd probably need more staff, but only time will tell. I'm also going to see if I can get a wine licence. It would be great if the customer could order dinner and the wine to go with it all under the same roof.'

'You've given this a lot of thought, haven't you?'

'I've had lots of time to,' Dominic said with a wry smile.

'Have you figured out how much it would cost? Putting in a commercial kitchen and changing the layout of the shop won't be cheap.'

'No, but I've talked to the bank and they're willing to back me.'

Marina looked reproachful. 'You've done all this yet you never said a word.'

'I'm sorry, darling, but I wanted to be sure it would work before I said anything because—'

'Yes?'

Dominic reached over and took her hand. 'I wanted to know exactly what my prospects were before I asked you.'

'Asked me what?'

'This is not the way it should be,' Dominic apologised, looking around the busy café. 'I hadn't intended to do this.'

'Dominic.' Marina tugged on his hand.

'Okay.' Dominic swallowed hard. 'Marina, will you marry me?'

'Yes.'

'Don't you want time to think about it?'

'No.'

'Maybe talk to your mother or even to Josh?'

'No. I love you, that's all that matters. Mum will be happy for me and Josh will get used to the idea. It's just been the two of us for so long he's bound to be jealous at first. Give him time. I know he'll come to love you as much as I do. I don't need to ask them.'

'Oh, Marina, I don't know what to say. Damn, I don't even have the ring with me.'

Marina's eyes widened. 'You've bought me a ring?'

'Yes, but the jeweller said I could change if you didn't like it. Apparently that happens quite a lot.'

'I'm sure I'll love it,' Marina told him, hoping fervently that she would.

'I hope you don't want a long engagement,' he murmured, taking her hand and kissing it.

'No, I don't think there's any need for that. But I want a very small wedding.'

He looked surprised. 'I thought you'd want the church, the dress, the works!'

'Been there, done that,' Marina said sadly. 'Anyway, we must think of the business. That comes first.'

'Oh, Marina, you're wonderful,' Dominic said, his smile tender. 'I don't deserve you.'

'Funny, that's what I was thinking,' Marina laughed.

'I'm not much of a prospect. A failing business and a tiny house. Are you sure you don't want to think about this?'

'Are you withdrawing your proposal?'

'No!'

'Then shut up. You can offer me something that money can't buy. You love me and you've been so good to Josh.'

'It's easy to love you and Josh is a part of you. But I don't think he'll be happy about having a stepfather.'

'He'll be fine,' Marina assured him. 'Now, tell me,

where's the best place to hold a cheap wedding?'

Dominic's eyes twinkled. 'Let's go to Las Vegas!'

Marina clapped her hands. 'What a wonderful idea! We could get married in one of those dinky little wedding chapels.'

'Your mum will probably think we're mad.'

'The only problem we'll have with my mum is dragging her away from the slot machines long enough to attend the service!'

'Richard could be my best man and Celine could be your bridesmaid.'

Marina's eyes moistened. 'And Joshie will make such an adorable pageboy.'

Tracy wandered over, a wide smile on her face. 'Can I get anything else for you two?'

Marina smiled at Dominic. 'No, I think we've got everything we need.'

Celine gathered up her bag and jacket as the train pulled into Arklow station. Babs, Rose's sister, had offered to pick her up and Celine was amused to see that the woman was a brunette version of her sister. Equally small, curvy and pretty, she was a bit more vocal, chatting non-stop until they pulled up outside a small bungalow on the outskirts of the town. As Celine got out of the car, she was thrilled to see Rose standing unaided in the doorway. 'Look at you!' she exclaimed, rushing over to hug her boss.

'Hello, Celine, it's lovely to see you.'

'Now you two go on out to the garden,' Babs told them. 'and I'll make us some tea.'

Rose led Celine through the house, into a pretty conservatory and out into a garden abundant with flowers.

'This is definitely the perfect spot for recuperation,' Celine said, helping Rose into her chair before flopping into a comfortable lounger.

'Isn't it?' Rose agreed.

'So tell me, how are you feeling?'

'Not bad at all. Getting in and out of the bath and dressing is still a bit of a struggle but apart from that I'm doing very well. How about you? I hope you're not finding managing the shop too stressful.'

'On the contrary, I'm enjoying it. It's nice to be doing something that involves my brain. My last job wasn't exactly challenging.' Knowing that Rose would want to know everything, Celine went on to give her a run down on the stock that had come in, the customers Rose would be interested in, and she finished up with the good news that the takings were up. Babs appeared with a heavy-laden tray and set it down on the table beside them.

'I think I'll stay here with you, Babs, this girl is running the place better than I did!'

'I wouldn't say that,' Celine protested. 'I'm not so good with the staff.'

Rose chuckled. 'Is Sadie driving you mad?'

Celine put her head on one side. 'Let's say I couldn't see us ever sharing a flat.'

'Ha!' Rose clapped her hands delightedly. 'I'm glad it's not just me. I mean, the poor woman means well but—'

'She whines,' Celine supplied. 'Whines, whinges, moans. Constantly.'

'Oh, my,' said Babs as she poured the tea. 'How do you put up with her?'

'I've learned to tune her out,' Celine replied.

'Me too,' Rose admitted, 'It's the only way.'

Babs handed Celine a cup of tea and pushed the tempting plate of cakes towards her. 'Then I'm glad you're not planning to return to work for a while, Rose, because that kind of thing wouldn't be good for you.'

'She's a terrible fusspot,' Rose told Celine, but she patted Babs' hand affectionately. 'But I was thinking of staying on here for a while longer, Celine – would that be okay with you?'

'Of course it's okay. Take as long as you like.'

'Bless you, love. So tell me, is there any news? How are Dominic and Richard?'

'Fine. Dominic's in an especially good mood. In fact, I'd go so far as to say he's in love.'

Rose's eyes lit up. 'Really? Not with one of those women from the musical society, I hope?'

Celine shook her head and laughed. 'No, with Marina.'

'Your friend?'

'That's right.'

'My goodness, how amazing.'

'I know. I introduced them one day, didn't think any more about it, and the next thing I know they're dating.'

'She must be something special,' Rose murmured. 'Dominic hasn't been out with a woman since he moved to Dublin.'

'Is that the nice Englishman who was jilted on his wedding day?' Babs asked.

Rose nodded. 'When I first met him he was a broken man. The shop and buying that dilapidated house is what got him through that terrible time. But, though he got plenty of invitations, Dominic never looked at another woman. He threw himself into the musical society, worked out in the gym and played squash with Richard, but any time a woman came on to him he ran a mile.'

Celine smiled. 'I'd have thought Marina was the last person he'd end up with. You met her, Rose, you know what she's like.'

Rose nodded at her sister. 'A real beauty, she's a model, you know, and very outgoing. She's a lot younger too, isn't she, Celine?'

'Thirty-five, but don't tell her I told you.'

'Well, I'm flabbergasted,' Rose admitted. 'No offence, Celine, I know she's your friend, but she won't hurt him, will she?'

'I don't think so, Rose, she seems mad about the man. They make a lovely couple.'

'I'm so glad. Now if I could just find someone for Richard.' She shot Celine a sly glance.

Celine rolled her eyes at Babs. 'Has she always been such a matchmaker?'

Babs nodded. 'She has poor Fergus driven mad. I keep telling her he's still young but she won't be happy until she sees him march down the aisle. What?' She stopped when she saw the grim look on Rose's face. 'Oh, sorry, I've put my foot in it, haven't I?'

'It's okay, Babs.' Celine looked her boss in the eye. 'You are allowed to talk about your son in front of me, Rose, I won't fall to pieces. Now, after all that tea, I really must use your loo.'

When she returned the sisters were careful to keep the conversation innocuous until it was time for Celine to leave.

'It's a pity you couldn't take the later train,' Rose said with a sigh.

'I have a business to run,' Celine reminded her. 'Anyway, I think I've tired you out.'

Babs nodded. 'Yes, it's time you had a nap, Rose. I'll get her settled and then I'll take you to the station, Celine.'

'Stop fussing, Babs,' Rose complained, but she allowed her sister to lead her back into the house and Celine noticed she was leaning rather more heavily on her sister's arm.

'Is she okay?' Celine asked Babs when they were on the way back to the station.

'She tires easily but the nurse says she's making a very good recovery.'

'I'm so glad. She was in such pain before the operation.'

'She's had a tough time but at least she can relax knowing the shop is in good hands.' Babs pulled into a parking spot outside the train station. 'Now, my dear, you had better hurry or you'll miss your train. It was lovely to meet you.'

Chapter 32

The following Thursday, Celine was in the parish hall an hour earlier than everyone else. The altered dresses were hanging up on one rack, clearly labelled. The remainder of the clothes she had sorted into size. She had wanted to sort them per scene but it transpired that most of the cast would be in the same outfits for much of the show so that wasn't possible. The only clothes she had for the men were the morning suits for the Ascot scene, suits for the wedding scene and suits for Henry Higgins and Colonel Pickering. They would bring in old clothes for the other scenes.

'You look busy.'

She looked up to see Dominic smiling down at her. 'Well, well, well, if it isn't the bridegroom!'

He smiled shyly. 'You've heard then.'

Celine hugged him. 'I think all of Dublin has heard! I'm delighted for you both. It's wonderful news.'

'I can't quite believe it,' Dominic admitted. 'I never expected to find someone, never mind a ready-made family.'

'And Marina tells me you're opening a deli too.

It's guaranteed to be a success with me living next door.'

He laughed. 'Let's hope there are plenty more like you.'

'When do you plan to start trading?'

'Hopefully September. I had a meeting with the builder today and he says the work should take about six weeks. Now I should let you get on with your sewing. You know, you're doing a wonderful job, Celine, we really appreciate it.'

Celine chuckled. 'I don't think all the ladies would agree with you. Between you and me, there's some fierce rivalry among them.'

Dominic groaned. 'Don't I know it, but I hope it hasn't frightened you off. You're a great addition to the society.'

Celine frowned. 'You may not think so once Mary Boyle tells everyone what I'm really like.'

'Sorry?'

'It's a bit embarrassing but—'

'Hello, you two.' Cathy Donlon marched in, laden down with scripts, scores and what looked like a box of wigs. 'Give me a hand, would you, Dominic?'

'Where did you get these?' Celine asked as she peered into the box that Dominic had set down on the floor. She pulled out a blonde wig and a feather boa.

'Had them for years,' Cathy told her. 'Some of them are falling apart but that's showbusiness.'

Celine blew dust off the wig, coughed and put it on.

'Ooh, Mae West, as I live and breathe!' Dominic laughed.

'Come up and see me sometime,' Celine replied sticking her chest out.

'It's a pity you insist on being behind the scenes,' Cathy complained. 'You'd be such an asset to our production.'

Celine removed the wig, laughing. 'Thank you but no thank you.'

'What was it you were going to tell me about Mary Boyle?' Dominic murmured as Cathy went to set out the chairs.

Celine dragged a hand through her hair. 'She was in the shop one day when I had a visit from—' She paused, wondering how to describe Eileen. 'From the wife of a friend of mine. We had words and it got rather heated. Good old Mary enjoyed every minute of it.'

'Sounds like our nosey neighbour.'

'I'm sure she's spent her week telling her cronies all about it.'

'I wouldn't worry.' Dominic patted her shoulder. 'Mary is always bad-mouthing someone. She'll probably have forgotten all about it by now.'

'I doubt that very much,' Celine murmured but Dominic was already crossing the room to help Cathy.

It wasn't long before Celine's worst fears were realised.

'I can't believe she has the nerve to show her face in here tonight,' Mary said in a stage whisper to the ladies nearest her. 'I'm sure poor Rose Lynch would be shocked if she knew what kind of person she had working for her.'

Celine pretended not to have heard the woman's vicious tongue but every time she looked up from her sewing, Mary was whispering in yet another ear and pointing in her direction. Dominic seemed unaware of the growing tension. He, Cathy and Tom Callen – Colonel Pickering – were working on a scene at the far end of the room. The ladies were supposed to be practising their songs but there was more talking than singing going on. Celine kept her head down but when she heard the word 'slut', she flipped. Standing up she clapped her hands. 'Can I have your attention, please? Sorry to interrupt,' she added as Cathy looked around in surprise. 'I just need to put the ladies straight on something. Mary Boyle has been telling you all about a visitor I had in my shop last week.' She paused and you could have heard a pin drop. 'She heard only one side of a very complicated story and I think you should remember that.'

'Then tell us the other half,' retorted one of Mary's closest friends.

'I, well, it's not true.'

'So you're not sleeping with the woman's husband?' Mary piped up.

'No I'm not!' Celine reddened, her eyes flickering

over the accusing faces and coming to rest on Dominic's bemused one.

'You heard her.' Cathy had moved silently up the room and was now standing at Celine's side. 'Not that I think it's any of our business one way or another,' she added, looking at Mary Boyle. 'Now can we get back to work, please? There's still a lot of work to do.'

'Thanks,' Celine murmured when the ladies had resumed their rehearsal.

'Mary can be a nosey old biddy, don't mind her,' Cathy advised.

'I wouldn't have wanted any customer to have overheard that – exchange – but Mary Boyle.' Celine sighed. 'I wouldn't mind so much if the woman ever bought anything.'

Cathy laughed. 'Look on the bright side. You'll be off her list of eligible brides for Gerry.'

Celine's smile was shaky. 'Do you mind if I head home, Cathy?'

'Not at all, love, you go on.'

'Thanks.' Celine packed up some costumes to take with her and headed for the door, aware that all eyes in the room were on her back.

'Are you all right?' Dominic had followed her outside.

Celine nodded. 'She's got it wrong, Dominic—' She stopped as he put his finger to her lips.

'You don't have say another word, Celine. I know you would never behave like that.'

Celine closed her eyes briefly. 'Oh, Dominic.'

'What?'

'You're a lovely man, Marina's lucky to have found you.'

He beamed like a schoolboy. 'I think I'm the lucky one. Good night, Celine, take care.'

Celine walked back to the flat feeling like a total tart. As soon as she got inside she picked up the phone and dialled Kevin's mobile. 'We need to talk,' she said without preamble.

'I'll be there as soon as I can,' he promised.

She opened a bottle of wine and took down two glasses. They were both going to need a drink. The buzzer went and Celine froze. It was unlikely to be Kevin, it must be Richard. The buzzer went again and she went to answer it. 'Hello?'

'Celine, it's Dominic.'

Celine sighed with relief. 'Come on up.' She opened the door and watched him climb the stairs. 'Is everything okay?'

'That's what I came to ask you. Cathy thought you might be upset.'

'I'll survive.'

Dominic noticed the two glasses and bottle of wine on the counter and smiled. 'Ah, you're expecting Richard I see.'

Celine looked from the glasses back to Dominic. 'Er, well, actually—'

'I'll leave you to it.' He turned to leave. 'Oh, by the

way, Cathy said that now you've sorted out most of the costumes you don't have to come to all the rehearsals.'

'She is so nice,' Celine said as she went downstairs with him.

'She is, and between us, she's not Mary's greatest fan.'

Celine laughed. 'I got that impression.' When she opened the door, Kevin was standing there, his finger poised in front of the buzzer.

He smiled at her and then noticed Dominic hovering behind her. 'Oh, hello, again.'

Dominic nodded curtly and barely looked at Celine as he stepped past her.

'Dominic, let me explain—'

He turned and gave her a cool smile. 'No need, good night.'

Celine groaned as she turned to go back upstairs.

'What was all that about?' Kevin asked as they went into the flat.

'I hardly know where to begin.' Celine handed him a glass of wine and took hers over to sit on the window ledge. 'I had a visit from Eileen last week.'

Kevin slopped some wine on his pale grey suit. 'Shit!' He took out an immaculate handkerchief and dabbed at the stain. 'I don't understand, what did she want?'

'It seems she followed you the last time you came to see me.'

'Followed me?' Kevin repeated. 'But why?'

'Oh, Kevin, because she loves you and she's jealous, of course!'

Kevin gave a short laugh. 'I don't think so.'

'Kevin, she was crying.'

'Crying?'

'I wish you'd stop repeating everything I say.'

'I can't remember the last time I saw her cry,' Kevin was saying, almost to himself.

'She was devastated when she thought we were still seeing each other. I'm telling you, Kevin, she really loves you.'

'Why doesn't she say so? Why doesn't she show me how she feels? She's never shown any interest in what I do.'

'Go home, Kevin, talk to her. Maybe she'll surprise you.'

Kevin put down his glass and stood up. 'Okay. I suppose I've nothing to lose. Thanks, Celine. I'll be in touch.'

Celine smiled. 'I don't think that's a good idea, do you?'

Chapter 33

Celine felt she'd only just closed her eyes when a noise woke her. She sat up in bed, rubbing her eyes. There it was again. It was the sound of breaking glass, not in the flat but very close. She peered out of the bedroom window but could see nothing. She went into the sitting room and looked out of the window. Nothing, although . . . she was sure something was different about the yard below. It took her a moment and then she realised that the table had been moved against the wall, under the window— 'Jesus, we've got burglars!' She groped behind her for the phone, afraid to take her eyes off the yard below and dialled 999. 'Police, please.' When she'd given her name and address, she rang off and phoned Richard. 'Come on,' she muttered as the phone rang and rang. Where the hell was he? She rang off and dialled his mobile but it was switched off. Damn, she'd have to call Rose. But what was the point in that? She couldn't do anything and why worry her unnecessarily? 'Damn, damn, damn.' She felt her way across the room in search of her handbag. After she'd found it and pulled out her address book, she took it and the phone into the bedroom and turned on the light. Hesitantly, she keyed the number into the phone and waited.

'Hello?'

'Fergus? It's Celine Moore.'

'Celine? What's wrong?'

'Someone is breaking into the shop. I've called the police but I thought you should know.'

'I'm on my way.'

'Are you sure—' she started but he'd already hung up. Celine hoped that the police would arrive before he did. She switched off the light and went back to her post by the window. She couldn't hear or see anything, maybe they'd left. She hurried back into the bedroom, pulled off her pyjamas and climbed into jeans and a sweatshirt. Then she went downstairs and opened the door a fraction. It felt like hours but it was only a few minutes before a police car pulled up outside. She opened the door wider. 'They got in through the back,' she whispered, as two policemen got out of the car.

'How do we get out there?' one of them asked.

'There's a fire escape from my flat down to the yard at the back.'

'Have you got keys to the shop?' the other one asked.

Celine handed them over as another police car pulled up. After a brief, whispered confab, two policemen went up to the flat with her while the other two positioned themselves at the front.

'Stay here,' one of them told Celine – rather unnecessarily, she thought – before they climbed out of her window and onto the fire escape.

'Be careful,' she whispered and then hurried back downstairs. She stepped out onto the street just in time to see one of the policemen reappear. 'All clear, love, but it's a bit of a mess in there. Is there anyone you can call?'

'The owner's son is on his way.'

'He's here.'

Celine turned to see Fergus standing behind her, grim and white-faced.

'What's the story?' he asked.

'The shop has been done over. I'm afraid they got away. It looks like they left the way they came in. There's a deserted property at the back with a side entrance so they probably came in that way.'

'Was there anything taken?' Celine asked as she followed the policeman and Fergus into the shop.

'The till was broken into. Was there much in it?'

Celine shook her head. 'Only change. I lodge the takings in the bank every evening.'

Another policeman came over to join them. 'I'm Sergeant Jim Thomas, and you are?' He looked at Fergus.

'Fergus Lynch. My Mother, Rose Lynch, owns this place. She's in Arklow staying with her sister at the moment. This is Celine Moore, the manager.'

'And you live upstairs?'

Celine could only nod as she looked around at the devastation. All the rails had been tipped over and it looked like they'd taken the contents of the kitchen cupboards and fridge and trampled them into the clothes.

'It's a bit of a mess, isn't it?' the sergeant was saying. 'They must have been pissed off because there was no cash.'

Fergus stood silently looking around him.

'The window at the back has been smashed in,' the sergeant told him. 'You'd better get a glazier out first thing. It might be an idea to get bars put on that window too.'

'I'll take care of it,' Fergus said.

'And you'll need to talk to your insurance company. It's a clear-cut break-in so there shouldn't be a problem.'

'But why didn't the alarm go off?' Celine asked. 'It was serviced only a few weeks ago.'

'It was the smaller window they came through so it probably isn't alarmed.'

'I don't understand,' Celine murmured. 'There's a newsagent's next door with cigarettes, sweets – why break into a boutique?'

'The newsagent's may have been their target but coming in from the back they could have got disoriented. I'm afraid, love, it was probably just bad luck.'

'The stock is ruined,' Celine groaned. 'Oh, Fergus, what are we going to tell Rose?'

'Don't worry about that now. Let's get this place sorted first.'

After the police had taken a statement, they left, promising to return in the morning to check for fingerprints. 'Not that we have much hope of catching the little buggers,' the sergeant said cheerfully.

When they were gone, Celine slumped against the counter. 'I don't know where to begin.'

'Put on the kettle,' Fergus told her, 'and I'll get started here.'

Celine obediently went into the back room, picked the kettle off the floor and filled it from the tap. But when she opened the cupboards she realised that everything had been thrown around the shop and the mugs were in smithereens on the floor. 'If we want a cuppa we'll have to go upstairs,' she said, coming back into the shop to stand beside Fergus. 'They've cleared everything out of the fridge and the cupboards.'

'Tell me about it,' Fergus muttered, as he wrung milk out of a black silk shirt. He righted the rails and hung up clothes that were dry. The wet stuff he threw in a corner. 'I'll stay here tonight.'

'You can't do that,' Celine protested. 'They're hardly going to come back.'

'I don't like leaving you here alone. We could ask Richard to come over, I suppose.'

'I called him first,' Celine admitted, 'but there was no answer.'

'Then I'm staying.'

Celine saw the determined look on his face and

capitulated. 'Okay, then, but you're sleeping on my sofa. I wouldn't get a wink of sleep if you were down here alone.'

Fergus glanced at his watch. 'It's nearly five. Why don't you go back to bed and I'll be up in a few minutes?'

Celine, suddenly feeling very weary, agreed and handed Fergus her keys. 'Don't be long.'

'I'll just mop out the floor and block up the window,' Fergus promised.

Celine went back to bed fully clothed but couldn't sleep. When she heard Fergus come in nearly an hour later, she went out to join him. 'You said you wouldn't be long.'

'I couldn't find anything to block up the window. I ended up using some of Ma's suit holders.'

'That's fine. Want a beer, tea, or would you prefer to get some sleep?'

'Beer, please.' Fergus sat up on a stool. 'I don't really feel like sleeping.'

'Me neither.' Celine took a beer from the fridge and handed it to Fergus. 'God, what's your mother going to say?'

'Once she knows no one was hurt she won't care,' Fergus assured her.

Celine nodded, realising the truth of this. 'Thanks for coming over.'

Fergus grinned suddenly. 'You'd never have asked me if Richard had been around.'

'No,' she admitted.

'You know, if I could change the past—'

Celine held up a hand. 'I don't want to talk about it.'

'Sorry.'

Celine looked at his crestfallen expression and relented. 'In my heart, I do know that it wasn't your fault. But Dermot only went there to see you.'

Fergus looked at her helplessly. 'If there was something I could do, I'd do it.'

Celine nodded. 'Is he out of jail?'

'He's dead,' Fergus replied, knowing immediately that she was talking about Dermot's killer. 'He managed to get drugs inside and took an overdose.'

'No one told me,' she murmured.

'He was lucky,' Fergus muttered. 'If I'd ever caught up with him when he got out he wouldn't have had such an easy escape.'

'You wouldn't have gone after him?'

'Damn right I would! Celine, you lost a husband and I lost the best friend I've ever had. Dermot saved my life long before that night.'

'Then I'm glad the bastard died in prison. It would be awful if you were locked up because of him and it wouldn't bring Dermot back.'

Fergus said nothing.

'He was very proud of you.'

'He was?'

'Yeah, he talked about you all the time. That morning, at the funeral, I recognised you immediately from his description.'

'Long and skinny.' A ghost of a smile played around Fergus's lips.

Celine smiled too. 'Yeah. He told me that he used to smuggle burgers into rehab for you.'

'The food in there was shite,' Fergus remembered. 'Not that I felt much like eating.'

'That's what scared him. You were so thin he was afraid you wouldn't make it.'

'With the pressure from him and Ma, I'd have been afraid not to!'

'You and Rose are very close.'

'We are now. When I was a teenager, though, we were always at each other's throats. I don't know how she put up with me for as long as she did.'

'Why did you start taking drugs?'

Fergus smiled slightly. 'You know, someone else asked me that question recently. I was shy, I wanted to fit in and I gave in to the pressure from kids in school. Then I realised that when I was high I was confident. I felt like one of the gang and everyone liked me. That's very hard to resist when you've been a loner.'

Celine nodded. 'I can understand that. How long were you using before Rose found out?'

'A couple of years.' Fergus saw her surprised look. 'You see, she was happy that I was finally mixing with other kids. She put down the changes in me to being part of a gang. She didn't really approve of them, they were too rough for her liking, but it was preferable to me spending all my spare time in front of the computer in my bedroom. When she finally realised what was going on she did everything she could to help me but I was too far gone. Finally she threw me out.'

'Is that when you met Dermot?'

He shook his head. 'No, he'd been on the scene for a while before that.'

'But he couldn't help?'

Fergus shrugged. 'I wasn't ready to be helped. It wasn't till I saw someone have a bad trip that I realised if I wanted to live I'd have to kick the habit. As soon as he knew I was serious, Dermot got me into rehab and that was that. Ma sold the house and by the time I got out she'd moved to Hopefield. Sometimes I think she decided to move here because of the name.'

Celine smiled. 'Sounds like Rose.' Her thoughts returned to the devastation downstairs. 'When do you think we should tell her about the break-in?'

'Let's wait until we've talked to the insurance people. There's no point in worrying her until we know what's happening.' He looked at his watch. 'I should get back down there and start the clean-up.'

Celine shook her head. 'First let me buy you breakfast. Café Napoli should be open by now.'

Fergus shot her a shy grin. 'That would be great.'

Chapter 34

He should have felt better after his conversation with Celine but Fergus actually felt worse. She had been so nice, so grateful for his help cleaning up the shop, but then she didn't know that he was responsible for the break-in. He had no doubt that this was the handiwork of one of Mick Garvey's gang. Mick obviously meant business and Fergus was going to have to deal with him. Although how he would do that he had no idea. He opened the door of the small house he and Rose had shared for the last six years and climbed the stairs. He felt tired now and couldn't wait to get his head down. Vincent Burke had been very understanding when he had phoned and told him about the break-in. He had arranged for someone to stand in for him today and tomorrow as well if he needed more time. And the way he felt now, he probably would, Fergus thought as he flopped on the bed and closed his eyes.

Celine blinked at the apparition in the doorway.

Marina, resplendent in old jeans, T-shirt, hair tied

back in a scarf and rubber gloves under her arm smiled at Celine. 'I thought you could use some help.'

'How did you know?' Celine asked, a lump in her throat.

'Dominic called me first thing. He'll be in later to help, although,' Marina paused as she looked around, 'it doesn't look too bad.'

'Fergus just left. He cleaned up most of it.'

'Fergus?' Marina stared at her, wide-eyed.

'I had to call him. It's his mum's shop, after all.'

Marina picked her way around the shop. 'Oh no,' she groaned, picking up a Chanel suit that was torn and filthy.

'Heartbreaking, isn't it? Some of the stuff will be fine once it's cleaned but a lot of the stock is ruined. I'll have to close for a few days.'

Marina touched a silk shift dress with reverential hands. 'Poor Rose, she must be devastated.'

'She doesn't know yet. Fergus decided not to tell her until we'd figured out the extent of the damage and talked to the insurance people. Come on, let's go across the road for a coffee.' Celine took her keys and went to the door. 'I need a break.'

Tracy smiled as they came through the door. 'Back again, Celine.'

Celine nodded wearily. 'I'm not getting much done,' she admitted.

'Once you've had your coffee you should lie down for a few hours,' Marina told her. 'It's been a very traumatic night.'

'But I have to sort through the clothes—'

'I can do that,' Marina retorted.

Celine smiled and nodded. Marina could always be trusted when it came to handling clothes.

'Where's Richard?'

'No idea.' Celine's tone was clipped. 'I haven't been able to get hold of him. Thank goodness Fergus was around. I don't know what I'd have done without him.'

Marina smiled. 'Did you ever think you would say those words?'

'No, never,' Celine admitted with a sigh. 'He's a good kid, Marina. I've been very unfair to him.'

'It's human nature, Celine, don't be too hard on yourself.'

They sipped their coffee in silence for a moment.

'Is Dominic disgusted with me?' Celine asked.

Marina laughed. 'Don't be ridiculous, Dominic's your biggest fan.'

'He hasn't told you then.'

'Told me what?'

'I got a bit upset at rehearsal the other night.' She held up a hand at Marina's questioning look. 'That's another story, but anyway, Dominic dropped by later to see if I was okay. He was just leaving when Kevin arrived.'

'Kevin?' Marina looked shocked. 'You're still seeing Kevin?'

'No, of course not! But Dominic obviously thought I was. God, Marina, the look he gave me.' Celine shivered.

'He just jumped to the wrong conclusion. Tell me about Kevin.'

Celine brought her up to date on the whole sorry saga. 'I never thought I'd feel sorry for Eileen,' she said finally. 'But I'm sure she really loves him. Unfortunately, when she was calling me all the names under the sun, a woman from the musical society was present and she told everyone what happened.'

Marina groaned. 'Oh, bloody hell!'

'Dominic didn't believe a word of it, of course, which made it worse. I felt awful. He dropped in on his way home to make sure I was okay.'

Marina smiled. 'No wonder I love him.'

'Anyway, when he arrived I was about to open a bottle of wine so he assumed that Richard was on his way over. Kevin arrived as he was leaving.'

'You had invited Kevin again?' Marina raised her eyebrows.

'Only to tell him about Eileen. He's never believed that she cared about him and I had to tell him he was wrong.'

'What did Dominic say?'

'He just gave me a filthy look and left.'

Marina gave her hand a sympathetic squeeze. 'Don't worry, I'll set him straight. Does Richard know about all this?'

'Not unless Dominic has told him. I suppose it's only matter of time. Now, if you don't mind I'm going for that nap. Call me if the police or insurance people call.'

'Sure.' Marina paid for their coffee and then guided her tired, miserable friend across the road.

Moments after Marina had opened the shop, Dominic appeared in the doorway. 'Hi.'

Marina moved forward to kiss him, careful not to touch his jacket with her dirty gloves. 'Hello, there. Are you avoiding Celine by any chance?'

He grimaced. 'Is it that obvious?'

'To me, yes.'

'I'm sorry, darling, but it was such a shock. I felt so stupid the way I was prattling on that she would never do something like that.' He gave a short laugh. 'I'm obviously not as good a judge of character as I thought I was.'

'Indeed you are!' Marina retorted. 'Celine hasn't been involved with Kevin for months. She asked him over last night to tell him that his wife loved him and he should give his marriage a chance. She's the first to admit she's made mistakes, Dominic, but she's doing her damnedest to put things right.'

'I'm afraid I jumped to the wrong conclusion,' Dominic admitted.

Maria hugged him. 'I can see why. But I don't see any reason why Richard should hear anything about this, do you?'

'I suppose not.'

'Excellent! Because I think Celine's got enough to worry about at the moment.'

'Is there a lot of damage?'

'It's not as bad as it looks. This pile is all fine.' She patted the clothes on the counter. 'That lot over there needs to be cleaned. And the clothes by the window need some minor repairs. Celine will have that done in no time.'

'What about them?' Dominic pointed to the clothes in the middle of the floor.

'They're for the bin, I'm afraid.'

'You've done a great job cleaning up,' Dominic replied.

'Not me, Fergus,' Marina said with a delighted grin. 'Talk about every cloud has a silver lining. Celine couldn't get hold of Richard last night so she called Fergus. He was here all night. I don't know how much they talked but certainly the ice is broken. It has to be the best thing for both of them.'

'Rose will be pleased.'

Marina made a face. 'Pity it had to happen under these circumstances. I don't know what kind of thugs would do such a thing. It's not as if they got anything.'

'The police seem to think they may have been trying to get into my place.'

'It would make more sense, I suppose.'

Dominic clapped his hands. 'Enough talk, what can I do to help?'

Marina smiled. 'Take that lot down to the cleaners and use your charms to get a good price and fast service.'

'I'll do my best.'

*

While he was gone, Marina dressed the window, hung up all of the undamaged stock and then arranged the rails so that the shop wouldn't look quite so bare. She was carefully folding scarves in tissue paper when Celine reappeared.

'The window display is wonderful, Marina!' One mannequin was dressed in a black suit and the other in a long black dress. Marina had contrasted the black with colourful scarves and hats at raunchy angles.

Marina smiled, delighted that her handiwork was appreciated. 'It's not bad, is it?'

'It's great. You've got quite a flair, Marina. When you've had enough of modelling, you can take over here.'

'I think I'd quite like that,' Marina admitted. 'It's lovely to be surrounded by such beautiful things.'

'Not so beautiful at the moment,' Celine murmured, looking at the pile of torn clothes in the corner. 'Hang on, that bundle looks a lot smaller.'

'That's the stuff that needs to be repaired. Dominic took the dirty clothes to the dry-cleaners. They've promised to get some of it back in the morning and the rest the day after.'

'That's wonderful. I'd better get to work with a needle and thread on the rest.'

'Take it upstairs,' Marina suggested, 'and I'll look after things down here.'

Celine shook her head. 'That's okay, I'm not opening the shop today.'

'In that case I'll wash the delicate stuff while you

sew. We'll have everything done in no time at all.'

'Thanks, Marina, I don't know what I'd do without you.'

'Don't worry about it,' Marina said with a wink. 'I'll expect a special discount in future.'

Chapter 35

Fergus had checked back in with Celine and was delighted to see the shop looking so well. The insurance people had visited and everything seemed very straightforward. Celine's concern about the alarm not going off didn't appear to be a problem.

'The kids always slip in the small windows,' the claims inspector had told her. 'They're usually in and out before anyone even notices.' The main problem that Celine had to face was replacing the stock. Fergus was happy to leave her and Marina to discuss that. Once they had some ideas, he and Celine would go down to visit his mother. After dropping in to say a quick hello to Dominic, Fergus went over to Richard's apartment. He'd tried to call him a couple of times but there was still no answer. This was a bit odd, Fergus thought, given that Richard had promised Rose he'd keep an eye on Celine and the shop.

He pressed the buzzer for Richard's apartment twice before it was answered.

'Hello?'

Fergus grinned at the groggy voice. 'Richard, it's Fergus.'

'Come on up,' Richard muttered.

When Fergus stepped out of the lift, the door to the apartment was open. He went in, closed the door and headed for the kitchen. Richard, predictably, was standing at the fridge with a carton of juice to his mouth.

'I thought you sounded a bit seedy,' Fergus said climbing onto a stool.

'Don't look so bloody cheerful,' Richard said, before going in search of painkillers. 'What time is it?'

'Five o'clock in the afternoon. What have you been up to?'

'Working,' Richard told him and then added with a lopsided smile, 'and celebrating.'

'You didn't have your phone with you?'

'I forgot it. Why, were you looking for me?'

'Me, Celine, Dominic.' Fergus ticked the names off on his fingers.

Richard frowned. 'Celine? Is something wrong?'

'The shop was broken into last night.'

'Shit! Is she okay?'

'Fine. They made an awful mess of the shop though.'

'She called you?'

Fergus smiled. 'Yeah.'

'God, I'm glad you were around.'

'I didn't do much,' Fergus admitted. 'The cops had arrived by the time I got there and the thieves were long gone.'

'Did they get much?'

'Nothing. They just wrecked the place. Cheers,' he said as Richard handed him a bottle of lager. 'The police think it was probably kids and that the news-agent's was their real target.'

Richard slouched against the counter and watched him through narrowed eyes. 'But you don't agree.'

Fergus hesitated for a moment and then shook his head. 'I'm pretty sure I know who's behind it.'

'Some of your old pals from Sandhill?'

'One. A guy called Mick Garvey. He's a dangerous character. A club member, would you believe? Who says crime doesn't pay.'

'Has he been giving you a tough time?'

'He wants me to work for him.'

'Dealing?' Richard straightened, his hangover for-gotten.

Fergus nodded. 'I said no, of course, but then he found out where I lived, where the shop was.' He shot Richard a worried look. 'He doesn't like to take no for an answer.'

'You need to tell the police.'

'Tell them what?'

'About the break-in for a start.'

'Waste of time,' Fergus told him. 'Mick will have arranged that through one of his contacts. You can bet that the lads who did it don't even know Mick's name.'

'There must be something we can do. If he's capable of this God knows what he'll do next.'

'He's not the sort to give up,' Fergus admitted. 'Ma will kill me when she finds out.'

'It's not your fault, Fergus.'

'I should never have taken the bloody job.'

'Then she'll have to kill me too as I got you that bloody job.'

Fergus ran a shaky hand through his short hair. 'Sorry. The job's great.'

'Vincent owns a couple of other centres. We could ask him to transfer you.'

'There's no point now that Mick knows where I live. Short of disappearing again, there's no solution to this.'

'We could get Mick arrested.' Richard smiled slightly.

'I told you, we don't have anything on him. I need to get out of Dublin. Maybe even Ireland.'

'There's no guarantee he'd leave Rose alone.'

Fergus sat down and put his head in his hands. 'What the fuck am I going to do?'

Richard sat down next to him and patted his back. 'We'll think of something.'

When Fergus had gone, Richard showered, dressed and walked the short distance to Close Second. It was closed and in darkness so he pressed the buzzer for Celine's flat.

'Hello?'

'Celine, it's Richard.'

She didn't answer but pressed the release on the door.

Marina, who was hanging clothes out on the fire escape, stuck her head in the window. 'Do you want me to leave?'

Celine shook her head. 'There's no need.' She opened the door and greeted Richard with a cool smile.

'Celine, I heard what happened. I'm so sorry I wasn't around.'

'I coped and luckily I managed to get hold of Fergus.'

'Yeah, I was just talking to him. Oh, hi, Marina,' he added as she stepped into the room.

'Just washing some of the stock,' she explained. 'Dominic took another load to the dry-cleaners. It's all hands on deck at times like this,' she added pointedly.

He nodded. 'What can I do to help?'

'We have everything under control, thanks,' Celine replied.

Richard looked nonplussed and then brightened. 'If you like I could drive you and Fergus to see Rose tomorrow.'

Celine picked up her sewing. 'I'm not sure I'll be able to go tomorrow.'

Marina glanced from one to the other and picked up her bag. 'I'd better go, Celine, but I'm not working tomorrow so if you need me—'

Celine stood up and embraced her friend. 'Thanks for everything, Marina, I really appreciate it.'

Marina kissed her cheek. 'That's okay, darling, what are friends for? Bye, Richard.'

'Goodbye, Marina.'

Celine stood in the doorway until Marina had let herself out on to the street.

'Come and sit down,' Richard said from the sofa.

'I think I'll have a coffee, would you like one?'

Richard sighed. 'Sure.'

Celine made the coffee in silence and then sat on a stool at the bar to drink it, leaving him alone on the sofa. Richard stood up and came over to stand beside her. 'Are you angry because I wasn't here last night?'

'Last night was difficult. It didn't help that I had to drag Fergus over here. The agreement was that you would be my contact if I had any problems.'

'I know that and I'm sorry. I went away for a couple of days and I forgot to take my mobile.'

Celine forced a smile. 'These things happen.' Where the hell had he been? Who had he been with?

'Let's go out and get something to eat.'

'I don't think so, I'm very tired.'

'You need to keep up your strength,' he insisted.

Celine wished he wouldn't be nice to her. 'Okay, then.'

Richard closed and locked her window and then stood over her as she locked the hall door.

'You don't think they'll come back, do you?' She shot him a nervous look as they walked to the Chinese restaurant.

'Of course not. Sorry, I suppose I'm guilty of shutting the stable door after the horse has bolted. I wish I'd been here with you. You must have been terrified.' He put an arm around her shoulders and gave her a squeeze.

Celine swallowed hard. 'It wasn't so bad,' she lied.

'You handled it very well. Fergus was telling me the police were already here when he arrived.'

'I called them first.'

'Which was exactly the right thing to do,' he said, his voice soothing and gentle.

When they were seated he picked up the wine list. 'I think we should have some champagne.'

'Are you trying to be funny? The shop that I manage has been destroyed by thugs and you think we have something to celebrate?' Her voice rose into an indignant squeak.

'I think we should celebrate the fact that no one was hurt and that you have managed to salvage so much of the stock,' Richard replied quietly.

The menu in Celine's hands began to shake uncontrollably. 'I lied when I said it wasn't so bad, Richard,' she whispered. 'I was scared out of my wits.'

He pushed the menu out of the way and took her cold hands in his. 'It's okay, Celine, you're safe now.'

Chapter 36

Early the next morning, Celine slipped out of bed and tiptoed out of the bedroom. After making a cup of coffee, she opened the living-room window and sat down on the ledge to enjoy the sunshine. She leaned her head back and closed her eyes, relishing the warmth on her skin. She smiled as she relived the previous night. Richard had told her as he'd led her into the bedroom that he was going to make her forget all about the break-in and he'd certainly delivered on his promise.

'Good morning.'

Her eyes flew open and her smile broadened when she saw him standing over her dressed only in boxer shorts. 'Hello.' She stretched up a hand and pulled him down next to her.

'How are you this morning?' he asked after a gentle kiss.

'Fine.'

Richard raised an eyebrow. 'You do look rather . . . pleased with yourself.'

'Pleased, satisfied, content, sated.' Celine looked at him through her lashes. 'And full of energy.'

He faked a yawn. 'Woman, you'll wear me out! Any chance of a cup of coffee first?'

Celine laughed and went to get him one.

'What are you going to do today?' he asked when she'd returned.

She nodded towards the pile of clothes on the chair opposite. 'Keep working on that lot, I suppose.'

He rubbed a hand absently up and down her bare leg. 'Let's go and see Rose. If we set off early we could have a leisurely lunch on the way back.'

'What about Fergus?'

'He doesn't really need to come, does he? And I'm sure he'd rather not take any more time off work.'

'I'll phone him and see what he says.'

Richard glanced at his watch. 'It's too early to phone. We'll have to think of something to keep us occupied for a while.'

Celine stood up slowly and untied the sash of her robe. 'I don't know about you but I'm going for a shower.'

'Excellent idea,' he murmured. 'I feel positively filthy.'

Celine giggled as she pulled him towards the bathroom. 'A very long, hot shower for you then.'

'Will you scrub the bits I can't reach?' he asked.

'And the rest,' she promised.

Half an hour later they fell back into bed, wrapped in towels.

'Maybe we should just stay here for the day,' Richard said with a wide yawn.

Celine laughed as the phone started to ring. 'I don't think that's going to be possible.' She stretched across him to lift the handset. 'Hello?'

'Hi, Celine, it's Fergus.'

'Fergus! I was just about to call you.' Celine pushed Richard away as he started to tug on her towel. 'Richard was going to take me down to see your mum today.'

'Oh, right. Do you want me to come along?'

Celine was happy to hear the lack of enthusiasm in his voice. 'I don't think it's necessary, unless you do.'

'No, I don't think so. Tell her I'll be down next weekend. I'll phone her to let her know what train I'll be on.'

'I'll tell her.'

'Thanks, Celine. How are you doing? I don't suppose you got much sleep last night.'

'Not a lot,' Celine agreed, grinning at Richard, 'but I'm fine. Marina and I were able to repair a lot of the clothes yesterday and that made me feel much better.'

'Good, I'm glad. Will you give me a call later and let me know how you got on?'

'Sure. Bye, Fergus.'

As Celine reached to put the phone back, Richard slipped his hand between the folds of her towel. 'You two seem very friendly.'

Celine curled up like a cat next to him. 'Amazing, isn't it?'

Richard ran his fingers through her hair. 'It's great. Fergus is a good kid.'

Celine raised her head to look at him. 'Kid? He's only three years younger than me.'

'Ah, but you're more mature and sophisticated,' Richard said quickly.

Celine smiled. 'No, I know what you mean. He seems very vulnerable. I can understand why Rose is so protective of him. It's probably just as well he got the job in Sandhill. Independence will be good for him.' Richard didn't answer. 'Are you gone asleep again?'

'Me, asleep, no.' He pretended to snore.

Celine started to tickle him. 'Come on, mate, you promised me a long, lazy lunch, remember?'

'Mmnn.'

She pulled his towel off and slapped his bare butt. 'Ow!'

'There, that woke you up.' Celine hopped out of bed before he could retaliate.

'You're a tough woman,' Richard complained but obediently climbed out of bed.

Celine studied his lean body appreciatively and had to steel herself not to reach out a hand to touch him. If she did that she knew they'd never get to Arklow. Selecting a pair of cotton trousers and a light top from her wardrobe, she carried them into the bathroom.

'Are you getting shy on me?' Richard taunted.

'No, just playing safe. I happen to know that your

intentions are far from honourable.' And she closed the door with a decisive click.

An hour later they were travelling down the coast road, with the top down on Richard's SLK Merc. Marina would have been horrified at the state of her hair, Celine thought with a smile, but she loved the feel of the wind in her face.

'Are you okay?' Richard asked, putting his hand on her knee.

'Fine,' she shouted back and reclined her seat slightly. Talking was impossible so she might as well catch up on sleep. It seemed only seconds later that Richard was calling her.

'We're just coming into the town, Celine.'

'Already?' She sat up and rubbed her eyes.

'Would you like me to stop so that you can tidy up?'

Celine grinned. 'Bad as that, eh?'

'A bit windswept,' he admitted.

Celine rummaged through her bag for a comb and some lipstick while Richard pulled into the side of the road. When she'd finished with the comb she passed it to him. 'Your turn.'

Once they were both presentable, Richard drove through the town and out towards Babs' house.

'You seem to know your way around here,' Celine observed.

He nodded. 'Yeah, I've brought Rose down a few times. Driving got difficult for her in the last year.'

'You're a real nice guy, aren't you?' she teased.

'Substitute nice for boring,' he muttered as he turned into the driveway.

Celine frowned as she noticed Babs' car was missing. 'Gosh, I hope they're in.'

'There's only one way to find out,' Richard said and rang the doorbell.

After several moments, it opened and Rose was looking at them, a mixture of surprise and delight on her face. 'Celine! Richard! What a lovely surprise. Come in.'

Celine embraced her and then moved aside as Richard gave Rose a gentle hug.

'You look well, Rose,' he told her.

'I'm fine. Come on through. Babs should be back in a minute. She just went to the supermarket. How on earth did you persuade Sadie to look after the shop on a Saturday?' She smiled at Celine but there was concern in her eyes.

'The shop is shut,' Celine told her as they sat down at the large kitchen table.

When Rose saw Richard putting on the kettle she looked worriedly from him back to Celine. 'What is it? What's happened? It's not Fergus, is it?'

'Fergus is fine,' Celine assured her.

Richard drew up a chair beside Rose and took her hand. 'The shop's been broken into, Rose. Nothing was taken and no one was hurt.'

'Oh, is that all?' Rose closed her eyes and put a hand to her chest. 'For a moment I thought you were going to tell me . . . something terrible.'

Celine looked at her and smiled. 'Fergus was right. He said you wouldn't be bothered once you knew no one was hurt.'

Rose seemed to have only heard part of the sentence. 'You talked to Fergus?'

The kettle boiled and Richard went to make the tea.

Celine nodded. 'After I'd called the police I tried to phone Richard but I couldn't get him. There was no way I was going to call you at that hour of the night so I phoned Fergus.'

Richard set the teapot between them with two mugs. 'I think I'll leave you to it. I'll be in the garden if anyone wants me.'

'He came over straight away,' Celine said as Rose poured. 'When the police were gone he cleaned up the mess. I'm afraid they really trashed the place, Rose. Anyway, once Fergus had cleaned up the worst of it he said he was going to stay in the shop for the rest of the night. Well, I couldn't let him do that so I told him he could sleep on the sofa.'

Rose smiled. 'Thanks, love.'

'I'm afraid he didn't get any sleep in the end. We did a lot of talking.'

'Oh?'

Celine sighed. 'Yes, we covered a lot of ground. About the drugs, about Dermot, about the bastard who murdered him. Do you know, Rose, I didn't even know that he was dead?'

'I'm surprised the police didn't inform you.'

'They probably tried,' Celine said with a guilty smile. 'They got in touch a few times over the years but I refused to talk to them. I just couldn't. Daddy stepped in and he did whatever was necessary. He used to try and talk to me about what was going on but I didn't want to know. Nothing was going to bring Dermot back.'

Rose wiped her eyes. 'I'm so glad you've talked. I don't know about you, Celine, but I think it will help Fergus a lot.'

'I'm sorry it took me so long, Rose. I've been very selfish.'

'Don't be silly, love, no one thinks that.'

'I do.'

'Grief hits people in different ways. If you'd had a child it would have been easier for you. Having a dependant forces you to get on with things.'

Celine blinked hard as she stared into her mug.

'Would you have liked children?' Rose asked.

Celine nodded. 'In retrospect, yes, but not at the time. I was just starting out and we were looking forward to finally having some spare cash. We were going to have fun, we were going to travel. But when Dermot died, I prayed I was pregnant. Marina had a lousy marriage and yet, if she hadn't met Ray, she wouldn't have Josh. And Josh, little menace though he is, means the world to her.'

Rose looked out of the window at Richard. 'You're very young, Celine. You can still be a wife, a mother.

You could still be an award-winning dress designer too if you put your mind to it.'

Celine shook her head and laughed. 'Don't you start nagging me, I get enough of that from Marina.'

Rose smiled. 'Okay then, I'll say no more. Let's get back to our current problem. Tell me how bad things are at the shop.'

Celine gave her the full story about the break-in and then a quick inventory of the stock situation.

'We need more stock and quickly.' Rose chewed on her lip.

'Give me some names and numbers and I'll get on it.'

'No, love, you've enough to do. Making a few phone calls won't hurt me and no offence, but I've more chance of success.'

Celine shook her head. 'I completely understand.' Working in the second-hand game required a sensitive touch and Rose had developed an excellent rapport with her customers.

Richard appeared in the doorway. 'How's it going?'

'Great.' Celine grinned at him. 'We should be back in business in no time.'

'Give yourself till Wednesday,' Rose suggested. 'Monday and Tuesday are always quiet anyway.'

'We'd better go, Celine.' Richard shot her a meaningful look.

'Oh, but you must stay for some lunch,' Rose protested. 'Babs will be back soon.'

'Sorry, Rose, but I have to get back for an important meeting.'

Rose shot him a look of pure disbelief. 'You have an important meeting? Would you believe that, Celine?' She turned to wink at her manager who was bent over her notebook, her face red. 'Ah, I see.'

'What do you see?' Richard's eyes twinkled.

'Nothing, nothing, you two go on.' Rose almost pulled the chair from under Celine and pushed her towards the door. 'I must start making these phone calls.'

'Your son will be down next weekend,' Richard told her. 'He said he'd call and let you know what train he's on.'

'Grand.'

At the doorway, Celine turned to hug her. 'I'm sorry to have brought you such bad news.'

Rose waved away the apology. 'I could understand you apologising if you'd left the door wide open or the alarm off but there's nothing you could have done about it. I want to thank you for all the hard work you've done to redeem the situation and please pass on my thanks to Marina. The next time she spots something she likes, Celine, you tell her it's on me.'

Celine smiled. 'She'll be ecstatic.'

Richard hugged Rose. 'Take care of yourself.'

'You too, Richard, and thanks for bringing Celine down. It was very obliging of you.'

Richard grinned at Rose's knowing look. 'My pleasure.'

*

'She took that very well,' Celine said when they were sitting in a small Italian bistro in Blackrock.

'That's Rose,' Richard said, biting into a breadstick. 'She has her priorities right.'

Celine took a sip of Chianti. 'I should be back at the shop working instead of sitting here boozing at lunchtime.'

'I think we deserve a break.'

'Perhaps you're right. If there's one thing I've learnt in the last couple of days it's that I should be living for today, not worrying about the past.'

Richard raised his glass. 'That's something to drink to.'

They had a pleasant meal, talking about nothing hugely important, teasing and flirting. Celine closed her eyes as they sped back to Hopefield and revelled in the warm wonderful feeling of new love.

'Hey, sleepyhead, we're here.'

Celine opened her eyes and yawned widely. 'Couldn't you go round the block a couple of times?'

Richard laughed as he got out of the car and came around to help her.

'Thank you, kind sir,' Celine said as she reached up to kiss him.

'Well, miss, you are really something else!'

They turned to see Mary Boyle standing on the pavement, a picture of disapproval.

'Good afternoon, Mrs Boyle,' Richard said but Celine had gone rigid in his arms.

'You must be married then, Mr Lawrence,' the woman continued. 'She only goes for the married ones. Does your wife know about her?'

Richard's smile faded. 'I'm not married and I have no idea what you are talking about, Mrs Boyle.'

'Ask her.' Mary shot a spiteful glance at Celine. 'She's the adulteress.'

Dominic, attracted by the raised voices, came out of his shop. Taking in the situation in an instant he moved to stand between Celine and Mary. 'I think you've said enough, Mary, don't you?'

'It's disgusting!' she snorted and walked away, her nose in the air.

Richard glanced from Dominic to Celine. 'Would one of you like to tell me what all that was about?'

Chapter 37

Fergus whistled under his breath as he mopped out the floor of the snack bar. He was feeling more cheerful than he had in days. Sarah had stayed over again last night and it had been wonderful to wake up beside her this morning. Also, there had been no sign of Mick Garvey and Fergus began to wonder if he'd jumped to the wrong conclusion about the shop. Maybe it had had nothing to do with Mick after all. Maybe Mick had got tired of hassling him and moved on to annoy someone else. Maybe, Fergus grinned, he'd been arrested and was sitting cooling his heels in a jail somewhere. His thoughts were interrupted by the beep of his mobile indicating that he had a text message. He pulled it out of his pocket and pressed the button to read it.

MEET ME IN LOCAL AT 12. NO EXCUSES. MG.

Fergus froze. He should have known that the little bastard wouldn't give in that easily. Garvey was vindictive and nasty and he wouldn't rest until Fergus agreed to work for him. Realising that he was out of his depth and that his actions would affect

Rose, Sarah, possibly even Celine, he decided to call Richard.

'Yes?' Richard barked.

Fergus held the phone away from his ear. 'Er, sorry to disturb you, Richard, it's Fergus here.'

'Fergus, hi, sorry, I was just in the middle of something. Is there a problem?'

''Fraid so.' Fergus told him about the text message.

Richard thought for a moment. 'Okay, go ahead and meet him.'

'What?'

'Meet him, don't be confrontational and buy us some time. We need to keep him happy for the moment while I try and figure out what to do. For God's sake don't agree to anything. Fergus, are you still there?'

'Yeah, I'm here,' Fergus replied, trying to quell the sick feeling in his gut.

'Call me after you meet him and don't worry, Fergus, you're not alone. I will do everything I can to help you on this.'

'Thanks, Richard,' Fergus said and hung up. He believed him but Richard didn't know what a scumbag Mick Garvey was. Fergus was frightened and he knew he had every reason to be.

Richard stared at the phone hard and tried to concentrate on the problem that was Mick Garvey. It wasn't easy because all he could think about was Celine and Kevin Gilligan. He'd known that there was something between them that night in her flat but it came as a shock to find out that not only was he married but he was still on the scene. Of course she said it was over but he wasn't sure he believed her. He felt cheated somehow. He'd opened himself up to Celine in a way he hadn't with any other woman. He was attracted to her physically but on top of that he loved her honesty and guileless nature. Now he realised she was just like all the rest, incapable of honesty and unworthy of the trust he'd placed in her. It hurt like hell because he'd thought they had a future. She had tried to get around him, tried to explain, but Richard was not about to believe those innocent grey eyes again. He wouldn't be anybody's fool. With supreme effort he turned his mind back to Fergus's problem. He'd been playing around with an idea of how to sort out this Garvey character and now it was time to put it into action. He flicked through his address book and then dialled a number. 'Inspector Declan Murphy, please.'

Mick was already at the bar when Fergus walked in. 'Get the drinks in,' he instructed and walked over to a table on the far side of the room.

Fergus bought two pints of Guinness and carried them over. The temptation to throw them over Mick's head was almost irresistible.

'Glad ye came to your senses, Gus. I'd have been pissed off if ye hadn't shown up.'

'Did you break into me ma's shop?'

Mick looked back, wide-eyed. 'Gus, how could ye think such a thing? Sure I'd never get through one of those little windows!' He threw back his head and laughed.

'Keep away from there or I'll fucking kill you,' Fergus warned.

Mick's smile disappeared. 'Don't ever talk to me like that, Gus, do ye understand? If ye know what's good for you and yer ma ye'll do exactly what I tell ye.'

Remembering Richard's words Fergus nodded. 'Yeah, sorry.' He clutched his pint with both hands wishing it was Mick's neck.

Mick sat back and the smile returned. 'That's better.'

'What do you want me to do?'

'Not so fast,' Mick murmured. 'How do I know I can trust ye?'

'To coin a phrase, Mick, you know where I live,' Fergus drawled.

Mick sniggered. 'Funny man, Gus, yer a very funny man. So yer interested in a bit of action?'

Fergus shrugged. 'Not really but you're right, I could do with the money.'

'Making snacks for yuppies in a gym doesn't pay that well, does it?'

Fergus shook his head.

'Okay then, I'll think about it.'

Fergus looked at him. 'Is that it?'

Mick frowned. 'Don't get lippy, mate. I'll be in touch when I've got something for ye.'

'Not in the centre,' Fergus warned.

Mick glared at him. 'Get the fuck out of here, yer giving me a headache.'

Fergus left without another word. It wasn't until he was back out on the street that he noticed spots of blood where he'd dug his nails into his palms. Feeling sick, he wiped them on his jeans and prayed that it would be the last time there would be blood on his hands.

'I don't know about this, Richard,' Declan said after he'd taken a sip of his pint. 'Garvey is a nasty piece of work. Are you sure this lad of yours isn't involved?'

'No, Declan, I told you, Fergus is as straight as they come.'

'But he was in trouble before.'

'Only because he was using and that was years ago,' Richard pointed out. He knew he couldn't rush Declan into this. He hadn't changed much since their schooldays.

'This isn't "The Bill", you know. We don't usually set up stings in Dublin Central.' He chuckled as he lit a cigarette.

'I realise that, but what else do you suggest? Garvey has already done over the shop.'

'We don't know that.'

'No, but it's a safe bet. He made enough threats. Who do you know that would be interested in doing over a boutique?'

Murphy grinned. 'I know plenty, Richard. Thieves

aren't always that smart, especially if they're off their heads.'

'Come on, Declan, you know this has Garvey's name written all over it. I thought you'd be glad of the opportunity to put a character like him away. A feather in your cap, surely, to put away a drug dealer.'

Declan pulled on his moustache as he digested this. 'I'd need your friend's total cooperation and he'd have to do exactly what he's told.'

'Of course.'

Declan threw back the remainder of his pint and stood up. 'Okay, leave it with me.'

'Thanks, Declan, I appreciate it.'

'Don't thank me, I haven't done anything yet.'

Richard was nursing a second pint when Fergus finally arrived. 'What will you have?'

'Nothing. I need to get back to work.' Fergus shifted from one foot to the other.

'So what did he have to say?' Richard asked.

'The usual.' Fergus pulled out twenty Rothmans and lit one with shaky hands. He'd been trying to give up but he'd figured without Mick Garvey coming back into his life. 'He was definitely behind the break-in, though.'

'Do you think we can get him on that?'

'Not a chance.'

'So what does he want you to do?'

'I don't know. He's being very cagey, said he'd be in touch.'

'What did you say?'

'I told him I could do with the extra money.'

'Good. I've had a word with a friend of mine, he's an inspector.'

Fergus's eyes widened. 'Jesus, Richard!'

'Don't worry, I've explained everything, he's on your side. He's going to find a way to get Garvey but he'll need your help.'

'I don't know—'

'Do you have any better ideas?' Richard hissed.

Fergus dragged deeply on his cigarette. 'You just don't know what he's capable of.'

'Of course I do and more to the point, the police do. They're professionals, Fergus, and they're your only hope of getting him off your back for good.'

Fergus stubbed out his cigarette and, looking defeated and frightened, nodded slowly. 'I'll do whatever you want.'

Celine finished ironing a pair of palazzo pants, hung them up and went to put on the kettle. She hadn't got much done this morning as she'd had visits from her father and Sadie. It had taken all of her patience to deal with Sadie, who wanted every last detail about the break-in and Rose's reaction to it. Celine assured her that it would be business as usual on Wednesday and that they would have plenty of stock. She wasn't sure how true that was. Though Rose had called many of her contacts no one had been in touch with Celine yet.

Her dad had been more philosophical. 'Little thugs, I know what I'd do with them if I got my hands on them!'

Celine smiled as she made her coffee. Her father believed that a kick in the arse was a lot more effective than a spell in a prison cell and it saved the taxpayer's money.

The one person she wanted to see was keeping his distance. Richard's reaction to Mary Boyle's outburst had annoyed her. A shutter had come down over his face and he'd turned into a frosty stranger. Dominic had looked from one to the other and left them to it and, with a heavy heart, Celine suggested they go up to her flat. Even as she explained what had happened she knew that Richard had already made up his mind. He was polite, too polite, and when she had finished he'd headed for the door without a word.

'Richard? Where are you going? Aren't you going to say something?'

He'd stopped in the doorway and looked at her, his beautiful brown eyes sad. 'I have to go. I'll call you later.'

And he was gone. Celine doubted now if he'd be back. She massaged the crick of her neck and closed her eyes. Would she ever stop paying for her affair with Kevin Gilligan? Their relationship had been the biggest mistake of her life and she regretted it more every day. Yesterday, she'd glimpsed a happy future spreading out in front of her. Now she was alone again and likely to stay that way. She didn't think she'd ever fall in love again after Dermot but then Richard had emerged from her airing cupboard and everything had changed. She glanced at her watch and decided to take the repaired stock back down to the shop. She was just walking out the door when the phone rang. She thought of ignoring it but it could be a customer or Brenda or even Rose. She hurried over and picked it up. 'Hello?'

'Celine, it's me.'

'Hi, Marina.' Celine took the phone over to the window.

'Are you okay? Dominic told me what happened. How are things with Richard? What did he say?'

Celine decided to answer the last question first. 'He didn't say anything.'

'Oh, so everything's okay?'

'I didn't say that. He didn't say anything, he just left. I suppose you could say actions speak louder than words.' Celine was trying to be glib but she was surprised by the catch in her voice. Marina heard it too. 'Oh, Celine, I'm sorry! But he'll come round. You need to explain things. I mean, did you tell him that it was all over with Kevin before you even moved to Hopefield?'

Celine closed her eyes. 'But it wasn't.'

'You mean you were still seeing Kevin? You never told me that! Jesus, Celine, you'd think you'd have learnt your lesson.'

'Give it a rest, Marina, it was just a couple of times.'

Marina sighed. 'Yeah, sorry.'

'Unfortunately one of the nights that he came to see me Richard was here.'

There was a gasp at the other end of the phone as Marina digested this. 'So they've met?'

The tears that Celine had managed to keep a lid on so far threatened to spill over. 'Yes,' she sniffed, realising how it must look from Richard's perspective.

'Oh, Celine. Look, I'll come over later. Hang on in there, pet, I'll see you around six.'

Celine hung up and went into the bathroom to wash her face. She stared at herself in the mirror. Red-eyed and pale, she looked exactly how she felt, miserable. She splashed cold water on her face, ran a comb through her hair and went to get the clothes. It took her three journeys to take them all back to the shop but once Celine had arranged them on the rails she felt a little more cheerful. The place was beginning to look normal again. She turned around as there was a rap on the door and smiled when she recognised one of Rose's regular customers laden down with bags and suit carriers. She flung open the door and relieved the woman of some of the bags. 'Hello! My goodness, this is wonderful!'

The older woman laughed. 'Rose did me a favour. I've been meaning to clean out my wardrobes for months. I didn't realise I had quite so much stuff.'

'This is all yours?'

'Lord, no! I nagged my daughter and next-door neighbour to have a rummage through their stuff too.'

'It's marvellous,' Celine murmured as she removed covers from some beautifully tailored suits. 'I don't know how to thank you.'

'I'd murder a cup of tea.'

Celine laughed. 'I'll put on the kettle.'

Chapter 38

Fergus stood outside the pub, shifting from one foot to the other and checking his watch every five seconds.

'Yo, Gus.'

Fergus swung round to see Mick grinning up at him. 'Where the hell were you? We said twelve.'

'Jeez, relax, man, will ye?' Mick opened the door and led the way into the dimly lit pub.

'Just give me the stuff and let me get out of here,' Fergus muttered, his eyes on the crowds around them.

Mick chuckled. 'For fuck's sake, get me a pint and pull yerself together. Ye may as well have a sign over yer head saying "I'm up to something".'

Fergus went to the bar and breathed deeply while the barman poured Mick's drink. He had to calm down or he could blow the whole deal. He paid for the pint and carried it back to the table, concentrating hard on not spilling it all over the place.

Mick grinned. 'Not joining me then?' He took a sip of his drink while Fergus watched him impatiently.

'That's better. Now, listen carefully. Ye do what I tell ye and we'll get on just fine.'

Fergus listened to his instructions, nodding occasionally.

'Have ye got all that?' Mick said when he'd finished.

Fergus nodded. 'Yeah, course I do.'

'Right.' Mick slipped a small package into Fergus's hand. 'That'll keep ye going for a few days.'

Fergus shoved it into his pocket and stood up. 'Okay, I'm off. Will you be in the club later?'

Mick's expression sobered. 'Nah, I've got to go and see someone. There's a piece of shit trying to move in on my patch. He needs to know that I'm not happy about it.' He slid a knife out of his pocket. 'It's not a good idea to mess me around, Gus, remember that.'

Fergus almost ran out of the pub and began to walk towards O'Connell Street. His heart was thumping and he could feel sweat dripping from his forehead. He ran for a bus, jumped on and flashed his monthly ticket. After a couple of stops, he got off, crossed the road and boarded another one going in the opposite direction. After the bus had cleared town, he got off again and walked to the nearest phone box. Taking out a piece of paper he dialled a number and waited. 'I'm here.'

'We're in the blue Mondeo parked across the road,' Declan Murphy told him.

Fergus hung up, crossed the road and climbed into the car.

'Did it go as planned?' Declan asked.

'Yeah, fine.' Fergus handed over the package and then wiped his forehead on his arm.

Declan opened it to reveal a clear packet of tablets. 'How many?'

'Ninety.'

'When do you see him again?'

Fergus shrugged. 'He said he'd call me.'

'What patch did he give you?'

'The nightclub and the pubs in Sandhill.'

Declan cursed. 'The clever bugger is keeping his eye on you. We'll have to move fast.'

'I don't think I can do this.' Fergus closed his eyes and dug his fingers into his seat.

'You don't have a choice.'

Marina was on the train on her way to a swimwear shoot in Brittas Bay when the manageress of Josh's nursery called.

'He has a temperature, Mrs Flynn, and a bad cough. I really think he should be in bed.'

'I'm not in Dublin, Miss Brennan, I'll have to call my mother and see if she can pick him up. I'll call you back in five minutes.' Marina hurriedly dialled her mother's number and prayed that she was home.

'Hello?'

'Oh, Mum, thank God.'

'Marina? What's wrong?'

'It's Josh. I just got a call from the school. He's not very well.'

'I'll go and get him straight away.'

'Oh, thanks, Mum. And could you—'

'Take him to the doctor? Of course, love.'

'Thanks, Mum, I owe you one. I'll call the nursery and tell them you're on your way.'

'And I'll call you as soon as we get home,' Kay promised.

After thanking her mother again, Marina called Miss Brennan and then sat back in her seat to worry for the remainder of the journey.

'A nasty infection,' the doctor pronounced, patting Josh on the head. 'His throat and his ears, poor little lad. I'll write you a prescription for an antibiotic and give him Calpol or Neurofen to get his temperature down.'

Kay hugged Josh against her. 'And would some ice cream help, Doctor?'

'I insist that he has plenty of ice cream.' The doctor winked at Josh.

Kay was alarmed at the lack of response from her grandson. Usually any mention of ice cream or chocolate had him swinging from the rafters. But today he was lolling back against her, his eyes half closed and his cheeks roaring red.

'He'll be fine in a day or so,' the doctor promised. 'Plenty of drinks, sleep and some TLC is all he needs. Don't worry if he doesn't want to eat.'

Kay thanked him and led Josh out into the packed waiting room.

'I'm tired, Granny,' Josh murmured, sounding frail and frightened.

'I know, love, I'll have you home in no time.'

An hour later, Josh was propped up on the sofa, with a soft blanket tucked around him and his favourite teddy clutched in his little hands. Kay set the video and when she was satisfied that Josh was engrossed in the latest Teletubbies adventure, she crept outside to phone Marina.

'Is he all right, Mum? I've been worried sick.'

'He's fine, Marina, don't worry. The doctor gave him an antibiotic. He has an ear, nose and throat infection, but he should be fine in a couple of days.'

'The poor lamb! Can I talk to him, Mum?'

Kay brought the phone into Josh and after he'd answered his mother's questions with monosyllables, Kay told her daughter not to worry and hung up. 'How about that ice cream now, love?'

'No thanks, Granny, but will you sit with me?'

Kay, a lump in her throat, sat down and put an arm around him. 'That's a grand idea.'

Josh leaned his head against her chest and smiled for the first time that day.

Marina, bent one way, then another, tossed her hair and smiled into the camera, but in her head she was at home with Josh.

'Hey, darling, pull your cozzie up, the editor doesn't want too much boob.'

Marina adjusted her top and thought back to the time when photographers had urged her to show more. She noticed the goose bumps standing out on her chest and hoped that they'd be able to airbrush them out. It was always a hazard doing these kind of shots in Ireland even in summertime. As Marina's face and feet began to ache, she thought how nice it would be if she could give it all up and stay home with Josh. It was awful not to be with him when he was poorly. Thank God her mum was with him. Josh didn't like babysitters at the best of times but when he was ill he hated them. She risked a quick glance at her watch. It was nearly seven and it would be a miracle if she was home in time to give Josh his bath. Marina felt a lump in her throat as she imagined his tears. Kay would be at her wits' end.

'I think we'll do a few more shots in the sand dunes,' the photographer told her and started to march across the beach.

'Great,' Marina muttered, hurrying after him.

It was after nine before she finally got in. The house was in darkness and after taking her shoes off she tiptoed upstairs but a quick search revealed that the three bedrooms were empty. He must have got worse and her mum had taken him back to the doctor or even to the hospital. She went downstairs and rushed into the living room in search of the note that Kay would surely have left.

'Hello, love,' Kay whispered from her position on the sofa.

'Mum! Josh!' Marina fell in a heap at the feet of her sleeping son. 'God, I thought you'd taken him to the hospital. Why are you sitting down here in the dark?'

'He didn't want to go to bed alone so I decided to let him fall asleep in front of the television. He's only just nodded off, poor pet.'

Marina brushed his hair back out of his eyes with gentle fingers. 'Did he eat?'

Kay shook her head. 'He's had nothing but water.'

'My God, he must be sick.'

'Miserable,' Kay agreed, 'but his temperature's down. I'm sure he'll be fine after a night's sleep. Why don't you take him upstairs and I'll put on the kettle?'

'Great.' Marina gathered Josh up in her arms and took him up to bed. After she'd tucked him in and kissed him she went downstairs to her mother.

'You look exhausted,' Kay remarked as she set the table.

'I'm frozen.' Marina shivered, folding her slim arms to try to warm herself. 'I think I must be coming down with the same bug that Josh has. Only in this country could you get an infection in the summertime.'

Kay chuckled. 'To hell with the tea, I'll make you a nice hot toddy and you can take it to bed.'

'Thanks, Mum, I don't know what I'd do without you.'

*

When Marina was in bed, Kay took her tea into the sitting room and settled in front of the television. There was a film starting that she'd been wanting to see for ages but as she sat there she found her mind wandering back over the last few hours. In sickness, Josh had been a different child. There had been no cheekiness and no tantrums. He had curled up close to her and held on tight to her hand with his pudgy little fingers. It was the first time in years that Kay had felt close to him and, realising that he must be feeling really bad, she'd sung, told stories, done anything that would bring a smile to those tiny lips and big blue eyes. For the first time he'd reminded her of Marina when she was small. Kay sniffed as she remembered what a beautiful child her daughter had been. Women used to stop her in the supermarket to admire the blonde curls, large blue eyes and the pretty smile that never seemed to be far away. Kay was convinced that Josh's acerbic nature was due to the absence of his father. Marina had over-compensated for his absence and given Josh whatever he asked for. What the boy actually wanted was the love and presence of his father but Ray just swanned in and out of his life when it suited him.

Kay decided that instead of sitting on the sideline criticising maybe it was time she waded in and helped raise Josh to be the great kid she knew he could be. There was no doubt he was smart but at the moment he used his intelligence to outwit his mother. Perhaps it would be different when Marina and Dominic were married. Dominic was a sensible and kind man and would be a good influence on both her daughter and grandson. It was too soon for him to become a figure of authority in Josh's life but thankfully he seemed to realise that. He wasn't going out of his way to win Josh over but he was friendly and approachable. Of course, Josh was still treating him like a leper but Kay had noticed a softening in his behaviour lately. Especially when Dominic played football with him. How Josh would feel when he had to share Marina full-time though was another story.

Kay yawned, switched off the television and stood up. There was no point in staying up to watch the film when she wasn't even following the plot. It had been a long day and it was unlikely that Josh would sleep through the night. Best to get some sleep while she could.

She felt she had only settled her head on the pillow when Josh started to cry. By the time she dragged herself out of bed and went into his room, Marina was already there.

'I want Granny,' Josh was whining.

'Darling, it's Mummy.' Marina stroked his face and bent to kiss him.

He pushed her away. 'I want Granny,' he repeated, sounding slightly hysterical.

'Go on back to bed, love.' Kay put a hand on her daughter's shoulder. 'I'm a novelty, that's all. Get some sleep and you can take over in the morning.'

Marina hesitated for a moment but as Josh started to cry even louder, she got to her feet and left the room.

'Now, Josh, calm down.' Kay sat on the edge of the bed and reached for the beaker of water she'd left on his bedside table. 'Have a drink,' she said, helping him to sit up.

'My throat hurts,' he sobbed, large tears rolling down his cheeks.

'I know. Take a drink and I'll go and get some medicine.' She felt his forehead and as she'd expected it was hot and damp. She hurried into the bathroom to get the Calpol. When she returned, Josh had stopped crying. 'Now, love, open wide.'

Josh obediently opened his mouth and swallowed the medicine.

'Good boy. Now, lie down and I'll tuck you in.'

'Granny, will you stay with me?'

'Of course I will.'

'And rub my back?'

Kay smiled. 'Okay, then. But only if you promise to close your eyes.'

'Promise,' Josh mumbled and stuck his thumb in his mouth.

Kay stayed with him, humming softly and rubbing his back until his breathing was even. She crept out of his room and was about to go back to bed when she noticed that Marina's door was ajar. 'Marina, are you awake?' she whispered, sticking her head into the darkened room.

'Yeah.'

As her eyes grew accustomed to the darkness, Kay saw her daughter sitting cross-legged on the end of the bed. 'He's fine, love,' she said, sitting down beside her.

'I think I should give up work, Mum,' Marina replied. 'He obviously resents the fact that I wasn't here today.'

Kay chuckled. 'That's rubbish. He's acting up because he's sick. In the morning he'll have forgotten all about it and will hate me again.'

'He doesn't hate you,' Marina protested.

'He doesn't love me like he loves his mummy either.'

Marina's eyes looked even larger in the dim light. 'Sorry, Mum, I know I'm being silly. It's just that I love him so much.'

Kay squeezed her hand. 'Of course you do.'

'I'm glad he feels so safe with you.'

'You know I'll always look after him, Marina. I'm here whenever you need me.'

Marina hugged her. 'Thanks, Mum.'

'Now I think we should both get some sleep before the little man wakes up again.'

Long after Kay had left her, Marina lay staring at the ceiling and thinking about her life. In the freezing cold on the beach today she'd realised that the attraction of modelling had finally worn off. It was just a job and a job that took her away from her son too often. Now that she was in her thirties she had to go where the work was and that was often outside of Dublin. That wasn't so bad while they were living with Kay but when they moved in with Dominic, Josh was going to need her more. Especially when he started school. Marina didn't want Kay to be the one meeting him at the school gate every day. She was his mother, that was her job. She couldn't believe the searing jealousy she'd felt when Josh had called for his granny. It had hurt so much, although she'd tried to comfort herself that it was just because he was sick and tired. Still, much as she wanted her Mum and Josh to be close, she didn't want to be replaced. It was time to take stock. Time to reevaluate her situation.

Chapter 39

A few days later she was lying in Dominic's bed mulling over her options once more.

'Are you going to tell me what's on your mind?' he said, raising himself up on one elbow to look down on her. 'I find it a bit insulting when you're this distracted.'

Marina smiled and stroked his face. 'Oh, I'm sorry, darling, I was just thinking about Josh. He was so sick it gave me quite a fright.'

'But he's okay now.'

Marina hugged the duvet around her. 'I know that, but it's made me think.'

'Sounds serious.'

'I've decided to give up modelling.'

'Really?'

'It just doesn't do it for me any more and I hate not being there for Joshie.'

'He seems happy with your mother.'

'Exactly,' Marina muttered.

Dominic laughed. 'You're jealous!'

'I know – isn't it pathetic? It was so tough when we

first moved in but now the two of them are much closer. Last night he even helped tidy his toys away.' Marina shook her head in wonder. 'He'd never do that for me.'

'She's wonderful with him,' Dominic agreed. Josh could be a handful but he seemed to have settled down a little recently. There was no doubt that it was all due to Kay's influence. Though she was strict with him she was also generous with her time. One night, Dominic and Marina had arrived home to find a sheet draped over the kitchen table and Josh and Kay crouched underneath 'camping'.

'I could get a part-time job.'

'You could always help me at the deli. I'm sure we'd make a great team.'

Marina's eyes widened. 'But I don't know anything about running a shop and as for food, well, I can screw up boiling an egg.'

He laughed. 'I wasn't planning on asking you to do the cooking. Why don't you think about it?'

Celine set out for the community centre with a heavy heart. She hadn't heard from Richard in days, Marina seemed to be spending all of her time with Dominic and her father had gone on a golf holiday with an old friend to the Algarve. He had waited until Alan returned from London before he arranged it. When he'd dropped into the shop to tell Celine he was in buoyant mood.

'They're getting on like a house on fire,' he'd told

Celine. 'I met them in the club last night and you wouldn't believe the difference. Brenda was blushing like a bride and Alan couldn't take his eyes off her.'

'Brenda called me yesterday. The counselling seems to be doing the trick.' Celine had yawned and brushed her hair back out of her sunken eyes.

Frank looked at her. 'Are you okay? You're looking a bit peaky.'

'I'm not sleeping very well.'

'Are you afraid here on your own? You know you could always move in with me. I could cancel the holiday—'

'Daddy, no, don't be silly, I'm fine.'

Frank looked relieved. 'If you're sure?'

'I'm sure.'

Celine turned into the centre and climbed the steps to the door. Thankfully, she had managed to convince her father she was fine and sent him on his way. It was true that she wasn't sleeping though. It reminded her of the first few months after Dermot's death. She went to bed tired but sleep wouldn't come. Now she felt worn out and the thought of facing Mary Boyle and her pals tonight did nothing to raise her spirits. At least she had finished most of the costumes and with luck she'd be ready to go before they broke for coffee. That way she wouldn't have to talk to anyone, not that anyone would probably want to talk to her.

Slipping into the back of the auditorium, Celine edged her way around the cast and went through the partition into what had become her sewing room. Almost immediately, Cathy appeared in the doorway. 'Hello there, I thought I saw you creep past.'

Celine grimaced. 'Sorry.'

'You have nothing to be sorry for,' Cathy assured her. 'You're helping out this society, I appreciate that, and so do the others though that's not always apparent.'

'I'll be honest, Cathy, I'm going to finish up tonight and then you won't see me for dust.'

'That's a shame. I hope you'll still come to the show.'

Celine grinned. 'I'll be the one in the wig and the trench coat.'

Cathy gave her a brief hug. 'I'll watch out for you.'

Celine watched her walk back to join the cast and then turned her attention to the work at hand. She was quite pleased with how the costumes had turned out. Some of them had been quite badly made and hung like sacks, but by ripping out a seam here and there, changing necklines, removing sleeves, she had made them fairly presentable. She worked steadily and was surprised when Dominic appeared at her side with a cup of coffee.

'You seem to be working very hard.'

Celine took the cup and thanked him. 'Yeah, well I wanted to leave early.'

'Going somewhere? Oh, sorry, I didn't mean—'

Celine smiled at the look of dismay on his face. 'It's okay, Dominic. No, I'm not going anywhere.'

'You must come out with Marina and me one night.'

Celine raised an eyebrow. 'And play gooseberry? I don't think so.'

'Would you feel better if Josh came too?'

She smiled. 'Yeah, thanks. How is Josh?'

Dominic laughed. 'Well, he's stopped trying to trip me up so I suppose that's progress! I'll let you get back to work.' Dominic turned to leave.

'Right. Dominic?'

He turned back.

'Thanks for the coffee.'

He smiled. 'You're welcome.'

Half an hour later, Celine left when they were all in the middle of a chorus of 'Get Me To The Church On Time'. She was glad that Dominic had come to talk to her. She realised it probably hadn't been easy for him and he'd more than likely done it for Marina's sake, but at least he'd made the effort. She realised how appalled he must be at her behaviour. From Marina she knew that Dominic believed in the sanctity of marriage and adultery was completely abhorrent to him. Of course Celine agreed. When she was married she'd never looked at another man and would have been devastated if Dermot had been unfaithful. But of course that would never have happened. They had been madly in love, with eyes only for each other. That certainly wasn't the case in Kevin and Eileen's relationship. Kevin had slept with plenty of other girls before Celine came along. Of course that was no excuse for her behaviour, Celine realised as she let herself into the flat. She'd have to stop thinking that way. She deserved the names that she was being called. She deserved Dominic's disappointment and Richard's distrust.

She dumped her bag on the sofa and turned on the lamp with a heavy sigh. It was time to stop blaming everything and anything else for her mistakes. Instead of being defensive with Richard she should explain everything and accept the blame for her behaviour. If he couldn't cope with that then she'd just have to accept it. Silent tears rolled down her cheeks as she realised that she'd blown her second chance of real happiness. She stood up and went to the phone but stopped, her hand on the receiver. It wasn't fair dumping on Marina all the time, especially now that she was involved with Dominic. She moved away from the phone and went to the fridge for a can of Coke. She fancied something stronger but now that she was solely responsible for the shop, Celine had eased off the booze. One or two drinks would be fine of course but she didn't trust herself to leave it at that tonight. She took her Coke back to her favourite spot by the window and sat down. She had come to Hopefield to escape her life but it had followed her. Now she had to decide whether to stay and live with the consequences or move on to pastures new.

As Rose was soon to return the decision might be out of her hands. If she wasn't working in Close

Second she could hardly stay in a flat owned by
Richard. He would want her out, she was sure of it.
He wouldn't say so now because he would put up
with the situation for Rose's sake. But as soon as she
returned, Celine knew her days were numbered.
Crunching the empty can in her fingers, Celine
decided that she'd prefer to go before Richard asked
her to leave. That would be just too hard to take.

Chapter 40

Marina pulled the bedclothes up around Josh and tiptoed out of the room. She looked at her watch and smiled. It was just eight o'clock and he'd gone to bed like a lamb and even turned off the light himself after she'd read only one story. She went downstairs and joined Kay in front of the telly. Unable to sit still or concentrate on the programme that Kay was engrossed in, Marina decided to manicure her nails.

'Cup of tea, love?' Kay asked as the break came on.

'Sorry? Oh, stay where you are, Mum, I'll make it.' Marina leapt to her feet and went out to the kitchen. As she arrived back in with the tray, Kay turned down the volume, took off her glasses and looked at her daughter. 'What's up?'

'Sorry?'

'You've been walking around in a daze for the last few days, love – what's on your mind?'

'I do have something to tell you,' Marina admitted. 'Two things actually. I've decided to give up modelling and Dominic's asked me to move in with him. The two are sort of connected,' she hurried on. 'He'll be supporting us until I get another job.'

Kay's expression clouded. 'I see.'

'I know you'll miss Josh, Mum, but we would have been moving out in a few weeks anyway.'

'True.'

'You don't look impressed.' Marina looked at her mother's tight-lipped expression.

'Well, of course I'm going to miss you both but, well, do you think it's a good idea to give up work? It can get very boring in the home with only a child to talk to.'

Marina chuckled. 'Oh, really, Mum, just because I'm not working doesn't mean I won't be out and about.'

'I'm telling you it's not the same,' Kay warned.

Marina frowned. 'This isn't about me cracking up at home, is it? You want me to hang on to my job in case things don't work out with Dominic.'

'That's not what I meant,' Kay protested, but she wouldn't meet Marina's eyes.

'He's not like Ray, Mum.'

'I know that.'

'And if he does walk out on us I can always go back to modelling. Provided I don't let myself go I could take it up again any time I feel like it. But I won't have to because Dominic loves me.'

'I know he does, I'm sorry.'

Marina smiled. 'It's okay, Mum, I know you worry about us. I've given you enough cause over the years.

But this time I really think it's going to be okay. Dominic is different.'

Kay blinked and managed a wobbly smile. 'Yes, he is. I'm sure the three of you are going to be very happy.'

Marina hugged her. 'So you don't mind us moving out?'

'Mind having my house back to myself, are you mad?'

Marina laughed. 'Don't relax too much. I think Josh plans to visit often.'

'His room will always be there for him,' Kay sniffed. 'I'm going to miss the little terror.'

'I'm very grateful for what you've done for him, for us.'

Kay gathered her into her arms. 'Oh, love, it's been my pleasure.'

Marina sat back and wiped her eyes. 'What are we like, sitting here blubbering?'

Kay stood up, laughing. 'This tea is freezing, I'll make us a fresh pot.'

'To hell with the tea, Mum, let's have a drink.'

Kay lay awake for a long time when they finally went to bed. If Marina had told her a month ago that she was moving out she'd probably have thrown a party. Now she felt sad at the thought of losing her daughter and grandson. It was nice to hear other voices around the house. It was wonderful to listen in as Josh talked to his toys. It often brought a lump to

her throat when he cuddled up against her and
slipped his little hand into hers. The house would
seem so empty and lonely without him. Still, it would
be good for Josh to have Dominic as a stepfather,
even if he didn't realise that yet. Kay could bear to
part with him as long as he was going to be happy.
She wiped her eyes and blew her nose. If he wasn't
happy they'd have her to deal with!

Celine waved Sadie off, shut the door and flicked
around the closed sign. With a feeling of pride, she
looked around the shop, chock-full with wonderful
stock. When word had got around about the break-in,
Rose's customers had come up trumps and arrived in
with armfuls of the most amazing clothes. Celine
seemed to spend half of her time on the phone to
Arklow telling her boss about the latest acquisitions.
The best part was that the stock was going out the
door as fast as it was coming in and takings had never
been better. A sharp rap on the door interrupted her
reverie and she hurried to answer it.

Richard, clad in his usual uniform of jeans and
rugby shirt, was standing on the doorstep. Celine
ventured a nervous smile. 'Hi.'

'I won't keep you.' Richard breezed past her. 'I just
wanted to arrange a convenient time for you to meet
the accountant.'

'Accountant?'

'Yes, didn't Rose tell you? He does the books every
quarter.'

Celine nodded, trying to concentrate. 'Yes, of course, she did mention it.'

'So when do you want to do it?'

'I suppose Monday would be the best day. That's when Sadie's here.'

'Right, I'll set it up,' Richard said, moving back towards the door.

He hadn't looked at her during the whole exchange, Celine realised. 'Is that it?'

He paused, his hand on the door. 'Unless there's anything you want to discuss.'

Celine nodded. 'There is actually. Let me close up and we can go up to my flat.'

For the first time there was a hint of a smile in the brown eyes. 'To talk business?'

Celine's eyes widened, all innocence. 'Of course!' As she led the way upstairs her stomach was in a knot. He'd managed a smile, surely that was a good sign? 'Drink?' she asked, going straight into the kitchen.

Richard walked across to the window. 'A beer would be nice.'

Definitely a good sign, Celine thought, taking two bottles from the fridge and opening them.

'Thanks.' Richard took his beer and raised it to his lips.

Celine watched him drink and experienced a moment of pure lust.

'So?' He leaned against the wall and studied her.

'What? Oh, right.' Celine was about to sit down on

the sofa but thought better of it. This was going to be hard enough without having him towering over her while she talked. Instead she moved across to the breakfast bar and perched on a stool. 'I want to explain. About Kevin.'

Richard's face was expressionless. 'There's no need.'

'I think there is.' Celine forced herself to look him in the eye. 'And you want to hear it. You could have phoned me to arrange the appointment with the accountant.'

Richard looked away. 'I was passing.'

'Of course you were. Anyway, back to Kevin.'

Richard grunted but he seemed slightly more at ease.

'I met him at my health club over a year ago. We got talking, went for a coffee – it became something of a ritual. Finally he asked me out for a drink and, well, it took off from there.'

'But you knew he was married?'

'Yeah, I knew Eileen.' She looked away from the disgust in his eyes. She'd promised herself she was going to tell him everything but she wasn't sure she could look at him as she was doing it. She got off the stool and went to her favourite spot by the window, staring out at the rooftops of Hopefield. 'I told myself that it didn't matter because she obviously didn't care about him.'

'I suppose he told you that.'

'Yep, and I believed it. Probably because I wanted

to. Anyway, Eileen found out eventually and had a go at me in the middle of the golf club.'

Richard laughed. 'Good for her!'

'My dad and Brenda, that's Dermot's sister, were pretty upset and I started to get these notes in the door telling me to get out of Killmont.'

'So you applied for the job in Close Second?'

She nodded. 'It seemed the perfect answer.'

Richard cleared his throat. 'So you left Killmont.'

Celine sighed and turned her eyes back to the rooftops of Hopefield. 'Yeah, I was nervous about it but I knew it would be better for everyone if I left. Unfortunately, Kevin followed.'

'You could have sent him away.'

'I did try to finish with him but he can be very persuasive. He said that once we kept a low profile for a while we could carry on as before. That Eileen didn't care about the affair but she didn't want to be made a fool of publicly.'

Richard's hand tightened around the neck of the bottle. 'So you continued the affair?'

Celine looked at him. 'Do you remember the night that you met him?'

'Oh, yes, I remember.'

'That was the night I finished it.'

Richard looked at her, a cynical smile playing around his lips. 'Sure you did.'

'It's true. When you left, Kevin wanted to go to bed.'

Richard flinched.

'But I couldn't. I didn't want to. I wanted you. So be disgusted with me for having an affair with him, that's okay, but don't accuse me of being unfaithful to you. I've seen Kevin only twice since that night and that was only because it took a while to convince him that it was over and that his marriage wasn't the sham he thought it was.'

'What do you mean?'

'Eileen came to see me in the shop. She'd followed Kevin to my flat one night and she came to warn me off. That was the conversation Mary Boyle overheard. The woman was distraught, Richard, and for the first time I realised that she really did love Kevin. I promised her that it was over and I'm saying the same to you now.'

Richard looked down at her in silence.

'Do you believe me?'

'Yes.'

Celine sighed. 'But it doesn't make any difference, does it?'

'I don't know,' Richard admitted.

Celine sank back down onto the window ledge. 'I understand.'

'I have to go.'

Celine nodded without looking up. 'Sure.'

He bent and kissed her hair. 'I'll call you.'

'Right.' Celine closed her eyes as the door shut behind him.

Chapter 41

When Celine heard the buzzer later that night, she flew across the room to press the button. He's come back. Everything's going to be okay. 'Yes?' she said, breathless.

'Celine, it's me, Fergus.'

'Fergus? Come on up.' Celine opened the door and watched his unsteady progress up the stairs. 'Are you okay?'

Fergus reached the top and looked at her with bloodshot eyes. 'Not really. Got any beer?'

'I think you should have some coffee.'

'Don't want coffee.'

'It's your funeral,' Celine said, going to the fridge.

'Ha! My funeral! That's funny.' Laughing, he collapsed on to the sofa.

Celine came back with two beers. 'What's up?'

'Oh, Celine, it's all such a bloody mess.'

'What is?'

'I have to go. There's no other way. I just have to go.'

Celine frowned. 'What is it, Fergus, what's wrong?'

'They don't understand, Celine. They don't realise how dangerous he is. I should never have listened to Richard.' He lit a cigarette with shaking fingers.

'Jesus, you're scaring me, Fergus. Will you tell me what the hell is going on?'

Over the next twenty minutes and three cigarettes, Celine managed to get the facts out of Fergus, although not necessarily in the right order. 'So, this guy Mick thinks you're working for him and the police want you to set him up?' Ignoring Fergus's pleas for another beer, Celine had gone the other side of the breakfast bar to make some strong coffee.

'Yeah.'

'Well, that's good, isn't it? Once he's in jail you can get on with your life.'

Fergus shot her a pitying look and lit another cigarette. 'Mick has more contacts in Dublin than I've had hot dinners. It'll take him about thirty seconds to figure out I shopped him and then he'll send his mates after me. And it won't be just me, Celine.'

'What do you mean?'

He put his head in his hands. 'Mick was behind the break-in.'

Celine placed a mug in front of Fergus and sat down on the window ledge. 'Shit.' She stared at him, her eyes large.

'Exactly. I can handle him coming after me but I can't let him destroy Ma. And the break-in was just a warning. Next time someone could get hurt.' He looked at her. 'You could get hurt. Jesus, it's not enough that I got Dermot killed, now I'm putting you in danger.'

'It's not your fault—' Celine broke off as Fergus's mobile rang. After looking at the display, he disconnected the call. 'Who was it, Mick?'

'The law.'

'Shouldn't you talk to them?'

He shook his head. 'I'm not going to do it. I can't do it.'

'But then won't you be in trouble?'

He gave a short laugh. 'I think I'm in trouble whatever happens.'

Celine closed her eyes. 'But if you help the police surely they'll take care of you afterwards?'

'Yeah, right. Trust me, Celine, I know what Mick and his gang are like. They'll find me wherever I go.'

'So what are you going to do? If you do a runner now won't Mick still come after you? And the police, they'll be after you as well. And if they don't get you they might come after Rose—' She broke off as she saw the look of terror in his eyes. 'I'm going to call Richard.'

'No!' Fergus shouted, making her jump. 'Sorry, Celine, but he's just going to insist I go along with whatever the police say.'

She moved over to sit beside him and put an arm around his thin shoulders. 'Maybe he's right, Fergus. If you don't deal with this now you're going to spend your life running away.'

Fergus sniffed back the tears. 'I know.'

'Let me call Richard. Between the three of us maybe we'll come up with something.'

Fergus nodded reluctantly and she grabbed the phone and took it into the bedroom.

'Richard?'

'Celine, hi.'

'Can you come over, Richard? Fergus is here.'

'What is it, what's wrong?'

'Nothing, everything, oh, please just come over.'

'I'll be five minutes,' he promised and she hung up.

'He's on his way,' she said as she went back into the living room. 'Fergus?' He was no longer on the sofa but, backtracking, she saw that the door to the loo was closed. 'He's on his way,' she called again and then went out to the kitchen to make more coffee.

True to his word, Richard arrived moments later. 'Where is he?' he asked looking around the room.

'In the loo. Do you want some coffee?'

'Yeah, thanks. So what's going on?'

'He's told me everything.'

'Oh yeah?'

Celine handed him a mug. 'Yeah, and I think you should have told me.'

'It wasn't up to me. Given the history that you and Fergus share I thought you'd be the last person he'd tell.'

'He's afraid I might be in danger because I live over the shop.'

'I suppose you could have been, but now that the police are involved everything will be fine.'

He sat down on the edge of the sofa and Celine sat cross-legged on the floor, her back against the window.

'Don't you think that's a bit naïve?'

'No.'

Celine sighed. 'Look, I know you mean well, Richard, and I'd probably have gone to the police too.'

'Well, thanks for the vote of confidence,' he drawled.

She ignored his sarcastic tone. 'But like Fergus says, this Mick character is bound to have plenty of friends who'll come after him when they find out what he's done.'

'But they won't find out.'

'Why not?'

'Because when Mick gets arrested, Fergus will be arrested too. He'll get off on a technicality, of course, but no one will suspect that he was in any way involved with Mick going down.'

'Oh.' Celine absorbed this for a moment.

'What the hell is he doing in there?' Richard muttered.

Celine's eyes widened. 'Oh!'

'What?'

'Well, I didn't actually *see* him go in. I went into the bedroom to phone you and when I came out he was gone. The loo door was shut so I just presumed—'

'Bloody marvellous! Well done, Celine, he's got at least fifteen minutes head start thanks to you.'

'Well, I didn't think—'

'No, you didn't, did you?' Richard stood up and started to punch numbers into his mobile. 'Jesus, Celine, how could you be so bloody stupid?'

Before she could answer, the bathroom door opened and Fergus ambled out. 'Oh, hi, Richard, what's all the noise about?'

'Richard thought you'd done a runner,' Celine told him.

'Sure why would I do that?' Fergus muttered as he sat down and lit a cigarette. 'I haven't finished my coffee yet.'

Richard met Celine's eyes. 'Okay, sorry, I'm sorry.' He sat back down opposite Fergus. 'Celine says you're worried about Mick. There's no need.'

Fergus's look was scathing. 'Anyone with any sense is scared of Mick. You've no idea what you're dealing with.'

'But the police do,' Richard replied, his voice calm and quiet. 'You have to trust them.'

'This is a very small town and Mick has a lot of contacts. If there is even the slightest suggestion that I might have been involved in his arrest I'm a dead man. If I do a runner, he'll come after me ma.'

'No one will know,' Richard replied.

Celine said nothing but she was as sceptical as Fergus. Dublin was a very small place and all it would take was a copper with a big mouth to put Fergus in danger.

'I should tell Ma,' Fergus decided. 'I should tell her

everything and we should get the hell out of here for good.'

'Oh, Fergus, no,' Celine began but Richard cut in.

'Where would you go?'

'Dunno. Cork, maybe.'

'And you think that Mick's contacts are limited to Dublin, do you?'

'Then we'll go to England, to Spain, anywhere, I don't give a fuck!'

Celine sat up beside him and put an arm around his shoulders before glaring across his head at Richard.

'Look, I'm not trying to scare you, Fergus,' Richard said, rubbing his eyes with a weary hand. 'But you have to think this through. You can't run for ever. You can't spend your life looking over your shoulder. And you can't ask your mother to do it either. She's been through enough.'

Celine sighed. 'He's right, Fergus. Your only hope is to help the police. Then at least you'll have them on your side.'

Fergus nodded. 'I suppose.'

'When is it all going to happen?' Celine asked.

'Don't answer that,' Richard instructed him. 'The less any of us know about it the better.'

Fergus patted her hand. 'He's right.'

'So aren't we going to tell Rose?' she asked.

'God, no, she'd be just worried sick.'

'It's for the best,' Richard assured her. 'Fergus doesn't need any distractions right now.'

Fergus gave a mirthless chuckle. 'No, I need my wits about me, don't I?' He stood up. 'Sorry for laying all this on you, Celine.'

'That's okay.' She stood up too and hugged him.

'I'll give you a lift,' Richard said.

'No, I could do with the walk.'

'Keep in touch,' Celine begged.

'I don't think I will,' he told her with a sad smile.

'But how will I know that you're all right?' She looked at him in dismay.

'Trust me, if anything happens it will be on the news and all over the newspapers. Would you do something for me, Celine?'

'Of course.'

'If anything happens, if I don't come out of this, look after Ma for me.'

Celine swallowed hard and nodded. 'Of course I will but I'm sure you'll be fine, Fergus.'

'Yeah, sure I will.'

Celine and Richard stood in silence as he ran down the stairs and let himself out on to the street. 'Do you think he'll be okay?' she asked, wiping her eyes.

He slipped an arm around her shoulder and pulled her to him. 'He'll be fine.'

Celine pulled away from him and walked into the kitchen. 'You don't know that,' she snapped.

He followed her. 'Why are you taking this out on me?'

'You were the one who got him into this mess. You called the police.'

'Only because Fergus came to me terrified. He couldn't have handled this on his own. Mick wanted him to deal and it would only have been a matter of time before Fergus got hooked again.'

Celine closed her eyes and slumped against the counter. 'You're right. I'm sorry. It's just that I hate feeling so helpless.'

'I know.'

'Do you want a drink?'

'Yeah.'

She fetched two more beers and went back to sit on the window ledge.

Richard laughed. 'I don't know why I bothered buying you chairs.'

She smiled. 'They come in handy for visitors.' They drank in silence for a moment. 'Will your inspector friend tell you what's going on?' she asked after a while.

'Not the details.'

'They will look out for Fergus, won't they? I mean they won't put him in danger.'

'I don't believe so. They've checked him out and they know he hasn't been in any trouble since he kicked the habit.'

Celine's eyes were solemn as she looked at him over the rim of her glass. 'If anything happens to him Rose will kill us.'

'Nothing is going to happen to him, Celine. He's doing the right thing.'

Chapter 42

Celine was finding it hard to keep her mind on her work the next morning. Her thoughts kept turning to Fergus and her stomach was in a knot wondering if today was going to be the day. It didn't help when Rose phoned for a chat. Celine was consumed with guilt and as a result chattered away nineteen-to-the-dozen. Rose was immediately suspicious.

'Is everything okay, Celine?'

'Yes, sure, of course, why?'

'You just sound a bit . . . hyper.'

Celine closed her eyes and took a deep breath. 'Sorry.'

'Is it Richard?' Rose's voice was quiet and concerned.

Celine's eyes flew open and she smiled. 'Yes, yes, it's Richard. We had words last night. When the phone rang, well, I thought it was him.'

'Oh, well, I'd better go and leave the line free so he can ring and grovel!'

Celine's laugh was nervous and shrill – God, she was a lousy actress. 'Yeah, right, thanks, Rose.'

'Bye, love, good luck. And if you see that son of mine tell him to phone his mother.'

Celine gulped. 'Yeah, I will. Bye.' She put down the phone and nipped into the back between customers to make a restorative cup of coffee. She had only taken one sip when the bell went again heralding another customer. She hurried back into the shop and smiled when she saw Marina rifling through the rail by the desk. 'Hello there!'

Marina turned and smiled. 'Hi, how are you?'

'Fine. I just made a coffee – would you like one?'

'Love one, thanks.' Marina followed her outside and sat down at the small table. 'You don't look fine. Is it Richard?'

Celine debated telling Marina about Fergus and decided against it. It was too risky. 'We talked but it didn't do much good.'

'Oh, Celine, I'm sorry.'

Celine placed a mug of coffee in front of her friend and sat down. 'That's life.'

'He may still come round.'

'I doubt it. The sooner Rose gets back the better.'

'You're definitely leaving then?'

'Definitely.'

'Are you going to go back to Killmont?'

Celine laughed. 'I don't think so. No, I'll probably sell the house.'

'But where will you go?'

Celine shrugged – she hadn't actually given it any thought. 'Maybe London, who knows?'

'Have you told your dad?'

'No point until I have a plan.'

'I wish you'd reconsider. You could buy a house here in Hopefield, we could be neighbours!'

Celine tapped a fingernail against her mug. 'Very cosy. No, I think it would be better if I made a clean break.'

'Another one,' Marina muttered.

Celine laughed. 'Well, at least this time nobody's sending me hate mail.'

'You know, I was thinking about those red envelopes. I bet it was Eileen who sent them after all.'

'It could have been,' Celine agreed. 'She was a lot more upset than I realised. I made her life a misery.'

Marina drained her cup and stood up. 'Stop beating yourself up, Celine. You've done all you can to put things right. Now, relax and finish your coffee. I'll see myself out.'

'Bye, Marina,' Celine called after her friend. Standing up, she rinsed the two mugs and left them on the draining board. The day seemed to be dragging but at least, she thought as she went back into the shop, she had one thing to look forward to. Tonight she was going to Brenda and Alan's for dinner.

'Nothing fancy,' Brenda had warned her, 'just roast chicken, but it's probably better than the rubbish you're surviving on.'

Celine had laughed. 'Sounds great.' It was wonderful to hear Brenda sounding like her old self again. Although she wasn't the same. She was softer and more confident, an excellent advertisement for counselling. The arrival of a mother and her two daughters looking for wedding outfits kept Celine occupied until lunchtime. As she nibbled on some crackers and cheese, she pondered calling or texting Fergus. Probably not a good idea, of course, because he could be with anyone, maybe even Mick. She shuddered at the thought. The doorbell jangled again and she dabbed her mouth with a piece of kitchen towel before going into the shop.

Richard turned to smile at her. 'How are you?'

She smiled back. 'Fine, well, distracted.'

'Yeah, I know what you mean.'

'Did you hear from Fergus?'

Richard shook his head. 'But I called Declan Murphy.'

'So what did he say?'

'Not a lot. So I just told him to look after Fergus or Mick Garvey would be the least of his worries!'

'Rose phoned,' Celine told him. 'I felt awful not telling her.'

'What would be the point?'

'He's her son, Richard, she'd want to know.'

'Well, he doesn't want her to and it's his decision,' Richard warned her.

'I never said a word,' she snapped.

'Yeah, right, sorry. Look, why don't we go out for a drink tonight or you could come over to my place and we could order some pizza, watch a movie, it would take our minds off things.'

'I can't, sorry, I'm going over to see Brenda and Alan tonight.'

'Oh, right. Pizza for one then.'

'I'm sorry—'

'Not a problem!' Richard was already halfway out the door, a polite smile on his face. 'I'll let you know if there's any news. Bye.'

'Bye,' Celine replied but she was already alone. Damn and blast. Richard seemed to have thawed, tonight they might even have sorted everything out. She was sure he thought that she'd lied about going to Brenda's tonight and probably wouldn't ask again. Still, she told herself, this was the twenty-first century, there was nothing stopping her inviting him over. If nothing else it would give him the chance to turn her down. Lord, they were behaving like a couple of teenagers. Still, at least they were talking, even if it was only about Fergus. Fergus. She sobered as she wondered where he was, what he was doing, who he was with. His problems made hers look pathetic. She went into the back room, dumped the remainder of her lunch in the bin and made another coffee. On days like today she wished she smoked.

Later that evening she stood on Brenda's doorstep clutching a bottle of chilled champagne and a bunch of flowers. Alan threw open the door and wrapped her in a warm hug. 'Celine, it's been ages, how are you?'

She pulled back to look up into his happy smiling face. 'Not as good as you,' she laughed.

'Champagne!' he exclaimed as she handed him the bottle. 'Very appropriate.'

'I thought so.'

'Celine!' Brenda ran out to join them and hugged her sister-in-law. 'It's lovely to see you. And what lovely flowers.'

Celine, surprised at this show of affection, hugged Brenda back. 'How are you, Brenda?'

'Fine, fine. Come on into the kitchen and talk to me while I arrange these.'

Another surprise. Brenda rarely invited guests into her kitchen when she was cooking. Celine obediently followed her into the inner sanctum. 'Something smells good.'

Brenda flashed her a grateful smile. 'Why don't you open the champagne, Alan? Celine, I'm sorry I haven't been over to see you. How are things at the shop?'

'Wonderful. Rose has some very good friends. The stock is better now than before the break-in.'

The cork popped and Alan poured the liquid gold into three glasses. 'Did they ever find out who did it?'

Celine took a sip from her glass and shook her head.

'At least no one was hurt.' Brenda placed the vase of flowers in the window and came to join them. 'This is nice. You are kind, Celine.'

'You look really well, Brenda.'

Brenda put an arm around Alan. 'That's because I'm happy.'

Celine watched the look of pure love that passed between them and felt a pang of envy.

'Thanks for looking after Brenda while I was away,' Alan said. 'You and Frank were wonderful.'

'I can't take any credit but Daddy was great.'

'He gets back from Portugal tomorrow, doesn't he?' Brenda said, going over to the oven to check the roast potatoes.

'Tomorrow night,' Celine confirmed.

'I could collect him from the airport if you like.'

Celine smiled. 'Thanks, Alan, that would be great.'

'No problem. One of these days you girls should learn to drive.'

Celine and Brenda exchanged looks and laughed. 'I suppose we should,' Brenda agreed.

'Rubbish. I don't want to end up eaten up with road rage.'

Alan winked at her. 'Then you'll have to find yourself a permanent chauffeur.'

Celine's smile wavered. 'Don't hold your breath.'

Brenda flashed Alan a look. 'As it's such a nice evening I thought we'd eat outside. Is that okay with you, Celine?'

'Lovely. Can I do anything to help?'

'Just grab the plates and cutlery and take them outside. Alan, would you get some napkins and open the wine?'

Ten minutes later they were sitting out on the deck

tucking into the succulent chicken. 'Your gravy is always gorgeous, Brenda,' Celine marvelled. 'What's your secret?'

'Booze,' Alan told her and Brenda laughed.

'I always put a dash of wine in,' Brenda explained. Alan snorted. 'Dash! More like half a bottle!'

'Then it's a good job I don't drive!' Celine laughed. 'No wonder my dad always falls asleep in the chair after one of your dinners!'

They talked and laughed over the meal and by the time they'd moved on to the coffee the topics of conversation had turned more serious. Brenda spoke about her counselling and Celine told her about Fergus – leaving out of course the whole Mick Garvey situation.

'I can't believe that you've met him again after all this time,' Brenda marvelled.

'Dublin is a small place,' Alan remarked.

'Don't I know it,' Celine muttered. 'If you feel up to it, I'll introduce you sometime, Brenda.'

'Yes, I think I'd like that. Meeting him has obviously helped you.'

'Yes, it has, although I wouldn't have anything to do with him at the beginning. If it hadn't been for the break-in I might never have talked to him.'

'Every cloud has a silver lining.' Alan nodded gravely, making Brenda and Celine burst out laughing. 'What?' He looked at them, confused.

'Nothing, darling, don't worry about it. Has Frank met Fergus?'

'Not yet. Maybe when Rose gets back to Dublin I'll arrange a dinner for the four of us.'

'Ooh, wouldn't it be great if you could fix Rose up with your dad?'

Celine laughed. 'My God, you want to fix everyone up, don't you? I wouldn't mind but you haven't even met Rose!'

'Speaking of love lives, how is yours?'

Celine rolled her eyes. 'God, I think I preferred you when you didn't talk to me. Am I going to get the third degree every time I come here?'

'There's no such thing as a free dinner,' Brenda grinned.

Alan, who had slid down in his chair, started to snore softly.

'There is someone,' Celine admitted, staring into her glass. 'His name is Richard, he's my landlord.'

'So? Tell me about him.'

And Celine did. As she talked, a smile played around her lips and her eyes lit up. Brenda watched, fascinated.

'He sounds perfect for you,' she said when Celine paused to take a drink.

'He wouldn't agree.'

'Why not?'

'He found out about Kevin Gilligan.'

'But how?'

Celine sighed. 'Eileen came after me. She thought I was still seeing Kevin and she came to the shop to warn me off. Unfortunately the nosiest woman in

Hopefield was in there at the time and lost no time in telling everyone that I was an adulterous harlot.'

'Oh, Celine, I'm sorry.'

Celine arched an eyebrow. 'I thought you'd say I got what I deserved.'

Brenda winced. 'I've been a judgemental cow, haven't I?'

Celine gaped at her. 'Well, no, you were right—'

'I was not right to turn my back on you.' She sighed. 'It's just that it brought all the sordid details of Alan's fling back into my head. My psychiatrist says that when you are depressed some things take on an importance that they wouldn't normally have. I think that's true. I've been so paranoid and scared for so long. I was convinced that Alan wanted to leave me and I made his life so miserable I nearly drove him away.'

Celine glanced at the sleeping man. 'No chance of that now. He seems very happy.'

Brenda smiled and nodded. 'We've decided to try and adopt a child.'

'Oh, Brenda, that's wonderful!'

'There are no guarantees that we'll succeed, of course,' Brenda said quickly.

'Weren't you able to have children?'

'It never happened, I don't know why. We didn't go for any tests. Then as time went on, we stopped trying. We didn't talk about it but it was always there like a shadow in the background. It's amazing under the circumstances that our marriage survived.'

'You love each other.'

Brenda nodded. 'Yes, yes we do. I haven't met Richard but if he's ready to give up on you based on gossip and your past, then maybe he's not for you anyway.'

'But he's made me happier than I ever thought possible,' Celine said, her voice barely a whisper. 'I never thought it could be like that again.'

Brenda reached over and squeezed her hand. 'In that case, Celine, don't let him go without a fight.'

Chapter 43

'Excuse me, I asked for fresh orange juice.'

'Sorry.' Fergus took the grapefruit juice from the woman and poured her an orange juice. He'd been making mistakes all day. It had been more than a week since he'd heard from Mick and he was in agony wondering what the hell was going on. It didn't help that Declan Murphy was on the phone all the time asking what the story was. Fergus knew he suspected that Mick had got to him and he wasn't going to go along with the sting.

'Gotcha!' Sarah crept up behind him and grabbed him round the waist. Fergus jumped.

'Jesus, Sarah, don't do that!'

She scowled. 'For God's sake, Fergus, it was just a joke. Do you remember what a joke is?' she added.

'Sorry.'

'That's okay. You can make it up to me by bringing me for a pizza tonight.'

'Sorry, I can't.'

'Listen, Fergus, if you want to finish with me just say so.'

'I don't! Look, things are a bit difficult at the moment.'

'So you've said, but I'm getting a bit tired of that excuse. You know, if you don't want to take me out there's plenty of guys that do.'

'Yeah, whatever,' Fergus said, only half-listening to her.

Sarah looked stunned. 'Right! Well! Now I know where I stand. See you around, Fergus.'

He watched her flounce off. 'Sarah?' He groaned as he realised that he must have put his foot in it – again but he was finding it impossible to concentrate on anything, including his gorgeous girlfriend. He'd been tempted to tell her what was going on but knew it was too dangerous. Sarah was a great girl but discretion wasn't her forte. Still, he'd make it up to her when life got back to normal. If he survived.

Celine's nerves weren't much better. Fergus had gone to ground and she had pestered Richard for news. He swore he knew nothing and she could tell he was just as worried as she was. She turned on the radio for the news every hour and scoured the papers every morning, but nothing. When the phone rang she pounced on it and when it was Rose at the other end it took all of her will power to hold a normal conversation.

'She's going to kill us if anything happens to him,' she'd said more than once to Richard.

Tonight, they were going out for a meal together at Richard's suggestion. 'It will distract us for a while and at least we can talk to each other. I'm very glad that Dominic is so busy with his building work because I don't think I could go drinking with him and carry on a normal conversation.'

Celine smiled. 'He's so caught up with the deli and his wedding plans that I don't think he'd notice.'

'True. Has anyone noticed your preoccupation?' he asked.

Brenda and Marina had, but put it down to the breakdown of her relationship with Richard though she wasn't going to tell him that. 'I'm avoiding everyone,' she said instead. 'It's easier.'

She was hoping that the fact that he was taking her to the dimly lit Indian restaurant was a good sign. He had been a lot friendlier and relaxed with her so perhaps he was ready to put the past behind him. She was going to do her damnedest to tempt him. Brenda was right, he was too special to let go without a fight. Sadie was looking after the shop today and she was going to treat herself to a hairdo, a manicure – Marina would be impressed – and she was going to buy something very feminine to wow him with.

In the hair salon, she gave in when the stylist suggested some auburn highlights and a softer fringe than she usually went for. The results were amazing and Celine smiled as she examined herself in the mirror. Once her nails were polished a rich plum colour, she set off for Grafton Street and a spot of designer shopping. Though Close Second had some wonderful clothes, it didn't have the kind of funky, sexy pièce de résistance that she was looking for this evening. It had to be special but not so special that it looked like she'd made too much effort. After unsuccessfully trawling through all the big shops she finally found what she wanted in a tiny boutique she'd never been in before but would definitely be visiting again. It was a chiffon top in various shades of blue and aquamarine with a frill around the low neck that suggested rather than exposed her cleavage. The colour made her eyes look almost green and she knew that, teamed with her black suede hipsters and high sandals, it would look great. Nipping back into Brown Thomas she found a matching bracelet and necklace of blue stones that would complement the outfit perfectly. 'Okay, Richard, I'm ready for you,' she breathed as she boarded a bus for home. The driver gave her a wink and she smiled. The hairdo was working anyway!

Richard smiled when she opened the door later that night. 'You look good. New top?'

'This?' Celine plucked at her top in an off-hand fashion. 'No, picked it up in a market a couple of months ago.'

'And you did something different to your hair,' he said as he helped her into the car.

'Went to the salon. It was my day off and I had to do something to take my mind off Fergus. I don't suppose you've heard anything.'

Richard pulled out into traffic. 'Just that apparently Mick hasn't been in touch with Fergus.'

'Isn't that good?'

'The police don't think so and I think they suspect Fergus of changing sides.'

'He'd never do that,' Celine protested.

'I told Declan that. So the other theory is that Mick's figured out what's going on and has gone to ground until the dust settles.'

'If that's true then Fergus has to be in danger.'

Richard nodded. 'I know. Maybe we should have let him do a runner.'

Celine put a comforting hand on his knee. 'That wouldn't have been a solution.'

Richard covered her hand and smiled at her. 'I'm so glad we're talking again.'

'Me too,' she said with a shy smile.

'Friends are important at times like this.'

Celine's smile faltered. Friends? 'Yes, they are.'

'Let's try and put this business out of our minds for tonight, shall we?'

She nodded.

'I don't know about you but I'm starving.'

'Famished,' Celine lied.

In an effort to lighten the mood, Celine told Richard about her father's exploits in Portugal.

'He's a terrible man for haggling, I remember Mum used to walk away from him in shops. Anyway, he went to this market and bought Brenda a vase. He haggled for ages and was delighted with himself when he finally got it for half the price. Until he saw it in the airport for a tenner cheaper! He was furious.'

Richard laughed. 'How was the golf?'

'Wonderful. You know, I wouldn't be surprised if he buys himself a place out there. He just loves the weather.'

'Would he leave Ireland for good?' Richard asked, helping himself to another poppadom.

'God, no, not unless I went too. Family is very important to him.'

Richard stared into the distance. 'That's nice.'

'Sorry,' Celine mumbled.

'Why?' He looked surprised.

'I don't suppose you want to be reminded that you don't have any. Family, that is.'

He shrugged. 'I had my uncle up until last year, I can't complain. And I never had a brother or sister so I don't know what I'm missing. How did you feel about being an only child?'

She leaned her head on one side and thought about it. 'I quite liked it. It's nice always to be the centre of attention. I was a very spoilt little girl.'

'I don't believe that.' Richard smiled at her.

Celine's heart lurched. He had that look in his eye, that special look that sent shivers down her spine. 'Just ask my dad.' She gave a nervous laugh.

'He adores you, I can relate to that.'

Celine looked away. 'I adore him. Oh, good, here are our starters.' She pretended more interest in her kebabs than they strictly deserved, licking her fingers in between mouthfuls. 'How's your bhaji?' she asked politely when she looked up and caught him staring at her.

'Fine,' he murmured, not taking his eyes off her.

'Stop it, Richard.'

'Stop what?'

'Staring.'

'I can't help it. I've never seen anyone eat in such a sexy way before.'

She grinned at him as she sucked each finger slowly. 'Really?'

He laughed. 'You trollop!'

She laughed. 'I didn't think we'd ever have a night out like this again. I've missed it.'

'Me too.'

There was a small silence. This is where he's supposed to tell me how he's been a fool and he wants us to be a couple again. But he didn't. She stood up and excused herself. 'Sticky fingers,' she explained before escaping to the ladies. As she held her hands under the cold tap she took some deep breaths in an attempt to get her emotions under control. She didn't want to make a show of herself and throw herself at him only to be rejected. At the same time, she wanted him to know that she was still interested – boy, was she interested! She re-applied her plum lipstick – bought to match the nails – ran her fingers through her feathered fringe and psyched herself up for battle. 'Don't give up without a fight, don't give up without a fight,' she murmured under her breath as she returned to the table.

'Celine, will you come home with me tonight?' Richard asked as soon as she was seated.

'Try and stop me,' she replied, longing to hurl herself across the table and into his arms.

Their main courses arrived and Richard sighed. 'I suppose we'd better try and eat some of this first.'

Celine's eyes flickered between his mouth and his eyes. 'I suppose.'

Twenty minutes later they were in the car on the way home, kissing every time they stopped at traffic lights.

'It's just as well you have tinted windows,' Celine murmured after one particularly fevered exchange.

'We could just park and no one would have any idea what we were up to.'

'The car rocking from side to side might give them a hint,' Celine replied, sliding her hand up his thigh.

Richard groaned. 'I have to warn you I'm not bringing you back for coffee.'

'I'm glad to hear it.' She pulled his head down to hers as they waited for the apartment gates to open.

They barely got into the apartment before they started to pull at each other's clothes. 'Lovely top,' Richard murmured, throwing it over his shoulder. 'Great trousers,' he added, his hands on the zip.

Celine pulled at the buttons on his shirt with shaky fingers. 'Why aren't you wearing a rugby shirt?' she complained.

He obliged by pulling the offending garment over his head and dragging her towards the balcony.

'Where are you going?' she hissed.

'I thought it might be nice to snuggle up under the stars.'

Celine stopped and stared at him. 'You want to do it outside?'

'Unless you're worried about low-flying aircraft,' he grinned.

Celine smiled slowly. 'I forgot there were advantages to living on the top floor.'

'Of course, there's a guy in the next block with a telescope,' he told her as he slid the door open.

'Then we'll have to give him something worth looking at,' Celine replied, shedding the last of her clothes.

Chapter 44

Dominic eyed the suitcases lined up in Kay's hall. 'I've no idea where we're going to put all of this,' he murmured.

Kay laughed. 'That's only her clothes. Wait until you see what's in the garage!'

'What's that?' Marina emerged from the kitchen clutching a large box. Even though she was wearing jeans and a white T-shirt, she still managed to look glamorous.

'I was just warning Dominic about the garage.'

Marina smiled as she handed over the box. 'Don't, Mum, he might change his mind.'

'No chance of that,' Dominic said, 'although I hope you're a good nurse. Because I'm not sure my back is up to this.'

'Henry Higgins in a wheelchair,' Kay laughed.

'You are coming to the show, aren't you, Kay?' Dominic asked his future mother-in-law.

'I wouldn't miss it.'

'It should be quite a night,' Marina said excitedly.

'Richard is having a party afterwards in his penthouse – I can't wait to see it.'

'I'll be coming straight home to Josh,' Kay said.

'You know you could stay at Dominic's with him if you want.'

'That's okay, we'll be fine here.'

Dominic paused on his way out to the car with two suitcases. 'You have to stop calling it "Dominic's". It's your home now too.'

Marina grinned at her mother. 'It's going to take some getting used to.' She watched Dominic piling the cases into the car. 'I hope I'm doing the right thing, Mum.'

'Of course you are, love. Everything's going to be just fine. Oops' – she looked at the clock – 'I'd better go and collect Josh. Why don't I take him for an ice cream and give you two a bit more time?'

'That would be great, Mum, thanks. I want to get his room ready first. If I set up his light and posters and put the Thomas the Tank Engine duvet cover on the bed it should make him feel right at home.'

'He'll settle in just fine. You know he loves Dominic's garden.'

Marina nodded, smiling. 'And Dominic's going to clear out the shed and turn it into a sort of playhouse.'

'Ah, sure, he won't miss this place at all.'

Marina hugged her. 'He'll always want to come and visit his granny.'

Kay pulled away, blew her nose and collected her bag and car keys. 'Okay, then, I'll see you two later.'

Dominic shut the back door of his car and turned to Marina. 'Right, I'll drop this lot over. I should be back in half an hour or so.'

Marina kissed him lightly on the lips. 'Are you having any second thoughts?'

'None, you?'

'None.'

He kissed her again. 'I'll pick up some black sacks on my way back and we can put Josh's toys in them.'

'Right, bye.' Marina stood in the doorway until he'd driven off and then went back upstairs. With the exception of some books and photographs her room was empty. On a sudden impulse she decided to strip the bed and put the clothes into the washing machine. She laughed as she carried the pile downstairs. Her mother would be in shock! Then she went up to Josh's room and stood in the doorway. She would leave some toys here – Kay had insisted she was keeping the room exactly the same for whenever Josh came to stay – the rest would come with them. She opened the wardrobe and drawers and started to fold his clothes into a neat pile on the bed. Some she put to one side. Josh was growing and this stuff could go to the charity shop. She would be buying him some new things for the trip to Nevada anyway. At least having the wedding in the US meant there was no reception to organise. She could focus all her energies on clothes and shopping, her favourite pastime. It was going to be quite a challenge on a budget. The bank loan was paying for the shop conversion but Dominic and

Marina still needed to watch every penny until they were up and running.

By the time Dominic returned, Marina had finished with Josh's stuff and was out in the garage.

'Wow, your mother wasn't kidding,' he said with a low whistle as he came to stand beside her.

'We can sell it,' Marina offered, but he saw the sadness in her eyes.

'No way, some of this furniture is beautiful.'

'Do you really think so?' Next to clothes, Marina's passion was antiques. She regularly trawled through shops and markets but only bought when she fell completely in love with something.

'Absolutely! I've always wanted to buy some good furniture for the house but I don't have the eye or the know-how or the money.'

Marina wrapped her arms around him. 'You know, I think you and I are going to get along just fine.'

Dominic kissed her. 'I never doubted it. Look, let's leave the furniture for today. It would be great if we had Josh's room ready before he arrives.'

They packed the last of the bags into the car and drove over to Dominic's. While Marina went to work on Josh's new bedroom, Dominic made a plate of sandwiches and a fresh pot of coffee.

'Everything okay?' Dominic asked when Marina joined him.

'Perfect!' she announced and bit into a sandwich. 'I can't wait to show him his room.'

'Why don't you ask Kay to stay tonight? Josh might feel happier having her in the room with him on his first night.'

'That's a great idea,' Marina agreed, 'I'll ask her.'

Josh and Kay were playing in the garden when they went back to collect them.

'Mummy, Mummy!' Josh came running and she scooped him up into her arms and swung him around.

'Hello, darling, are you having fun with Granny?'

'Yes, we had ice cream and now we're playing football.'

Marina looked at her red-faced mother. 'Well, I think you should finish that game in Dominic's – in our new house.' She smiled over his head at Dominic.

Josh scowled. 'I don't want to move. I want to stay with Granny.'

'But look at the wonderful garden you'll have to play in,' Kay pointed out. 'Much nicer than Granny's. And Dominic can play football much better than me.'

'Will you play football with me, Dominic?' Josh asked.

'Sure I will, pal.'

'Okay, then.'

Marina shot her mother a grateful look. 'Mum, will you come with us too? You could stay the night.'

Kay hesitated. 'Is that a good idea?' She lowered her voice so Josh wouldn't hear. 'Maybe a clean break would be better.'

'Josh, go and wash your hands, we'll be going in a

minute.' When he'd run inside, Marina turned to Dominic. 'What do you think?'

He shrugged. 'It's up to you, but I don't think there's a need for a clean break, Kay. There's a bed for you in our house and you're welcome to use it whenever you want.'

Kay smiled. 'Well, that's very kind of you, Dominic, thank you.'

'So, Mum, will you come?'

Kay stood up. 'Just let me go and pack an overnight bag.'

When they were alone in the garden, Marina hugged Dominic. 'I never thought I could be this happy. Now if we could just get our bridesmaid and best man together, everything would be perfect.'

Dominic, who'd seen Celine and Richard walk past the newsagent's this morning hand in hand, smiled. 'I think your wish may have already come true.'

Chapter 45

Fergus had just got home when there was an urgent knocking on the back door. With his heart pounding in his chest, he went into the kitchen and edged his way towards the door. The banging came again.

'Fergus! It's Inspector Murphy, open this fucking door!'

Hastily, Fergus complied. 'What the hell are you doing here?' He let Declan in, closed the door and locked it. 'What if the house is being watched?'

'The only one who's watching it is my lads,' Declan assured him. 'Now what the hell's going on?'

Fergus shook his head. 'I don't bloody know. I haven't heard a word from Mick and he hasn't been at the club either.'

Declan frowned. 'Do you think he's done a runner? Could he have found out we were after him?'

'Dunno.' Fergus lit a cigarette and dragged on it long and hard.

'Tell me exactly what he said to you the last day you met.'

'I've told you that a dozen times already—'

'Tell me again,' Declan barked.

With an impatient sigh, Fergus reeled off the short conversation that he'd had with Garvey. 'Then I asked him would he be in the club later and he said no, that he was going to see someone.'

Declan's head jerked up. 'You never told me that before. Who was he going to see? Think, Fergus!'

'I don't know. It was someone who was trying to muscle in on his patch. Then he showed me a knife and said that it was a mistake to mess around with him.'

Declan stared at him, incredulous. 'And you never thought to mention this before?'

Fergus stubbed out his cigarette. 'Sorry.'

Declan pressed the speed-dial on his phone. 'Yeah, it's me, look I need you to check something out for me. Do a search on the system for any other new dealers in the Sandhill area and anywhere in a ten-mile radius. Ring me back as soon as you find anything.' Declan hung up. 'Right, I'll be in touch.'

'What are you going to do?'

'Never mind. Just carry on as normal and if Garvey makes contact you know what to do.' Declan unlocked the back door and left. There was no side entrance and the garden walls were high, but when Fergus looked out of the window there was no sign of the policeman. He went out to the hall, picked up the phone and called Richard. 'I, er, was just wondering if I could talk to you about the shop,' he said when the phone was answered. 'Me ma wanted me to check the books.'

'Oh, right, yes of course. Do you want to meet me there in half an hour?'

'That would be fine.'

Richard hung up, left his apartment and walked the short distance to Close Second. The closed sign was up but he could see Celine moving around inside. He tapped on the door and she turned and smiled.

'This is a nice surprise,' she said as she let him in.

He kissed her. 'I got a call from Fergus. I think he's okay but we'll know for sure in about twenty minutes. He's on his way over.'

'He's coming here? Why? Do you think it's all over?'

Richard shrugged. 'Like he said, we'd have heard if Garvey had been arrested.'

'In that case something's gone wrong,' Celine said miserably.

'There's no point in guessing. Let's wait and ask him.'

'I'll make some coffee.'

Richard followed her out to the back, sat down in a chair, stood up again and began to pace the tiny room. 'Hurry up, Fergus,' he muttered, 'hurry up.'

When there was a sharp rap on the door, Richard almost ran to open it.

'Let's go in the back,' Fergus said, slipping in the door and walking past him. 'Howaya, Celine.'

Celine hugged him. 'It's good to see you, Fergus. Are you okay?'

He collapsed in a chair and pulled out his cigarettes. 'My nerves are gone but apart from that I'm fine.'

'What's happening?' Richard asked, leaning against the fridge.

'I wish I knew. Mick has disappeared. I just had a visit from your inspector friend. He seems to think I know something' – he looked directly at Richard – 'which I don't.'

Richard nodded. 'Okay, so what had Declan got to say about it?'

'He thinks I'm a bit of a gobshite,' Fegus muttered. 'Mick said something the last day I met him and I never told the cops.'

'What did he say?' Celine asked, sitting down at the table, her eyes never leaving Fergus's face.

Fergus sighed. 'He said he was going to see some guy who was trying to muscle in on his patch.' He broke off and looked up at Richard. 'He took a knife with him.'

'A knife?' Celine's eyes widened in horror. 'But if there had been a fight, we'd know about it, surely?'

'I don't know.' Fergus stubbed out his cigarette. 'Murphy says I'm to carry on as normal and let him know if Garvey makes contact. Carry on as normal, it's easy for him to say! I can't even manage to serve coffee without spilling it and I don't know how many cups and glasses I've broken this week.'

Celine took his hand. 'Hang in there, Fergus, it can't go on for much longer.'

'No,' Richard agreed. 'Now that you've told Declan that Garvey was going looking for trouble I'm sure they'll find him.'

'I'd better go to work' – Fergus stood up – 'while I still can.'

Celine walked with him to the door. 'Please be careful and keep in touch. Just call and say something about the shop just so that I know—'

He smiled slightly. 'I'm still alive? Bye.'

He slipped quietly out the door and Richard gathered Celine into his arms. 'He'll be fine.'

'I'm not so sure.'

'Declan will look out for him. Now, are you finished here? I want to take you to dinner.'

Celine smiled. 'Oh?'

'Yes, we have some talking to do.'

She frowned. 'Sounds ominous.'

He sighed. 'Not at all. I just need to clear up a few things.'

'Then let's go.'

As it was another warm evening, they went to the beer garden behind Donnelly's pub and ordered a smoked salmon salad for Celine and a burger and fries for Richard.

Celine was quiet, her mind still on Fergus. She kept wondering what Rose would say when she found out that they'd kept this from her. Celine had seen some evidence of the woman's temper but had never been on the receiving end.

'What are you thinking about?' Richard asked, pushing his empty plate away.

'Fergus, Rose. She'll be furious with me for keeping this from her.'

He shrugged. 'You're respecting Fergus's confidence. Anyway, what good would it do telling her? It's not like she can do anything.'

'Yes, ignorance is definitely bliss at the moment. I feel so bloody helpless. Why don't you call this inspector and ask him what's happening?'

'Okay, okay.' Richard pulled at his mobile and tapped in the number. 'Declan? It's Richard Lawrence. Just wondering if there's any news on Garvey.' He listened for a moment and Celine moved closer in the hope of hearing the reply. 'Yes, I spoke to Fergus, he told me that . . . No, I told you, Declan, Fergus is straight up . . . yes, right, okay . . . thanks.' Richard put down the phone.

'Well?' Celine asked.

'They have an idea who Garvey was going after.'

'And?'

'They're looking for him – for both of them.'

'He doesn't really think Fergus is involved, does he?'

Richard shook his head. 'I don't believe so. Declan is just naturally cautious.'

'I suppose you have to be in that job.'

'Now,' Richard took her hand, 'can we forget about all that for the moment and talk about us?'

She smiled and took a sip of wine. 'I suppose we could do that. Anything in particular?'

'Yes, I want to apologise.'

'What on earth for?'

'For the way I reacted over the whole Kevin Gilligan business.'

'Don't worry about it,' Celine told him, not particularly keen to bring that subject up again.

'No, I need to tell you something.' He sighed. 'Rose told you I was no angel and she was right. I was involved with a married woman a couple of years ago.'

'Ah.'

'Yes, and it got very messy.'

'You were found out too.'

'Yes and he left her.'

'Oh.'

'She wanted me to move in but, to be honest, I didn't even love her.'

'Did she love you?'

'I don't believe so. I think she was just bored.'

'So what happened?'

'They sold their house, split the proceeds and she moved to Spain.'

'That was convenient for you,' Celine said, knowing she sounded bitchy.

'Like I said, I'm not proud of myself.'

Celine sighed. 'And neither am I, Richard. I demonised Eileen in my head but she didn't deserve it. It must have been awful to be humiliated the way she was.'

'How do you feel about Gilligan now?' he asked.

'Sad. Sad that he's wasted so much time. I just hope that it's not too late for him and Eileen.'

'You've done what you can. It's up to Kevin now. Anyway, I just wanted you to know that I had no right to be so judgemental. Basically I was just sick with jealousy.'

Celine smiled. 'That's nice.'

'There's nothing nice about jealousy. Anyway, I apologise.'

She kissed him. 'Apology accepted.'

'Now, I need to explain something else to you. It's about the night of the break-in.'

'Oh?' Celine stiffened. She had wondered where he'd disappeared to that night and why he hadn't taken his mobile with him but she'd refused to ask.

'I was in Kerry, painting.'

Celine relaxed. 'Really?'

He laughed. 'Yeah, I just got this urge and I had to go. I think you inspired me.'

'But why didn't you say?'

'I wanted to see what I could do first. I have this little house in the middle of nowhere and that's where I go when I have some ideas. Oh, Celine, I had a great couple of days, I even worked through the night. Then I had a few beers to celebrate on the train back to Dublin.' He rolled his eyes. 'I crashed as soon as I got home and didn't wake up until Fergus came banging on my door. I am so sorry I wasn't here for you.'

'That doesn't matter.' She waved away his apology. 'When can I see the paintings?'

'As soon as you finish your drink. Although, I must admit, I'm a bit nervous.'

She frowned. 'Why?'

His brown eyes stared into hers. 'Because your opinion matters.'

She swallowed hard. 'If I tell you they're brilliant, will you promise to have an exhibition?'

'I'll make a deal with you,' he told her, taking her hand. 'I'll have an exhibition if you start designing again.'

She pulled her hand away. 'It's not the same—'

'It's exactly the same,' he insisted. 'You told me that you gave up design because with Dermot gone there was no point. What about now?'

'What do you mean?'

'You've got me now, doesn't that count for anything?'

Celine looked at him. 'Have I got you?'

He smiled and kissed her fingers. 'You know you have.'

Celine swallowed hard. 'I don't know what to say.'

'Say you'll go back to designing,' he urged. 'What were you planning to do when Rose got back?'

'Leave,' she replied without thinking.

'Leave Hopefield? But why?'

'Like you say, Rose won't need me soon. I thought it might be time to make a fresh start.'

Richard frowned. 'But what about us?'

'What about us, Richard? Is there an "us"?'

'Of course there is! I love you, Celine. I want to spend the rest of my life with you.'

She stared at him, not quite trusting her own ears. He'd said he loved her, hadn't he? 'Are you sure?'

'I've never been more sure of anything in my life, Celine. Stay in Hopefield, move in with me. I'll even share my studio with you.'

Celine laughed. 'I don't know what to say.'

'Just tell me one thing. Do you love me?'

Celine threw her arms around him. 'Of course I love you, you silly man, you must know that.'

He grinned. 'I had my suspicions. But when I heard Gilligan was back on the scene—'

'Kevin was never back on the scene,' Celine told him. 'Do you believe that?'

'I do.' He kissed her long and hard.

Celine pulled away, flushed and happy. 'We're starting to get some funny looks,' she murmured.

'Then let's go back to my place and continue our, er, discussion there.'

They strolled back to his apartment arm-in-arm, talking about the future.

'So when do you think you'll have your exhibition?' Celine asked as they stepped into the lift.

'You don't give up, do you?' He opened the apartment door and stood back.

Celine arched an eyebrow. 'I thought we had a deal.'

'Do you mean it?'

She smiled, nodding. 'It's been on my mind lately. Working with all those lovely clothes – some of them designed by people I was in college with – really got me thinking.'

He hugged her. 'You know, getting all of those nasty anonymous letters can't have been nice but I'm beginning to think that the day you left Killmont was a red letter day for both of us!'

She smiled. 'I suppose that's true.'

'So what next? Will you set up your own label, your own shop?'

'I think I could do with some work experience first. It would be nice to work for a while in established design houses, maybe even spend some time in London, Milan or Paris.'

His face fell. 'I didn't think you'd want to go away, but I suppose it makes sense.'

She smiled. 'I wouldn't mind some company. I would have thought an artist would have jumped at the chance of spending time in such places.'

'Now there's an idea.'

'Could you get away from work?' she asked.

'I'm the boss, aren't I?'

'So, come on, show me.'

'What?'

'These wonderful paintings, I want to see them.'

He led the way down the corridor to the studio and swung open the door. One large canvas stood on the easel in the centre of the room but it was facing the other way.

Celine walked around, putting her hand to her mouth as she realised what she was looking at.

'I had to work from memory but I think I got it about right.'

Celine stared at the nude portrait of herself. 'I think you were very kind.'

He looked at her face, his eyes anxious. 'Do you like it?'

'I love it,' Celine said, not taking her eyes off the painting. 'You make me look so, so, remote. It's like I'm not aware of being nude, that I don't care about the artist, I'm in another world.'

'You've got it exactly!' Richard said, delighted. 'That's what I wanted to capture about you.'

Celine looked surprised. 'Are you saying that I'm remote?'

He bent to kiss her lips. 'Not now, but that's the way you were when I first met you: beautiful, very nice but just that little bit distant.'

'I think since Dermot died I've felt as if I'm on the sidelines watching life pass by.'

'And now?' he asked.

She smiled. 'Now I feel happy, alive, in love.' She looked back at the portrait. 'Thank you for this.'

'Do you still want me to exhibit it?'

She closed her eyes and groaned. 'I will die of embarrassment if anyone recognises me but you have to exhibit it. It's truly beautiful.'

'I won't sell it,' Richard told her, pulling her into

his arms. 'Although I plan to paint you many, many times.'

'I thought you usually did landscapes.'

'I didn't have the right model before. Now' – he started to open the buttons of her shirt – 'I'd like to check some details.'

She smiled as he peeled her clothes away. 'I'd no idea you were such a perfectionist.'

'You wouldn't believe,' he murmured, pushing her down on to the wooden floor.

'Ooh, it's a bit cold,' she giggled.

'I'll soon warm you up.'

Chapter 46

Marina sat in Dominic's kitchen reading while Josh played at her feet with his cars. She smiled down at her son's blond head, delighted to see him so happy. He'd been to stay with Kay once already and he thought it was a great adventure altogether. Marina was thrilled, as she'd been terrified that he'd throw a tantrum when he realised he was moving here for good but he hadn't been too bad at all. His playhouse had probably helped, and the fact that he now had someone to play football with. Marina had told Dominic that he didn't have to entertain her son all the time but it soon became obvious that he enjoyed it as much as Josh did. Marina often felt herself close to tears when she saw the two of them together. To find a new love at thirty-five was wonderful. To find someone willing to take your child on too was amazing. Even Ray was happy with the arrangement and had wished her and Dominic well. Probably because once Marina remarried he wouldn't have to cough up maintenance any more – not that he'd ever done so on a regular basis.

Marina washed her cup and started to prepare

lunch. It was Celine's day off and Dominic was going to collect her after a meeting with the builders. The conversion was going very well so far and was due to be finished while they were on their honeymoon. As she washed the salad leaves, Marina smiled at the thought of two weeks touring around Nevada. She hadn't been out of Ireland in years and it would be Josh's first time on a plane – she'd no doubt that he'd love it. Kay had offered to take him home to Ireland after the wedding but Dominic had insisted he come with them.

'You'll never be able to truly enjoy yourself if you leave him behind,' he'd told Marina.

No wonder she loved him. He was so considerate. She and Celine had landed on their feet when they'd met Dominic and Richard. They were both good men. Dominic seemed thrilled too that Celine and Richard had finally settled their differences. She chuckled as she remembered how emotional he'd got the night Celine and Richard had dropped by to give them the good news.

Marina sliced the chicken portions she'd cooked earlier and arranged them on the salad. The short time under Kay's roof had broadened her range of recipes but she was still careful not to get too ambitious. She was setting the table when she heard the car doors slam on the car in the driveway.

'Joshie, Aunty Celine's here.'

Josh jumped up and ran to open the door. 'Hello, Aunty C'line, hi, Dominic!'

Celine looked taken aback when Josh hugged her knees before running to Dominic, who swung him up into the air.

Marina kissed her on both cheeks and led her inside. 'It's a pity Richard couldn't join us.'

'He's in town visiting an art gallery who are interested in exhibiting his work.'

Dominic shook his head as he opened the wine. 'I still can't believe he's an artist.'

'And a great one,' Marina chipped in. After much persuasion and several glasses of wine, Richard had agreed to show them around his studio. They had been as impressed as Celine and implored him to go public. Richard had laughed and told them about the deal he and Celine had struck. Marina had whooped with delight. 'It's about time the women of Ireland got to wear an original Celine Moore. They've been deprived for far too long.'

Now she raised her glass in a toast and smiled at her friend. 'To the success of our two artistic friends.'

'To Celine and Richard.' Dominic lifted his glass and drank.

'Thank you, thank you,' Celine said, laughing. Once she'd agreed to the deal it seemed her brain had been in overdrive and she was sketching every chance she got. Working at the shop helped enormously as she watched women of all shapes and sizes try on the different clothes. Her pencil moved across the page at an alarming rate when she was there. Sometimes she even got irritated when she had to put down her pad to go and serve a customer!

Marina went to the counter to make the dressing, leaving Dominic and Celine talking about the show.

'I can't believe it starts tomorrow night,' Celine was saying. 'Are you nervous?'

Dominic shrugged. 'A little but once I get on stage I'm usually fine. I actually enjoy it if I'm honest.'

'I'm not surprised, you're so good at it. I'm sure you could take it up professionally.'

Dominic threw back his head and laughed. 'No thank you, it's strictly a hobby.'

'So how's the deli coming along? I had a peek in this morning and it looks like a bombsite.'

'Yes, it is a bit of a mess but they seem to be on schedule. The kitchen is nearly finished. The ovens, fridges and freezers will be delivered next week but we won't get them hooked up until we get back from Nevada.'

'Did someone mention Nevada?' Marina said carrying their salads to the table. 'I can hardly wait.'

'The most gorgeous cocktail dress came into the shop yesterday, it would be perfect for your holiday.'

Marina beamed at her. 'I hope you didn't put it on a rail.' She fetched sandwiches and a cup of milk for Josh.

'No, it's stuffed under the counter,' Celine admitted. 'As long as Sadie doesn't find it, it's yours.'

Marina sat down beside Celine and shook out her napkin. 'I have a favour to ask.'

'Oh, yes?' Celine grinned as she popped some chicken into her mouth.

'Would you design my wedding dress?'

Celine almost choked on her food and reached for her wine glass.

'Oh, sorry.' Marina patted her on the back. 'Are you okay?'

Josh looked up at her, his eyes full of concern. 'Are you okay, Aunty C'line?'

Celine smiled at him. 'Thanks, Josh, I'm fine now.'

He nodded. 'Good. Mummy, can I have some ice cream?'

'After you've eaten your sandwiches,' Marina said firmly.

Celine waited for the screams but Josh just went back to his sandwich without a word of protest. 'He's so good,' she marvelled.

'All thanks to Mum,' Marina admitted. 'Anyway, you haven't answered me. My wedding dress?'

'I don't know what to say, Marina. Are you sure you want me to do it?'

'I would be thrilled if you would.'

'Then I'll do it,' Celine said and was almost suffocated in a hug.

Dominic smiled. 'That's wonderful, thank you, Celine.'

'It's my pleasure but there's one condition.'

'Anything.'

'It's my present to you.'

'Oh, no, Celine, that wouldn't be right—'

'I won't do it otherwise.'

Marina sighed. 'I don't know what to say.'

'Thank you?' Dominic suggested.

'Thank you, thank you, thank you,' Marina said, hugging her friend once more.

'Now will you put the girl down and let her eat her lunch?' Dominic said.

Celine laughed. 'And it's a nice lunch too! Is Kay hiding in the garden?'

'Cheek!' Marina nudged her. 'No, this is all my own work. Some of my mother's talents rubbed off while we were living together. Although if we invite you to dinner I promise I'll leave the cooking to Dominic.'

'Or we could order from our new deli,' he pointed out.

'Oh, yes, won't that be handy? I'll be able to call you each evening and place my order. We need never cook again!'

'That brings a whole new meaning to the words "eating the profits"!' Dominic excused himself as his mobile started to ring.

'Are you missing work?' Celine asked Marina as he went into the garden to take the call.

'Not at all. I'm sure I'll probably get bored after a while but for now I'm quite happy to stay at home.'

'Are you really at home much? I'd have thought you'd be shopping morning, noon and night.'

Marina laughed. 'Guilty as charged! And between that and organising our trip there's plenty to keep me busy. You know, I think it's awfully decent of you and Richard to get it together. If you had other partners we'd have had to pay for four flights instead of two!'

'You're not paying for us,' Celine protested.

'Now it's my turn to insist. You and Richard are our witnesses and you are our guests.'

Celine bowed her head. 'Okay then, if that's what you want but who's going to give you away?'

'Josh, of course,' Marina murmured, sneaking a look at her son, who was trying to hide the remainder of his ham sandwich under his napkin. 'But he doesn't know it yet.'

Celine clapped her hands together. 'What a marvellous idea. I thought it might be Kay.'

'That was my original plan but she suggested Josh. She thought it was important to give him a definite role in the ceremony.'

'Your mother is a very wise woman.'

'I'm beginning to realise that,' Marina agreed.

'I wonder if she—' Celine broke off as Dominic came back into the room, his face grim. 'What's wrong, Dominic?'

'What is it, darling?' Marina looked at him, her eyes anxious. 'It's not Mum—'

'No, no, nothing like that but there's been a fire down at the community centre.'

'Was anyone hurt?' Celine asked.

Dominic shook his head. 'But I'm afraid some of the costumes were destroyed.'

'Oh, no, that's terrible,' Marina clutched Celine's hand. 'After all your hard work.'

'Maybe I could repair them,' Celine offered, although she wasn't sure how she could do it with the show opening tomorrow night.

'There's nothing to repair.' Dominic sat down and took a drink. 'I think we're going to have to cancel the show.'

Marina sighed. 'Oh, that would be such a shame, all the tickets are sold.'

Dominic shrugged. 'I don't see what else we can do.'

'Why don't we go over there and examine the damage?' Celine suggested.

'Good idea.' Dominic stood up again and reached for his car keys.

'Does Cathy know?'

'She's down there already.'

'Then let's go. Sorry for eating and running, Marina.' Celine gave her a quick hug.

'Don't worry about it.'

Dominic kissed her. 'I'll phone you and let you know what's happening.'

Chapter 47

Cathy was standing in the car park with a few other people when Dominic and Celine arrived. She threw up her hands in a gesture of resignation when she saw them.

Celine climbed out of the car and hurried over, Dominic hot on her heels.

'Is there much damage?' she asked.

'Not much at all,' Cathy told them. 'A chip pan went on fire when they were preparing the old folks' dinner.'

Celine frowned. 'But I don't understand, the costumes—'

'Were in the storeroom that backs onto the kitchen. Only a stud wall separates them and that went up in smoke straight away.'

'We could hire some costumes,' Dominic suggested.

Cathy shook her head. 'Not at such short notice and anyway, it would cost a small fortune.'

'Let me see the costumes, I might be able to do something.'

Cathy led the way inside. 'Be my guest, Celine, but

I don't see how you could sort this lot out in twenty-four hours.'

Inside, rails of clothes now stood in the middle of the hall. They were soaked, stank of smoke but were undamaged. Cathy fingered one suit. 'The fire brigade were here in minutes but unfortunately the water does nearly as much damage as the fire.'

'Rubbish,' Celine retorted as she moved from rail to rail. 'We can easily get these cleaned in time.'

'Maybe,' Dominic agreed, 'but what about that lot?' He nodded towards the rail that stood just outside the burnt-out store room.

Celine groaned as on closer examination she discovered that she was looking at the scarred remains of the Ascot dresses. 'Of all the lousy luck. If it were the ballgowns we'd have had some chance of replacing them but where are we going to find fourteen cheap gowns in black and white?'

Dominic turned back to Cathy. 'We could explain the situation to the audience at the beginning of the show and let the women wear ordinary dresses.'

Cathy nodded. 'I suppose that would be better than cancelling.'

'Or we could postpone,' he continued.

Cathy shook her head. 'No, the centre is booked up for months ahead and, anyway, we still couldn't afford new gear.'

Celine had been looking speculatively at the tables laid for lunch, the white cloths now blackened with soot. 'Could the budget stretch to a few tablecloths?'

'I suppose,' Cathy replied, following her gaze. 'But you don't have to worry about the damage to the centre. That's covered under the insurance.'

Celine smiled. 'Good. Will we definitely be able to use the hall tomorrow night?'

'Yeah, I got the all clear on that. The kitchen will be boarded off and obviously we won't be able to serve tea and coffee at the interval but apart from that, once we clean the hall and it has had a good airing, it should be fine.'

'Thank goodness we're having a summer this year,' Dominic murmured, looking up at the cloudless sky. 'Even if it is still smelly we can leave the doors and windows open.'

'And I think I can sort out the Ascot gowns,' Celine told them.

'How on earth can you do that?' Cathy stared at her.

'Leave it with me. Can you organise that the rest of the costumes are laundered?'

'Of course.'

'Right. Dominic, can you take me to the shopping centre?'

'Sure.'

'And I'm going to need some help. Can I use your house as a base?'

'Of course.'

'Great. Now, if you could call Marina and ask her to get Kay and Rose to meet us there around eight.'

'Rose? Is she back?'

'Just for the show, she wouldn't miss that for the world.'

'Right, well, I'd better arrange to pick her up.' Dominic went back to the car to make his calls.

Celine turned to the producer. 'Cathy, can you phone around the cast and get them to arrive an hour earlier tomorrow night? That way we can have a try-on and I can do a quick fix if there are any problems.'

'Sure! Celine, I really appreciate this.'

'Wait until you see some results before you thank me. I'll see you later.' Celine climbed in beside Dominic just as he was finishing his call.

'All organised,' he said, starting the car.

Dominic followed her around the shopping centre, mystified at the kind of things Celine was buying. She'd spent nearly an hour in Roches Stores household department, finally emerging triumphant with twenty tablecloths. Then she'd gone to the office equipment shop and bought a large stapler and then spent what seemed to Dominic like hours in an accessory shop selecting flowers, scarves, feathers, beads, and various other bits and pieces. Her last port of call was the hardware where she bought three containers of black dye and some Superglue. She burst out laughing when she saw the expression on Dominic's face. 'Don't worry, Dominic, all will become clear.'

When they finally returned to the car with their purchases it was almost five o'clock. Celine urged

Dominic to drive faster and got very annoyed when he refused to use the dedicated bus lane.

'Everyone else does,' she protested.

'If I did, I'd be caught,' Dominic replied calmly. 'Now instead of criticising my driving why don't you make a few phone calls and check how everyone else is doing?'

Celine scowled at him but obediently phoned Cathy.

'Hi, Celine, how's it going?'

'Not bad, what about you?'

'We've got three different dry-cleaners working on the costumes and, get this, they're doing it for free!'

'How did you manage that?' Celine asked, impressed.

Cathy laughed. 'I got the parish priest to ask them.'

'Very clever. Will they be ready on time though?'

'We've to pick some of them up in the morning, the rest, they promise, will be ready by five.'

Celine winced. 'That's cutting it fine. I just hope nobody's put on any weight.'

'If they have they can leave buttons and zips open,' Cathy said airily. 'That's the great thing about theatre. The audience are too far away to see the detail.'

Celine absorbed this piece of useful information. 'Right, Cathy, I'll talk to you later. Bye.' She hung up before the woman had a chance to answer. 'Dominic, we need to go by my flat on the way.'

'Well, I know that,' he retorted. 'We have to get all your sewing paraphernalia, don't we?'

Celine laughed. 'We do,' she agreed as she dialled Marina. After she'd filled her friend in on her progress so far and Marina had confirmed that both Rose and Kay were coming over, Celine rang off and called Richard.

'Hey, stranger, how are you?'

Celine told him quickly about the fire and the work that lay ahead of her.

'And I thought I'd had an exciting day,' he murmured.

'Oh, Richard, I completely forgot! How did it go at the gallery?'

'Not bad.'

'What does that mean?' she asked impatiently.

'They're going to give me a solo exhibition in October.'

'You're kidding? Solo? That's fantastic.'

'Yeah, I know, I can hardly believe it. They seemed really impressed and they're planning to send out invites to all the important people, including the press.'

'That's wonderful.' Celine beamed at Dominic and gave him the thumbs up. 'Listen, I have to go. We're setting up a sewing room at Dominic and Marina's and Rose will be there too. Why don't you come over? I'm sure Dominic would welcome some male company.'

'Ask him could he collect Rose,' Dominic said.

Celine passed on the message and nodded at Dominic. 'Great, thanks, Richard.'

'No problem, see you later. Bye, love.'

'Bye,' Celine said and wondered as she hung up if she'd ever get used to this gorgeous man calling her 'love'.

When they got to her flat, Celine whizzed around collecting all her stuff and then she went down to the shop to get some more accessories. Ten minutes later she was back in the car, slightly out of breath. 'Let's go,' she breathed.

Marina flung open the door as Dominic turned into the driveway and rushed out to help with the bags.

She frowned as she peered into some of them and Celine grinned. 'Don't ask.'

'All, apparently, will be revealed,' Dominic added.

They brought everything into the kitchen and Marina laughed when she spotted the stapler. 'That old trick!'

'What?' Dominic asked.

'If clothes don't fit the models properly at a fashion show,' she explained, 'they're pinned to fit us.'

'But you're going to use a stapler?'

'A stapler would damage good material,' Celine told him, 'but it's fine for a situation like this.'

'And there's more likelihood of the clothes staying on,' Marina chipped in.

Dominic grabbed Josh and headed for the garden. 'Come on, mate, let's leave them to it.'

Celine quickly explained to Marina what she was planning to do and sent her up to the bathroom with seven of the tablecloths and the dye. 'Make sure you use gloves,' she warned.

Marina raised her eyebrows. 'Since when did you have to tell me how to take care of my hands?'

Celine laughed. 'Go!' she ordered.

'Yessir!' Marina saluted and hurried out of the room.

When she was alone, Celine set out her booty on the kitchen table, took her pad and pencil from her bag and began to sketch. As she completed each design she took the accessories she needed for it and put them to one side with the sketch and a label. She hummed as she worked, engrossed in the job at hand.

'If I didn't know any better I'd say you were enjoying yourself,' Dominic said from the doorway.

Celine jumped. 'Dominic! I didn't hear you come in.'

'Sorry, I didn't mean to startle you. I just need to get a snack for one hungry little footballer.'

Celine laughed. 'Go ahead.'

'So how's it going?' he asked, taking apple juice and yoghurt from the fridge.

'Not bad, although it's hard to tell until I get my models to try the clothes on.'

Dominic frowned. 'Models?'

Celine smiled. 'Marina, size ten, Rose, size twelve and Kay, who's somewhere between a fourteen and sixteen but don't tell her I told you that.'

'So that's why you need them – very clever, I'm impressed!'

Celine grimaced. 'Let's hope it works.'

'I'll let you get on with it. Once Josh has finished his snack I'll take him up for his bath so he's not in the way.'

'Ah, the bath . . .'

Dominic grinned. 'Or maybe a shower would make a nice change.'

'Thanks, Dominic.' Celine smiled. 'I promise to give you your house back before bedtime.'

'Hey, you're single-handedly saving our show, don't worry about it.'

Marina appeared shortly after with some of the cloths. 'I haven't left these for as long as it says on the bottle but if I did we'd never be ready on time.'

'Don't worry about it, I'm sure they'll be fine. Put them in the washing machine on a rinse, spin cycle and then into the tumble dryer.'

Marina did as she was told and then came back to the kitchen to look at Celine's handiwork. 'Isn't some of this stuff from the shop?'

Celine nodded. 'They'd better look after it or Rose will have my guts for garters.'

'How much longer is she going to stay in Arklow?' Marina asked.

'I'm not sure.' Silently, Celine prayed it would be

until Mick Garvey was out of the way and Fergus could breathe again. She was glad she was so busy this evening and had a good excuse for not talking to her boss. Tomorrow night, however, would be a different matter. Once the show was over it would be hard to avoid Rose and her questions. She'd just have to spend all of her time in the kitchen when they went back to Richard's. She smiled and started to sing under her breath, 'That's why you'll always find me in the kitchen at parties . . .'

'You're really enjoying this.' Marina smiled.

Celine, who'd forgotten her friend was still there, shrugged. 'It's a buzz I suppose. I don't have time to think too much about the designs, I just have to trust my instincts.'

Marina's eyes roamed over the sketches scattered on chairs around the room. 'I'd say your instincts are pretty good. Right, I'll go up and check on my other cloths. Shout if you need me.'

Marina and Kay were taking the last of the cloths from the dryer when Rose and Richard arrived. Celine flew out to greet her boss and give her a warm hug.

'Rose, how are you? You look wonderful.'

'I'm fine,' Rose confirmed with a pain-free smile.

'She'll be hitting the nightclubs in no time,' Richard confirmed.

'I don't know about that but I wouldn't mind getting back to my ballroom dancing. Well, Celine, Richard tells me that you've been hard at work all day. I knew you were planning on taking up designing again, but not this quickly.'

Celine laughed. 'I think it's called being thrown in at the deep end. Anyway, I must get back to work. We'll use the bedroom to put the dresses together,' she added, and then shot Marina a guilty look, 'if that's okay?'

'Fine.'

'What do these labels mean, twelve A, fourteen C?' Kay asked, after she and Rose had been introduced.

'They're the different sizes of the cast,' Celine explained. 'We have two size tens, three size twelves, four size fourteens and five size sixteens.'

'So Marina doesn't have much work to do.' Rose chuckled.

'Our cast like their food,' Celine confirmed.

'Why don't we all go into the sitting room and leave Celine in peace until she calls us?' Kay suggested.

Celine shot her a grateful look. The last thing she needed at the moment was an audience. 'That's a good idea – you relax and have a glass of wine.'

Kay winked at Rose. 'I think I might enjoy being a model.'

'Marina, you're first,' Celine told her.

'Can I just get the drinks? Oh, and I want to nip up and say good night to Josh.'

'Can I come?' Kay asked.

'You go on, Marina, I'll get the wine,' Richard suggested.

'Thanks, Richard, come on, Mum. Won't be a minute, Celine.' When she returned she had Dominic with her. Kay had stayed behind to read Josh a story.

'Where is everybody?' he asked.

'Richard and Rose are in the living room drinking your wine.'

'Then I'll go and help them!'

When Dominic had gone, Celine and Marina carried everything upstairs. 'Celine, why didn't you just buy material in the fabric shop at the centre?' Marina asked as she laid the cloths across the bed. When she looked up Celine was staring at her.

'There's a fabric shop in the centre?' They stared at each other and then collapsed into fits of laughter. 'I never noticed,' Celine said after she'd pulled herself together and wiped her eyes. 'I wonder why Dominic didn't mention it?'

Marina shrugged. 'He's a man! Now, do you want me to strip?'

'Just down to bra and pants.' Celine glanced at the large window. 'You're not overlooked here, are you?'

'We'll find out if I start to get funny looks from the neighbours,' Marina laughed as she took off her clothes, whirled them around her head and threw them in a corner.

'You're quite mad,' Celine said, wrapping a black tablecloth around her. 'Now hold still,' she said as she went to work with her stapler. Within minutes she'd fashioned a strapless dress with a strip of white cloth around the top and a white sash around the waist that fell in folds down the back of the dress. 'What do you think?' she asked Marina as she turned her to face the mirror.

Marina appraised herself, turning this way and that. 'It's fantastic, Celine!'

'With the hat and gloves I think it should be okay.'

'It's a masterpiece. Oh, I can't wait until you start on my wedding dress!'

Celine smiled. 'Okay, take that off very carefully and I'll get ten B.'

'What about the hem?'

'She's not as tall as you so I won't do that until tomorrow night.'

'Right-ho!' Marina opened the Velcro fastening Celine had stapled to the back of the dress and slid it down over her hips.

The night flew by with much laughter and oohing and aahing over Celine's creations. By gluing on feathers and beads and changing the necklines she'd made sure that none of the dresses were identical.

'I can't wait to see this scene tomorrow night,' Rose said as she surveyed herself in the mirror. 'With the hats and the gloves these dresses are going to look amazing. Have you got plenty of costume jewellery, Celine?'

'Oh, yes, in fact Marina helped me select it.'

'Excellent, she has a very good eye. It should be a wonderful night.'

'You don't mind me borrowing stuff from the shop, do you?'

Rose waved a hand. 'Of course not, we have to play our part in helping a community project. And it's wonderful advertising.'

Celine laughed. 'I can see you haven't lost your head for business. Right, you can take that off now – carefully.'

Rose sighed. 'I've really missed the shop, you know. I'm just not cut out for lazing around.'

Celine smiled. 'I know. So when do you think you'll be back?'

'I thought just before Marina and Dominic's wedding would make sense.'

'That would be great.'

Rose hung her dress on a hanger. 'And looking at this dress, I have a feeling that you'll be ready to move on.'

'I won't leave you until you're ready to work full-time,' Celine promised, 'but yes, I've been bitten by the bug again.'

Rose hugged her. 'I'm so glad. And I'm thrilled that you and Richard are together. I just knew you'd be perfect for each other. Now, tell me, has my son been behaving himself?'

Celine turned away and buried her head in her sewing bag. 'Yes, absolutely. He seems to be very busy at work, we've hardly seen him lately.' At least that was true, she thought, turning Rose around so she didn't have to look her in the eye and draping a white cloth over her shoulder.

'I must admit that I wasn't keen on him working at that leisure centre but it seems to have worked out for the best.'

Celine grunted, glad of the pins between her teeth.

'Although he's acting very strange lately – I think he's keeping something from me,' Rose continued.

Celine froze.

'Everything okay, dear?'

'Fine, yes, fine.'

Chapter 48

'She's suspicious,' Celine hissed in Richard's ear later when she'd finished the dresses and was flopped on the sofa beside him.

'Don't worry about it,' he replied out of the corner of his mouth. 'Drink your wine and relax.'

'Relax!' Her eyes widened in disbelief. 'How can I do that?'

'Top-up, Celine?' Dominic stood over her with the bottle in his hand.

She shook her head. 'No, I'm falling asleep as it is.'

'You've done a fantastic job,' Kay told her.

'I think we should have a fashion show, Dominic, what do you think?' Richard winked at his friend.

'Great idea. Come on, ladies!'

Marina stood up. 'Yeah, why not?'

'We're not modelling them all,' Kay protested.

'Just one each,' Rose suggested.

The three of them disappeared upstairs, laughing.

'I really appreciate all your hard work, Celine,' Dominic said. 'The cast will be overjoyed.'

Celine sat up suddenly. 'Damn, I was supposed to phone Cathy!'

'I did it already,' Dominic soothed. 'You had enough on your plate.'

'Thanks. You know I don't mind the work, it's just avoiding Rose's questions about Fergus that's the real challenge.'

'Why, what's up with Fergus?' he asked.

Celine put her hand over her mouth and looked at Richard.

'We may as well tell him,' Richard said.

'Tell me what?'

As quickly as he could, Richard filled Dominic in on the situation, swearing him to secrecy.

'The poor lad,' Dominic said when he'd finished. 'But I think you should contact him and get him to talk to Rose.'

Richard dragged a weary hand through his hair. 'I would if I could. I've been calling him all day but his phone's switched off. And' – he glanced at Celine's worried face – 'I'm afraid he didn't turn up for work today.'

'Ta-da! Whadayathink?' Marina swept into the room with Rose and Kay on her heels.

'Amazing!' Dominic stood up and clapped and Richard whistled. Only Celine sat silent, staring into space.

'Celine? Are you okay?' Marina bent down to look into her friend's face.

Richard hugged Celine. 'She's just worn out, aren't you, darling?'

Celine forced a smile and nodded. 'Yeah, sorry.'

Dominic was gazing at the three women, his expression incredulous. 'You have nothing to be sorry for. Celine, these are better than the original costumes!'

She reddened. 'Now you're exaggerating.'

Rose shook her head. 'I've been in the fashion business for years and you know I wouldn't lie to you, Celine. You have a very special talent.'

Marina pulled Celine to her feet and hugged her. 'I told you years ago you were a natural! Dominic, I think we should open a bottle of bubbly.'

Dominic saw the look on Celine's face. 'It's late, darling, and we've a big day tomorrow. Let's save the champagne for after the show.'

Richard stood up too. 'I promise, Marina, I'll have it on ice.'

'You'd better,' she warned, releasing Celine and leading the other women back upstairs to change.

'Come on, darling, I think you need your sleep.' Richard took Celine's hand.

'What about the costumes?'

'Leave them here,' Dominic replied. 'I'll bring them down to the community centre tomorrow afternoon.'

'Okay then.' Celine suppressed a yawn and went to the bottom of the stairs. 'Thanks for the help everyone,' she called.

'Any time. I haven't had so much fun in ages,' Kay told her as they emerged from the bedroom.

'Me neither,' Rose agreed. 'Do you think Richard would mind dropping me home, Celine?'

'Of course not.'

'Maybe that son of mine will be there.'

'I doubt it,' Richard said. 'To be honest, Rose, I think Fergus has found himself a girlfriend in your absence.'

Celine stared at him and he nodded slightly.

'Why didn't you tell me before, Richard?' Rose protested.

'Ah, Rose, the last thing the lad needs at the moment is an interfering mother.'

'Bloody cheek, I never interfere!' She smiled. 'To be honest, I'd be delighted if he'd found himself a nice girl. Ooh, I wonder what she's like.'

Richard steered her towards the door. 'You must promise to say nothing until he tells you, Rose,' he warned.

'Of course not, what do you take me for?'

They left after much kissing and hugging and then Kay went in search of her handbag. 'I must be going too.'

Marina linked her arm through her mother's and walked out to the car with her. 'Thanks, Mum, you've been great.'

'Pleasure, love.' Kay kissed her cheek before getting into her car. 'Now, what time are you picking me up tomorrow night?'

'Sevenish?'

'Fine.'

'And don't forget your overnight bag.'

'Are you sure Josh is going to be okay with that new babysitter?'

'Oh, yes, he adores Jenny. She lets him play with the games on her phone.'

'Right then, dear, if you're sure. Good night.'

Dominic came out to the gate. 'Good night, Kay, drive carefully.'

Marina stepped back from the car and waved. ''Night, Mum.'

After she'd driven away, Marina slipped her hand into Dominic's and they walked back into the house. 'What's going on, Dominic?'

'Let's see to the dresses and then I'll fill you in.'

They went back upstairs and Marina sighed as she gazed at the gowns. 'Aren't they beautiful?'

'Beautiful,' he agreed. 'But I think we'd better put them in the living room and lock the door or Josh may decide to add some touches of his own!'

Marina laughed. 'Um, yes, good idea.' After they'd carefully moved the gowns downstairs, Marina led the way into the kitchen. 'So?' she prompted, sitting down.

Dominic sat down opposite her and told her what Richard had told him.

'Why didn't you tell me before?' she asked, looking hurt.

'I only found out myself this evening. Celine let

something slip. And don't give her a hard time about it,' he warned, 'because the police told them to say nothing. The more people who know about this the more dangerous it gets.'

Marina shivered. 'And now he's missing.'

'We don't know he's actually missing. Maybe he just forgot to recharge his phone.'

'He wasn't at work though,' she pointed out.

Dominic sighed. 'No.'

'You're going to have to tell Rose. She deserves to know what's going on.'

'That's Richard and Celine's decision.'

'I don't envy them.'

'No, neither do I. For God's sake, Marina, don't mention this to anyone. Not even Richard or Celine.'

'Of course I won't.'

'Good. Now, let's go to bed. I promised Cathy I'd be down at the centre first thing in the morning to help clean the chairs.'

Marina pretended shock as she stood up. 'But you're the star of the show!'

Dominic didn't laugh. 'It all seems so frivolous when you consider what Fergus might be going through.'

Marina put her arms around his neck and kissed him. 'You can't think like that. You have a full house tomorrow night, people have paid money to come and see this show. Put everything else out of your mind and give it your best shot.'

Dominic kissed the tip of her nose. 'You're much too sensible for a dumb blonde.'

Marina pushed him away, laughing. 'That's a lovely way to talk to your fiancée!'

Chapter 49

On the other side of town, Fergus stood outside a shabby town house trying to work up the courage to knock on the door. He had, as the police had instructed, sat tight for days but his nerves couldn't take it any longer. If Mick wouldn't come to him, then he was going after Mick. He had started his search early in the day but had no luck until he stopped off in one of the seedier pubs in Sandhill. He was nursing his second pint when the door opened and a guy came in that he recognised from his schooldays.

'Can I buy you a drink, Robbie?'

The other man whirled around at the sound of his name and a smile slowly started to spread across his face. 'Fergus? Fergus Lynch?'

Fergus stood up to shake hands. 'That's me.'

'God, it's been years, man, howaya?'

Fergus grimaced. 'I'd be grand if my memory wasn't so lousy. What are you having?'

'A pint of lager. Why, what's wrong with your memory?'

After ordering the drink, Fergus beckoned Robbie

to come closer. 'I was supposed to give Mick Garvey a call, he has a bit of business for me, and I can't remember the bloody number he gave me.'

Robbie laughed. 'Ye stupid gobshite, Mick'll kill ye!'

Fergus rolled his eyes. 'Don't I know it. I wouldn't mind but I could do with the cash. I don't suppose you have any idea where he hangs out these days?'

Robbie shrugged. 'Mick doesn't stay anywhere for long, mate, if ye know what I mean.'

'Yeah, that's what I thought. Oh, well, that's it then.'

'Unless—'

'Yeah?' Fergus wondered if Robbie could hear his heart beating in his chest.

'He could be at the girlfriend's.'

Fergus struggled to keep his voice normal. 'Oh, yeah?'

'Yeah. She's got a place down on Templar Row.'

'I know it. I don't suppose you know what number?'

'Haven't a clue, mate, but the front door is the most disgusting colour orange – it's hard to miss.'

Fergus beamed at him. 'I think, Robbie, you may have saved my life. How about a chaser?'

'A Jameson would go down nicely,' Robbie agreed.

And now here he stood at the orange door. Fergus raised his hand to knock but before he could, the door was thrown open and he was confronted by a young girl with a white tear-stained face. 'Who are you?'

'Gus. I'm a friend of Mick's. Is he in?'

She let out a strangled sob and went down the hall. Fergus stepped in, closed the door and followed. 'Er, are you okay?'

'No, I'm bloody terrified! Two fellas came to the house about an hour ago. They took Mick away.'

Fergus stared at her. 'Were they cops?'

'I don't think so.'

'What did Mick say?'

'He just told me not to worry.'

Fergus shrugged. 'Then I'm sure he'll be fine.'

She shook her head. 'I watched them from the window. They shoved him into the back of a car. They weren't mates, no way.'

Fergus thought quickly. 'Okay, love, calm down. Why don't you tell me all you can about these guys and their car and I'll put the word out. Someone will know what the story is.'

She nodded gratefully and stammered through a reasonably good description of the men and a vague one of the car.

Fergus smiled at her. 'Well done. Can I use your phone?'

'It's through there.' She pointed into the other room.

'Great, er, any chance of a cuppa?'

She nodded and went to put on the kettle while he went into the next room and closed the door.

He dialled the number that by now he knew off by heart.

'Detective Murphy, please.'

After Fergus had given the detective all the information and the address of Mick's girlfriend, Declan upbraided him for not following orders.

'I've made more progress in one day than you have all week,' Fergus retorted.

'Right then, Rambo, stay put and leave the rest to us.'

'You want me to stay here?'

'Yeah, just in case Mick comes back or anyone else turns up. I'll be in touch.'

'You'll have to phone the house number, the battery's flat on my phone.' Fergus gave him the number written under the keypad and then hung up. He went out to the kitchen to find Mick's girlfriend – God, he didn't even know her name! 'Okay, er, sorry, I don't know your name.'

'Lindsay.'

'Right, Lindsay, I've talked to some of the lads and they're going to keep an eye out for Mick.'

She nodded. 'Okay, thanks. Is there anything I can do?'

He grinned at her. 'Any biscuits to go with that tea?'

Her anxious face brightened. 'Are you staying, then?'

'Of course I am. Sure Mick would never forgive me if I left you on your own in this state.'

'You're very good. Thanks,' she said and went in search of some biscuits.

Fergus felt a pang of guilt as he watched her. It wasn't in his nature to be so devious but he didn't have much choice. Until he knew exactly where Mick was or who had taken him, Fergus had to maintain the illusion that he was a mate. He just hoped that the cops would hurry up and find him.

By one in the morning there was still no news and Fergus persuaded Lindsay to go to bed.

'But what about you?' she asked.

'I'll be fine on the sofa, sure it's as good as any bed.'

'Okay, thanks, Fergus. Good night.'

He wasn't sure what time the phone rang but there was some light in the sky and the cramp in his leg told him he'd been asleep for some time. He hopped to the phone, shut the door and jammed the receiver against his ear. 'Yeah?'

'Fergus? It's Detective Murphy. Get yourself down to the station.'

'What about Mick? Did you find him?'

'Yeah, we found him.'

'Is he . . . ?'

'Let's say he won't be bothering you again.'

'Jesus! What happened?'

'I'll fill you in when you get here.'

'But what about Lindsay, Mick's girlfriend?'

'We'll send someone around to see her. You just get over here, okay?'

Fergus let himself quietly out of the house. He felt bad not saying goodbye to Lindsay but what could he tell her? He walked the two miles to the station in town and asked for Declan Murphy. The sergeant nodded. 'Fergus, is it? Yeah, he's expecting you.'

Chapter 50

Celine slept late the next morning and had to throw on her jeans and shirt to go down and open up for Sadie. She had just switched on the lights when the woman arrived.

Sadie looked at her clothes and sniffed. 'You'd better go before any customers see you.'

Celine rolled her eyes. 'I'm sure they won't decide to shop elsewhere just because I'm wearing jeans.'

'Will you be back in later?'

'Yes, Sadie, I told you I would. But I'll be leaving early to go to the community centre.'

'What about the alarm?'

'Richard will drop by to shut the shop.'

'Oh.' Sadie looked slightly mollified.

'Anything else?'

'No, you go on back to bed.'

Celine bit her lip to prevent herself saying something she'd regret. 'Rose is up to see the show tonight,' she said when she could trust herself to remain polite. 'She may drop by to see how you're getting on.'

'Oh, right.'

'See you later.' Celine left, chuckling quietly as she ran back up to the flat. That should keep Sadie on her toes. Now that she was up, Celine didn't feel like going back to bed. Though she felt very tired she couldn't get Fergus out of her head. Going to the phone, she called Richard. 'Did I wake you?' she said when he answered.

'Nah, I've been up for a while.'

'You're worrying too.'

'It's hard not to.'

'Why don't you phone your inspector friend?'

'Already did, but he's not available. God, it's so frustrating.'

'I think we should tell Rose.'

'Not yet, Celine, at least let her enjoy the show.'

'Okay.'

'What are you doing today?'

'Nothing much. I have to put in a couple of hours at the shop later and then I need to be at the centre by six.'

'Let's have a leisurely breakfast at the Napoli,' he suggested.

'Yeah, why not?'

'See you there in five.'

He'd hung up before Celine could tell him she wanted to shower first. 'He can wait,' she decided, pulling off her shirt.

*

Richard was on his second cup of coffee when she walked in. 'And about time,' he said, putting down his newspaper.

Celine raised an eyebrow as she slid into the booth opposite him. 'You should know that it takes a woman more than five minutes to get ready.' She looked pointedly at his tousled hair and crumpled shirt. 'Some of us have standards.' She turned to smile at Tracy, who'd followed her to the table. 'Hi, Tracy. I think you'd better give this man the works, he's a terrible grouch this morning.'

Tracy laughed. 'Aren't they all?'

Richard growled. 'Enough of your lip, woman! I want the full Irish breakfast and quick about it!'

'Yes sir!' Tracy said, laughing. 'How about you, Celine?'

'Toast and coffee, please.'

'You can't start the day on just toast and coffee,' Richard protested.

Celine winked at Tracy. 'Oh, okay, I'll have the works too!'

'Right away. I'll bring your coffee first.'

'Thanks, Tracy.'

Richard took Celine's hand. 'Did you sleep well?'

'Yes, although I was a bit lonely.'

'You were exhausted and I was afraid you wouldn't get any sleep if I spent the night.'

'That's okay, you can make up for it tonight. After one of Bob's breakfasts you should have energy to burn for days.'

He laughed. 'Ah, yes, except Dominic's roped me in to help out at the centre.'

'He's a persuasive man. What time are you picking up the food for the party?'

He clapped a hand to his head. 'I forgot completely about that!'

Celine stared at him. 'You did organise some food?'

'Of course I did, I just forgot that I had to pick it up. I'll give them a call and ask them to deliver.'

'And who'll let them in?' Celine asked, wide-eyed.

'Shit! Would you—?'

She smiled. 'Seeing as you asked so nicely, yes I will. But tell them to come before one.'

'You're an angel. And, by the way, you're also an incredibly talented designer.'

Celine's eyes were anxious. 'Do you honestly think so?'

He squeezed her hand. 'I do. I felt so proud of you last night. Those dresses would look good on any catwalk.'

'What do you know about catwalks?' Celine scoffed, but her cheeks were flushed.

'I know what I like looking at. Although I don't think someone like Mary Boyle is going to do justice to your creation.'

Celine laughed. 'I'm delighted to say that she's not in the Ascot scene.'

'She'll be disgusted. Ah, sustenance!' he cried as Tracy set down a loaded tray between them.

Celine winced when she saw the pile of food. 'We'll have to lie down after eating this lot.'

'If you insist,' he said cheerfully and Tracy moved away, chuckling to herself.

Between them they polished off the food and as they sat over their coffee, Celine nodded towards Richard's mobile. 'Try again.'

'Fergus or Declan?'

'Both.'

Richard dialled, sighed and disconnected. 'Still out of service.' He dialled Declan's mobile and got an answering service. 'Declan, it's Richard Lawrence again. Can you call me as soon as possible? Thanks.'

'We'd better go.' Celine stood up.

Richard walked to the desk to pay Tracy. 'You are coming to my place after the show tonight, aren't you?'

'Wouldn't miss it,' she assured him. 'And I'm looking forward to the show too.' She smiled at Celine. 'I can't wait to see your dresses.'

Celine stared at her. 'How on earth do you know about that?'

'Dominic was in earlier,' she laughed. 'Anyway, everyone knows everything that goes on in Hopefield.'

Celine rolled her eyes. 'Don't I know it!'

That evening when Celine arrived at the community centre, laden down with all her sewing gear, most of the cast were already there.

'She's here!' Cathy shouted and one by one they started to applaud. She cringed when Dominic broke into a chorus of 'For she's a jolly good fellow' but was thrilled with the warm hugs and kisses she received.

'I can't wait to try my dress on,' Maggie Doyle, one of the larger ladies, told her. 'I've never worn anything as glamorous.'

'Just move carefully,' Celine warned her. 'They're all only stapled together.'

'They're magnificent, Celine.' Cathy kissed her. 'I can't believe you managed to do all that work in one night.'

Celine caught Dominic's eye and smiled. 'I had lots of help. Now, if you don't mind, I'd like the ladies to have a fitting. I haven't done any of the hems yet.'

'Of course.' Cathy clapped her hands and directed the ladies from the Ascot scene to the dressing room.

Celine spent most of the next hour on her knees, her trusty stapler in hand. The room was swarming with women admiring each other, fixing hair and trying on different hats and jewellery.

'Thirty minutes to curtain,' Cathy called from the doorway and there was a groan from some, excited giggles from others.

'I don't know how you do it,' Maggie Doyle said to Celine as she admired her gown.

Celine laughed. 'I don't know how you go out and perform in front of a room full of people. I'd die of fright.'

'Not at all, it's great fun!'

Celine stood up and glanced around at her handi-work. 'Is everyone okay?'

There was a chorus of assent.

'Okay then. Please get changed for the first scene and please, please be careful. Remember there are only a few staples between you and nudity!'

Everyone laughed. 'Now that would bring the punters in!' one of the women said.

'I think the parish priest might faint.'

'Rubbish, he'd love it!'

Celine gathered up her stuff as they joked amongst themselves. 'Ladies, I'm going to check on the boys but holler if you need me.'

'Thanks, Celine!'

'Cheers, Celine!'

She was smiling as she left the room.

'Everything okay?' Dominic asked.

'Fine. You look very handsome. How do you feel?'

'Sick.'

'You'll be great. Do all your costumes fit okay?'

'All three of them?' he grinned. 'Yeah, they're fine.'

'Do me a favour and stick your head into the men's dressing room and see if anyone needs me.'

Dominic did as he was told but there was a chorus of 'fine', 'grand', 'ace' – this from the only man in his twenties! 'Looks like you're off the hook,' he told Celine.

'Right then, I'll go out front and see how things are

going.' She reached up to kiss Dominic's cheek. 'Break a leg!'

Before she left backstage, she went in search of Cathy to let her know where she'd be if she was needed. 'And I'll come backstage to help the ladies and Eliza with their ballgowns.'

Cathy smiled. 'Bless you. Now all I have to do is persuade Eliza that her voice is fine and we'll be ready to go.'

Celine was still chuckling as she went down to the hall. Phyllis Jenkins was a very nervous, anxious woman with the voice of an angel. Unfortunately she never thought it was good enough. But no doubt Cathy would reassure her.

'What's so funny?' Richard asked, appearing at her side.

'Just the leading lady's suffering with her nerves. Is everything ready out here?'

'Seems to be.'

'Any news?'

He shook his head.

She sighed. 'I think we'll have to spend the evening dodging Rose.'

'But we'll tell her tomorrow.'

'Do you think so?'

'We can't leave it any longer than that. He's her son.'

By the time the curtain went up, the hall was full and except for a slight smell of smoke, no one would have known of the previous day's crisis. Celine was standing at the back of the room, grateful she had an excuse not to sit with Rose. 'I need to go backstage for some of the costume changes,' she'd explained after introducing her dad, Brenda and Alan to everyone. Richard wasn't so lucky. Rose had patted the seat beside her and he'd thrown Celine a desperate look. 'Enjoy the show!' she'd said with a sympathetic smile and slipped away. Now at least she was able to forget about Fergus for a little while and get lost in the story of Eliza Doolittle and Henry Higgins. The time raced by and before she knew it, it was time to go backstage again. The dressing room was full of hushed excitement. 'You're all fantastic,' Celine told them honestly. 'The audience are really enjoying it.'

They hurriedly put on the ballgowns and Celine moved among them, helping with hair, fastening necklaces, touching up make-up and supplying a safety pin when necessary. She had deliberately worn her lightweight cotton jacket with the large pockets that were laden with pins, buttons, combs and even Superglue for real emergencies! After a frantic five minutes, she was alone again as the women hurried to their positions in the wings. Celine hadn't expected this buzz from an amateur production but there was an amazing atmosphere in the cramped backstage area. She hurried back out front so that she could see the full effects of the costumes from the hall. A ripple went through the audience as the curtains opened revealing the ballroom scene. Celine smiled. If only they knew that under the corsage pinned to Eliza's waist there was a tear; that the elaborate feathers attached to another gown hid a nasty burn and that the gauzy net material adorning some of the ball-gowns had come from some old net curtains!

At the break, Celine went to find her dad and Brenda to see what they thought.

'Excellent!' her dad pronounced. 'That Eliza Doolittle has a beautiful voice.'

Brenda shook her head. 'No, I think Henry – Dominic – is better.'

Marina joined them and beamed at Brenda. 'He is wonderful, isn't he?'

'He's marvellous!' Rose told her. 'Kay and I were just saying he could go professional.'

'The costumes are wonderful, Celine.' Brenda smiled at her sister-in-law. 'You've done a great job.'

'She's done an amazing job,' Richard said, putting an arm around Celine.

'Wait until you see the Ascot scene,' Rose told Brenda.

'Kay told us about the fire,' Frank said. 'You did well, love, to get the new dresses finished on time.'

'I enjoyed every minute,' Celine admitted.

Brenda's eyes lit up. 'Really?'

Alan laughed. 'I think, Rose, that Celine may not be working for you for much longer.'

Rose nodded. 'Yes, I know, but at least I'll be able to buy and sell her clothes.'

Frank looked at his daughter. 'Are you really going back to dress design?'

She nodded. 'I even have my first customer.'

'She's making my wedding dress,' Marina told them.

Frank hugged Celine tightly to him. 'That's wonderful.'

There was an announcement telling them to return to their seats. 'I'll see you later,' Celine said, squeezing his hand. She kissed Richard as they left to go back to their seats. 'I'll go back to the apartment with Daddy after the show.'

'And Alan can follow me. Rose said she'll go with them.'

'They all seem to be getting on well,' she remarked.

He grinned. 'Like one big happy family.'

As the lights went down, Celine went backstage to help the women into their gowns but by the time she got to the dressing room most of them were already dressed.

'We couldn't wait,' Maggie told her. 'But we could do with some help with our hats.'

'And can you fix my feathers, Celine?'

'Have you got your stapler, Celine?' another shouted, 'I think my boobs are going to fall out!'

This was greeted with laughter and Cathy ran in to hush them. 'You all look beautiful,' she whispered, 'but keep the noise down.'

As they went to take their positions, Cathy drew Celine into the wings. 'You can watch from here for a few minutes. You'll be able to see the audience's reaction.'

When the curtain went up there was an audible gasp. Then someone started to applaud and soon the entire audience were applauding.

'That's for you,' Dominic whispered in Celine's ear.

'Daddy and Richard probably started it,' she joked but her heart was thumping in her chest. She hurried down to the hall so she could judge the dresses for herself. Her heart thumped even faster and her eyes filled with tears as she studied her own designs and admitted to herself that they were good. 'You were right, Dermot,' she murmured under her breath. 'I can do it.'

Chapter 51

'More champagne?' Richard moved from group to group, a bottle in each hand.

'The champagne's never going to last at the rate he's pouring it,' Marina said as Celine loaded another tray of vol-au-vents into the oven.

'It doesn't matter, there's plenty of beer and wine.'

'You should be out there with your adoring public,' Marina told her.

'No chance. Anyway, this is Phyllis and Dominic's big night. Weren't they sensational?'

'Wonderful,' Marina agreed, misty-eyed.

'Can I help?' Brenda walked in and put her empty glass on the counter.

Celine looked up and smiled. 'Perfect timing, Brenda, we're just about to start the food. Can you take the sandwiches and sausages around?'

'No problem.' Brenda took a bunch of napkins, the two plates and went out again.

'I can't believe the difference in that woman,' Marina remarked as she arranged canapés on a plate.

'I know, isn't it great? I think if Alan's grin gets any bigger it's going to split his face!'

'Speaking of grins, my mum and your dad haven't stopped nattering all evening.'

'I hope Rose doesn't feel left out.'

'Rose? Not at all! She's holding court in the studio and Richard's pal from the art gallery is hanging on her every word.'

'You're kidding!'

'Nope.' Marina loaded a tray with food and napkins. 'I'll see what else is going on and report back.'

Celine wiped her hands on a cloth and sat down on a stool to enjoy her champagne.

'What are you doing out here all alone?' Richard asked, walking up behind her and slipping his arms around her waist.

Celine rested her head against his chest. 'Someone has to look after the guests.'

'Is there no end to your talents?' He leaned across her to take a spring roll. 'Mmmn, these are good!'

'Have you called again?' she asked.

Richard sat down on the stool beside her and pulled out his mobile. 'Several times. I left a message for Fergus telling him everyone would be here after the show.'

'Did you tell him Rose was here?'

'About three messages ago.'

'What about Declan?'

'I phoned the station but they said he wasn't available.'

'All this waiting is driving me mad. What if something's happened to Fergus?'

'What's going on?'

Celine whirled around. 'Rose! I didn't see you there.'

'Obviously. What's happened to Fergus?'

Richard went to her and put an arm around her shoulders. 'Rose, there's nothing to worry about—'

She shook his arm off. 'Don't treat me like a child, Richard. I want the truth and I want it now.'

Richard met Celine's eyes and she shrugged.

'Let's go outside,' he said. 'It's quieter.'

When they were sitting on the sofa in the hallway outside the apartment, Richard started at the beginning and told Rose everything.

She paled at the mention of Mick Garvey but listened in silence as Richard talked.

'Why didn't you tell me?' she said when they were finished, tears rolling silently down her face.

Celine crouched at her feet. 'He begged us not to. He didn't want to worry you.'

'I'm his mother, that's my job,' Rose said wearily. 'He did this to protect me, to protect the shop? As if I give a damn about the bloody shop! I'd gladly move to Timbuktu if necessary.'

'If this works, Mick Garvey will go down for a very long time.' Richard pointed out.

'But at what cost?' Rose snapped.

'The police will look after him,' Celine murmured and hoped it was true.

'How the hell can they look after him if they don't even know where he is?'

Celine shot Richard a helpless look.

Rose stood up, wiping here eyes on her sleeve. 'I'm going down there.'

Richard stared at her. 'To the station? There's really not much point, Rose—'

'Don't try and stop me! I'm going down there and I'm not leaving until I get some answers.'

She walked over to the lift and pressed the button.

Richard nodded. 'I'll drive you. Hang on and I'll get my keys.'

On arriving at the police station, Rose and Richard were shown into the same room that Fergus had been in hours earlier.

Minutes later, Declan Murphy walked in and Richard introduced Rose.

'So what can I do for you?' he asked.

'I want to know where my son is.'

Declan frowned. 'Isn't he at home?'

'Jesus, Declan, if he was at home I wouldn't have been phoning you constantly for the last two days!' Richard exploded.

Declan shook his head in confusion. 'Hang on a minute, folks, I think we have our wires crossed. Fergus was here today but now he's gone home. Haven't you seen him?'

'Well, no,' Rose told him, 'but then we've been out all evening.'

Declan's face cleared. 'That explains it then. You don't know what's happened.'

'Why don't you fill us in?' Richard suggested.

The inspector gave them a brief summation of Fergus's detective work over the last couple of days.

'Bloody fool,' Rose muttered. 'When will he ever learn?'

A smile flickered across Declan's face. 'I said something along those lines myself. Anyway, it was lucky for him he didn't track Mick down earlier. Two lads from a rival gang had beat him to it and taken Mick away. We found his body early this morning.'

Rose's hand went to her mouth. 'Holy Mother of God!'

'So its over?' Richard asked his friend.

'As far as Fergus is concerned, yes.'

'Are you sure? What's to stop these characters coming after Fergus?' Rose looked anxiously at the detective.

'They don't even know of Fergus's existence,' Declan assured her.

'What about Mick's cronies? Won't they be looking for Fergus?' Richard asked.

'Unlikely. Mick kept his cards pretty close to his chest and Fergus was a new recruit. But we'll be keeping an eye on things for a while and Fergus knows what to do if he's approached by anyone.'

Rose shook her head. 'The lad will spend his life looking over his shoulder.'

The inspector looked her straight in the eye.

'There's really no need, Mrs Lynch. Fergus was a tiny cog in a very big wheel and no one will think it unusual that he disappears now that Garvey is dead. There will be a lot of characters disappearing into the woodwork, believe me.'

Let's go and see him, Rose,' Richard suggested, standing up.

Rose nodded. 'Thank you, Inspector. No offence, but I sincerely hope we never have to meet again.'

Declan nodded, 'Likewise, Mrs Lynch.'

'Give Fergus my love,' Celine said and put the phone down.

'Well?' Dominic said.

Celine smiled. 'He's safe.'

'Thank God,' Marina murmured. 'Are they still at the station?'

'Fergus is at home and Richard is taking Rose there now.'

'We'll stay with you until he gets back.'

'No, Marina, there's really no need. Now that I know he's safe I'll be fine. Anyway, Richard says he won't be long. He's just going to drop Rose and he'll be straight home.'

'If you're sure?' Dominic said.

She reached up to kiss him. 'I'm sure. And congratulations again on a wonderful performance.'

'Lock up after us,' Dominic instructed, 'and go to bed. You'll have plenty of time to hear about Fergus's exploits in the morning.'

'I will. Goodnight.' Celine closed the door after them and wandered back into the living-room. The place was a mess but she couldn't face cleaning up tonight. She didn't feel much like going to bed alone either. In the end she decided to make some coffee and wait for Richard. She knew she wouldn't be able to sleep until he got home.

Though Fergus was dog-tired when he got home he couldn't face going to bed. Instead, he got a beer from the fridge and went into the living-room. Stretching out on the sofa, he went over the last couple of days in his head and knew that he'd been very lucky to walk away from this mess unscathed. As he finished his beer, his eyelids began to droop. He'd go up to bed in a minute. As soon as he'd locked up properly. Fergus settled himself more comfortably, closed his eyes and slept.

He was dreaming of knives and blood when he heard the front door bang. Almost catapulting out of the chair, he ran to the door.

'Fergus? Fergus, love, are you here?'

Sagging against the wall, Fergus gave his mother a shaky smile. 'Hiya, Ma.'

Richard's head was in turmoil as he drove home. It had been a relief to see Fergus safe and well but it all could have turned out so different. And it would all have been his fault. He'd contacted Declan Murphy.

The sting had been his idea. If Fergus had been with Mick when those men had come to get him – 'Jesus!' he muttered as he turned into the aparment complex. He had taken ridiculous chances with another man's life and he wouldn't blame Fergus or Rose if they never wanted to talk to him again.

The apartment was silent when he got in. Celine was probably tucked up in bed. He went out to the kitchen, checked that the oven was off and switched off the lights. As he crossed the living-room, he noticed that Celine was curled up on the sofa, fast asleep. Sitting down beside her, he pulled her gently into his arms and closed his eyes.

She stirred. 'Richard?' she said sleepily.

'Yeah, I'm here. Everything's fine, Celine. Go to sleep.'

Epilogue

'That was a lovely service,' Celine said as they emerged into brilliant sunshine.

Dominic struggled with the cork on the bottle of champagne.

'It was certainly fast!' Marina laughed as she held out her glass.

'I'm so glad you decided against Elvis.' Kay dabbed her eyes.

'We have our own little Elvis right here!' Richard swung Josh up onto his shoulders. 'Isn't that right, champ?'

'Uh-huh,' Josh said and they all laughed.

'He looks wonderful,' Celine said, smiling at the little boy resplendent in a white suit with his hair greased back. He had been positively angelic in the chapel, walking up the aisle with Marina exactly as Kay had taught him.

'A beautiful bride and a handsome stepson, I'm a lucky man.' Dominic said happily.

Marina did look ravishing in a cream silk halter dress that hung in soft folds to her ankles. Her hair was piled into an intricate knot on the top of her head and with her eyes shining, she looked every inch the beautiful bride.

'Come on, guys, our car awaits!' Dominic lifted Josh down and held his hand as they crossed the road.

Celine lifted Marina's short train as they went over to the car.

'Isn't this tacky?' Marina laughed as she climbed into the white stretch limousine.

'The only way to travel in Las Vegas,' Dominic said as he popped another cork.

Kay covered her glass with her hand. 'I'll be drunk before we get to the hotel at this rate!' she protested.

Dominic laughed. 'It is still an Irish wedding. Tell me, Kay, should I call you Mum now?'

'Not if you want to make it back to Ireland in one piece,' Kay retorted and they all laughed.

They returned to the hotel, where they enjoyed a wonderful dinner in the rooftop restaurant and afterwards, when Kay and Josh had retired to their room, the others danced to the mellow sound of the small blues band.

'Happy?' Dominic asked, looking down at his new wife.

'Very,' she assured him reaching up to kiss his lips. 'Coming here was one of your better ideas.'

'Well, enjoy it because it's going to be hard work when we get home. And lord only knows when we'll be able to afford another holiday.'

'Who needs holidays? We have a home, a nice garden and each other. What more do we need?'

Dominic smiled as Richard and Celine glided past. 'I have a feeling we might be going to another wedding in the not too distant future.'

Marina followed his gaze. 'It's wonderful to see Celine so happy. But it's not all down to Richard.'

'Oh?'

'No, I think she's thrilled to be designing again.'

'It's certainly what she's good at.' Dominic's eyes travelled over Marina's slim figure in the silk dress that clung to every curve. 'Let's hope her talents are recognised. I wonder if it was their creativity that drew them to each other. I still can't believe the paintings that Richard has produced. I mean he's a builder, for God's sake!'

'As they say, don't judge a book by its cover.'

As the song ended they all returned to their seats and Dominic looked around for a waiter.

'Just coffee for me,' Celine said. 'If I have any more to drink I'll never be up on time for that flight in the morning.'

'It's a pity you have to go back so soon,' Marina complained.

'It is,' Richard agreed,' but I'm afraid we have an awful lot to do, what with moving Celine's things out of the house and getting ready for my exhibition.'

'And I don't like to leave Rose for too long,' Celine added.

'When are Fergus and Sarah moving into your flat?' Dominic asked.

Celine laughed. 'Probably five minutes after I move out!'

'I'm still amazed Rose is letting him leave home,' Richard marvelled.

'It's only because he's moving in over the shop,' Dominic pointed out, 'and she'll be able to keep an eagle eye on them both.'

'It's hardly surprising that she's protective after all he's been through,' Marina defended Rose. 'It's not easy being a parent, as you two will soon find out.'

Celine rolled her eyes at Richard. 'Dear God, I haven't moved in with you yet and she's at us about kids!'

'Well, we shouldn't leave it too long, I suppose,' Richard remarked. 'I'm not getting any younger. And your dad is dying to dangle a grandchild on his knee.'

'Not an illegitimate one,' she shot back with a wink at Marina.

'Then I suppose we'd better get married.'

'Well, that has to be the least romantic proposal I've ever heard!' Marina laughed.

'Proposal? It sounded more like a statement to me,' Celine remarked, her cheeks flushed.

Richard looked at her steadily. 'You know as well as I do that it's a foregone conclusion.'

Celine nodded slowly, only vaguely aware of the fact that Dominic and Marina were holding their breaths. 'Yes, I suppose it is.'

'Sod the coffee, Dominic,' Marina spluttered, 'get some more champagne!'

Celine laughed as Richard leaned over to kiss her. 'I love you,' she murmured.

'You don't feel press-ganged, do you?' he asked, his eyes suddenly concerned. 'I don't want to rush you—'

She put a finger to his lips. 'You're not.'

Marina watched as they kissed again and sighed. 'Well, this has been the most perfect day.'

As the champagne was served, Dominic stood up. 'Come on, Marina, they're playing our song.'

'They are?' She looked confused.

'They are,' he said firmly and led her away.

'No regrets?' Richard asked when they were alone.

Celine shook her head. 'None.'

'What about the house? Are you sure you're ready to sell it?'

'Yes, it's time.' Her tenants had moved out a week ago and she'd gone over to see the place, curious as to what effect it would have on her. She was relieved that she was able to smile and think of the happy memories she and Dermot had shared. Before she had left, she'd taken the anonymous letters in their distinctive red envelopes from the drawer in Dermot's desk. After reading them one more time, she took them into the living-room, threw them into the grate and set fire to them. She'd smiled as she'd watched them burn, realising that she'd finally started a new stage in her life. 'This really is a red

letter day,' she'd murmured and walked out of the
house with a smile on her face.

'Celine?'

'Sorry, I was just thinking about the anonymous
letters I was sent.'

'Only small-minded busybodies with too much
time on their hands send anonymous letters.'

'But like you said, if it hadn't been for them, I might
never have come to Hopefield.'

'True.'

'Will you help me clear out the house when we get
back?' she asked.

'Are you sure I won't be intruding?'

She took his hands in hers. 'Richard you are my life
now and Dermot would be happy for me that I'd
found you. That house was our home and a very
happy one but that part of my life is over now. I'm
ready to say goodbye.'

'I hope you two are ready for company again,'
Marina said, sinking back into her chair, 'because
these heels weren't made for dancing.'

Celine smiled. 'Your feet may be sore but you still
look beautiful.'

Marina gave her a quick hug. 'Well, thank you,
darling. Now I know why we've been friends for so
many years!'

'You'll have to get used to having sore feet
when you're working in the shop,' Dominic pointed
out.

'I'll slip off my shoes when I'm behind the counter. Oh, Celine, I am so looking forward to working in Close Second.'

'Rose is looking forward to it too. She can't believe her luck that you agreed to take the job.'

'It's wonderful that I'll be just working mornings. I really didn't want Josh to go to a childminder after school.'

'I suppose it's more glamorous than working in a deli,' Dominic said, pulling a long face.

'Oh, I'm sorry, darling, but you know that I really wouldn't have been much use to you.'

'She'd have told off the customers if they bought anything fattening,' Celine agreed. 'You'd have been out of business in no time.'

Dominic laughed. 'Okay, okay, I'm convinced.'

'Of course I won't be bringing in nearly as much money than if I was modelling,' Marina said, her expression anxious.

Dominic shook his head. 'We've been through this. Josh is more important.'

Marina's eyes were bright as she smiled at Celine. 'Isn't he wonderful?'

Richard groaned. 'I can't take much more of this lovey-dovey stuff. We should really get some sleep, Celine, or we'll never make that flight.'

She stood up and stretched. 'You're right. Goodnight, you two. Don't bother joining us for breakfast, we have to be up much too early.'

Marina stood up and hugged her friend. 'Thanks

for being here, Celine. It wouldn't have been the same without you.'

'Wouldn't have missed it for the world. Look after her, Dominic,' she said, turning to hug him.

'Always,' he assured her. 'Safe home, you two, and look after my mother-in-law.'

'Promise.' Richard shook hands with his friend and then bent to kiss Marina. 'Have a wonderful holiday.'

'That depends on Josh,' Marina replied. 'And without my mother's firm hand, God only knows what we're letting ourselves in for!'

'Leave the boy alone,' Dominic admonished. 'He's just high-spirited.'

Celine and Richard looked at each other and smiled. 'Goodnight,' they said and made their way through the large hotel towards the bank of lifts.

'They're so happy,' Celine mused.

'Nearly as happy as us,' Richard agreed.

'I'm not sure you'd have hung around if there was a "Joshie" on the scene,' she laughed.

'I'm not sure you would have either! I think Dominic's life may prove a little rocky for a while. Our son will be different.'

She raised an eyebrow as she stepped into the lift and pressed the button for the eighth floor. 'Our son?'

'Yes, we'll have a boy first. And he will be handsome, funny and will want to follow in his father's footsteps.'

'Would that be the footsteps of the property developer or the artist?'

He frowned. 'Good question. We could do with someone to take over the family business.'

'Our daughter can do that.'

'You think?' He slipped an arm around her shoulders as they stepped out of the lift and walked towards their room.

'Yeah, no problem. She'll be tough, but not hard and she'll be nobody's fool.'

'Don't you think she'll be a designer like her mother?'

Celine shook her head as he opened the door to their room. 'No, our second son is going to be the designer.'

'Second son, eh?'

'That's right.' She kicked her shoes off and squealed as he pulled her down on to the bed. 'What do you think you're doing, Mr Lawrence?'

'Well, if we're going to have three kids I think we should get in a bit of practice.'

'Only three?' she murmured as his mouth came down on hers.